A STAINED WHITE RADIANCE

James Lee Burke is the author of ten previous novels, including four starring the detective Dave Robicheaux.

Burke grew up on the Texas-Louisiana Gulf Coast. He now lives with his wife in Missoula, Montana, and spends several months each year in New Orleans.

By the same author

The Neon Rain
Heaven's Prisoners
Black Cherry Blues
A Morning For Flamingos

A STAINED WHITE RADIANCE

James Lee Burke

ARROW

First published 1992

1 3 5 7 9 10 8 6 4 2

© James Lee Burke 1992

Chapter 8 is an adaptation of a short story
by the author entitled "Texas City 1947"
which appeared in the Summer 1991 issue of *The Southern Review*

James Lee Buurke has asserted his
right under the Copyright, Designs and Patents Act, 1988
to be identified as the author of this work

First published in the U.S.A. by Hyperion in 1992

Arrow edition 1993
Random House, 20 Vauxhall Bridge Road, London SW1V 2SA

Random House Australia (Pty) Limited
20 Alfred Street, Milsons Point, Sydney,
New South Wales 2061, Australia

Random House New Zealand Limited
18 Poland Road, Glenfield
Auckland 10, New Zealand

Random House South Africa (Pty) Limited
PO Box 337, Bergvlei, South Africa

Random House UK Limited Reg. No. 954009

A CIP catalogue record for this book
is available from the British Library

ISBN 0 09 914491 3

Printed and bound in Great Britain by
Cox & Wyman Ltd, Reading, Berkshire

I would like to thank the following people for all the support and help they have given me over the years: Fran Majors of Wichita, Kansas, who typed and copyedited my manuscripts and was always my loyal friend; Patricia Mulcahy, my editor, who put her career on the line for me more than once; Dick and Patricia Karlan, my film agents whose commitment and faithful advocacy I will never be able to repay; and finally my literary agent, Philip G. Spitzer, one of the most honorable and fine men I've ever known, the only agent in New York who would keep my novel *The Lost Get-Back Boogie* under submission for nine years, making the rounds of almost one hundred publishers, until it found a home.

For Farrel and Patty Lemoine
and my old twelve-string partner, Murphy Dowouis

A
STAINED
WHITE
RADIANCE

1

I had known the Sonnier family all my life. I had attended the Catholic elementary school in New Iberia with three of them, had served with one of them in Vietnam, and for a short time had dated Drew, the youngest child, before I went away to the war. But, as I learned with Drew, the Sonniers belonged to that group of people whom you like from afar, not because of what they are themselves, but because of what they represent—a failure in the way that they're put together, a collapse of some genetic or familial element that should be the glue of humanity.

The background of the Sonnier children was one that you instinctively knew you didn't want to know more about, in the same way that you don't want to hear the story of a desperate and driven soul in an after-hours bar. As a police officer it has been my experience that pedophiles are able to operate and stay functional over long periods of time and victimize scores, even hundreds, of children, because no one wants to believe his or her own intuitions about the symptoms in the perpetrator. We are repelled and sickened by the images that our own minds suggest, and we hope against hope that the problem is in reality simply one of misperception.

Systematic physical cruelty toward children belongs in the same shoebox. Nobody wants to deal with it. I cannot remember one occasion, in my entire life, when I saw one adult interfere in a public place with the mistreatment of a child at the hands of another adult. Prosecutors often wince when they have to take a child abuser to trial, because usually the only witnesses they can use are children who are terrified at the prospect of testifying against their parents. And ironically a successful prosecution means that the victim will become a legal orphan, to be raised by foster parents or in a state institution that is little more than a warehouse for human beings.

As a child I saw the cigarette burns on the arms and legs of the Sonnier children. They were scabbed over and looked like coiled, gray worms. I came to believe that the Sonniers grew up in a furnace rather than a home.

It was a lovely spring day when the dispatcher at the Iberia Parish sheriff's office, where I worked as a plainclothes detective, called me at home and said that somebody had fired a gun through Weldon Sonnier's dining-room window and I could save time by going out there directly rather than reporting to the office first.

I was at my breakfast table, and through the open window I could smell the damp, fecund odor of the hydrangeas in my flower bed and last night's rainwater dripping out of the pecan and oak trees in the yard. It was truly a fine morning, the early sunlight as soft as smoke in the tree limbs.

"Are you there, Dave?" the dispatcher said.

"Ask the sheriff to send someone else on this one," I said.

"You don't like Weldon?"

"I like Weldon. I just don't like some of the things that probably go on in Weldon's head."

"Okay, I'll tell the old man."

"Never mind," I said. "I'll head out there in about fifteen minutes. Give me the rest of it."

"That's all we got. His wife called it in. He didn't. Does that sound like Weldon?" He laughed.

People said Weldon had spent over two hundred thousand

dollars restoring his antebellum home out in the parish on Bayou Teche. It was built of weathered white-painted brick, with a wide columned porch, a second-floor verandah that wrapped all the way around the house, ventilated green window shutters, twin brick chimneys at each extreme of the house, and scrolled ironwork that had been taken from historical buildings in the New Orleans French Quarter. The long driveway that led from the road to the house was covered with a canopy of moss-hung live oaks, but Weldon Sonnier was not one to waste land space for the baroque and ornamental. All the property in front of the house, even the area down by the bayou where the slave quarters had once stood, had been leased to tenants who planted sugarcane on it.

It had always struck me as ironic that Weldon would pay out so much of his oil money in order to live in an antebellum home, whereas in fact he had grown up in an Acadian farmhouse that was over one hundred and fifty years old, a beautiful piece of hand-hewn, notched, and pegged cypress architecture that members of the New Iberia historical preservation society openly wept over when Weldon hired a group of half-drunk black men out of a ramshackle, back-road nightclub, gave them crowbars and axes, and calmly smoked a cigar and sipped from a glass of Cold Duck on top of a fence rail while they ripped the old Sonnier house into a pile of boards he later sold for two hundred dollars to a cabinetmaker.

When I drove my pickup truck down the driveway and parked under a spreading oak by the front porch, two uniformed deputies were waiting for me in their car, their front doors open to let in the breeze that blew across the shaded lawn. The driver, an ex-Houston cop named Garrett, a barrel of a man with a thick blond mustache and a face the color of a fresh sunburn, flipped his cigarette into the rose bed and stood up to meet me. He wore pilot's sunglasses, and a green dragon was tattooed around his right forearm. He was still new, and I didn't know him well, but I'd heard that he had resigned from the Houston force after he had been suspended during an Internal Affairs investigation.

"What do you have?" I said.

"Not much," he said. "Mr. Sonnier says it was probably an accident. Some kids hunting rabbits or something."

"What does Mrs. Sonnier say?"

"She's eating tranquilizers in the breakfast room."

"What does she *say*?"

"Nothing, detective."

"Call me Dave. You think it was just some kids?"

"Take a look at the size of the hole in the dining room wall and tell me."

Then I saw him bite the corner of his lip at the abruptness in his tone. I started toward the front door.

"Dave, wait a minute," he said, took off his glasses, and pinched the bridge of his nose. "While you were on vacation, the woman called us twice and reported a prowler. We came out and didn't find anything, so I marked it off. I thought maybe her terminals were a little fried."

"They are. She's a pill addict."

"She said she saw a guy with a scarred face looking through her window. She said it looked like red putty or something. The ground was wet, though, and I didn't see any footprints. But maybe she did see something. I probably should have checked it out a little better."

"Don't worry about it. I'll take it from here. Why don't you guys head up to the café for coffee?"

"She's the sister of that Nazi or Klan politician in New Orleans, isn't she?"

"You got it. Weldon knows how to pick 'em." Then I couldn't resist. "You know who Weldon's brother is, don't you?"

"No."

"Lyle Sonnier."

"That TV preacher in Baton Rouge? No kidding? I bet that guy could steal the stink off of shit and not get the smell on his hands."

"Welcome to south Louisiana, podna."

Weldon shook hands when he answered the door. His hand was big, square, callused along the heel and the index finger. Even when he grinned, Weldon's face was bold, the eyes like buckshot, the jaw rectangular and hard. His brown-gray crewcut was shaved close to the scalp above his large ears, and he always seemed to be biting softly on his molars, flexing the lumps of cartilage behind his jaw-line. He wore his house slippers, a pair of faded beltless Levi's, and a paint-stained T-shirt that molded his powerful biceps and flat stomach. He hadn't shaved and he had a cup of coffee in his hand. He was polite to me—Weldon was always polite—but he kept looking at his watch.

"I can't tell you anything else, Dave," he said, as we stood in the doorway of his dining room. "I was standing there in front of the glass doors, looking out at the sunrise over the bayou, and *pop,* it came right through the glass and hit the wall over yonder." He grinned.

"It must have scared you," I said.

"Sure did."

"Yeah, you look all shaken up, Weldon. Why did your wife call us instead of you?"

"She worries a lot."

"You don't?"

"Look, Dave, I saw two black kids earlier. They chased a rabbit out of the canebrake, then I saw them shooting at some mockingbirds up in a tree on the bayou. I think they live in one of those old nigger shacks down the road. Why don't you go talk to them?"

He looked at the time on the mahogany grandfather clock at the far end of the dining room, then adjusted the hands on his wristwatch.

"The black kids didn't have a shotgun, did they?" I asked.

"No, I don't think so."

"Did they have a .22?"

"I don't know, Dave."

"But that's what they'd probably have if they were shooting rabbits or mockingbirds, wouldn't they? At least if they didn't have a shotgun."

"Maybe."

I looked at the hole in the pane of glass toward the top of the French door. I pulled my fountain pen, one almost as thick as my little finger, from my pocket and inserted the end in the hole. Then I crossed the dining room and did the same thing with the hole in the wall. There was a stud behind the wall, and the fountain pen went into the hole three inches before it tapped anything solid.

"Do you believe a .22 round did this?" I asked.

"Maybe it ricocheted and toppled," he answered.

I walked back to the French doors, opened them onto the flagstone patio, and gazed down the sloping blue-green lawn to the bayou. Among the cypresses and oaks on the bank were a dock and a weathered boat shed. Between the mudbank and the lawn was a low red-brick wall that Weldon had constructed to keep his land from eroding into the Teche.

"I think what you're doing is dumb, Weldon," I said, still looking at the brick wall and the trees on the bank silhouetted against the glaze of sunlight on the bayou's brown surface.

"Excuse me?" he said.

"Who has reason to hurt you?"

"Not a soul." He smiled. "At least not to my knowledge."

"I don't want to be personal, but your brother-in-law is Bobby Earl."

"Yes?"

"He's quite a guy. A CBS newsman called him 'the Robert Redford of racism.'"

"Yeah, Bobby liked that one."

"I heard you pulled Bobby across a table in Copeland's by his necktie and sawed it off with a steak knife."

"Actually, it was Mason's over on Magazine."

"Oh, I see. How did he like being humiliated in a restaurant full of people?"

"He took it all right. Bobby's not a bad guy. You just have to define the situation for him once in a while."

"How about some of his followers—Klansmen, American Nazis, members of the Aryan Nation? You think they're all-right guys, too?"

"I don't take Bobby seriously."

"A lot of people do."

"That's their problem. Bobby has about six inches of dong and two of brain. If the press left him alone, he'd be selling debit insurance."

"I've heard another story about you, Weldon, maybe a more serious one."

"Dave, I don't want to offend you. I'm sorry you had to come out here, I'm sorry my wife is wired all the time and sees rubber faces leering in the window. I appreciate the job you have to do, but I don't know who put a hole in my glass. That's the truth, and I have to go to work."

"I've heard you're broke."

"What else is new? That's the independent oil business. It's either dusters or gushers."

"Do you owe somebody money?"

I saw the cartilage work behind his jaws.

"I'm getting a little on edge here, Dave."

"Yeah?"

"That's right."

"I'm sorry about that."

"I drilled my first well with spit and junkyard scrap. I didn't get a goddamn bit of help from anybody, either. No loans, no credit, just me, four nigras, an alcoholic driller from Texas, and a lot of ass-busting work." He pointed his finger at me. "I've kept it together for twenty years, too, podna. I don't go begging money from anybody, and I'll tell you something else, too. Somebody leans on me, somebody fires a rifle into my house, I square it personally."

"I hope you don't. I'd hate to see you in trouble, Weldon. I'd like to talk with your wife now, please."

He put a cigarette in his mouth, lit it, and dropped the heavy metal lighter indifferently on the gleaming wood surface of his dining-room table.

"Yeah, sure," he said. "Just take it a little bit easy. She's having a reaction to her medication or something. It affects her blood pressure."

His wife was a pale, small-boned, ash-blonde woman, whose milk-white skin was lined with blue veins. She wore a pink silk house robe, and she had brushed her hair back over her neck and had put on fresh makeup. She should have been pretty, but she always had a startled look in her blue eyes, as though she heard invisible doors slamming around her. The breakfast room was domed and glassed-in, filled with sunlight and hanging fern and philodendron plants, and the view of the bayou, the oaks and the bamboo, the trellises erupting with purple wisteria, was a magnificent one. But her face seemed to register none of it. Her eyes were unnaturally wide, the pupils shrunken to small black dots, her skin so tight that you thought perhaps someone was twisting the back of her hair in a knot. I wondered what it must have been like to grow up in the same home that had produced a man like Bobby Earl.

She had been christened Bama. Her accent was soft, pleasant to listen to, more Mississippi than Louisiana, but in it you heard a tremolo, as though a nerve ending were pulled loose and fluttering inside her.

She said she had been in bed when she heard the shot and the glass break. But she hadn't seen anything.

"What about this prowler you reported, Mrs. Sonnier? Do you have any idea who he might have been?" I smiled at her.

"Of course not."

"You never saw him before?"

"No. He was horrible."

I saw Weldon raise his eyes toward the ceiling, then turn away and look out at the bayou.

"How do you mean?" I asked.

"He must have been in a fire," she said. "His ears were little stubs. His face was like red rubber, like a big red inner tube patch."

Weldon turned back toward me.

"You've got all that on file down at your office, haven't you, Dave?" he said. "There's not any point in covering the same old territory, is there?"

"Maybe not, Weldon," I said, closed my small notebook, and replaced it in my pocket. "Mrs. Sonnier, here's one of my cards. Give me a call if you remember anything else or if I can be of any other help to you."

Weldon rubbed one hand on the back of the other and tried to hold the frown out of his face.

"I'll take a walk down to the back of your property, if you don't mind," I said.

"Help yourself," he said.

The Saint Augustine grass was wet with the morning dew and thick as a sponge as I walked between the oaks down to the bayou. In a sunny patch of ground next to an old gray roofless barn, one that still had an ancient tin Hadacol sign nailed to a wall, was a garden planted with strawberries and watermelons. I walked along beside the brick retaining wall, scanning the mudflat that sloped down to the bayou's edge. It was crisscrossed with the tracks of neutrias and raccoons and the delicate impressions of egrets and herons; then, not far from the cypress planks that led to Weldon's dock and boathouse, I saw a clutter of footprints at the base of the brick wall.

I propped my palms on the cool bricks and studied the bank. One set of footprints led from the cypress planks to the wall, then back again, but somebody with a larger shoe size had stepped on top of the original tracks. There was also a smear of mud on top of the brick wall, and on the grass, right by my foot, was a Lucky Strike cigarette butt. I took a plastic Ziploc bag from my pocket and gingerly scooped the cigarette butt inside it.

I was about to turn back toward the house when the breeze blew the oak limbs overhead, and the pattern of sunlight and shade shifted on the ground like the squares in a net, and I saw a brassy glint in a curl of mud. I stepped over the wall, and with the tip of my pen lifted a spent .308 hull out of the mud and dropped it in the plastic bag with the cigarette butt.

I walked through the sideyard, back out to the front drive and my pickup truck. Weldon was waiting for me. I held the plastic bag up briefly for him to look at.

"Here's the size round your rabbit hunter was using," I said. "He'd ejected it, too, Weldon. Unless he had a semiautomatic rifle, he was probably going to take a second shot at you."

"Look, from here on out, how about talking to me and leaving Bama out of it? She's not up to it."

I took a breath and looked away through the oak trees at the sunlight on the blacktop road.

"I think your wife has a serious problem. Maybe it's time to address it," I said.

I could see the heat in his neck. He cleared his throat.

"Maybe you're going a little beyond the limits of your job, too," he said.

"Maybe. But she's a nice lady, and I think she needs help."

He chewed on his lower lip, put his hands on his hips, looked down at his foot, and stirred a pattern in the pea gravel, like a third-base coach considering his next play.

"There are a bunch of twelve-step groups in New Iberia and St. Martinville. They're good people," I said.

He nodded without looking up.

"Let me ask you something else," I said. "You flew an observation plane off a carrier in Vietnam, didn't you? You must have been pretty good."

"Give me a chimpanzee, three bananas, and thirty minutes of his attention, and I'll give you a pilot."

"I also heard you flew for Air America."

"So?"

"Not everybody has that kind of material in his dossier. You're not still involved in some CIA bullshit, are you?"

He tapped his jaw with his finger like a drum.

"CIA . . . yeah, that's Catholic, Irish, and alcoholic, right? No, I'm a coonass, my religion is shaky, and I've never hit the juice. I don't guess I fit the category, Dave."

"I see. If you get tired of it, call me at the office or at home."

"Tired of what?"

"Jerking yourself around, being clever with people who're trying to help you. I'll see you around, Weldon."

I left him standing in his driveway, a faint grin on his mouth, a piece of cartilage as thick as a biscuit in his jaw, his big, square hands open and loose at his sides.

▼

Back at the office I asked the dispatcher where Garrett, the new man, was.

"He went to pick up a prisoner in St. Martinville. You want me to call him?" he said.

"Ask him to drop by my office when he has a chance. It's nothing urgent." I kept my face empty of meaning. "Tell me, what kind of beef did he have with Internal Affairs in Houston?"

"Actually it was his partner who had the beef. Maybe you read about it. The partner left Garrett in the car and marched a Mexican kid under the bridge on Buffalo Bayou and played Russian roulette with him. Except he miscalculated where the round was in the cylinder and blew the kid's brains all over a concrete piling. Garrett got pissed off because he was under investigation, cussed out a captain, and quit the department. It's too bad, because they cleared him later. So I guess he's starting all over. Did something happen out there at the Sonniers'?"

"No, I just wanted to compare notes with him."

"Say, you have an interesting phone message in your box."

I raised my eyebrows and waited.

"Lyle Sonnier," he said, and grinned broadly.

On my way back to my office cubicle I took the small pile of morning letters, memos, and messages from my mailbox, sat down at my desk, and began turning over each item in the stack one at a time on the desk blotter. I couldn't say exactly why I didn't want to deal with Lyle. Maybe it was a little bit of guilt, a little intellectual dishonesty. Earlier that morning I had been willing to be humorous with Garrett about Lyle, but I knew in reality that there was nothing funny about him. If you flipped through the late-night cable channels on TV and saw him in his metallic-gray silk suit and gold necktie, his wavy hair conked in the shape of a cake, his voice ranting and his arms flailing in the air before an enrapt audience of blacks and blue-collar whites, you might dismiss him as another religious huckster or fundamentalist fanatic whom the rural South produces with unerring predictability generation after generation.

Except I remembered Lyle when he was an eighteen-year-old tunnel rat in my platoon who would crawl naked to the waist down a hole with a flashlight in one hand, a .45 automatic in the other, and a rope tied around his ankle as his lifeline. I also remembered the day he squeezed into an opening that was so narrow his pants were almost scraped off his buttocks; then, as the rope uncoiled and disappeared into the hillside with him, we heard a *whoomph* under the ground, and a red cloud of cordite-laced dust erupted from the hole. When we pulled him back out by his ankle, his arms were still extended straight out in front of him, his hair and face webbed with blood, and two fingers of his right hand were gone as though they had been lopped off with a barber's razor.

People in New Iberia who knew Lyle usually spoke of him as a flimflam man who preyed on the fear and stupidity of his followers, or they thought of him as an entertaining borderline psychotic who had probably cooked his head with drugs. I didn't know what the truth was about Lyle, but I always suspected that in that one-hundredth of a second between the time he snapped the tripwire with his outstretched flashlight or army .45 and the instant when the inside of his head roared with white light and sound and the skin of his face felt like it was painted with burning tallow, he thought he saw with a third eye into all the baseless fears, the vortex of mysteries, the mockery that all his preparation for this moment had become.

I looked at his Baton Rouge phone number on the piece of message paper, then turned the piece of paper over in my fingers. No, Lyle Sonnier wasn't a joke, I thought. I picked up my telephone and started to dial the number, then realized that Garrett, the ex-Houston cop, was standing in the entrance to my cubicle, his eyes slightly askance when I glanced up at him.

"Oh, hi, thanks for dropping by," I said.

"Sure. What's up?"

"Not much." I tapped my fingers idly on the desk blotter, then opened and closed my drawer. "Say, do you have a smoke?"

"Sure," he said, and took his package out of his shirt pocket. He shook one loose and offered it to me.

"Lucky Strikes are too strong for me," I said. "Thanks, anyway. How about taking a walk with me?"

"Uh, I'm not quite following this. What are we doing, Dave?"

"Come on, I'll buy you a snowball. I just need some feedback from you." I smiled at him.

It was bright and warm outside, and a rainbow haze drifted across the lawn from the water sprinklers. The palm trees were green and etched against the hard blue sky, and on the corner, by a huge live oak tree whose roots had cracked the curb and folded the sidewalk up in a peak, a Negro in a white coat sold snowballs out of a handcart that was topped with a beach umbrella.

I bought two spearmint snowballs, handed one to Garrett, and we sat down side by side on an iron bench in the shade. His holster and gunbelt creaked like a horse's saddle. He put on his sunglasses, looked away from me, and constantly fiddled with the corner of his mustache.

"The dispatcher was telling me about that IA beef in Houston," I said. "It sounds like you got a bad deal."

"I'm not complaining. I like it over here. I like the food and the French people."

"But maybe you took two steps back in your career," I said.

"Like I say, I got no complaint."

I took a bite out of my snowball and looked straight ahead.

"Let me cut straight to it, podna," I said. "You're a new man and you're probably a little ambitious. That's fine. But you tainted the crime scene out at the Sonniers'."

He cleared his throat and started to speak, then said nothing.

"Right? You climbed over that brick retaining wall and looked around on the mudbank? You dropped a cigarette butt on the grass?"

"Yes, sir."

"Did you find anything?"

"No, sir."

"You're sure?" I looked hard at the side of his face. There was a red balloon of color in his throat.

"I'm sure."

"All right, forget about it. There's no harm done. Next time out, though, you secure the scene and wait on the investigator."

He nodded, looking straight ahead at some thought hidden inside his sunglasses, then said, "Does any of this go in my jacket?"

"No, it doesn't. But that's not the point here, podna. We're clear on the real point, aren't we?"

"Yes, sir."

"Good. I'll see you inside. I have to return a phone call."

But actually I didn't want to talk with him anymore. I had a feeling that Deputy Garrett was not a good listener.

I called Lyle Sonnier's number in Baton Rouge and was told by a secretary that he was out of town for the day. I gave the spent .308 casing to our fingerprint man, which was by and large a waste of time, since fingerprints seldom do any good unless you have the prints of a definite suspect already on file. Then I read the brief paperwork on the prowler reports made by Bama Sonnier, but it added nothing to my knowledge of what had happened out at the Sonnier place. I wanted to write it all off and leave Weldon to his false pride and private army of demons, whatever they were, and not spend time trying to help somebody who didn't want any interference in his life. But if other people had had the same attitude toward me, I had to remind myself, I would be dead, in a mental institution, or putting together enough change and crumpled one-dollar bills in a sunrise bar to buy a double shot of Beam, with a frosted schooner of Jax on the side, in the vain hope that somehow that shuddering rush of heat and amber light through my body would finally cook into ashes every snake and centipede writhing inside me. Then I would be sure that the red sun burning above the oaks in the parking lot would be less a threat to me, that the day would not be filled with metamorphic shapes and disembodied voices that were like slivers of wood in the mind, and that ten A.M. would not come in the form of shakes so bad that I couldn't hold a glass of whiskey with both hands.

At noon I drove home for lunch. The dirt road along the bayou was lined with oak trees that had been planted by slaves, and the sun flashed through the moss-hung branches overhead like a heliograph. The hyacinths were thick and in full purple flower along the edges of the bayou, their leaves beaded with drops of water, like quicksilver, in the shade. Out in the sunlight, where the water was brown and hot-looking, dragonflies hung motionless in the air and the armored-plated backs of alligator gars turned in the current with the suppleness of snakes.

A dozen cars and pickup trucks were parked around the boat ramp, dock, and bait shop that I owned and that my wife, Bootsie, and an elderly black man named Batist operated when I wasn't there. I waved at Batist, who was serving barbecue lunches on the telephone-spool tables under the canvas awning that shaded the dock. Then I turned in to my dirt drive and parked under the pecan trees in front of the rambling cypress-and-oak house that my father had built by himself during the Depression. The yard was covered with dead leaves and moldy pecan husks, and the pecan trees grew so thick against the sky that my gallery stayed in shadow almost all day, and at night, even in the middle of summer, I only had to turn on the attic fan to make the house so cool that we had to sleep under sheets.

My adopted daughter Alafair had a three-legged pet raccoon named Tripod, and we kept him on a chain attached to a long wire that was stretched between two oaks so he could run up and down in the yard. For some reason whenever someone pulled into the drive Tripod raced back and forth on his wire, wound himself around a tree trunk, tried to clatter up the bark, and usually crashed on top of one of the rabbit hutches, almost garroting himself.

I turned off the truck engine, walked across the soft layer of leaves under my feet, picked him up in my arms, and untangled his chain. He was a beautiful coon, silver-tipped, fat and thick across the stomach and hindquarters, with a big ringed tail, a black mask, and salt-and-pepper whiskers. I opened one of the unused hutches, where I kept his bag of cornbread and dry cracklings, and filled up his food bowl, which was next to the water bowl that he used to wash everything he ate.

When I turned around, Bootsie was watching me from the gallery, smiling. She wore white shorts, wood sandals, a faded pink peasant's blouse, and a red handkerchief tied up in her honey-colored hair. In the shadow of the gallery her legs and arms seemed to glow with her tan. Her figure was still like a girl's, her back firm with muscle, her hips smooth and undulating when she walked. Sometimes when she was asleep I would put my hand against her back just to feel the tone of her muscles, the swell of her lungs against my palm, as though I wanted to assure myself that all the heat, the energy, the whirl of blood and heartbeat under her tanned skin were indeed real and ongoing and not a deception, that she would not awake in the morning stiff with pain, her connective tissue once more a feast for the disease that swam in her veins.

She leaned against the gallery post with one arm, winked at me, and said, *"Comment la vie,* good-lookin'?"

"How you doin' yourself, beautiful?" I said.

"I made *étoufée* for your lunch."

"Wonderful."

"Did Lyle Sonnier get hold of you at the office?"

"No. He called here?"

"Yes, he said he had something important to tell you."

I squeezed her with one arm and kissed her neck as we went inside. Her hair was thick and brushed in swirls, tapered and stiff on her neck and lovely to touch, like the clipped mane on a pony.

"Do you know why he's calling you?" she said.

"Somebody took a shot at Weldon Sonnier this morning."

"Weldon? Who'd do that?"

"You got me. I think Weldon knows, but he's not saying. The older Weldon gets, the more I'm convinced he has concrete in his head."

"Has he been in trouble with some people?"

"You know Weldon. He always went right down the middle. I remember once he got caught stealing food out of the back of the poolroom in St. Martinville. The bartender pulled him out of the kitchen by his ear and twisted it until he squealed in front of everybody in the room. Ten minutes later Weldon came back through the door with tears in his eyes and grabbed a handful of balls off the pool table and smashed every inch of window glass in the place.

"That's a sad story," she said.

"They were sad kids, weren't they?" I sat down at the table in front of my smoking bowl of crawfish *étoufée*. The roux was glazed with butter and sprinkled with chopped green onions. The white window curtains with tiny pink flowers on them rose in the breeze that blew through the oak and pecan trees in the sideyard. "Well, let's eat and not worry about other people's problems."

She stood close to me and stroked my hair with her fingers, then caressed my cheek and neck. I put my arm across her soft rump and pulled her against me.

"But you do worry about other people's problems, don't you?" she said.

"Under it all Weldon's a decent guy. I think it's a contract hit of some kind. I think he's going to lose, too, unless he stops acting so prideful."

"You mean Weldon's mixed up with the mob or something?"

"After he got out of the navy I heard he flew for Air America. It was a CIA front in Vietnam. I think that stuff involves a lifetime membership." I clicked my spoon on the side of the *étoufée* bowl. "Or maybe Bobby Earl has something to do with it. A guy like that doesn't forget somebody dragging him through the tossed salad by his necktie."

"Ah, a big smile on our detective's face."

"It would have made wonderful footage on the evening news."

She leaned over me, pressed my head against her breasts, and kissed my hair. Then she sat across from me and started peeling a crawfish.

"Are you busy after lunch?" she asked.

"What'd you have in mind?"

"You can't ever tell." She looked up and smiled at me with her eyes.

I am one of the few people I have ever known who has been given two second chances in his life. After investing years in being a drunk and sawing myself apart in pieces, I was given back my sobriety and eventually my self-respect by what people in Alcoholics Anonymous call a Higher Power; then after the murder of my wife Annie, Bootsie Mouton came back into my life unexpectedly, as though all the years had not passed and suddenly it was once again the summer of 1957 when we first met at a dance out on Spanish Lake.

I'll never forget the first time I kissed her. It was at twilight under the Evangeline Oaks on Bayou Teche in St. Martinville, and the sky was lavender and pink and streaked with fire along the horizon, and she looked up into my face like an opening flower, and when my lips touched hers she came against me and I felt the heat in her suntanned body and suddenly realized that I'd never had any idea of what a kiss could be. She opened and closed her mouth, slowly at first, then wider, changing the angle, her chin lifting, her lips dry and smooth, her face confident and serene and loving. When she let her hands slide down on my chest and rested her head against mine, I could hardly swallow, and the fireflies spun webs of red light in the black-green tangle of oak limbs overhead and the sky from horizon to horizon was filled with the roar of cicadas.

I stopped eating and walked around behind her chair, leaned down and kissed her on the mouth.

"My, what kind of thoughts have you been having this morning?" she said.

"You're the best, Boots," I said.

She looked up at me, and her eyes were kind and soft, and I touched her hair and cheek with my fingers.

Then she looked out the window toward the front road.

"Who's that?" she said.

A silver Cadillac with television and CB antennas and windows that were tinted almost black turned off the dirt road by the bayou and parked next to my pickup truck under the pecan trees. The driver cut the engine and stepped out into the yard, dressed in a suit that was silver-charcoal, a blue shirt with French cuffs, a striped red-and-blue necktie, and wrap-around black sunglasses. He pulled off his sunglasses gingerly with his right hand, which had only a carved, half-moon area where the two bottom fingers should have been, widened his eyes to let them adjust to the light, and walked over the layer of leaves and pecan husks toward the gallery. His black shoes were shined so brightly they could have been patent leather.

"Is that—" Bootsie began.

"Yeah, it's Lyle Sonnier. He shouldn't have come out here."

"Maybe he tried at the office and they told him you were home."

"It doesn't matter. He should have arranged to meet me at the office."

"I didn't know you felt that way about him."

"He takes advantage of poor and uneducated people, Boots. He used the Ethiopian famine to raise money for that television sideshow of his. Look at the car he drives."

"Shhhh, he's on the gallery," she whispered.

"I'll talk to him outside. There's no need to invite him in. Okay, Boots?"

She shrugged and said, "Whatever you say. I think you're being a little too hard."

Lyle grinned through the screen when he saw me walking toward the door. He had the same dark Cajun complexion as the other Sonniers, but Lyle had always been the thin one, narrow at the shoulders and hips, a born track runner or poolroom lizard and ultimately one of the most fearless grunts I knew in Vietnam. Except Vietnam and pajama-clad little men who hid in tunnels and spider holes were twenty-five years back down the road.

"What's happenin', Loot? he said.

"How are you, Lyle?" I said, and shook hands with him out on the gallery. His mutilated hand felt light and thin and unnatural in mine. "I have to feed the rabbits and my daughter's horse before I go back to work. Do you mind walking with me while we talk?"

"Sure. Bootsie isn't home?" He looked toward the screen. On the right side of his face was a shower of shrapnel scars like a chain of flesh-toned plastic teardrops.

"She'll be out directly. What's up, Lyle?" I walked toward the rabbit hutches under the trees so he would have to follow me.

He didn't speak for a while. Instead he combed his waxed brown conked hair in the shade and looked out toward my dock and the cypress swamp on the far side of the bayou. Then he put his comb in his shirt pocket.

"You don't approve of me, do you?" he said.

I opened the chicken-wire door to one of the hutches and began filling the rabbits' bowl with alfalfa pellets.

"Maybe I don't approve of what you do, Lyle," I said.

"I don't apologize for it."

"I didn't ask you to."

"I can heal, son."

I looked at my watch, opened up the next hutch, and didn't answer him.

"I don't brag on it," he said. "It's a gift. I didn't earn it. But the power comes through my shoulder, through my arm, right through this deformity of a hand, right into their bodies. I can feel the power swell up in my arm just like I was holding a bucket of water by the bail, then it's gone, from me into them, and my arm's so light it's like my sleeve is empty. You can believe it or not, son. But it's God's truth. I tell you another thing. You got a sick woman up in that house."

I set down the alfalfa bag, latched the hutch door, and turned to look directly into his face.

"I'm going to ask two things of you, Lyle. Don't call me 'son' again, and don't pretend you know anything about my family's problems."

He scratched the back of his deformed hand and looked up toward the house. Then he sucked quietly on the back of his teeth and said, "It wasn't meant as an offense. That's not my purpose. No, sir."

"What can I help you with today?"

"You've got it turned around. You went out to Weldon's, but he wouldn't tell you diddly-squat, would he?"

"What about Weldon's?"

"Somebody shot at him. Bama called me right after she called y'all. Look, Dave, Weldon's not going to cooperate with you. He can't. He's afraid."

"Of what?"

"The same thing most people are afraid of when they're afraid— facing up to the truth about something."

"Weldon doesn't impress me as a fearful man."

"You didn't know our old man."

"What are you talking about, Lyle?"

"The man with the burned-off face that Bama saw through her window. I've seen him, too. He was sitting in the third row at last Sunday's telecast. I almost pulled the mike out of the jack when my eyes got focused on him and I saw the face behind all that scar tissue. It was like holding up a photographic negative to a light until you see the image inside the shadows, you know what I mean? By the end of the sermon sweat was sliding off my face as big as marbles. It was like that old son of a buck reached up with a hot finger and poked it right through my belly button."

He tried to grin, but it wasn't convincing.

"You're not making any sense, partner," I said.

"I'm talking about my old man, Verise Sonnier. He was gone

when I went down into the audience, but it was him. God didn't make two of his kind."

"Your father was killed in Port Arthur when you were a kid."

"That's what they said. That's what we hoped." He grinned again, then shook the humor out of his face. "Buried alive under a pile of white-hot boilerplates when that chemical factory blew. Somebody shoveled up a pillow sack full of ashes and bone chips and said that was him. But my sister Drew got a letter from a man in the San Antonio city jail who said he was our old man and he wanted a hundred dollars to go to Mexico." He paused and stared at me a moment to emphasize his point, as though he were looking into a television camera. "She sent it to him."

"I'm afraid this has the ring of theater to it, Lyle."

"Yeah?"

"Why would your father want to hurt Weldon?"

He looked away into the trees, his face shadowed, and brushed idly at the chain of scar tissue that seemed to flow out of the corner of his eye.

"He has reason to want to hurt all of us. After we thought he was dead, we did something to somebody who was close to him." He looked back into my face. "We hurt this person bad."

"What did you do?"

"I've made my peace on it. Somebody else will have to tell you that."

"Then I don't know what I can do for you."

"I can tell you what Weldon did to him. Or at least what the old man thinks Weldon did to him." He waited, and when I didn't respond he continued. "When we were kids the old man had this obsession. He was going to be an independent wildcatter, a kind of legend like Glenn McCarthy over in Houston. He started off as a jug hustler with an offshore seismographic outfit, roughnecked all over Texas and Oklahoma, then started contracting board roads in the marsh for the Texaco Company. After a while he was actually leasing land in the Atchafalaya basin and buying up a bunch of rusted junk to put his first rig together. A geologist from Lafayette told him the best place to punch a hole was right there on our farm.

"Except the old man had a problem with that. He was a *traiture*, you know, and always claimed he could cure warts, stop bleeding in cut hogs, blow the fire out of a burn, cause a woman to have a boy or a girl, all that kind of 'white witch' stuff. But he also told us there were Indians buried in an old Spanish well in the middle of our sugarcane field, and if he drilled a hole on our property their spirits would be turned loose on us.

"He was afraid of spirits in the ground, all right, but I think of a different kind. My uncle got drunk once and told me the old man hired this black man for thirty cents an hour to plow his field. The black man ran the plow across a rock and busted it, then just lay down under a tree and took a nap. The old man found the busted plow and the mule still in harness in the row, and he walked over to the tree and kicked this fellow awake and started hollering at him. That black fellow made a big mistake. He sassed my old man. The old man went into a rage, chased him across the field, and broke open his skull with a hoe. My uncle said he buried him somewhere around that Spanish well."

"What does this have to do with Weldon?"

"Are you sure you're listening to me? As greedy and driven to be a success as he was, the old man was afraid to drill on his own property. But not Weldon, podna. That's where he built his first rig, and he cored right down through the center of that Spanish well, I think just to make a point. A floorman on that rig told me the drill bit brought up pieces of bone when they first punched into the ground."

"I'll keep all this in mind. Thanks for coming out, Lyle."

"You don't look upon it as the big breakthrough in your case?"

"When people go about trying to kill other people with forethought and deliberation, it's usually over money. Not always, but most times."

"Well, a man hears when it's time for him to hear."

"Is that right?"

"I was never a good listener. At least not till somebody up on high got my attention. I don't fault you, Dave."

"Do you know what passive-aggressive behavior is?"

"I never went to college, like you and Weldon. It sounds real deep."

"It's not a profound concept. A person who has a lot of hostility learns how to mask it in humility and sometimes even in religiosity. It's very effective."

"No kidding? You learn all that in college? It's too bad I missed out." He grinned with the side of his mouth, his teeth barely showing, like a possum.

"Let me ask you something fair and square, with no bullshit, Lyle," I said.

"Go ahead."

"Do you hold your last day against me?"

"What do you mean?"

"In Vietnam. I sent you into that tunnel. I wish we'd blown it and passed it on by."

"You didn't send me down there. I *liked* it down there. It was my own underground horror show. I made those zips think the scourge of God had crawled down into the bowels of the earth. It wasn't a good way to be, son." He flinched good-naturedly and raised his hands, palms outward, in front of him. "Sorry, it's just a manner of speaking."

I looked at my watch.

"I guess that's my cue to go," he said. "Thanks for your time. Say good-bye to Bootsie for me, and don't think too unkindly of me."

"I don't."

"That's good."

Without saying anything further, he turned and walked through the dead leaves toward his Cadillac. Then he stopped, rubbed the back of his neck hard, as though a mosquito had burrowed deep into his skin, then turned around and stared blankly at me, his jaw slack with a sudden and ugly knowledge.

"It's a disease that lives in the blood. It's called lupus. I'm sorry, Dave. God's truth, I am," he said.

My mouth fell open, and I felt as though a cold wind had blown through my soul.

The next morning was Saturday, and the sun came up as pink as a rose over the willow trees and dead cypress in the marsh and the clouds of mist that rolled out of the bays. Batist and I opened up the bait shop at first light, and the air was so cool and soft, so perfect with blue shadows and the smell of night-blooming jasmine, that I forgot about Lyle's visit and his attempt to appear omniscient about my wife's illness. I had concluded that Lyle was little different from any other televangelist huckster and that somebody close to Bootsie had told him about her problem. But regardless I wasn't going to clutter my weekend with any more thoughts about the Sonnier family.

Some people were born to take a fall, I thought, and Weldon was probably one of them. I also had a feeling that Lyle was one of those theological self-creations whose own neurosis would eventually eat him like an overturned basket of hungry snakes.

After we had rented most of our boats, Batist and I seined the dead shiners out of the aluminum bait tanks, poured crushed ice over the beer and soda pop in the coolers, and started the fire in the barbecue pit I had made by splitting an oil drum with an acetylene torch, hinging it, and welding metal legs on the bottom. By eight o'clock the sun was bright and hot in the sky, burning the mist out of the cypress trees, and on the wind you could smell the faint odor of a dead animal back in the marsh.

"You got somet'ing on your mind, Dave?" Batist asked. He had a head like a cannonball; a pair of surplus navy dungarees hung on his narrow hips, and his wash-torn undershirt looked like strips of white rag on his massive coal-black chest and back.

"No, not really."

He nodded, put a dry cigar in his mouth, and looked out the window at a tangle of dead trees and hyacinths floating past us in the bayou's current.

"It ain't bad to have somet'ing on your mind, no," he said. "It's bad when you don't tell nobody."

"What do you say we season the chickens?"

"She gonna be all right. You gonna see. That's what they got all them doctors for."

"I appreciate it, Batist."

I saw Alafair walk down through the pecan trees from the house with Tripod on his chain. She was in third grade now, a little bit fat across the stomach, so that her old gold-and-purple LSU T-shirt, with a smiling Mike the Tiger on it, exposed her navel and the top of her elastic-waisted jeans. She had shiny black hair cut in bangs, skin that stayed tan year-round, wide-set Indian teeth, and a smile that was so broad it made her dark eyes squint almost completely shut. Nowadays, when I would pick her up, she felt heavy and compact in my arms, full of energy and play and expectation. But three years ago, when I pulled her from a crashed and submerged plane out on the salt, one piloted by a Lafayette priest who was transporting illegal refugees from El Salvador, her lungs had been filled with water, her eyes dilated with terror as we rose in a rush of bubbles toward the Gulf's surface, her little bones as thin and frail as a bird's.

Tripod thumped out on the dock, rattling his chain across the board planks behind him.

"Dave, you left the bag of rabbit food on top of the hutch. Tripod threw it all over the yard," Alafair said. Her face was beaming.

"You think that's funny, little guy?" I said.

"Yeah," she said, and grinned again.

"Batist says you brought Tripod down to the bait shop yesterday and he got into the hard-boiled eggs."

Her face became vague and quizzical.

"Tripod did that?" she said.

"Do you know anyone else who would wash a hard-boiled egg in the bait tank?"

She looked across the bayou speculatively, as though the answer to a profound mystery lay among the branches of the cypress trees. Tripod zigzagged back and forth on his chain, sniffing the smell of fish in the dock.

I rubbed the top of Alafair's head. Her hair was already warm from the sunlight.

"How about a fried pie, little guy?" I said, and winked at her. "But you and Tripod show some discretion with Batist."

"Show what?"

"Keep that coon away from Batist."

I brought a tray of seasoned and oiled chickens out of the shop and began laying them on the barbecue grill. The hickory wood I used for fuel had burned into hot, white coal, and the oil from the chickens dripped into the ash and steamed away in the wind. I could feel Alafair's eyes on the side of my face.

"Dave?"

"What is it, Alf?"

"Bootsie told me not to tell you something."

"Maybe you'd better not tell me, then." I turned my head to smile at her, but her dark eyes were veiled and troubled.

"Bootsie dropped a fork on the floor," she said. "When she picked it up her face got all white and she sat down real hard in a chair."

"Was that this morning?"

"Yesterday, when I came home from school. She started to cry, then she saw me looking at her. She made me say I wouldn't tell."

"It's not bad to tell those kinds of things, Alf."

"Is Bootsie sick again, Dave?"

"I think maybe we need to change her medicine again. That's all."

"That's all?"

"It's going to be all right, little guy. Let me finish up here, and we'll get Boots and go to Mulate's for crawfish."

She nodded her head silently. I hoisted her up on my hip. Tripod ran in circles at our feet, his chain clanking on the wood.

"Hey, let's buy you some new Baby Squanto books today," I said.

"I'm too old to read Baby Squanto."

I pressed her against me and looked over the top of her head at the shadowed front of my house and thought I could feel my pulse beating in my throat with the urgency of a damaged watch that was about to run out of time.

I wasn't able to keep our weekend entirely free of the Sonniers after all. That afternoon, after we drove back from Mulate's in a rain shower, the phone was ringing as we ran from the truck through the pecan trees onto the gallery. I picked up the receiver in the kitchen and blotted the rainwater out of my eyes with the back of my wrist.

"I thought I'd check in with you before we left town," the voice said.

"Weldon?"

"Yeah. Bama and I are going to visit her mother in Baton Rouge. We'll probably be gone a week or so. I thought I should tell you."

"Why?"

"What do you mean 'why'? That's what you're supposed to do when you're part of a case, aren't you? Check in with the authorities, that sort of thing?"

"You weren't cooperative yesterday, Weldon. I think you have information you're not giving me. I have my doubts about our level of sincerity here."

"I get the feeling I shouldn't have bothered you today."

"Your brother Lyle paid me a visit. He told me a long story about your father."

"Lyle's a great entertainer. Did you know he had a zydeco band before he got hit with a bolt of religion?"

"He said the prowler your wife saw was your father. He said he's seen the same man in his TV audience in Baton Rouge."

"Years ago Lyle put so many chemicals in his head it glows in the dark. He has hallucinations."

"Was Bama hallucinating?"

"You're poking a stick in the wrong place, Dave."

Before I spoke again I waited a moment and looked out the screen at the rain falling through the limbs of the mimosa tree in my backyard.

"So there's nothing to Lyle's story, then?" I asked.

"As a matter of fact, there is. But it's not anything you might be interested in. The truth is that Lyle takes money from a lot of pitiful nigras and po' white trash who think heat lightning is a sign out of Revelation. But after the television cameras are off and the audience goes home, my brother has problems with his conscience. Instead of dealing with it, he's developed this obsession that our old man is back from the dead and is trying to thread our souls on a fish stringer."

"How long will you be gone?"

"A week or so."

"Give me your mother-in-law's address and phone number."

I wrote them down on a notepad.

"Did you make plaster casts of those footprints by the bayou?" he asked.

"We're a low-budget department, Weldon. Also, plaster casts usually tell us that the suspect wore shoes. Let me explain something to you. There's not a lot of interest down there about your shooter. Why is that? you ask. Because when the intended victim acts like Little Orphan Annie, with wide, empty eyes, it's hard to get other people to bite their nails over that person's fate. If you want to let a hired gumball cancel your ticket, maybe we figure that's your business."

In my mind's eye I could almost see his hand squeezing on the receiver.

"What do you mean 'hired gumball'?" he said.

"People around here usually kill only their friends and relatives. They usually do it in bars and bedrooms. A long-range shooter, a guy probably using a scope, a guy who got in and out without being seen, I think we're talking about a contract killer, Weldon. There was something else I didn't tell you. Our fingerprint man didn't find even a trace of a print on that shell casing. In all probability that means the shooter wiped each shell clean before he loaded the rifle. It sounds pretty professional to me."

"You're a smart cop."

I didn't answer and instead waited for him to speak again. But he remained silent.

"You don't want to tell me anything else?" I said.

"It's a story that involves a lot of players. You couldn't guess at it."

"When people get into trouble, it's over money, sex, or power. Always. It's not a new script."

"This one is. It's a real stomach churner."

I waited again for him to continue, but he didn't.

"How about it?" I said.

"That's all I have to say, except I'm not going to do time and I'm not going to get clipped by some gumball. If that doesn't float with somebody, or if they want more information on that, they might try dialing 1-800-EAT SHIT for assistance. How's that sound?"

"Who said anything about doing time?"

"Nobody."

"I see. Have a nice trip to Baton Rouge. Tell me, though, before you hang up, how bad did you and Lyle hurt your father's friend?"

"What? What did you say?"

"You heard me."

"Yeah, I did. You listen to me, Dave. You stay out of my goddamn family's history. It doesn't have anything to do with this. You understand that? Are we clear on that?"

"Call back when you have something of value to tell me, Weldon," I said, and softly replaced the receiver in the telephone cradle. I suspected that I left him with knives turning in his chest. But Weldon was one of those who became interested in the cathedral only after you barred its entrance to him.

▼

Sunday night it rained again, and Bootsie, Alafair, and I drove to New Iberia and had dinner at Del's on East Main, then went to a movie. Later, it stopped raining, and the moon rose over the freshly plowed sugarcane fields in a sky that looked like black ink wash. I was restless and couldn't concentrate on the book I was reading or the movie that Bootsie was watching on television, and I told Bootsie that I was going back into town to drop off some overdue bills at the post office. Then I drove out to Weldon's place.

Why? I can't say, really—except that I suspected he was involved in something that went way beyond the confines of Iberia Parish. Over the years I had seen all the dark players get to southern Louisiana in one form or another: the oil and chemical companies who drained and polluted the wetlands; the developers who could turn sugarcane acreage and pecan orchards into miles of tract homes and shopping malls that had the aesthetic qualities of a sewer works; and the Mafia, who operated out of New Orleans and brought us prostitution, slot machines, control of at least two big labor unions, and finally narcotics.

They hunted on the game reserve. They came into an area where large numbers of the people were poor and illiterate, where many were unable to speak English and the politicians were traditionally inept or corrupt, and they took everything that was best from the Cajun world in which I had grown up, treated it cynically and with contempt, and left us with oil sludge in the oyster beds, Levittown, and the abiding knowledge that we had done virtually nothing to stop them.

I parked my truck on the blacktop in front of Weldon's house and looked at his flood lamps in the mist, the lighted chandelier that he had left on in the living room, the lawn that sloped away toward Bayou Teche, his boathouse, and the dark line of cypress trees along the bank. The shooter had probably come before dawn, maybe in a boat, and had crouched behind the brick retaining wall until he saw Weldon enter the dining room. So the shooter knew something about the layout of Weldon's house and property, I thought, and maybe about Weldon's habits as well; perhaps he even knew Weldon and had been in his house. If not, the person who hired the shooter was probably on familiar terms with Weldon.

It wasn't a profound theory, nor was it that helpful. I drove back home with the heat lightning flickering whitely over the southern horizon, then lay in the dark beside Bootsie and tried to fall asleep. Why did I preoccupy myself with Weldon's troubles, I asked myself? The answer was not long in coming. I rubbed my hand lightly over the curve of Bootsie's back, kissed the smooth grain of her skin, stroked the short-cropped stiff hair on her neck, and wondered in awe at how the flush of health in her complexion could be so successful a part of nature's masquerade. I had fantasies in which we changed the blood in her whole vascular system and rinsed disease out of her body; saw faith and prayer drive the red wolf from her like an exorcised incubus; or simply awoke one fine morning to discover that a new drug as miraculous as penicillin or the polio vaccine had been invented, and that all our cares and worries about Bootsie had been illusionary and ultimately forgettable.

So when you have a problem that has no solution and you can no longer drink over it, you get psychologically drunk on somebody else's woe, I thought. And maybe I even resented and envied Weldon for what I thought was the simplicity of his problem.

The moon made a square of light on Bootsie's sleeping form. Her white silk gown looked almost phosphorescent, her bare shoulders as cool and bloodless as alabaster. I put my arm across her stomach and drew her against me, hooked one leg inside hers, and buried my face in her hair, as though anger and need were enough to hold both of us aloft, safe from the dark spin and pull of the earth beneath us.

Two days later I would learn that Weldon's problems were not simple ones, either, and my involvement with the Sonnier family would become much more than a dry drunk.

After I got home from work the
following Tuesday Batist and I closed up the bait shop early because
of an electrical storm that blew up out of the south. Three hours
later the rain was still pouring down, lightning bolts were popping
all over the marsh, and the air was heavy with the wet, sulfurous
smell of ozone. The thunder reverberated like echoing cannon
across the drenched countryside, and I could barely hear the dispatcher's voice when I answered the telephone in the kitchen.

"Dave, I think I made a mistake," he said.

"Speak louder. There's a lot of static on the line."

"I put my foot in something. A little bit ago a black man across
the bayou from Weldon Sonnier's called in and said he saw somebody behind Weldon's house with a flashlight. He said he knew Mr.
Weldon was out of town, so he thought he ought to call us. I was
about to send LeBlanc and Thibodeaux, but Garrett was sitting by
the cage and said he'd take it. I told him he wasn't on duty yet. He
said he'd take it anyway, that he was helping you with the investigation about the shooting. So I let him go out there."

"Okay . . ."

"Then the old man calls up and wants to know where Garrett is, that he wants to talk with him right now, that there's been another complaint about him. Garrett cuffed a couple of kids and put them in the tank for shooting him the finger. The kids live two houses from the sheriff. That Garrett knows how to do it, doesn't he? Anyway, he doesn't answer his radio now, and I already sent LeBlanc and Thibodeaux somewhere else. You want to help me out?"

"All right, but you shouldn't have sent him out there by himself."

"You ever try to say 'no' to that guy?"

"Send LeBlanc and Thibodeaux for backup as soon as they're loose."

"You got it, Dave."

I put on my raincoat and rain hat, took my army .45 automatic from the dresser drawer in the bedroom, inserted the clip loaded with hollow-points into the magazine, and dropped the automatic and a spare clip in the pocket of my coat. Bootsic was reading under a lamp in the living room, and Alafair was working on a coloring book in front of the television set. The rain was loud on the gallery roof.

"I have to go out. I'll be back shortly," I said.

"What is it?" she said, looking up, her honey-colored hair bright under the lamp.

"It's a prowler report out at Weldon's again."

"Why do you have to go?"

"The dispatcher messed it up and sent this new fellow from Houston. Now he doesn't answer his radio, and the dispatcher doesn't have a backup."

"Then let them mess it up on their own. You're off duty."

"It's my investigation, Boots. I'll be back in a half hour or so. It's probably nothing."

I saw her eyes become thoughtful.

"Dave, this doesn't sound right. What do you mean he doesn't answer his radio? Isn't he supposed to carry one of those portable radios with him?"

"Garrett's not strong on procedure. Y'all be good. I'll be right back."

I ran through the rain and the flooded lawn, jumped in the pickup truck, and headed up the dirt road toward town. The oak limbs overhead thrashed in the wind, and a bright web of lightning lit the whole sky over the marsh. The rain on my cab was deafening, the windows swimming with water, the surface of the bayou dancing with a muddy light.

When I pulled into Weldon's drive, the night was so black and rain-whipped I could barely see his house. I hit my bright lights and drove slowly toward the house in second gear. Leaves were shredding out of the oak trees in front of the porch and cascading across the lawn, and I could hear a boat pitching and knocking loudly against its mooring inside the boathouse on the bayou. Then I saw Garrett's patrol car parked at an angle by one corner of the house. I flipped on my spotlight and played it over his car, then across the side of the house, the windows and the hedges along the walls, and finally the telephone box that was fastened into the white brick by the back entrance. There was a line of dull silver-green footprints pressed into the lawn from the patrol car to the telephone box.

Smart man, Garrett, I thought. You know a professional second-story creep always hits the phone box first. But you shouldn't have gone in by yourself.

I left my spotlight burning, took a six-battery flashlight from under the seat, pulled back the receiver on my .45, eased a round into the chamber, and stepped out into the rain.

I stooped in a crouch until I was at the back of the house and past the side windows. The wiring at the bottom of the telephone box had been sliced neatly in half. I looked over my shoulder at the blacktop road, which was empty of cars and glazed with a pool of pink light from a neon bar sign. Where in the hell were LeBlanc and Thibodeaux?

I went up the steps to the back entrance to try the door, but two panes of glass, one by the handle and one by the night chain, had been covered with pipe tape and knocked out of the molding, and the door was open. I eased it back and stepped inside. My flashlight reflected off enamel, brass, and glass surfaces and made rings of yellow-green light all over the kitchen, which was immaculately clean and squared away, but already I could see the disarray that existed deeper in the house.

"Garrett?" I said into the darkness. "It's Dave Robicheaux."

But there was no answer. Outside, I could hear the rain pelting the bamboo that grew along the gravel drive. I moved into the dining room, with the .45 extended in my right hand, and swung the flashlight around the room. All the drawers were pulled out of the cabinets and emptied on the floor, the paintings on the walls were knocked down or askew, and the crystalware had been raked off a shelf and ground into the rug.

The front rooms were even worse. The divans and antique upholstered chairs were slashed and gutted, a secretary bookcase overturned on its face and its back smashed in, the marble mantelpiece pried out of the wall, an enormous grandfather's clock shattered into kindling and pieces of glinting brass. A sheet of lightning trembled on the front yard, and in my mind's eye I saw myself silhouetted against the window just as I heard a foot depress a board in the hardwood floor somewhere behind or above me.

I clicked off my flashlight and went back through the dining room to the stairway. There was a closed door at the top of it, but I could see a faint glow at the bottom of the jamb. The stairs were carpeted, and I moved as quietly as I could, a step at a time, toward the door and the rim of light at the bottom, my palm sweating on the grips of the .45, my pulse racing in my neck. I turned the doorknob, pushed it lightly with my fingers, and let the door drift back on its hinges.

The hallway was strewn with sheets, mattress stuffing, clothes, and shoes that had been thrown out of the doorways to the bedrooms. The only light came from behind a partially closed door at the end of the hall. Through the opening I could see a desk, a word processor, a black leather chair whose back had been split in a large X. I moved along the wall with the .45 at an upward angle, past two demolished bedrooms, a linen closet, a darkened bathroom, an overturned dirty-clothes hamper, a dumbwaiter, until I reached the last bedroom, which was only ten feet from the lighted room that Weldon probably used as a home office. I stepped quickly inside the bedroom door and swept my .45 back and forth in the darkness. The room was still intact, except for the fact that the box springs had been shoved halfway off the frame of the canopy bed, a warning that I didn't heed.

I caught my breath, squatted down at the base of the door, wiped the sweat and rainwater out of my eyes with my knuckle, then aimed the .45 along the wall at the lighted opening of the office.

"This is Detective Dave Robicheaux of the Iberia Parish Sheriff's Department. You're under arrest. Throw your weapons out in the hall. Don't think about it. Do it."

But there was no sound from inside.

"Right now it's breaking and entering," I said. "You can be smart and come out on your own. If we have to come in after you, we'll paint the walls with you. I guarantee it."

Beyond the opening in the door I saw a shadow break across Weldon's desk. I could feel the veins tightening in my head, the sweat dripping out of my hair. It wasn't going to go down right, I thought. When they think about it, they either freeze or become cunning. And my situation was all wrong. I had been forced to take up a position on the right-hand side of the hallway, so that I had to extend my right arm at an awkward angle around the doorjamb. I was getting a charley horse in my leg and a muscle twitch in my back. Where were LeBlanc and Thibodeaux?

"Last chance, partner. We're about to shift up into the dirty boogie," I said. But it was hard-guy flimflam. All I could do was contain whoever was in there and wait for the backup.

Then the shadow broke across the desk again, a shoe scraped against a piece of furniture, and I straightened my back, stiffened my right arm, and aimed the .45 in the middle of the door, my eyes burning with salt.

But I'd forgotten that old admonition from Vietnam: Don't let them get behind you, Robicheaux.

He came out of the bedroom closet like a spring exploding from a broken clock, a short crowbar raised above his head. His head was huge, his face full of bone, his torso knotted with muscle under his wet T-shirt. I tried to pivot, swing the .45 clear of the doorjamb and aim it at his chest, or simply stand erect and get away from the arch of the crowbar, but my knees popped and burned and seemed to have all the resilience of cobweb. The crowbar thudded into my shoulder and raked down my arm and sent the .45 bouncing across the carpet.

Then he was on me in earnest and I was rolling away from him, toward the canopy bed, my arms wrapped around my head. He hit me once in the back, a blow that felt just like a wild inside pitch that catches you flat and hard in the spine as you try to twist away from it in the batter's box, and I kicked at him with one foot, tripped backward over the box springs, and saw the bone-plated, muddy-eyed resolution in his face as he came toward me again.

"Get away, Eddy! I'm gonna blow up his shit!" a voice behind him said.

A toy of a man stood in the doorway. He looked like a racehorse jockey, except his little body had the rigid lines of a weight lifter's. In his diminutive hand was a blue revolver.

But they had intervened in each other's script and hesitated too long. I saw the .45 on the carpet, next to the hanging box springs, and I grabbed it and tumbled sideways into a half bathroom just as the toy man started firing.

I saw the sparks of gunpowder fly out in the darkness, heard two rounds *whock* into the tile wall and a third *whang* off the toilet bowl and blow the tank apart in a cascade of water and splintered ceramic; then he tried to change his angle of fire, and a fourth round ricocheted off a chrome towel rack and collapsed the shower door in a pile of frosted glass.

I was flat on the floor, in a spreading pool of water, my back and hair covered with bits of glass and tile caulking. But it had turned around on him, and he knew it, because he was already backing fast into the hallway when I raised up and started firing.

The roar of the .45 was deafening, the recoil as powerful and palm-numbing and disconnected as the kick of an air hammer; then the .45 felt suddenly weightless in my hand just before I pulled the trigger again. I fired four times at the bedroom entrance, then stood erect in a tinkle of glass at my feet, opening and closing my mouth to clear my eyes. The bedroom doorway was empty, the layered smoke motionless in the air. Out in the hall, an oil painting lay face down on the carpet, with three holes cored through the back of the canvas.

I could hear them on the stairway, but one of them obviously wanted the game to go into extra innings. He had the high-pitched, metallic voice of a midget.

"Give me your piece! I got that fuck bottled!"

"The boat's leaving, Jewel. Either haul ass or you're on your own," another man said.

I looked around the edge of the doorjamb and let off the .45—too quickly, high and wide, scouring a long trench in the wallpaper. But this time I saw three men—the man with the crow-bar, the toy man, who wore black, silver-studded cowboy boots and had short-clipped blond hair that looked like duck down, and a third, older man in a brown windbreaker, black trousers like a priest's, black, razor-trimmed hair, and a mouth full of metal fillings that reflected the light from Weldon's office. Or at least that's how the image of the three men froze itself in my mind just before I heard a sound that I thought was the unmistakable ring of opportunity, the cylinder of a revolver being clicked open and ejected brass cartridges rattling on a wood surface.

I gripped the handle of the .45 with both hands and started to step out into the hall and begin firing, but the man in the wind-breaker was a pro and had anticipated me. He had gone to one knee, three steps down from the landing, while the other two men had fled past him, and when he squeezed off his automatic I felt my raincoat leap out from my side as though a gust of air had blown through it. I spun back inside the cover of the doorway and heard him running into the darkness of the house below.

They'll drop you coming down the stairs, I thought. *Think, think*. They didn't have a car in front or out on the blacktop. There's no access road in the back. They came on the bayou. They have to go back to it on foot.

I crossed the hallway and went into a bedroom on the opposite side, one with French doors and a verandah that overlooked the driveway, the garage, and the bamboo border of Weldon's back-yard. A moment later I heard them running hard on the wet gravel.

They were visible for not more than two or three seconds, between the corner of the house and the back of the garage, but I aimed the .45 with both hands across the wood railing and fired until the clip was empty and the breech locked open and a solitary tongue of white smoke rose from the exposed chamber. Just before the three men crashed through the bamboo and disappeared into the rain, just as the man called Eddy was almost home free, the last round in the magazine ripped the corner off the garage and filled his face with a shower of wood splinters. He screamed, and his hand clutched his eye as though he had been scalded.

Then I saw a patrol car turn off the blacktop and head fast up the front drive, the rain spinning in the blue and red kaleidoscopic flashing of emergency lights. I felt in my pocket for my flashlight, but it was gone. I ran down the stairs and out the front door just as LeBlanc and Thibodeaux pulled abreast of the porch, their faces looking at me expectantly through the open passenger window.

"They're headed for the bayou, three of them. They're armed. One guy's hurt. Nail 'em," I said.

The driver stepped on the accelerator, and the car shot around the side of the house, scouring skid marks in the gravel, gutting a big potted plant by the edge of the rose bed. I pulled the empty clip from the magazine of the .45, inserted a full one, and followed them through the rain toward the back of the property.

But it was all comedy now. They drove through Weldon's bamboo, destroyed his vegetable garden, and spun sideways into the coulee. The back wheels of the car whined and smoked in the mud. Out in the darkness I heard an outboard engine roar away from the dock, up the bayou toward St. Martinville.

The driver rolled down his window and looked at me in exasperation.

"Get on the radio," I said.

"Sorry, Dave. I didn't know that goddamn coulee was there."

"Forget about it. Call an ambulance, too."

"Are you all right?"

"Yeah. But I think Garrett's not."

"What happened in there?" the other deputy said, getting out of the passenger's seat.

But I was already walking back toward the house, the rain cold on my head, the .45 heavy and loose in my coat pocket. I found him at the bottom of the cellar stairs. The green dragon on his right forearm was laced with blood. I didn't even want to look at the rest of it.

▼

An hour later the medical examiner and I stood on the columned marble front porch and watched the two ambulance attendants load the gurney into the ambulance and close the doors on it. The rain had stopped, and the ambulance lights made swinging red patterns in the oaks. I could hear the frogs out on the bayou.

"Have you ever seen one like that before?" the medical examiner said. He was a thin elderly man who wore gold-rimmed glasses and a white shirt and tie and carried a pocket watch on a chain. His sleeves were rolled, and he kept brushing at his wrist with a piece of wet paper towel.

"In New Orleans. When I was at the First District," I said.

He wadded up the towel and threw it into the flower bed. His face looked disgusted.

"It's a first for me," he said. "Maybe that's why I'll stay in New Iberia. Does he have family here?"

"I think he was single. I don't know if he has relatives back in Houston or not."

"If you have to talk with any of them, you can tell them he was probably out of it with the first shot."

"Is it true?"

"It's what you can tell them, Dave."

"I see."

"His eyes were open when he got the next one. He probably saw it coming. But where's the law say that relatives need to know everything?" A fingerprint man went out the door, and a deputy locked it behind him. They both got in their cars. "So you figure the shooter's from the mob?" the examiner said.

"Who knows? It's their signature."

"Why do they do it that way? Just to be thorough?"

"More likely because most of them are degenerates and sadists. But maybe I say that just because I'm tired." I tried to smile.

"How's your shoulder?"

"All right. I'll put some ice on it."

"I scraped a blood specimen off the corner of the garage. It might help you later."

"Thanks, doctor. I'd appreciate it if you'd send me a copy of the autopsy report as soon as it's ready."

"You're sure you're all right? It got pretty close in there, didn't it?"

"The bottom line is I should have figured someone was in that bedroom. He'd just started to toss it when he heard me in the hallway. I'm lucky I didn't get my eggs scrambled."

"If it's any consolation, the guy you wounded probably has a sizable slice of wood in his neck or face. He might show up at a hospital. My experience has been that most of these guys are crybabies when it comes to pain."

"Maybe so. Goodnight, doctor."

"Goodnight, Dave. Drive carefully."

The fields were white with mist as I drove back toward New Iberia. My collarbone throbbed and felt swollen and hot when I touched it. The pink neon sign over the roadside bar gleamed softly on the oyster-shell parking lot. In my mind I kept repeating something told me by a platoon sergeant during my first week in Vietnam: don't think about it before it happens, and never think about it afterward. Yes, that was the trick. Just put one logical foot after the other. I yawned and my ears popped like firecrackers.

▼

Back at the office, I called Weldon at his mother-in-law's home in Baton Rouge. I had waked him up, and he kept asking me to repeat myself.

"Look, I think it's better that you drive back to New Iberia in the morning and then we'll have a long talk."

"About what?"

"I don't think you listen well. The inside of your home is

virtually destroyed. Three guys tore it apart because they were looking for something that's obviously important to them. Meanwhile they murdered a sheriff's deputy. Do you want to know how they did it?"

He was silent.

"They shot him through the back, probably when he came down the basement stairs," I said. "Then they put one under his chin, one through his temple, and one through the back of his head. Do you know any low-rent wiseguys named Eddy or Jewel?"

I heard him cough in the back of his throat.

"I'm tied up here with some business for the next few days," he said. "I'm going to send some repair people out to the house. You've got this number if you need me."

"Maybe it's about time you plug into reality, Weldon. You don't make the rules in a murder investigation. That means you'll be in this office before noon tomorrow."

"I don't want to leave Bama by herself, and I don't want to bring her back there, either."

"That's a problem you're going to have to work out. We're either going to be talking in my office tomorrow morning, or you're going to be in custody as a material witness."

"Sounds like legalese doodah to me."

"It's easy to find out."

"Yeah, well, I'll check my schedule. You want to have lunch?"

"No."

"You've sure got a dark view of things, Dave. Lighten up."

"The warrant gets cut one minute after twelve noon," I said, and hung up.

As was typical of Weldon, which was to do everything possible in a contrary and unpredictable fashion, he came up the front walk of the sheriff's department at eight o'clock sharp, dressed in a pair of khakis, sandals without socks, a green-and-red-flowered shirt hanging outside his trousers, and a yellow panama hat at a jaunty angle on his head. His jaws were clean and red with a fresh shave.

He helped himself to a Styrofoam cup of coffee from the outer office, then sat in a chair across the desk from me, folded one leg over the other, and played with his hat on his knee. My shoulder still throbbed, down in the bone, like a dull toothache.

"What were they after, Weldon?" I asked.

"Search me."

"You have no idea?"

"Nope." He put an unlit cigar in his mouth and turned it in circles with his fingers.

"It wasn't money or jewelry. They left that scattered all over the place."

"There're a lot of weird guys around these days. I think it's got something to do with the times. The country has weirded out on us, Dave."

"I haven't had to talk with any of Deputy Garrett's family yet. It's something I don't want to do, either. But I hope I have something more to offer them than a statement about the country weirding out on us."

He looked momentarily shamefaced.

"What do you want me to say?" he asked.

"Who are these guys?"

"You tell me. You saw them. I didn't."

"Eddy and Jewel. What do those names mean to you? Who's the guy with a mouthful of metal?"

"I'm sorry about your friend in the basement. I wish he hadn't gone in there."

"It was his job."

He gazed out the window at a cloud that hung on the edge of the early sun. His face became melancholy.

"Do you believe in karma? I do. Or at least I came to believe in it when I was in the Orient," he said. His eyes wandered around the room.

"What's the point?"

"I don't know what's the point. You ever hear of a flyer named Earthquake McGoon? His real name was Ed McGovern, from New Jersey. He was kind of a legend among certain people in the Orient. He was a huge fat guy, and one time he and his copilot, this Chinese kid, got locked up in a Chinese jail. Earthquake kept yelling at the guards, 'Goddamn it, you haven't fed me. Give me some goddamn food.' They told him he'd already had his rice bowl and to shut his mouth. That night when the guards went home Earthquake bent the bars apart and told his copilot to beat it, then he pushed the bars back into shape. The guards came back in the morning and said, 'Where's the other guy?' Earthquake said, 'I told you to feed me, and you wouldn't do it, so I ate the sonofabitch.'

"He was one of those indestructible guys. Except he was doing a supply drop for the French at Dien Bien Phu and he got hit by some ground fire. He tried to get his parachute on but he was too fat. He told his kickers to jump and he was going to set it down on Highway One going into Hanoi. They said if he was going to ride it down, they would, too. He came in like a powder puff. It looked like they were home free, then his wing tipped a telephone pole, and they flipped and burned."

He looked at me as though I should find meaning in his face or his story.

"That's what karma is," he said. "Highway One outside of Hanoi is waiting for us. It's all part of a piece. I'm sorry about your friend."

"Have you ever been in jail?" I said.

"No. Why?"

I walked around the side of the desk.

"Let me see your hand," I said.

"What are you talking about?"

"Let me see your hand."

"Which hand?"

"It doesn't matter." I lifted his right hand off the chair arm and snipped one end of my handcuffs around his wrist. Then I locked the other end to the D-ring on the floor.

"What do you think you're doing, Dave?"

"I'm going to have some breakfast. I'm not sure when I'll be back. Do you want me to bring you anything?"

"You listen—"

"You can start yelling or banging around in here if you want and somebody'll move you to the tank. I think today they have spaghetti for lunch. It's not bad."

He looked simian in the chair, with one shoulder and taut arm stretched down toward the floor, his square face discolored with anger. Before he could speak again I closed the door behind me.

I walked across the street in the sunshine and bought four doughnuts at a café, then returned to the office. I wasn't gone more than ten minutes. I unlocked the handcuff from his wrist.

"That's what it's like," I said. "Except it's twenty-four hours a day. You want to eat now?"

He opened and closed his right hand and rubbed his wrist. His eyes measured me as though he were looking down a gun barrel.

"You want a doughnut?" I repeated.

"Yeah, why not?"

"You don't trust people, Weldon. And maybe I can understand that. But it's not a private beef anymore."

"I guess it's not."

"Who are the three guys?"

"I've heard the name Jewel before. In New Orleans."

"In connection with what?"

"I flew for some people. Down in the tropics. A lot of different kinds of stuff goes in and out of there, you get my drift?" He closed his eyes and pinched the bridge of his nose. "I never saw the guy. But you get in bad with the wrong people and guys like that get turned loose on you sometimes."

"Which people?"

One tooth made a white mark on the corner of his lip.

"I can't tell you any more, Dave. If you want to lock me up, that's the breaks. I'm living in a dark place, and I don't know if I'm ever going to get out of it."

His face looked as flat and empty as melted tallow.

▼

That same afternoon I drove out to his sister Drew's place on East Main. East Main in New Iberia is probably one of the most beautiful streets in the Old South or perhaps in the whole country. It runs parallel with Bayou Teche and begins at the old brick post office and the Shadows, an 1831 plantation home that you often see on calendars and in motion pictures set in the antebellum South, and runs through a long corridor of spreading live oaks, whose trunks and

root systems are so enormous that the city has long given up trying
to contain them with cement and brick. The yards are filled with
hibiscus and flaming azaleas, hydrangeas, bamboo, blooming myrtle
trees, and trellises covered with roses and bugle vine and purple
clumps of wisteria. In the twilight, smoke from crab boils and fish
fries drifts across the lawns and through the trees, and across the
bayou you can hear a band or kids playing baseball in the city park.

Like the other Sonnier children, Drew had never been one to
live a predictable life. She had used her share of Weldon's oil strike
on her father's farm to buy a rambling one-story white house,
surrounded with screened-in gallerys, on a rolling, tree-shaded lot
next to the old Burke home. She had been divorced twice, and any
number of other men had drifted in and out of her life, usually to
be cut loose unexpectedly and sent back to wherever they came
from. She never did anything in moderation. Her love affairs were
always public knowledge; she took indigent people of color into her
home; she was inflexible in matters of principle and never gave an
inch in an argument. She was robust and merry and big-shouldered,
and sometimes I'd see her at the health club in Lafayette, clanking
the weights up and down on the Nautilus machines, her shorts
rolled up high on her thighs, her face hot and bright with purpose,
a red bandana tied in her wet black hair.

But she did surprise us once, at least until we thought about it.
She gave up men for a while and became a lay missionary with the
Maryknolls in Guatemala and El Salvador. Then she almost died of
dysentery. When she returned home she formed the first chapter of
Amnesty International in New Iberia.

I found her behind her house, trimming back the grapevines on
the gazebo with two black children. She was barefoot and wore
dirty pink shorts and a white T-shirt, and there were twigs and flecks
of dead leaves in her hair.

She had a pair of hedge trimmers extended high up on the vine
when she turned her head and saw me.

"Hi, Dave," she said.

"Hello, Drew. How've you been?"

"Pretty good. How's it with you?"

"I've been kind of busy of late."

"I guess you have."

I looked down at the two black children, both of whom were about five or six years old. "I have a six-pack of Dr. Pepper on the seat of my truck. Why don't you guys go get it for us?" I said.

They looked at Drew for approval.

"Y'all go ahead," she said.

"You know a sheriff's deputy was murdered last night at Weldon's house?" I said.

"Yes."

"Why would some people want to kill your brother, Drew?"

"Isn't he the one to ask?"

"He seems to think that being a standup guy is the same thing as allowing someone to blow his head off. Except now an innocent man is dead."

She wiped the sweat out of her eyebrows with the back of her hand. The sun winked brightly off the bayou.

"Come inside and I'll give you some iced tea," she said, wiped both of her hands on her rump, and walked ahead of me into the shade at the rear of her house. She pulled her damp T-shirt off her breasts with her fingers and shook the cloth as she opened the screen door. There was something too cavalier about her attitude, and I had the feeling that she had anticipated my visit and had already made a private decision about the outcome of our conversation.

She took a pitcher of tea out of the icebox, picked up two glasses, and we walked through a dark, cool room that gave onto a side porch. On the wall above her desk were several framed photographs: Weldon in a navy aviator's uniform; Lyle with his zydeco band, the name CATAHOULA RAMBLERS written in white letters at the bottom; and a cracked black-and-white picture of two little boys and a little girl standing in front of a man and woman, with a Ferris wheel in the background. The little girl had a paper windmill in her hand, and the boys were smiling over the tops of their cotton candy. The woman was expressionless and thick-bodied, her shoulders slightly rounded, her straw purse the only ornament or bright thing on her person. The man was dark and had a narrow face and wore cowboy boots, a bolo tie, and a cowboy hat at a slant on his head. He was looking at something outside the picture.

Drew had stopped in the doorway to the porch.

"I was just admiring your photographs. Are those your parents?"

She didn't answer.

"I don't remember them very well," I said.

"What are you asking me, Dave?"

"Lyle says your father's alive."

"My father was a sonofabitch. I don't concern myself thinking about him."

"His picture's hanging here, Drew."

She set down the iced tea and the glasses on the porch and came back in the room.

"I keep it because my brothers and mother are in it," she said. "It's the only one I have of her. The day he drove her out of the house her car went through the railing on the Atchafalaya bridge. She drowned in fifty feet of water, down where it was so dark they had to use electric lights to find her."

"I don't think your father has any connection with this case. But I had to ask anyway. I'm sorry to bring up bad memories."

"It's the past. Who cares about it?"

"But if you thought your father had anything to do with it, you'd tell me, wouldn't you, Drew?" I looked her directly in the eyes. Her stare remained as intent as mine.

"You should discount most of what Lyle tells you, Dave."

"And if you knew, you'd also tell me why three guys would tear Weldon's house apart?"

She pushed her tongue into her cheek and let her eyes rove over my face. No matter what the situation, Drew always gave me the feeling that she was about to step two inches from my face.

"Come outside and sit down," she said.

I followed her out onto the porch, and after I had sat down in a canvas chair, she sat on the corner of a wrought-iron table, with her legs apart, and looked down at me. I looked away through the screening at some bluejays playing in the birdbath on the lawn.

"I'm going to ask you to accept something," she said. "I can't help you out about Weldon. If I try to, I may hurt him. That's something I'm not going to do."

"Maybe it's not yours to decide what degree of involvement you'll have with the law, Drew."

"You want to put that a little more clearly?"

I raised my eyes to hers.

"Earlier today I cuffed your brother to a D-ring in my office. It was for only a few minutes, but I hope the lesson wasn't lost on him."

"A what?"

"It's an iron ring, like a tethering ring, inset in the floor. Sometimes we handcuff people in custody to it until we can move them into a holding area."

"That was supposed to impress Weldon? Are you serious?"

I felt the skin of my face tighten.

"Do you know the kind of life he had growing up?" she said. "I won't even try to describe it to you. But no matter how bad it was, he'd give whatever he had to me and Lyle. And I mean he'd take the food out of his mouth for us."

I looked out at the lawn again.

"You've got something to say?" she said.

"I'm at a loss."

"We perplex you?"

"Your family didn't have the patent on hard times."

She rubbed the heels of her hands idly on her thighs.

"You'll never get my brother to cooperate with you by pushing him," she said.

"What's he into, Drew?"

"Forget the D-ring clown act and maybe one day he'll tell you about it."

"I should revise my methods? That's the problem?"

"Stop acting like a simpleton."

"You always knew how to say it."

I could have pressed on with my questions, but Drew was not one to be taken prisoner. Or at least that's what I told myself. I put my iced tea back on the table and stood up.

"See you around," I said.

"That's it?"

"Why not? You've been straight with me, haven't you?"

I walked across the blue-green lawn through the shade trees and could almost feel her troubled, hot eyes on my neck.

▼

I went back to the office and talked with our fingerprint man, who told me that trying to sort out the prints in Weldon's home was a nightmare. There was no single, significant object, such as a murder weapon, for him to work with, and virtually every inch of space inside the house had been touched, handled, or smeared by family members, house guests, servants, meter readers, and a crew of carpenters that Weldon had evidently hired to refurbish several rooms. The fingerprint man asked me if I would present him with an easier job next time, like recovering prints from the Greyhound bus depot.

When I got home I found a note from Bootsie on the kitchen table, saying that she had taken Alafair with her to the grocery store in town. The evening was warm, the western sky maroon with low-hanging strips of cloud, and I put on my gym shorts and running shoes and did three miles along the dirt road by the bayou's edge. Gradually I could feel the fatigue and concerns of the day leave me, and at the drawbridge I turned around and hit it hard all the way home, the blood pounding in my neck, the sweat glazing on my chest. The house was in shadow now, the notched and pegged cypress planks as dark and hard-looking as iron, and I went into the backyard, where I could still see the late sun above the duck pond and the roofless barn at the foot of my property, and began alternating six sets of push-ups, leg lifts, and stomach crunches.

I propped my feet on the bench of the redwood picnic table that we kept under the mimosa tree and did each push-up as slowly as I could, my back straight, touching my forehead lightly against the clipped grass, my muscles tightening across my ribs and through my shoulders and biceps. I was old enough to know that most of it was a narcissistic vanity, but at a certain age you're given the luxury of no longer having to be an apologist for yourself. Sometimes it feels good to be over a half-century old and to still be a player, a bit scarred perhaps, but still out there on the mound, messing them up with sliders and spitters when your fastball won't hum anymore. I had a round scar the diameter of a cigar on both sides of my left shoulder, where a psychopath had cored a hole right below my collarbone with a .38 round; a pungi-stick scar on my stomach that looked like a flattened gray worm; and a spray of raised welts across my thigh, like Indian arrowheads wedged under the tissue, a lover's kiss from a bouncing Betty that lighted me on a night trail in Vietnam with such a heated brilliance that I believed my soul left my breast and I could look down and count my bones inside my skin.

But I was all right, I thought. I no longer had dreams about the murder of my wife Annie, and the nocturnal film strips from Vietnam had become less and less distinct, as though the flattening elephant grass under the whirling helicopter blades, the grunts piling out of the Hueys and racing for the cover of the banyan trees, their pots clamped on their heads with one hand, the thump of mortars in a ville across the rice paddy, were all now part of someone else's experience, not really mine anymore or maybe I had finally come to realize that I was only a small part of an army made up of blacks and slum kids and poor-whites from cotton-gin and lumber towns who had a collective cross dropped on them that no one should have to bear. But at least I knew now that it wasn't mine to bear alone anymore, and so maybe I didn't have to bear it at all.

As always in my moments of self-indulgent reverie I had failed to notice an aluminum pot that was sitting in the middle of the redwood table. It was filled with shelled shrimp and an okra and tomato roux, and a red line of ants went from a crack in the table, up one side of the pot and down inside. I picked it up, took a spade from the tool shed, cleaned out the spoiled food in the vegetable garden by the coulee, and buried it.

The doctors at Baylor in Houston and the specialist we used in Lafayette had tried to explain in their best way (and, like most physicians, they were inept with language, even though the compassion was obviously there in their voices) that there was no one answer for lupus. The steroids and medicines that we used to control it, to alleviate its symptoms, to knock it into remission, to protect the connective tissue and the kidneys, were hard to put into perfect balance, and sometimes an imbalance caused moments of hallucination, even temporary periods of psychosis.

I had seen her sway once to music that was not there and had dismissed it; then on a second occasion she told me that perhaps in fact dead people had called me up on the phone when I was having delirium tremens years ago, because just minutes earlier the phone had rung and she had picked up the receiver and had heard the voice of her dead sister.

An hour later she was fine and laughing at her own imagination.

Tomorrow I would call the specialist in Lafayette and make another appointment. It was dusk now, and the purple air was thick with birds. I walked down to the dock to help Batist close up. He wore cutoff Levi's, a tank top, and canvas boat shoes with no socks. His black body looked so hard and muscular you could break barrel slats across it. He was in the back of the bait shop, flinging cases of Jax and Dixie beer into a stack against the wall, an unlit cigar shoved back in his jaw like a stick.

I seined some dead shiners out of the bait tank, then began restocking one of the coolers with long-necked bottles of beer.

"Somet'ing wrong, Dave?" he asked.

"No, not really."

I could feel his eyes on me.

"Too much work at the office, I suppose," I said.

"That's funny. It don't usually bother you."

"It's just one of those days, Batist."

"When I got some trouble at home, sometimes trouble with my wife, my kids, I don't like to tell nobody about it. So I just study on it. It ain't smart, no."

"I worry about Bootsie. But there's nothing for it."

"Don't pretend you be knowing that. You don't know that at all."

I didn't say anything more. I pushed the bottles of beer deep into the crushed ice. The bare electric bulb overhead glinted dully off the smooth metal caps and filled the inside of the bottles with a trembling gold-brown light. My hands were numb up to my wrists.

"We don't need to ice down no more. We got enough for tomorrow," Batist said.

"I'll finish closing up. Why don't you go on home?"

"I got to sweep out."

"I'll do it."

"I ain't in no hurry, me."

I took another case of Jax off the wall and laid the bottles flat on the ice, between the necks of the bottles I had already loaded horizontally into the cooler. I slid the aluminum top shut with the heel of my hand.

Batist was still watching me. Then he lit his cigar, flipped the match out the window into the dark, and began sweeping the plank floor. He was a good and kind man, and even though it might be a cliché for a southern white man to talk about the loyalty of a black person, I was convinced that if need be he would open his veins for me.

I said goodnight to him and walked back up to the house. In the kitchen Bootsie and Alafair were taking pieces of pizza out of a box and putting them on plates.

3

The next morning I left early for New Orleans and spent two hours looking through mug books at my former place of employment, First District headquarters just outside the French Quarter, but I did not see any of the three men who had been inside Weldon's house. Most of the men I used to work with were gone—burnt-out, transferred, retired, or dead—and the two detectives I talked with were of no help. One was a new man from Jefferson Parish, and the other was bored and uninterested by a case that had nothing to do with his workload. In fact, he kept yawning and playing with his empty coffee cup while I described the three intruders to him. Finally I said, "They don't sound like local talent, huh?"

"They don't clang any bells for me."

I had given him my business card. His cup had already made a half-moon coffee print on it.

"But you'll rack your memory, won't you?" I said.

"What?"

"If I wanted to have somebody whacked out in New Orleans, who would I have to see?"

His face began to grow attentive with the suggestion of the insult.

"What are you getting at?" he asked.

"There are at least four guys in the Quarter who can arrange a contract hit for five hundred dollars. Do you know who they are?"

"I don't care for your tone."

"Maybe it's just one of those off days. Thanks for the use of your mug books. I'd appreciate your keeping my card in your desk in case you need to call me."

I drove on over to Decatur by the river and parked my truck down the street from Jackson Square and walked into the French Quarter. The narrow streets were still cool with morning shadow, and I could smell coffee and fresh-baked bread in the cafés, strawberries and plums from the crates set out on the sidewalks in front of small grocery stores, the dank, cool odor of old brick in the courtyards. It had rained just before dawn, and water leaked out of the green window shutters on the pastel sides of the buildings and dripped from the rows of potted plants on the balconies or hanging from the ironwork.

I walked down St. Ann in the shadow of the cathedral to a one-story stucco building with a piked gate and a domed brick walkway that led to an office just off a flagstone courtyard. The courtyard was bordered with tight clumps of untrimmed banana trees. Painted on the frosted glass office window were the words CLETUS PURCEL INVESTIGATIVE SERVICES.

He had been my partner in the First District and one of the best cops I ever knew. Among the lowlifes, the wiseguys, the psychopaths, even the contract hit men out of Houston and Miami, he'd had a reputation that was notorious even by the standards of the New Orleans Police Department. Hard-nosed, mainline recidivists who laughed at the threat of ten-year jolts in Angola would swallow with apprehension and reconsider their point of view when they were told that Clete had taken an interest in their situations. Once a recently discharged convict from Parchman, a man who had shot out his wife's eye with a BB gun and whom I busted in a hot-pillow joint on Airline Highway, said he was coming back to New Orleans to cool out the cop who was responsible for his grief. Clete met him at the Greyhound depot, walked him into the restroom, and poured a container of liquid soap down his mouth. We never heard from him again.

But his marriage went bad, and eventually he got into trouble with whiskey, prostitutes, and shylocks, and a teaspoon at a time he began to serve the forces and people he had hated all his life. Finally he took ten thousand dollars to get rid of a witness in a federal investigation and barely made the flight to Guatemala, three minutes before his fellow detectives were racing down the concourse behind him with a murder warrant. Later the murder charge was dropped and he became head of security at two casinos in Las Vegas and Reno and the bodyguard of a Galveston mobster by the name of Sally Dio. I had marked Clete off as a turncoat, a pitiful facsimile of the friend I'd once had, but I came to learn that his loyalty and courage went far deeper into his character than his personal problems. His resignation from the mob came in the form of Sally Dio's private plane exploding all over a mountaintop in western Montana. Sally Dio and his entourage had to be combed out of the ponderosa trees with garden rakes. The National Transportation Safety Board said they suspected that someone had put sand in the fuel tanks.

"How's it hanging, noble mon?" he said from behind his desk when I opened his office door.

He wore a candy-striped shirt that looked like it was about to burst on his huge shoulders, a tie pulled loose at the throat, a blue-black .38 revolver in a nylon shoulder holster, and a powder-blue porkpie hat pushed down low on his forehead. His eyes were green and intelligent, his hair sandy, and his face always had a flush to it because of his weight and high blood pressure. A scar the texture and color of a bicycle patch ran down through one eyebrow and across the bridge of his nose, where he'd been bashed with a length of pipe when he was a kid.

I had already called him and told him about my problems with the Sonnier investigation.

"How'd you make out down at the First?" he said.

"I didn't recognize anyone in the mug books. I didn't get any help from anyone, either. I got the feeling I was a tourist from the provinces."

"Let's face it, mon. They didn't hold a going-away party when either one of us hung it up."

"How do you like the PI business?" I sat down across from him in a straw and deer-hide swayback chair. The walls of his office were decorated with bullfight posters, wine bags, and festooned *banderillas*. Through the back window I could see the courtyard and Clete's barbells and weight bench next to a stone well that leaked water at the top.

"It's good," he said. "Well, maybe the word's *easy*. You don't get rich at it, but the competition isn't exactly the first team. You know, ex-cops who majored in stupid, redneck jocks from Mississippi who think the big score is working security at Walmart. I'm clearing around five hundred a week after the overhead. It beats running a nightclub for greaseballs, I guess."

"Sounds all right."

He took a cigarette out of his package of Camels and held it for a moment in his big hand, then he set it down on the desk blotter and put a stick of gum in his mouth. His eyes smiled at me while he chewed.

"The problem is that a lot of it's a drag," he said. "Discovery investigations for lawyers, stuff like that. It's not like the old days in Homicide when we used to really make them wince. You remember when we—"

"No, I don't remember, Clete."

"Come on, Dave. It was all full-tilt boogie rock 'n' roll back then. You loved it, mon. Admit it." He kept grinning, and his teeth clicked while he chewed his gum.

"Why the piece?"

"It gets interesting once in a while. I run down bail jumpers for a couple of bondsmen. Pimps, street dealers, bullshit like that. What a bunch. I think the Orkin Company ought to get serious in this town. I'm not kidding you, New Orleans is turning to shit. The fucking lowlifes have crawled out of the cracks."

I looked at my watch.

"You're worried about your parking meter or something?" he said.

"Sorry. I just need to be back in New Iberia this afternoon."

"How's everything at home?"

"It's okay. Good."

The smile went out of his eyes. I looked away from him.

He spread his fingers on the desk blotter. His hands looked as big as skillets.

"Bootsie's having trouble again?" he said.

"Yes."

"How bad?"

"You never know. One day's fine and full of bluebirds. The next day the gargoyles come out of the closet."

He took the gum out of his mouth and dropped it in the wastebasket. I heard him take a deep breath through his nose.

"Let's walk on over to the Pearl and have some oysters," he said. "Then we'll talk about these three buttwipes you're looking for."

"I'm a little tapped out right now."

"I've got a tab there. I never pay it, but that's what tabs are for. Let's get out into this beautiful day."

We walked down Bourbon, which was becoming more crowded with tourists now, past the T-shirt shops, jazz clubs and strip joints that advertised nude dancers and French orgies, to the corner of St. Charles and Canal, where we went inside the Pearl and sat at the long counter that ran the length of the restaurant. The tables were covered with checkercloth, wood-bladed fans turned overhead, and three black men in aprons were shucking open raw oysters over the ice bins behind the bar. We ordered two dozen on the half-shell, a glass of iced tea for me and a small pitcher of draft for Clete.

"Run it by me again," he said.

I went over all the details of Garrett's murder, the shootout, the description of the three intruders, the names I had heard them call each other while my ears had roared like the sea with the sound of my own blood.

Clete was silent, his green eyes thoughtful under his porkpie hat while he squeezed a lemon on his oysters and dotted them with Tabasco sauce.

"I don't know about the guy named Eddy or the guy with the scrap metal in his mouth," he said. "But this sawed-off character named Jewel sounds like a local I used to know. I haven't seen him around in a while, but I think we might be talking about Jewel Fluck."

"What?"

"You heard me. That's his name. His family came from Germany and he grew up in the Channel. He tried to make it as a jockey out at Jefferson Downs, but he was too heavy and so he worked as a hot-walker till they caught him doping a horse. He's a mean little bastard, Dave."

"*Fluck?*"

"You got it. Maybe his name screwed him up. When you think of Jewel Fluck, think of a hornet somebody just poured hot water on."

"Why doesn't he have a record?"

"He does. In Mississippi. I think he did four or five years in Parchman."

"What for?"

"Cutting up a colored guy who was scabbing on a job. Or something like that. Look, the only reason I know about this guy is he hid out a bail jumper I was looking for. The jumper was in the AB. I heard Fluck is, too."

"The Aryan Brotherhood?"

"Integrated jails breed them like fungus. I used to think it was the Black Muslims we had to worry about. But this is your genuine psychopathic white trash with a political cause up their butts. Hitler would have loved them."

He signaled the bartender for another pitcher of beer.

"Something wrong with your oysters?" he said.

"I'm just trying to figure this guy's tie-in with Weldon Sonnier," I said.

"Maybe it was just a robbery gone bad, Dave. Maybe it's not that complicated a deal."

"You didn't see the inside of the house. They really did a

number on it. They were after something specific."

"Maybe this Sonnier guy is holding some dope. We live in funny times. The coke money's a big temptation. A lot of straights have nosed up to the trough."

"It could be. When's the last time you saw Fluck?"

"A year or so ago. I don't think he's around town. I'll ask around, though. Look, Dave, from what you've told me, this Sonnier character has invited a pile of shit into his life. He also sounds like one of these white-collar cocksuckers who think cops have about the same status as their yardmen. Maybe it's time he learned the facts of life."

"Sir, could you watch your language, please?" the bartender said.

"What?" Clete said.

"Your language."

"What about my language?"

"We're okay here," I said to the bartender. He nodded and walked farther down the bar and started mixing a drink. Clete continued to stare after him.

"Does Fluck still have relatives in New Orleans?" I asked.

"I don't know," he answered, his eyes coming back into mine. "His mother probably wishes she'd thrown him away and raised the afterbirth. Forget about Fluck a minute. I've got a thought, a funny memory about somebody. The guy with the crowbar, the one named Eddy, tell me what he looked like again."

"His head was real big, his face full of bone. The kind you break your fist on."

"Did he have a tattoo?"

"I don't remember."

"A red and yellow tiger on his right arm?"

I tried to see it in my mind's eye, but the only image that came back was the bone-heavy face and the ridges of muscle under the T-shirt.

"Maybe I couldn't even pull him out of a lineup with any certainty," I said.

"There's one guy around town, he has a head like a pumpkin.

His name's Raintree, from Baton Rouge. I don't know his first name, though."

"Go on."

"I get a security retainer out at the yacht club. Sometimes I check out backgrounds on potential members, keep out the riffraff supposedly, which means the south-of-the-border crowd. The tomato pickers are very big on clubs these days. But I also do security at dances, receptions, Republican geek shows, that kind of stuff. So one night Bobby Earl has a big gig out there. It's black-tie stuff, respectable, people from the Garden District, no Red Man spitters allowed, get the picture? You couldn't get the word 'nigger' out of this bunch at gunpoint.

"Except a guy shows up who Bobby Earl wasn't planning on. Some character from the old States' Rights party, a real oil can, Vitalis running out of his hair, shiny suit, enough cologne to make your nose fall off. He was hooked up with those Klansmen who dynamited that colored church in Birmingham back in the sixties and killed those four children. Anyway, he's shaking hands with Bobby on the steps of the yacht club and this weird-looking kid from a radical newspaper takes their picture.

"That's when this guy Raintree, the guy with the pumpkin head and a red and yellow tiger on his arm, comes down the steps and takes the kid by the arm and walks him through the parking lot down to the lake. When I got there he'd punched the kid in the stomach and thrown his camera in the lake."

"What did you do?"

"I told Raintree to leave the grounds. I told the kid he ought to go home and leave these guys alone."

His eyes shifted away from me. He lit a cigarette. When I didn't speak, he turned on the stool and looked at me, a pinched light in his eyes.

"So it's not noble stuff. If I'd had my choices, I'd have clicked off Raintree's switch with a slapjack. But I don't get a city paycheck anymore, Dave."

"No, that's not what I was thinking about. You just tied the ribbon on the box, partner."

"You mean the connection between Jewel Fluck, the AB maybe, and this racist politician? But what's Bobby Earl got to do with your man in New Iberia?"

"Weldon Sonnier is his brother-in-law."

▼

Five minutes later we were walking under a colonnade on our way back to Clete's office. The sun had gone behind a cloud, and the air had become close with the smell of rain and the ripe fruit that was stacked in boxes on the sidewalk.

"What are you going to do?" Clete said. His face was heated from our pace.

"Head back to New Iberia and check out this guy Raintree."

"You think that's the way we ought to do it?"

I looked at him.

"Leave that procedure dogshit to the paper shufflers," he said.

"Clete, I don't think the word 'we' figures into the equation here."

"Oh yeah?"

"Yeah."

"You got a lot of help from the guys at the First, did you? You got a lot of backup when those three gumballs were trying to paint the furniture with your brains?"

We turned up Toulouse toward Bourbon. He stopped in front of a cigar and news stand. A black man was shining the shoes of a man who sat in an elevated chair. Clete touched me on the jacket lapel with his finger.

"I won't tell you what to do," he said. "But when they try to kill you, it gets personal. Then you play it only one way. You go into the lion's den and you spit in the lion's mouth."

"I don't have any authority here."

"That's right. So they won't be expecting us. Fuck, mon, let's give them a daytime nightmare." He stuck a matchstick in the corner of his mouth and grinned. "Come on, think about it. Is there anything so fine as making the lowlifes wish they were still a dirty thought in their parents' mind?"

He snapped his fingers and rhythmically clicked his fists and palms together. His green eyes were dancing with light and expectation.

▼

If you grew up in the Deep South, you're probably fond, as I am, of recalling the summertime barbecues and fish fries, the smoke drifting in the oak trees, the high school dances under a pavilion that was strung with Japanese lanterns, the innocent lust we discovered in convertibles by shadowed lakes groaning with bullfrogs, and the sense that the season was eternal, that the world was a quiet and gentle place, that life was a party to be enjoyed with the same pleasure and certainty as the evening breeze that always carried with it the smell of lilac and magnolia and watermelons in a distant field.

But there is another memory, too: the boys who went nigger-knocking in the little black community of Sunset, who shot people of color with BB guns and marbles fired from slingshots, who threw M-80s onto the galleries of their pitiful homes. Usually these boys had burr haircuts, jug ears, half-moons of dirt under their fingernails. They lived in an area of town with unpaved streets, garbage in the backyards, ditches full of mosquitoes and water moccasins from the coulee. Each morning they got up with their loss, their knowledge of who they were, and went to war with the rest of the world.

When we meet the adult bigot, the Klansman, the anti-Semite, we assume that he was bred in that same wretched place. Sometimes that's a correct conclusion. Oftentimes it's not.

"Did this guy grow up in a shithole or something?" Clete said.

We were parked in my truck across from Bobby Earl's home out by Lake Pontchartrain.

"I heard his father owned a candy company in Baton Rouge," I said.

"Maybe he was an abused fetus." He blew cigarette smoke out the window and looked at the piked fence, the blue-green lawn and twirling sprinklers, the live oaks that formed a canopy over the long white driveway. "There must be big bucks in sticking it to the coloreds these days. I bet you could park six cars on his porch." He looked at his watch. The sky was gray over the lake, and the waves were capping in the wind. "Let's give it another half hour, then I'll treat you to some rice and red beans at Fat Albert's."

"I'd better head back pretty soon, Clete."

He formed a pocket of air in one jaw.

"You always believed in prayer, Streak," he said.

"Yes?"

"Don't you AA guys call it 'turning it over'? Maybe it's time to do that. Worrying about Bootsie and what you can't change is putting boards in your head."

"It sure is."

"So?"

"What?"

"Why set yourself up for a lot of grief?" He was looking straight ahead now, his porkpie hat resting on his brow. "I know you, noble mon. I know the thoughts you're going to have before you have them. Turn the dials on yourself long enough, tamp them down till you got all the gears shearing off against each other, and pretty soon the old life looks pretty good again."

"That's not the way it is this time."

"Yeah, probably not. I shouldn't be handing out advice, anyway. When I started drinking my breakfast there for a while, I got sent by the captain to this shrink who was on lend-lease from the psychology department at Tulane. So I told him a few stories, stuff that I thought was pretty ordinary—race beefs when I was growing up in the Irish Channel, a hooker who dosed me while I was married, the time you and I smoked that greaseball dope dealer and his bodyguard in the back of their Cadillac—and I thought the guy was going to throw up in his wastebasket. I always heard these guys could take it. I felt like a freak. I ain't kidding you, the guy was trembling. I offered to buy him a drink and he got mad."

I couldn't help laughing.

"That's it, mon. Lighten up," he said. "Nothing rattles the Bobbsey Twins from Homicide. And my, my, what do we have here?" He adjusted the outside mirror with his hand. "Yes indeedy, it's the All-American peckerwood. You know this guy's got broads all over New Orleans? That's right, they really dig his rebop. I've got to learn his technique. Come on, fire it up, Streak."

I turned the ignition and followed the white, chauffeur-driven Chrysler toward the entrance.

"I'm out of my jurisdiction, Clete," I said. "No Wyatt Earp stuff. We don't bruise the fruit. Right? Agreed?"

"Sure. We're just out here to visit. Talk some trash, maybe drink some mash. Get some political tips. Step on it, mon." His arm was pressed flat against the side of the truck door, his face bright, like a man anticipating a carnival ride.

The Chrysler drove through the gate and on up the drive toward the white stucco, blue-tiled home with the sweeping porch and an adjacent swimming pool that was bordered with banana and lime trees and flaring gas torches. A man in pressed black pants and shined shoes, white shirt and black tie, with oiled red hair combed straight back on his head, swung the gate closed and walked away as though we were not there.

Clete got out of the truck and walked to the gate.

"Hey, bubba, does it look like we're from Fuller Brush?" he said.

"What?" the man said.

"We're here to see Bobby Earl. Open up."

"He's got dinner guests. Who are you?"

"Who am I?" Clete said, smiling, pointing at his chest with his thumb. "Good question, good question. You see this badge? Dave, do you know who we're talking to here?"

He folded his private investigator's badge and replaced it in his coat pocket when the man reached for it.

"I bet you didn't think I recognized you, did you?" Clete said. "Gomez, right? You were a middleweight. Lefty Felix Gomez. I saw you fight Irish Jerry Wallace over in Gretna. You knocked his mouthpiece into the third row."

The gateman nodded, his face unimpressed. "Mr. Earl don't want to be bothered by anybody tonight," he said. "That badge you got. Pawnshop windows are full of them."

"Sharp eye," Clete said, his mouth still grinning. "I remember another story about you. You beat up a kid in a filling station. A high school kid. You fractured his skull."

"I told you what Mr. Earl said. You can come back tomorrow, or you can write him care of the state legislature. That's where he works."

"Nice tie," Clete said, reached through the gate, knotted the man's necktie in his fist, and jerked his face tightly against the bars. "You've got a serious problem, Lefty. You're hard of hearing. Now, you get on that box and tell Mr. Earl that Cletus Purcel and Detective Dave Robicheaux are here to see him. Is my signal getting through to you? Are we big-picture clear on this?"

"Let him go, Clete," I said.

A tall, good-looking man with angular shoulders in a striped, gray double-breasted suit, his silk shirt unbuttoned on his chest, walked down the drive toward us.

"Sure," Clete said, and released the gateman, whose face had gone livid with anger except for the two diagonal lines where the flesh had been pressed into the iron bars of the gate.

"What's the trouble, Felix?" the man in the suit said.

"No trouble, Mr. Earl. We want a few minutes of your time. I don't think your man here was passing on the information very well," Clete said.

"I'm Detective Dave Robicheaux of the Iberia Parish sheriff's office," I said, and opened my badge in my palm. "I'm sorry for the late hour, but I'm in town only for today. I'd like to talk with you about Mr. Raintree."

"Mr. Raintree? Yes. Well, I'm having someone for dinner, but—" His thick brown hair was styled and grew slightly over his collar, giving him a rugged and casual look. His skin was fine-grained, his jaws cleanly shaved, and his smile was easy and good-natured. The only strange characteristic about him was his right eye, whose pupil was larger than the one in his left eye, which gave it a monocular look. "Well, we can take a minute or two, can't we? Would you like to sit down by the pool? I'm not sure that I can help you, but I'll try."

"I appreciate your time, sir," I said, and followed him up the drive.

"Hey, Lefty, I forgot to tell you," Clete said, winking at the gateman. "When you were in the ring, I always heard they tried to match you up with cerebral-palsy victims."

We sat on canvas deck chairs by a swimming pool that was shaped in the form of a cross. The underwater lights were on, and the turquoise surface glistened with a thin sheen of suntan oil. On the flagstone patio a linen-covered table was set with candelabra and service for two. Bobby Earl walked to the side door of his house and spoke to his chauffeur, who had changed into a white butler's jacket. Then a young blonde woman in a pink bathing suit, terry-cloth robe, and high heels came out the door and began arguing with Bobby Earl. His back was to us, but I could see him raise his long, slender hands in a placating gesture. Then she slammed the screen and went back inside.

"I told you he was a gash hound," Clete said.

"Clete, will you ease up? I mean it."

"I'm mellow, I'm extremely serene. Don't sweat it. Hey, I didn't mention something else about the gateman back there. He was a coke mule for Joey Gouza and the Giacano family. It's funny he's out here with the white man's hope."

"We'll run him later. Now stop shaking the screen on the zoo cage."

"You've got no sense of humor, Streak. The sonofabitch is scared. Watch the corner of his mouth. Now's the time to squeeze his peaches."

Bobby Earl came back to the pool, with his butler behind him. The butler set a bowl of popcorn crawfish down on a folding table between me and Clete.

"Would you gentlemen like something from the bar?" he said. His face was flat, with a small nose, close-set eyes, and a chin beard.

"Nothing for me, thanks," I said.

"How about a double Black Jack, no ice, with a 7 on the side?" Clete said.

"I'll have a vodka collins, Ralph," Bobby Earl said, sat down across from us, and folded one leg across his knee. I studied his handsome face and tried to relate it to the 1970s newspaper photograph I had seen of him in silken Klan robes when he had been imperial wizard of the Louisiana Grand Knights of the Invisible Empire.

"Does Mr. Raintree work for you?" I asked. I opened a small notebook in my hand and clicked my ballpoint pen with my thumb.

"No."

"He doesn't work for you?" I said.

"You mean Eddy?"

"Yes, Eddy Raintree."

"He did at one time. Not now. I don't know where he is now."

Then I saw what Clete had meant. The skin at the corner of his mouth wrinkled, like fingernail impressions in putty.

"When's the last time you saw him?" I asked.

"It's been a while. I tried to help him a couple of times when he was out of work. Has Eddy done something wrong? I don't understand."

"I'm investigating the murder of a police officer. I thought Eddy might be able to help us. Do you know if Eddy has ever been up the road?"

"What?"

"Has he ever done time?"

"I don't know." Then his peculiar, mismatched eyes focused on me thoughtfully. "Why do you ask me if he's been in prison? As a police officer, wouldn't *you* know that?"

"I didn't know his first name until you told me," I said, and smiled at him.

The butler brought the drinks from the poolside bar and served them to Clete and Bobby Earl. Earl took a deep drink from his without his eyes ever leaving my face. When he lowered his glass his mouth looked cold and red, like a girl's.

"When was the last time you talked to him?" I asked.

"It was a while back. I don't remember."

I nodded and smiled again while I wrote in my notebook. Clete put a handful of popcorn crawfish in his mouth, drank out of his glass of 7 Up and cracked the ice between his molars.

"This is a great place," he said. "You own it?"

"I lease it."

"I hear you're going to run for the U.S. Senate," Clete said.

"Perhaps."

"Say, you ever see Jewel Fluck around?" Clete said.

"Who?"

"He's a little sawed-off guy. Hangs around with Eddy. He's in the AB."

"I'm not sure what you're saying."

"The Aryan Brotherhood," Clete said. "They're jailhouse Nazis."

"Well . . ." Bobby Earl began.

"You really don't know Fluck, huh?" Clete said.

"No."

"Streak would really like to talk with him and Eddy. They almost blew out his light. You get Streak mad and he'll throw elephant shit through your window fan."

Clete held up his glass for the butler to fill it again.

"I think we don't need to talk anymore," Bobby Earl said. "I'm not sure why you're here anyway. I have the feeling you'd like to provoke something."

"Here's my business card, Mr. Earl," I said. "But I'll be back in touch one way or another. How's Eddy's face?"

"What?"

"He had a lot of splinters in it the last time I saw him. Do you know why he'd want to tear up your brother-in-law's house?"

"Now, you listen—"

"He and two others executed a policeman. They blew his brains all over a basement floor at pointblank range," I said. "You'd better think up some better bullshit the next time cops come out to your house."

The blood had drained out of his cheeks. Then a strange transformation took place in his face. The skin grew taut against the bone, and there was a flat, green-yellow venomous glaze in his eyes, the kind you see only in people who have successfully worked for years to hide the propensity for cruelty that lives inside them.

"You got in here when you shouldn't have. Now you're on your way out," he said.

"That sounds serious. No J.D. refills?" Clete said.

The butler rested his hand on the back of Clete's chair. Through the banana trees I saw the gateman walking across the lawn toward us. I stood up to go. Clete lit a cigarette and flipped the match into the swimming pool. It was deep dusk now, and the trees were swimming with fireflies.

"Don't crowd the plate," he said, his eyes looking straight ahead.

The butler looked at Bobby Earl, who nodded his head negatively and rose from his chair.

"I get it," Clete said, rising also, his grin back in place. "You're cutting us some slack. Otherwise the hired help might just stomp the shit out of us. But this ain't niggertown. And it's no time for bad press, right? I've changed my mind about you, Mr. Earl. You've got real Kool-Aid. I dig it." He blew cigarette smoke at an upward angle into the violet air and gazed approvingly about the grounds. "What a place. I've been in the wrong line of work."

Then the butler fitted his hand around Clete's biceps to point him toward the driveway.

Clete pivoted and lifted his huge fist into the butler's stomach. It was a deep, unexpected blow, in the soft place right under the sternum, and the butler's face went white with shock. His mouth gasped, and his eyes locked open as big as half dollars.

Then Clete grabbed him by the back of his jacket and threw him spread-eagled across the table that had been set for two.

"Back off, Clete!" I said.

"Yeah? Take a look at the lollipop our man's got in his pocket?" He held up a leather-hided slapjack in one hand, and tossed it over his shoulder into the pool. "Let's see what other items Bonzo's holding. How about this? A .25-caliber Beretta. What were you going to do with this, fuckhead?"

The side of the butler's face was pressed flat against the table; spittle dripped into his chin beard.

"Answer me. You think this is Beirut?" Clete said, his hand tight on the back of the butler's neck.

Then he straightened his back, released the clip from the pistol's magazine, ejected the round in the chamber, and sailed the pistol over a hedge. He threw the clip and the ejected round into the pool.

The gateman's eyes flicked back and forth between us and

Bobby Earl; then he stepped hesitantly out on the flagstones, the skin around his mouth tight with expectation.

"You don't get paid enough money for it, partner," I said.

"You want me to call the cops, Mr. Earl?" he said.

Bobby Earl didn't answer him. Instead he looked at me.

"You've made a grave mistake," he said. The pupil in his right eye was round and black, like a large, broken drop of India ink.

"I don't think so," I said. "I think you're dirty. I think you're involved with the death of a police officer. In Louisiana you don't skate when you kill a cop. Do some research on the Red Hat and find out who they've processed through there."

"The what?" The rim below his right eye was red and trembling with anger.

"The Red Hat House. You're in the legislature. Call up at Angola and check it out. They used to have a sign on one wall that said, *This is where they knock the fire out of your ass.* I think they meant it."

Clete and I walked across the lawn toward my truck. I looked back over my shoulder before I opened the door. Bobby Earl was staring after us, his face bathed in the yellow-red light of a flaming gas torch by the pool. The blonde girl in the pink swimsuit and terry-cloth robe clung to his arm like a frightened acolyte, her mouth a silent O. The 1970s photograph of Bobby Earl in silken robes, a cross crawling with fire in the background, no longer seemed out of place and time.

4

The house was dark when I got back home. I looked in on Alafair, who was sleeping with her thumb in her mouth and her stuffed frog on the pillow next to her. Her room was filled with souvenirs from our vacation trips to Houston, Key West, Biloxi, and Disney World: an Astros space helmet, a Donald Duck cap with a quacking bill, conch shells, dried starfish, a huge inflated Goofy figure, rows of sand dollars, a coral-encrusted cannon ball that I had chopped out of Seven-Mile Reef. I took her thumb out of her mouth and stroked her hair when her eyes fluttered temporarily awake. Then I latched her screen window, which had become part of a silent conspiracy three or four nights a week when she forgot to hook it after letting Tripod in her room against house rules.

Then I undressed in the main bedroom and sat on the side of the bed in my skivvies next to Bootsie's sleeping form. The sky had cleared, and the pecan trees clicked with moonlight in the breeze off the bayou; I could smell the fecund odor of bream spawning in the marsh. In the distance I heard a freight train blowing down the line.

I tried to let go of the day's concerns, let all the heat and fatigue and anger drain out of my hands and feet; but I was genuinely wired, wrapped so tight that my skin felt like a prison. I could hear the tiger pacing in his cage, his paws softly scudding on the wire mesh. His eyes were yellow in the darkness, his breath as fetid as meat that had rotted in the sun.

Sometimes I imagined him prowling through trees in William Blake's dark moral forest, his striped body electrified with a hungry light. But I knew that he was not the poet's creation; he was conceived and fed by my own self-destructive alcoholic energies and fears, chiefly my fear of mortality and my inability to affect the destiny of those whom I could not afford to lose.

Then Bootsie rolled against me, and I felt her hand brush my thigh and touch my sex. I took off my shorts and undershirt and lay down next to her, slipped my arms around her back, and put my face in her hair. Her body was warm from sleep, and she spread one leg around my calf, placed me inside her, and pressed her palm in the small of my back. When we made love I always had several images in my mind of Bootsie and I never saw her as one person, maybe because we had both known each other since we were nineteen. I remembered her in an organdy evening dress and the bright redness of her sunburned shoulders under the Japanese lanterns when we first met at a college dance out on Spanish Lake; I saw the fearful innocence in her face when we lost our virginity together in my father's boathouse, the rain dripping out of the cypress trees into the dead water as loudly as the beating of our hearts; and I still saw the pain in her eyes when I rejected her, hurt her deeply, and caused her to marry another man, all because of my own self-loathing and inability to explain to anyone else the dark psychological landscape I had wandered in and out of since I was a child.

But just as Alafair had been given to me in a wobbling bubble of air below the Gulf's surface, I believed my Higher Power had given me back Bootsie when I had lost all claim to her, had undone my youthful mistakes for me, and had made that wonderful summer of 1957 as immediate and tangible and ongoing as the four o'clocks that bloomed nightly under the moon on Bayou Teche.

But how do you cast out the canker from the rose, I thought.

Then she put both her legs in mine, held me tightly inside her, her mouth open and wet against my cheek, and in my mind's eye I saw a wave bursting in a geyser of foam against the hard outline of a distant jetty, a coral boulder ripping loose from the ocean's floor, and a flurry of silver ribbon fish rising from the mouth of an underwater cave.

▼

By the next afternoon I had received the files and photos of Jewel Fluck and Eddy Raintree from the National Crime Information Center in Washington, D.C.; police departments in New Orleans, Jackson, Biloxi, and Baton Rouge; and Angola and Parchman penitentiaries. Both men belonged to the great body of psychologically misshapen people that I refer to as The Pool. Members of The Pool leave behind warehouses of official paperwork as evidence that they have occupied the planet for a certain period of time. Their names are entered early on in welfare case histories, child-abuse investigations, clinic admissions for rat bites and malnutrition. Later on these same people provide jobs for an army of truant officers, psychologists, public defenders, juvenile probation officers, ambulance attendants, emergency-room personnel, street cops, prosecutors, jailers, prison guards, alcohol- and drug-treatment counselors, bail bondsmen, adult parole authorities, and the county morticians who put the final punctuation mark in their files.

The irony is that without The Pool we would probably have to justify our jobs by refocusing our attention and turning the key on slumlords, industrial polluters, and the coalition of defense contractors and militarists who look upon the national treasury as a personal slush fund.

I looked at the mug shots of Fluck and Raintree and was reasonably sure that these were the same men who had been in Weldon's house (I say "reasonably sure" because a booking-room photograph is often taken when the subject is tired, angry, drunk, or drugged, and recidivists constantly change their hairstyles, grow and shave mustaches and hillbilly sideburns, and become bloated on jailhouse fare like grits, spaghetti, and mashed potatoes).

But Fluck's file told me little that I didn't already know, or couldn't have guessed at. At seventeen he had pushed another boy down a stairs at the Superdome and broken his arm, but the charge had been dropped. He had been banned for life from Louisiana racetracks after he was caught feeding a horse a speedball; he had been in the New Orleans city prison twice, once for beating up a taxicab driver, a second time for distribution of obscene film materials. His mainline fall had been at Parchman, where he did a five-year jolt and went out on what is called "max-time," which meant he either gave the hacks constant trouble and earned no good-time, or he refused parole because he didn't want to go back on the street under supervision.

But because he had gone out on max-time, Parchman had no address for him, and he hadn't been arrested again in the two years since his discharge. His parents were deceased, and neither the New Orleans phone directory nor any of the utility companies listed anyone by the name of Fluck.

Eddy Raintree's photo stared at me out of his file with a face that had the moral depth and complexity of freshly poured cement. He had a sixth-grade education, a dishonorable discharge from the Marine Corps, and had never had a more skilled job than that of fry cook and hod carrier. He had been in the Calcasieu, West Baton Rouge, and Ascension parish prisons for bigamy, check writing, arson, and sodomy with animals. He went down for three years in Angola for possession of stolen food stamps, and he spent two of those three years in lockdown with the big stripes (the violent and unmanagable) after he was suspected of involvement in a gang rape that left a nineteen-year-old convict dead in a shower stall.

He, like Jewel Fluck, had gone out max-time three years ago, and there was no current address for him. But at the bottom of Raintree's prison sheet was a notation that Captain Delbert Bean had recommended that this man be reclassified as a big stripe, and that no good-time be applied toward his early release from the farm.

Early Monday morning I drove up to Angola, north of Baton Rouge on the Mississippi River, rolled across the cattle guard between the gun towers and the fences topped with rolls of razor wire, and followed the narrow road past the Block, an enormous fenced compound where both the snitches and the big stripes were kept in lockdown, through fields of sweet potatoes and corn and freshly plowed acreage that dipped all the way down to the river basin. I passed the old prison cemetery, where those who die while incarcerated do Angola time for all eternity; the bulldozed and weedgrown foundations of the sweat boxes on Camp A (there had been two of them, upright, narrow cast-iron places of torment, with a hole the diameter of a cigar to breathe through, the space so tight that if a convict collapsed his knees and buttocks would wedge against the walls); the crumbled ruins of the stone buildings left over from the War Between the States (which for years had been used to house Negro inmates, including three of the best twelve-string blues guitarists I know of—Leadbelly, Robert Pete Williams, and Hogman Mathew Maxie); and finally the old Red Hat House down by the river bank, a squat, ugly off-white building that took its name from the red-painted straw hats worn by the big-stripe levee gangs who were locked there before the building became the home of the electric chair, which has since been moved to a more modern environment, one with tile walls that glow with the clean, antiseptic light of a physician's clinic.

The Mississippi was high and churning with mud and uprooted trees, and out on the flat, among the willows, I saw Captain Delbert Bean on horseback, a pearl-gray Stetson hat slanted on his head, working a gang of convicts who were filling sandbags out of a dump truck and laying them along the base of the levee.

That levee is a burial ground for an untold number of convicts who were murdered, some as object lessons, by prison personnel. Ask anyone who ever worked in Angola, or did time there. I will not use their names, but there used to be two old-time gunbulls, brothers, who would get sodden and mean on corn whiskey, sometimes take a nap under a tree, then awake, single out some hapless soul, tell him to start running, and then kill him.

Delbert Bean was a dinosaur left over from that era. He had been a prison guard for forty-seven years, and I don't believe that in his life he had ever traveled farther away from the farm than New Orleans or Shreveport. He had no family or friends that I knew of, no external frame of reference, little knowledge of change in the larger world. His eyes were a washed-out blue, his skin covered with brown spots the size of dimes, his liver eaten away with cirrhosis. His stomach looked like a watermelon under his long-sleeved blue shirt. The accent was north Louisiana hill country, the voice absolutely certain when he spoke, and the face absolutely joyless.

He was not a man whom you either liked or disliked. He had been jailing most of his life, and I suspected that at the center of his existence was a loneliness and perversion so great that if he ever became privy to it he would blow his brains all over the ceiling of the little frame house where he lived with others like himself in the free people's compound.

He handed the reins of his horse to a black inmate and walked with a cane up a path through the willows toward me. The bottom of the cane was seated inside a twelve-inch steel tube. A briar pipe protruded from inside the holster belt of his chrome-plated nine-millimeter automatic. He shook hands with the limpness of a man who was not used to social situations, filled his pipe, and pushed the tobacco down with his thumb while his eyes watched the men filling and hefting sandbags below us. I had known him for fifteen years, and I did not once remember his addressing me by name.

"Eddy Raintree," he said, acknowledging my question. "Yeah, he was one of mine. What about him?"

"I think he helped kill a deputy sheriff. I'd like to run him to ground, but I'm not sure where to start."

He lit his pipe and watched the smoke drift off into the wind.

"His kind used to run their money through their pecker on beer and women. Now they do it with dope. I caught him and another one once cooking down some blues to shoot in an eyedropper. They was using the edge of a dollar bill for an insulator. No more sense than God give a turnip."

"Was he in any racial beefs?"

"When you got nigger and white boys in the same cage, there ain't any of them wouldn't cut each other's throats."

"Do you know if he was in the AB?"

"The what?"

"The Aryan Brotherhood."

"We ain't got that in here."

"That's funny. It's the fashion everywhere else." I tried to smile. But he was not given to humor about his job.

"Let me sit down. My hip's hurting," he said. He raised his cane in the air and shouted, "Walnut!" A mulatto convict, his denims streaked with mud and sweat, dropped his shovel, picked up a folding chair, ran it up the incline, and popped it open for the captain.

"Tell Mr. Robicheaux what you're in for," the captain said.

"Suh?"

"You heard me."

The convict's eyes focused on a tree farther down the levee.

"Murder, two counts," he said, quietly.

"Whose murder?" the captain said.

"My kids. They say I shot bof' my kids. That's what they say."

"Get on back to work."

"Yes, suh."

The captain waited until the convict was back down the mud-flat, then said, pointing with the steel tip of his cane, "See that big one yonder, the one flinging them bags up on the levee, he raped an eighty-five-year-old woman, then snapped her neck. You tell these white boys they're gonna have to cell with niggers like them two out yonder or they'll lose their good-time, what do you think's gonna happen?"

"I'm not following you."

He drew in on his pipe, his eyes hazy with a private knowledge. It was overcast, and his lips looked sick and purple against his liver-spotted skin.

"We had two white boys shanked in the Block this year," he said. "One a trusty, one a big stripe. We think the same nigger got both of them, but we can't prove it. If you was a white person living up there, what would you do?"

"So maybe there's something *like* the AB in Angola?"

"Call it what you want. They got their ways. The goddamn Supreme Court's caused all this." He paused, then continued. "They carve swastikas, crosses, lightning bolts on each other, pour ink in the sores. The black boys don't tend to mess with them, then.

Wait a minute, I'll show you something. Shorty! Get it up here!"

"Yow boss!" A coal-black convict, with a neck like a fire hydrant, his face running with sweat, heaved a sandbag against the levee and lumbered up the incline toward us.

"What'd Boss Gilbeau put you in isolation for?" the captain asked.

"Fightin', boss."

"Who was you fighting with, Shorty?"

"One of them boys back in Ash." He grinned, his eyes avoiding both of us.

"Was he white or colored, Shorty?"

"He was white, boss."

"Show Mr. Robicheaux how you burned yourself when you got out of isolation."

"Suh?"

"Pull up your shirt, boy, and don't act ignorant."

The convict named Shorty unbuttoned his sweat-spotted denim shirt and pulled the tail up over his back. There were four gray, thin, crusted lesions across his spine, like his skin had been branded by heated wires or coat hangers.

"How'd you burn yourself, Shorty?" the captain said.

"Backed into the radiator, boss."

"What was the radiator doing on in April?"

"I don't know, suh. I wished it ain't been on. It sure did hurt. Yes, suh."

"Get on back down there. Tell them others to clean it up for lunch."

"Yes, suh."

The captain knocked his pipe out on his boot heel and stuck it back in his holster belt. He gazed out on the wide yellow-brown sweep of the river and the heavy green line of trees on the far side. He didn't speak.

"That's the way it is here, huh?" I said.

"Besides dope, Raintree's problem is his prick. He's got rut for brains. It don't matter if it's male or female, if it's warm and moving he'll try to top it. The other thing you might look for is fortune-tellers. He had astrology maps all over his cell walls. He give a queer in Magnolia a carton of cigarettes a week to read his palm. By the way, it ain't the AB you ought to have on your mind. Them with the swastikas I was telling you about, they get mail from some church out in Idaho called Christian Identity. Hayden Lake, Idaho.''

He raised himself up on his cane to indicate that our interview was over. I could almost hear his bones crack.

"I thank you for your time, captain," I said.

Then as an afterthought he said, "If you bust that boy, tell him he just as lief hang himself as come back here for killing a policeman."

His pupils were like black cinders in his washed-out blue eyes.

▼

I arrived back at my office just in time to shuffle some papers around on my desk and sign out at five o'clock. I was tired from the round-trip drive up to Angola; my shoulder still hurt where Eddy Raintree had caught me with the crowbar, and I wanted to go home, eat supper, take a run along the dirt road by the bayou, and maybe go to a movie in Lafayette with Alafair and Bootsie.

But parked next to my pickup truck was a waxed fire-engine-red Cadillac, with the immaculate white canvas top folded back loosely on the body. A man in ice-cream slacks lay almost supine across the leather seats, one purple suede boot propped up on the window jamb, a sequined sunburst guitar hung across his stomach.

"*Allons à Lafayette, pour voir les 'tites françaises,*" he sang, then sat up, pulled off his sunglasses with his mutilated hand, and grinned at me. "What's happening, lieutenant?"

"Hello, Lyle."

"Take a ride with me."

"How many of these do you own?"

"They actually belong to the church."

"I bet."

"Take a ride with me."

"I'm on my way home."

"You can blow a few minutes. It's important."

"Do you have anything against talking to me during office hours?"

"Somebody broke into Drew's house last night."

"I didn't hear anything about it. Did she report it to the city police?"

"No."

"Why not?"

"Maybe I'll explain that. Take a ride with me." He lifted his guitar over into the back seat. I opened the door and sat back in the deep flesh-colored leather seat next to him. We clanked across the drawbridge over Bayou Teche and drove out of town on East Main. He picked up a paper cup from the floor and drank out of it. A familiar odor struck my nostrils in the warm air.

"Did you give yourself a dispensation today?" I said.

"I preach against drunkenness, not drinking. There's a big difference."

"Where are we going, Lyle?"

"Not far. Right there," he said, and pointed across a sugarcane field to a collapsed barn, a rusted and motionless windmill, and some brick pilings that had once supported a house. The field behind the barn was unplowed, and in it were a half-dozen oil wells.

We pulled off the parish road into a weed-grown dirt lane that led back to the barn. Lyle cut the engine, removed a pint bottle of bourbon from under the seat, and unscrewed the cap with one thumb. His hair, which he wore on-camera in a waved conk that reminded me of a washboard, was windblown and loose and hanging in his eyes.

"I own a third of it, a third of them wells out there, too," he said. "But I'm not fond of coming out here. I surely ain't."

"Why are we here, then?"

"You got to go back where the dragons live if you want to get rid of them."

"I tried to make myself clear before, Lyle. I sympathize with the problems your family had in the past, but my concern now is with a murdered police officer."

"Drew came home last night from her Amnesty International

meeting and she noticed the light on the back porch was out. She went on into the house, and there was a guy in the kitchen, in the dark, looking at her. He had something in his hand, a screwdriver or a knife. She ran back out the front of the house to the neighbor's and tried to get hold of Weldon, then she called me up in Baton Rouge."

"Why didn't she call the cops, Lyle?"

"She thinks she's protecting Weldon from something."

"What?"

"I'm not sure. Neither one of them is real convinced about my religious conversion. They tend to think maybe my brain cells soaked up a little too much purple acid when I came back from Vietnam. So they don't always confide everything in me. But it doesn't matter. I know who that fellow was."

"Your father?"

"I don't have a doubt."

"Everybody else seems to, including me."

He took a sip from his pint bottle and looked away at the red sun over the bayou. The wind was warm, and I could smell the reek of natural gas from the wells.

"What does Drew say? What did this man look like?" I asked.

"She didn't see his face."

"I'll talk to her tomorrow. Now I'd better get back home."

"All right, I'm going to tell you all of it. Then you can do any damn thing you want with it, Loot. But by God, first, you're going to listen."

The scars dripping down the side of his face looked like smooth pieces of red glass in the late sunlight.

5

And this is the way Lyle told it to me, or as I have reconstructed it.

His mother had come home angry from her waitress job in a beer garden on a burning July afternoon, and without changing out of her pink uniform, she had begun butchering chickens on the stump in the backyard, shucking off their feathers in a caldron of scalding water. The father, Verise, came home later than he should have, parked his pickup by the barn, and walked naked to the waist through the gate with his wadded shirt hanging out the back pocket of his Levi's. His shoulders, chest, and back were streaked with sweat and black hair.

The mother sat on a wood chair, with her knees apart in front of the steaming caldron, her forearms covered with wet chicken feathers. Headless chickens flopped all over the grass.

"I know you been with her. They were talking at the beer joint. Like you some kind of big ladies' man," she said.

"I ain't been with nobody," he said, "except with them mosquitoes I been slapping out in that marsh."

"You said you'd leave her alone."

"You children go inside."

"That gonna make your conscience right 'cause you send them kids off, you? She gonna cut your throat one day. She been in the crazy house in Mandeville. You gonna see, Verise."

"I ain't seen her."

"You sonofabitch, I smell her on you," the mother said, and swung a headless chicken by its feet and whipped a diagonal line of blood across his chest and Levi's.

"You ain't gonna act like that in front of my children, you," he said, and started toward her. Then he stopped. "I said y'all get inside. This is between me and her."

Weldon and Lyle were used to their parents' quarrels, and they turned sullenly toward the house; but Drew stood mute and fearful under the pecan tree, her cat pressed flat against her chest.

"Come on, Drew. Come see inside. We're gonna play with the Monopoly game," Lyle said, and tried to pull her by the arm. But her body was rigid, her bare feet immobile in the dust.

Then Lyle saw his father's large, square hand go up in the air, saw it come down hard against the side of the mother's face, heard the sound of her weeping, as he tried to step into Drew's line of vision and hold her and her cat against his body, hold the three of them tightly together outside the unrelieved sound of his mother's weeping.

Three hours later her car went through the railing on the bridge over the Atchafalaya River. Lyle dreamed that night that an enormous brown bubble arose from the submerged wreck, and when it burst on the surface her drowned breath stuck against his face as wet and rank as gas released from a grave.

▼

The woman called Mattie wore shorts and sleeveless blouses with sweat rings under the arms, and in the daytime she always seemed to have curlers in her hair. When she walked from room to room, she carried an ashtray with her, into which she constantly flicked her lipstick-stained Chesterfields. She had a hard, muscular body, and she didn't close the bathroom door all the way when she bathed; once Lyle saw her kneeling in the tub, scrubbing her big shoulders and chest with a large, flat brush. The area above her head was crisscrossed with improvised clotheslines, from which dripped her wet underthings. Her eyes fastened on his, and he thought she was about to reprimand him for staring at her; but instead her hard-boned, shiny face continued to look back at him with a vacuous indifference that made him feel obscene.

If Verise was out of town on a Friday or Saturday night, she fixed the children's supper, put on her blue suit, and sat by herself in the living room, listening to the *Grand Ole Opry* or the *Louisiana Hayride,* while she drank apricot brandy from a coffee cup. She always dropped cigarette ashes on her suit and had to spot-clean the cloth with dry-cleaning fluid before she drove off for the evening in her old Ford coupe. They didn't know where she went on those Friday or Saturday nights, but a boy down the road told them that Mattie used to work in Broussard's Bar on Railroad Avenue, an infamous area in New Iberia where the women sat on the galleries of the cribs, dipping their beer out of buckets and yelling at the railroad and oil-field workers in the street.

Then one morning when Verise was in Morgan City a man in a new silver Chevrolet sedan came out to see her. It was hot, and he parked his car partly on the grass to keep it in the shade. He wore sideburns, striped brown zoot slacks, two-tone shoes, suspenders, a pink shirt without a coat, and a fedora that shadowed his narrow face. While he talked to her he put one shoe on the car bumper and wiped the dust off it with a rag. Then their voices grew louder and he said, "You like the life. Admit it, you. He ain't given you no wedding ring, has he? You don't buy the cow, no, when you can milk through the fence."

"I am currently involved with a gentleman. I do not know what you are talking about. I am not interested in anything you are talking about," she said.

He threw the rag back inside the car and opened the car door.

"It's always trick, trade, or travel, darlin'," he said. "Same rules here as down on Railroad. He done made you a nigger woman for them children, Mattie."

"Are you calling me a nigra?" she said quietly.

"No, I'm calling you crazy, just like everybody say you are. No, I take that back, me. I ain't calling you nothing. I ain't got to, 'cause you gonna be back. You in the life, Mattie. You be phoning me to come out here, bring you to the crib, rub your back, put some of that warm stuff in your arm again. Ain't nobody else do that for you, huh?"

When she came back into the house she made the children take all the dishes out of the cabinets, even though they were clean, and wash them over again.

It was the following Friday that the principal at the Catholic elementary school called about a large welt on Lyle's cheek. Mattie was already dressed to go out. She didn't bother to turn down the radio when she answered the phone, and in order to compete with Red Foley's voice she had to almost shout into the receiver.

"Mr. Sonnier is not here," she said. "Mr. Sonnier is away on business in Port Arthur. . . . No, ma'm, I'm not the housekeeper. I'm a friend of the family who is caring for these children . . . There's nothing wrong with that boy that I can see. . . . Are you calling to tell me that there's something wrong, that I'm doing something wrong? What is it that I'm doing wrong? I would like to know that. What is your name?"

Lyle stood transfixed with terror in the hall as she bent angrily into the mouthpiece and her knuckles ridged on the receiver. A storm was blowing in from the Gulf, the air smelled of ozone, and the southern horizon was black with thunderclouds that crawled with white electricity. Lyle heard the wind ripping through the trees in the yard and pecans rattling down on the gallery roof like grapeshot.

When Mattie hung up the phone the skin of her face was tight against the bone and one liquid eye was narrowed at him like someone aiming down a rifle barrel.

▼

That winter Verise started working regular hours, what he called "an indoor job," at a chemical plant in Port Arthur, and the children saw him only on weekends. Mattie cooked only the evening meal and made the children responsible for the care of the house and the other two meals. Weldon started to get into trouble at school. His eighth-grade teacher, a laywoman, called and said he had thumb-tacked a girl's dress to the desk during class, causing her to almost tear it off her body when the bell rang, and he would either pay for the dress or be suspended. Mattie hung up the phone on her, and two days later the girl's father, a sheriff's deputy, came out to the house and made Mattie give him four dollars on the gallery.

She came back inside, slamming the door, her face burning, grabbed Weldon by the neck of his T-shirt, and walked him into the backyard, where she made him stand for two hours on an upended apple crate until he wet his pants.

Later, after she had let him come back inside and he had changed his underwear and blue jeans, he went outside into the dark by himself, without eating supper, and sat on the butcher stump, strik-ing kitchen matches on the side of the box and throwing them at the chickens. Before the children went to sleep he sat for a long time on the side of his bed, next to Lyle's, in a square of moonlight with his hands balled into fists on his thighs. There were knots of muscle in the backs of his arms. Mattie had given him a burr haircut, and his head looked as hard and scalped as a baseball.

"Tomorrow's Saturday. We're gonna listen to the LSU-Rice game," Lyle said.

"Some colored kids saw me from the road and laughed."

"I don't care what they did. You're brave, Weldon. You're braver than any of us."

"I'm gonna fix her."

His voice made Lyle afraid. The branches of the pecan trees were skeletal, like gnarled fingers against the moon.

"Don't be thinking like that," Lyle said. "It'll just make her do worse things. She takes it out on Drew. She made her kneel in the bathroom corner because she didn't flush the toilet."

"Go to sleep, Lyle," Weldon said. His eyes were wet. "She hurts us because we let her. We ax for it. You get hurt when you don't stand up. Just like Momma did."

Lyle heard him snuffing in the dark. Then Weldon lay down

with his face turned toward the opposite wall. His head looked carved out of gray wood in the moonlight.

▼

Three days later the school principal saw the cigarette burn on Drew's leg in the lunchroom and reported it to the social-welfare agency in town. A consumptive rail of a man in a dandruff-flecked blue suit drove out to the house and questioned Mattie on the gallery, then questioned the children in front of Mattie. Drew told him she had been burned by an ember that had popped out of a trash fire in the backyard.

He raised her chin with his knuckle. His black hair was stiff with grease.

"Is that what happened?" he asked.

"Yes, sir." The burn was scabbed and looked like ringworm on her skin.

He smiled and took his knuckle away from her chin. "Then you shouldn't play next to the fire," he said.

"I would like to know who sent you out here," Mattie said.

"That's confidential." He coughed on the back of his hand. "And to tell you the truth, I don't really know. My supervisor didn't tell me." He coughed again, this time loud and hard, and Lyle could smell his deep-lung nicotine odor. "But everything here looks all right."

Weldon's eyes were as hard as marbles, but he didn't speak.

The man walked with Mattie to his car, and Lyle felt like doors were slamming all around them. She put her foot on the man's running board and propped one arm on his car roof while she talked, so that her breasts were uplifted against her blouse and her knees were wide-spaced below the hem of her dress.

"Let's tell him," Lyle said.

"Are you kidding? Look at him. She could make him eat her shit with a spoon," Weldon said.

It was right after first period the next morning that they heard about the disaster at Port Arthur. A ship loaded with fertilizer had been burning in the harbor, and while people on the docks had watched fire-fighting boats pumping geysers of water onto the ship's decks, the fire had dripped into the hold. The explosion filled the sky with rockets of smoke and rained an umbrella of flame down on the chemical plant. The force of the secondary explosion was so great that it blew out windows in Beaumont, twenty miles away.

Mattie got drunk that night and fell asleep in the living room chair by the radio. When the children returned home from school the next afternoon, Mattie was waiting on the gallery to tell them that a man from the chemical company had telephoned and said that Verise was listed as missing. Her eyes were pink with either hangover or crying, her face puffy and round like a white balloon.

"Your father may be dead. Do you understand what I'm saying? That was an important man from his company who called. He would not call unless he was gravely concerned. Do you children understand what is being said to you?"

Weldon brushed at the dirt with his tennis shoe, and Lyle looked into a place about six inches in front of his eyes.

"He's worked like a nigra for you, maybe lost his life for you. You have nothing to say?"

"Maybe we ought to start cleaning up our rooms. You wanted us to clean up our rooms," Lyle said.

"You stay outside. Don't even come in this house," she said.

"I have to go to the bathroom," Weldon said.

"Then you can just do it in the dirt like a darky," she said, and went inside the house and latched the screen behind her.

▼

The next afternoon Verise was still unaccounted for. Mattie had an argument on the phone with somebody, perhaps the man in zoot pants and two-tone shoes; she told him he owed her money and she wouldn't come back and work at Broussard's Bar again until he paid her. After she hung up she breathed hard at the kitchen sink, smoking her cigarette and staring out into the yard. She snapped the cap off a bottle of Jax and drank it half empty, her throat working in one long wet swallow, one eye cocked at Lyle.

"Come here," she said.

"What?"

"You tracked up the kitchen. You didn't flush the toilet after you used it, either."

"I did."

"You did what?"

"I flushed the toilet."

"Then one of the others didn't flush it. Every one of you come out here. Now!"

"What is it, Mattie? We didn't do anything," he said.

"I changed my mind. Every one of you outside. All of you outside. Weldon, you too, you get out there right now. Where's Drew?"

"She's playing in the yard. What's wrong, Mattie?" Lyle said.

Outside, the wind was blowing through the trees in the yard, flattening the purple clumps of wisteria that grew against the barn wall.

"Each of you go to the hedge and cut the switch you want me to use on you," she said.

It was her favorite form of punishment. If they broke off a large switch, she hit them fewer times with it. If they came back with a thin or small switch, they would get whipped until she felt she had struck some kind of balance between size and number.

They remained motionless. Drew had been playing with her cat. She had tied a piece of twine around the cat's neck, and she held the twine in her hand like a leash, her knees and white socks dusty from play.

"I told you not to tie that around the kitten's neck again," Mattie said.

"It doesn't hurt anything. It's not your cat, anyway," Weldon said.

"Don't sass me," she said. "You will not sass me. None of you will sass me."

"I ain't cutting no switch," Weldon said. "You're crazy. My mama said so. You ought to be in the crazy house."

She looked hard into Weldon's eyes, and there was a moment of recognition in her colorless face, as though she had seen a growing meanness of spirit in Weldon that was the equal of her own.

Then she wet her lips, crimped them together, and rubbed her hands on her thighs.

"We shall see who does what around here," she said. She broke off a big switch from the myrtle hedge and raked it free of flowers and leaves except for one green sprig on the tip.

Drew looked up into Mattie's shadow, and dropped the piece of twine from her palm.

Mattie jerked her by the wrist and whipped her a half-dozen times across her bare legs. Drew twisted impotently from Mattie's fist, her feet dancing with each blow. The switch raised welts on her skin as thick and red as centipedes.

Then suddenly Weldon ran with all his weight into Mattie's back, stiff-arming her between the shoulder blades, and sent her tripping sideways over a bucket of chicken slops. She righted herself and stared at him open-mouthed, the switch loose in her hand. Then her eyes grew hot and bright with a painful intention, and her jawbone flexed like a roll of dimes.

Weldon burst out the back gate and ran down the dirt road between the sugarcane fields, the soles of his dirty tennis shoes powdering dust in the air.

▼

She waited for him a long time, watching through the screen as the mauve-colored dusk gathered in the trees and the sun's afterglow lit with flame the clouds on the western horizon. Then she took a bottle of apricot brandy into the bathroom and sat in the tub for almost an hour, turning the hot-water tap on and off until the tank was empty. When the children needed to go to the bathroom, she told them to take their problem outside. Finally she emerged in the hall, wearing only her panties and bra, her hair wrapped in a towel, the dark outline of her pubic hair plainly visible.

"I'm going to dress now and go into town with a gentleman friend," she said. "Tomorrow we're going to start a new regime around here. Believe me, there will never be a recurrence of what happened here today. You can pass that on to young Mr. Weldon for me."

But she didn't go into town. Instead, she put on her blue suit, a flower-print blouse, her nylon stockings, and walked up and down on the gallery, her cigarette poised in the air like a movie actress.

"Why not just drive your car, Mattie?" Lyle said quietly through the screen.

"It has no gas. Besides, a gentleman caller will be passing for me anytime now," she answered.

"Oh."

She blew smoke at an upward angle, her face aloof and flat-sided in the shadows.

"Mattie?"

"Yes?"

"Weldon's out back. Can he come in the house?"

"Little mice always return where the cheese is," she said.

At that moment Lyle wanted something terrible to happen to her.

She turned on one high heel, her palm supporting one elbow, her cigarette an inch from her mouth, her hair wreathed in smoke.

"Do you have a reason for staring through the screen at me?" she asked.

"No," he said.

"When you're bigger, you'll get to do what's on your mind. In the meantime, don't let your thoughts show on your face. You're a lewd little boy."

Her suggestion repelled him and made water well up in his eyes. He backed away from the screen, then turned and ran through the rear of the house and out into the backyard, where Weldon and Drew sat against the barn wall, fireflies lighting in the wisteria over their heads.

No one came for Mattie that evening. She sat in the stuffed chair in her room, putting on layers of lipstick until her mouth had the crooked bright-red shape of a clown's. She smoked a whole package of Chesterfields, constantly wiping the ashes off her dark-blue skirt with a hand towel soaked in dry-cleaning fluid; then she drank herself unconscious.

It was hot that night, and dry lightning leaped from the horizon to the top of the blue-black vault of sky over the Gulf. Weldon sat on the side of his bed in the dark, his shoulders hunched, his fists between his white thighs. His chopped haircut looked like feathers on his head in the flicker of lightning through the window. When Lyle was almost asleep Weldon shook him awake and said, "We got to get rid of her. You know we got to do it."

Lyle put his pillow over his head and rolled away from him, as though he could drop away into sleep and rise in the morning into a sun-spangled and different world.

But in the false dawn he woke to Weldon's face close to his. Weldon's eyes were hollow, his breath rank with funk. The mist was heavy and wet in the pecan trees outside the window.

"She's not gonna hurt Drew again. Are you gonna help or not?" he said.

Lyle followed him into the hallway, his heart sinking at the realization of what he was willing to participate in. Mattie slept in the stuffed chair, her hose rolled down over her knees, an over-turned jelly glass on the rug next to the can of spot cleaner.

Weldon walked quietly across the rug, unscrewed the cap on the can, laid the can on its side in front of Mattie's feet, then backed away from her. The cleaning fluid spread in a dark circle around her chair, the odor as bright and sharp as white gas.

Weldon slid open a box of kitchen matches, and they each took one, raked it across the striker, and, with the sense that their lives at that moment had changed forever, threw them at Mattie's feet. But the burning matches fell outside the wet area. Lyle jerked the box from Weldon's hand, clutched a half dozen matches in his fist, dragged them across the striker, and flung them right on Mattie's feet.

The chair was enveloped in a cone of flame, and she burst out of it with her arms extended, as though she were pushing blindly through a curtain, her mouth and eyes wide with terror. They could smell her hair burning as she raced past them and crashed through the screen door out onto the gallery and into the yard. She beat at her flaming clothes and raked at her hair as though it was swarming with yellow jackets.

Lyle and Weldon stood transfixed in mortal dread at what they had done.

A Negro man walking to work came out of the mist on the road and knocked her to the ground, slapping the fire out of her dress, pinning her under his spread knees as though he were assaulting her. Smoke rose from her scorched clothes and hair as in a depiction of a damned figure on a holy card.

The Negro got to his feet and walked toward the gallery, a solitary line of blood running down his black cheek where Mattie had scratched him.

"Yo' mama ain't hurt bad. Go get some butter or some bacon grease. It gonna be fine, you gonna see," he said. "Don't be shakin' like that. Where yo' daddy at? It gonna be just fine. You little white children ain't got to worry about nothing."

He smiled to assure them that everything would be all right.

▼

"They put her in the crazy house at Mandeville," Lyle said, his face turned into the warm breeze off the bayou. "She died there about ten years later, I heard."

"And you've felt guilt about it all this time?" I asked.

"Not really."

"No?"

"We were kids. Nobody would help us. It was her or us. Besides, I think my sins are forgiven."

"I don't know what to tell you, Lyle. I just don't believe that your father has reappeared after all these years to do y'all harm. People just don't come back after that long for revenge."

He sipped from his bottle and shook his head sadly.

"The son of a buck was evil. If ever Satan took a human form, it was my old man," he said.

"Well, I'll have a talk with Drew about the intruder. But I want to ask you something else while we're out here."

"Go ahead. I got no secrets."

"If you really did get religion, was it because of something that happened in Vietnam that I don't know about?"

The oil wells clanked up and down in the unplowed field, which was now pink in the sun's afterglow.

"You think maybe you had something to do with it?" he asked. "Don't give yourself too much credit, Dave."

He snuffed dryly and touched at his nostrils with one knuckle.

"I killed a nun," he said.

"You did what?"

"I never told you about it. I climbed down into what I thought was a spider hole, but one tunnel went off into a room that they must have used as an aid station because there were bloody field dressings all over the floor. I saw something go across the door, and I opened up. It was a nun, a white woman. There were two of them in there. The other one was huddled up against the wall, trembling all over. They must have been from the school in the ville. You remember there were some French nuns in that one ville?"

I nodded silently.

"When I climbed back up, Charlie started firing from the ville and the captain called in the arty," he said. "Then we were all hauling butt. You remember? It was short. That's when Martinez got it. So I just never said anything about it. The next day we got into that minefield. I couldn't keep it all straight in my head anymore."

"It wasn't your fault, Lyle. You were a good soldier."

"No, I told you before, I dug it down there. The ragin' Cajun, sliding down the tunnel to give Charlie a red-hot enema. What a hand job."

"I'll give you some advice someone once gave me. Get Vietnam out of your life. We already fought our war. Let the people who made it grieve on it."

"I don't grieve. I believe I've been reborn. I don't care if you accept that or not. I give those people out there something they ain't found anyplace else. And I couldn't give it to them unless God gave it to me first. And if He gave it to me, that means I've been forgiven."

"What is it you give them?"

"Power. A chance to be what they're not. They wake up scared every morning of their lives. I show them it doesn't have to be that way anymore. I grew up uneducated, in foster homes, hustled drugs on the street, spent time in a couple of jails, washed dishes for a

living with this crippled hand. But the man on high got my attention, and, son, I ain't did bad. . . . Sorry, that word's just one I can't
seem to get away from."

"That sounds a little bit vain, Lyle."

"I never said I was perfect. Look, make me one promise. Watch
out for my sister. I suspect you've got personal feelings toward her
anyway, don't you?"

"I'm not sure I know what you mean."

"She said you poked her when y'all were in college."

I looked at the side of his face, the scars that leaked from one eye,
then I gazed at the bayou and a black man fishing in a pirogue and
drummed my fingers on the leather seat.

"I'd better get home now," I said. "The next time you have
information for me, I'd appreciate your bringing it to me at my
office."

"Don't get bent out of shape. Drew made it with a lot of guys.
So you were one of them. Why pretend you were born fifty years
old?"

"I changed my mind. I really don't need a ride all the way home,
Lyle. Just drop me at the four-corners. I'm going to ask Bootsie to
come in town for some crawfish."

"Whatever you want, Loot." He screwed the cap on his whiskey bottle, dropped it on the seat, and started the engine. "You
might think I have a head full of spiders, but if I do, I don't try to
hide them from anybody. You get my meaning?"

"I want you to take this in the right spirit, Lyle. You don't have
the franchise on guilt about Vietnam, and you're not the only guy
who had his life set back on track by some power outside himself.
I think the problem here is peddling it to other people for money."

"You ever see a bishop drive a Volkswagen?"

"I'll get off right there at the corner. Thanks very much for the
evening."

I stepped out onto the gravel road, closed the car door, and
walked toward a clapboard bar that vibrated with the noise from
inside. Lyle's fire-engine-red convertible grew small in the distance,
then disappeared in the purple shadows between the sugarcane
fields.

I had to wait to use the pay phone in the bar, and I drank a 7 Up at a table in the corner and watched a drunk black-haired girl in blue jeans dance by herself in front of the bandstand. Her undulating, slim body was haloed in cigarette smoke.

I hadn't meant to be self-righteous with Lyle. I truly felt for him and his family and what they had endured at the hands of the father and the prostitute named Mattie, but Lyle also made me angry in a way that I couldn't quite describe to myself. It wasn't simply that he pandered to an audience of ignorant and fearful people or that he misused the money they gave him; it went even deeper than that. Maybe it was the fact that Lyle had truly been inside the fire storm, had seen human behavior at its worst and best, had made a mistake down in a tunnel that perhaps beset his conscience with a level of pain that could only be compared to having one's skin ripped off in strips with a pair of pliers. And he sold it all as cheaply as you might market the plastic flowers that adorned the stage of his live TV show.

Yes, that was it, I thought. He had made a meretricious enterprise out of an experience that you share with no one except those who've been there, too. I don't believe that's an elitist attitude, either. There are events you witness, or in which you participate, that forever remain sacrosanct and inviolate in memory, no matter how painful that memory is, because of the cost that you or others paid in order to be there in that moment when the camera lens clicked shut.

How do you tell someone that a drunk blue-collar girl dancing in a low-rent Louisiana bar, her black hair curled around her neck like a rope, makes you remember a dead Vietnamese girl on a trail three klicks from her village? She wore sandals, floppy black shorts, a white blouse, and she lay on her back, with one leg folded under her, her eyes closed as though in sleep, the only disfiguration in her appearance a dried stream of blood that curled from the corner of her mouth like a red snake. Why was she there? I don't know. Was she killed by American or enemy fire? I don't know that either. I only remember that at the time I wanted to see a weapon near her person, to believe that she was one of *them*. But there was no weapon, and in all probability she was simply a schoolgirl returning from visiting someone in another village when she was killed.

That was my third day in-country. That was twenty-six years ago. I had news for Lyle. He might be honest about the spiders crawling around in his head, but he wouldn't get rid of them by trying to sell them through a television tube. You offer them the real thing, Brother Lyle, you tell them the real story about what happened over there, and they'll put you in a cage and take out your brains with an ice cream scoop.

6

The next morning I telephoned Drew to ask her about the intruder in her kitchen, but there was no answer, and later when I went by her house she wasn't home. I stuck my business card in the corner of her screen door.

As I drove back down East Main under the oaks that arched over the street, I saw her jogging along the sidewalk in a T-shirt and a pair of purple shorts, her tan skin glistening with sweat. She raised her arm and waved at me, her breasts big and round against her shirt, but I didn't stop. She could call me if she wanted to, I told myself.

I drove home for lunch and stopped my pickup at the mailbox on the dirt road at the foot of my property. Among the letters and bills was a heavy brown envelope with no postage and my name written across it with no address. I cut the engine, sorted out the junk mail, then sliced open the brown envelope with my pocket knife. Inside were a typed letter and twenty one-hundred dollar bills. The letter read:

We think this fell out of your pocket in Weldon Sonnier's house. We think you should have it back. The cop in the basement was an accident. Nobody wanted it that way. He could have walked out of it but he wanted to be a hard guy. Sonnier is a welsher and a prick. If you want to be his knothole, that's your choice. But we think you should mark off all this bullshit and stay in New Iberia. What you've got here is two large with more down the road, maybe some business opportunities too, if we get the right signals. Let Sonnier drown in his own shit. If you don't want the money, blow your nose on it. It's all the same to us. We just wanted to offer you an intelligent alternative to being Sonnier's main local fuck.

I replaced the hundred-dollar bills and the letter in the envelope, put the envelope in my back pocket, and walked down to the dock. Batist was squatted down on the boards in the sunlight, scaling a stringer of bluegill with a spoon. The sun was hot off the water, and sweat coursed down between the shoulder blades of his bare back.

"Did you see someone besides the postman up by the mailbox?" I asked.

He squinted his eyes in the glare and thought for a moment. The backs of his hands were shiny with fish mucus.

"A man pass on a mortorsickle," he said.

"Did he stop?"

"Yeah, I t'ink he stopped. Yeah, he sho' did."

"What did he look like?"

"I ain't real sure. I ain't paid him much mind, Dave. Somet'ing wrong?"

"It's nothing to worry about."

Batist tapped his spoon on the dock.

"I 'member he was dressed funny," he said. "He didn't have no shirt but he wore them t'ings on his pants, what you call them t'ings, you see them in the movies."

I tried to visualize what he meant, but I was at a loss, as I often was when I tried to talk with Batist in either English or French.

"What movies?" I said.

"The cowboy movies."

"Chaps? Big leather floppy things that fit over the legs?"

"Yeah, that's it. They was black, and he had tattoos on his back. And he had long hair, too."

"What kind of tattoos?"

"I don't 'member that."

"Okay, partner. That's not bad."

"What ain't bad?"

"Nothing. Don't worry about it."

"Worry about what?"

"Nothing. I'm going up to the house for lunch now. If you see this guy again, call me. But don't mess with him. Okay?"

"This is a bad guy?"

"Maybe."

"This is a bad guy, but Batist ain't suppose to worry, no. You somet'ing else, Dave. Lord, if you ain't."

He went back to scraping the fish with his spoon. I started to speak again, but I had learned long ago to leave Batist alone when I had offended him by underestimating his perception of a situation.

I walked up to the house, and Bootsie and I ate lunch on the redwood table under the mimosa tree in the backyard. She wore a flowered sundress, and had put on lipstick and earrings, which she seldom did in the middle of the day.

"How do you like the sandwich?" she said.

"It's really good." It was, too. Ham and onion and horseradish, one of my favorites.

"Did something happen today?"

"No, not really."

"Nothing happened?"

"Somebody put some money in our mailbox. It's a bribery attempt. Batist thinks it was a guy on a motorcycle. Somebody with riding chaps and tattoos on his back. So kind of look out for him, although I doubt he'll be back."

"Is this about Weldon Sonnier?"

"Yeah, I think Clete and I shook up somebody's cookie bag when we went to Bobby Earl's house."

"You think Bobby Earl's trying to bribe you?"

"No, he's slicker than that. It's probably coming from somewhere else, maybe somebody who's connected with him. I'm not sure."

"You got a call from Drew Sonnier."

"Oh?"

"Why did she call here, Dave?"

"I left my card at her house this morning."

"At her house. I see."

"Lyle said somebody broke into her house."

"Doesn't that involve the city police, not the sheriff's department?"

"She didn't report it to them."

"I see. So you're investigating?"

I looked at the mallards splashing on the pond at the back of our property.

"I promised Lyle I'd talk to her."

"Lyle made you promise? Is that right? I had the impression that you had a low opinion of Lyle."

"Ease up, Boots. This case is a pain in the butt as it is."

"I'm sure that it is. Why don't we ask Drew over sometime? I haven't seen her in a long time."

"Because I'm not interested in seeing Drew."

"I think she's very nice. I've always been fond of her."

"What should I do, Boots? Pretend she's not part of this case?"

"Why should you do that? I don't think you should do that at all."

I could see the peculiar cast coming into her eyes, as though inside her head she had seen a thought or a conclusion that should have been as obvious to the rest of the world as it was to her.

"Let's go to the track tonight," I said.

"Let's do. Will you call her this afternoon? I think you should."

I tried to read what was in her eyes. The mood swings, the distorted and fearful perception, took place sometimes as quickly as a bird flying in and out of a cage.

"I might talk to her," I said, and put my hand on top of hers, "but I don't think she'll be much help in the case. The Sonniers don't trust other people. But I have to try to do what I can."

"Of course you do, Dave. Nobody said otherwise." And she looked off at the periwinkles blowing in the shade next to the coulee. The light in her eyes was as private as a solitary candle burning in a church.

"We'll take Alafair to Possum's for *étoufée* before we go to the track," I said. "Or maybe we can just come home and rent a movie."

"That would be wonderful."

"The sandwiches were really good. It's sure nice to come home and have lunch with you, Boots. Maybe after I close the drawer on this case, I might take leave of the department. We're doing pretty well at the dock."

"Don't fool yourself. You'll never stop being a cop, Dave."

I looked into her eyes again, and they were suddenly clear, as though the breeze had blown a dark object away from her line of vision.

I squeezed her hand, rose from the wood bench, and went around behind her and kissed her hair and hugged her against me. I could feel her heart beating under my arms.

▼

At the office I gave the sheriff the envelope containing the two thousand dollars and the unsigned letter.

"It must be a cheap outfit," he said. "You'd think they'd pay a little more to get a cop on the pad."

He had run a dry-cleaning business before he became sheriff. He was also a Boy Scout master and belonged to the Lions Club, not for political reasons but because he thoroughly enjoyed being a Scoutmaster and belonging to the Lions Club. He was a thoughtful and considerate man, and I always hated to correct him or to suggest that his career as an elected police officer would probably always consist of on-the-job training.

"Seduction usually comes a teaspoon at a time," I said. "Sometimes a cop who won't take fifty grand will take two. Then one day you find yourself way down the road and you don't remember where you made a hard left turn."

He wore large rimless glasses, and his stomach swelled over his gunbelt. Through the window behind his desk I could see two black trusties from the parish jail washing patrol cars in the parking lot. He scratched the blue and red veins in his soft cheek with his fingernail.

"Who do you think it came from?" he asked.

"Somebody with long-range plans, somebody who's always looking around to buy a cop. Probably the mob or somebody in it."

"Not from Bobby Earl?"

"His kind only pay out money when you catch them sodomizing sheep. I'm pretty sure we're dealing with the wiseguys now."

"What do you think they'll do next?"

"If I stay out of New Orleans, there will probably be another envelope. Then they'll offer me a job providing security in one of their nightclubs or in a counting room at the track."

He put an unlit cigarette in his mouth and rotated it with his fingers.

"I've got a bad feeling about all this," he said. "I surely do."

"Why?"

"Don't underestimate Bobby Earl's potential. I met him a couple of times ten or twelve years ago, when he was still appearing in Klan robes. This guy could make the ovens sing and grin while he was doing it."

"Maybe. But I never met one of those guys who wasn't a physical and moral coward."

"I saw Garrett's body before the autopsy. It was hard to look at, and I was in Korea. Watch your butt, Dave."

His eyes were unblinking over his rimless glasses.

▼

By two P.M. it was ninety-five degrees outside; the sunlight off the cement was as bright as a white flame; the palm trees looked dry and desiccated in the hot wind; and my own day was just warming up.

I called Drew again and this time she answered. I was ready to argue with her, to lecture her about her and Weldon's lack of cooperation in the case, even blame her for my difficulties with Bootsie at lunch. In fact, my opening statement was "Who was this guy in your kitchen, Drew, and why didn't you report it?"

I could hear her breathing in the receiver.

"Lyle told you?" she said.

"As well as Lyle can tell me anything, without trying to sell glow-in-the-dark Bibles at the same time. I'll tell you the truth, Drew, I've pretty well had it with your family's attitude. I don't want to be unkind, but the three of you behave like y'all have been shooting up with liquid Drano."

She was quiet again, then I heard her began to weep.

"Drew?"

But she continued to cry without answering, the kind of un-relieved and subdued sobbing that comes from deep down in the breast.

"Drew, I apologize. I've had some bad concerns on my mind and I was taking them out on you. I'm truly sorry for what I said. It was thoughtless and stupid."

I squeezed my temples with my thumb and forefinger.

"Drew?"

I heard her swallow and take a deep breath.

"Sometimes I'm not very smart," I said. "You know I've always admired you. You have more political courage than anybody I've ever known."

"I don't know what to do. I've always had choices before. Now I don't. I can't deal with that."

"I don't understand."

"Sometimes you get caught. Sometimes there's no way out. I've never let that happen to me."

"Do you want to come into the office? Do you want me to come out there? Tell me what you want to do."

"I don't know what I want to do."

"I'm going to come over there now. Is that all right?"

"I have to take the maid home, and I promised to stop by the market with her. Can you come out about four?"

"Sure."

"You don't mind?"

"No, of course not."

"It doesn't make you uncomfortable?"

"No, not at all. That's silly. Don't think that way."

After I had hung up the phone, I looked wanly at the damp imprint of my hand on the receiver. Were her tears for her brother or herself, I wondered. But then what right had I to be judgmental?

Oh Lord, I thought.

I was almost out the door when the dispatcher caught me in the hallway.

"Pick up your line," he said. "A sergeant in the First District in New Orleans has been holding for you."

"Take a message. I'll call him back."

"You'd better get it, Dave. He says somebody stomped the shit out of Cletus Purcel."

▼

After I had finished talking with the sergeant in New Orleans, who had not been the investigative officer and who couldn't tell me much other than Clete's room number in the hospital off St. Charles and the fact that Clete wanted to see me, that somebody had worked him over bad with a piece of pipe, I told the dispatcher to send a uniformed deputy out to Drew's house and to call Bootsie and tell her that I would be home late and would call her from New Orleans.

The wind was hot through my truck windows as I drove across the causeway over the Atchafalaya marsh. The air tasted like brass, like it was full of ozone, and I could smell dead fish on the banks of the willow islands and the odor of brine off the Gulf. The willows looked wilted in the heat, and the few fishermen who were out had pulled their boats into the warm shade of the oil platforms that dotted the bays.

I thought of an event, a low moment in my life, that had occurred almost fifteen years ago. I had been sent to Las Vegas to pick up a prisoner at the county jail and escort him back to New Orleans. But the paperwork and the court clearance had taken almost two days, and I walked in disgust from the courthouse down a palm-lined boulevard in 115-degree heat to a casino and cool bar, where I began drinking a series of vodka collinses as though they were soda pop. Then I had a blackout and seven hours disappeared from my day. I woke up in a rented car out on the desert about 10 P.M., my head and body as numb and devoid of feeling and connection with the day as if I had been stunned from crown to sole with novocaine, the distant neon city blazing in the purple cup of mountains.

There was blood on my shirt and my knuckles, and a woman's compact was on the floor. My wallet was gone, along with my money, traveler's checks, credit cards, identification, and finally my shield and my .38 special. I remembered nothing except walking from the bar to a twenty-one table with my drink in my hand and sitting among a polite group of players from Ocala, Florida.

I drove trembling back to the hotel and tried to drink myself sober with room-service Jim Beam. By midnight I went into the DTs and believed that the red message light on my phone meant that once again I had received a long-distance call from the dead members of my platoon. When I finally became rational enough to pick up the receiver and talk to the desk clerk, I was told that I had a message from Cletus Purcel.

I had to use both hands to dial his number, while the sweat slid out of my hair and down the sides of my face. Six hours later he was standing in my hotel room in his Budweiser shorts, sandals, porkpie hat, and cutoff LSU T-shirt that looked like a tank top on a hippo.

He sat on the side of the bed and listened to my story again, chewing gum, nodding, looking between his knees at the floor; then he left and didn't come back until three in the afternoon. When he did, he dropped a paper sack on the dresser and said, smiling, "Time to pick up our prisoner and boogie on down the road. The Chinese broad got away with your traveler's checks, but I got your money, credit cards, your shield, and your piece back. The American guy working with her is heading back to the Coast by Greyhound to make some long-range dental plans. He's looking forward to it, he said. There's no paperwork on this one, mon."

"What Chinese? What are you talking about?"

"She and her pimp picked you up in a parking lot outside a bar at the end of the Strip. You were too drunk to start your car. They said they'd drive you back to the hotel. You're lucky he didn't put a shank in you. I took a gut ripper off him that must have been eight inches long."

"I don't remember any of it." My hands still felt thick and wooden when I tried to open and close them.

"Sometimes you lose. Forget it. Come on, let's eat a steak and blow this shithole. I think they got the architects for this place out of a detox center."

Then he looked at me quietly, and I saw the pity and concern in his eyes.

"You dropped your brains in a jar of alcohol for a few hours," he said. "Big deal. When I worked Vice I got rolled by one of my own snitches. Plus she gave me the gon. What bothers me is I think I knew she had it when I got in the sack with her."

He grinned and blew a stream of cigarette smoke into the stale refrigerated air.

That was my old partner before whiskey and uppers and shy-locks made him a fugitive from his own police department.

▼

His face whitened when he tried to sit farther up in bed and reach the water glass and the glass straw on the nightstand.

"Don't try to move around with broken ribs, Clete," I said, and handed him the glass.

His green eyes were red along the rims, and they blinked like a bird's while he sucked on the straw with the corner of his mouth. Divots of hair had been shaved out of his head, and his scalp was sewn with butterfly stitches in a half-dozen places.

"Man, what a drag," he said. "They say I'm supposed to be in here two more days. I don't think I can cut it. You ought to see my night nurse. She looks like the Beast of Buchenwald. She tried to shove a thermometer up my butt while I was asleep."

"They hit you with pipes?"

"No, the little guy had brass knuckles, and Jack Gates, the guy I made for sure, had a baton."

"The cop I talked to said they beat you up with pipes."

"Then they got it wrong in the report. They sound like the

same incompetent guys we used to work with."

"How'd they get into your apartment?"

"Picked the lock, I guess. Anyway, Jack Gates was behind the door when I walked in. He caught me right across the ear with the baton. Damn, those things hurt. I crashed right over my new TV set. Then that little fuck was all over me. The last thing I remember I was falling through the furniture, trying to get my piece untangled from my coat, those brass knuckles bouncing off my head, and Gates trying to get a clear swing to take me off at the neck. That's when I grabbed him around the head and tore the stocking off his face. The first thing I saw was all the metal in his teeth. Then it was lights out for Cletus. That sawed-off little fart caught me right at the base of the skull.

"It was just like you said, Gates has a scrap yard for a mouth. I should have made the connection before. He was a button man for Joey Gouza, but I heard he moved to Fort Lauderdale or Hallendale two or three years ago and got ice-picked by a chippy or something. But it was Jack Gates, mon, a real barf bucket. I heard Joey Gouza caught his brother-in-law skimming off his whores, so he told Gates to create an object lesson. The brother-in-law was a big, soft mushy guy who couldn't climb a stairs without pulling himself up the banister with both hands. Gates wined and dined him at Copeland's, got him stinking drunk, and kept telling him about these hot-assed Mexican broads over in Galveston. So the tub got his ovaries fired up, and Gates drove them out to a private airport in Kenner, all the time telling the tub what these broads would do for his sex life. Then ole Jack walked him out to the runway, lit a cigar for him, and pushed him into an airplane propeller."

"You think he's working for Gouza now?"

"He's got to be. You don't resign from Joey Meatballs. It's a lifetime job."

"Where'd he get that name?"

"His old man ran a spaghetti place on Felicity. In fact, Joey still owns three or four Italian restaurants around town. But the story is when he was a kid in the reformatory a redneck guard made Joey cook him meatballs all the time. Except Joey would always spit in them or mash up dead cockroaches in them. Have you ever seen him? His mother must have been knocked up by a street lamp."

"The little guy with the brass knuckles is probably Fluck, right?"

"Maybe. But a nylon stocking makes everybody look like Cream of Wheat. All I can tell you is I think he wanted to take my eyes out. . . . Why are you looking like that?"

"I got you into this, Clete."

"No, you didn't. It was my idea to go out to Bobby Earl's and pull on his tallywhacker. But I was right about the connection between Earl and Gouza, wasn't I? I told you that flunky at the gate used to be a mule for Gouza. I think we've got the ultimate daisy chain of Louisiana buttwipes here—Klansmen, Nazis, and wise-guys."

"You took the beating for me."

"Bullshit."

"You haven't heard it all. I received a bribe attempt earlier today. A couple of grand in my mailbox, a letter suggesting I spend a lot of time around New Iberia."

"Ah," he said. The streetcar rattled down the tracks on St. Charles. "The carrot and the stick."

"I think so."

"And I got the stick."

"They don't like to beat up cops."

"They did something else too, Dave, maybe a signal for you about their future potential. After they laid me out, they sprinkled a bagful of rainbows and black beauties all over the room to make it look like a drug deal gone sour. I cleaned them up before I called the First District. . . . Dave, I don't like what I'm seeing on your face."

"What's that?"

"Like you got a piece of barbed wire behind your eyes. You get those thoughts out of your head."

"You're mistaken."

"Like hell I am. Ole Streak turns on the Mixmaster and almost drives himself crazy with his own thoughts, then goes out and strikes a match to their balls. You wait till I'm out of here and we'll 'front these guys together. Are we straight on that, podjo?"

I looked at the square of sunlight on his sheets. The palm trees outside the window lifted and straightened in the breeze.

"I'm not supposed to be a player?" he said.

"You want me to bring you anything?"

"Don't go up against Gouza on your own. An Iberia sheriff's badge is puppy shit to these guys."

"What do you want me to bring you?"

"My piece. It's in a little sock drawer under my bed." He took his keys off the nightstand and dropped them in my palm. "There's also a fifth of vodka and a carton of cigarettes on the kitchen counter."

"I'll be back in a little while."

"Dave?"

"Yes?"

"Gouza's a weird combo. He's got an ice cube in the center of his head when it comes to business, but he's also a sadistic paranoid. A lot of the greaseballs in this town are scared shitless of him."

▼

I drove to Clete's apartment on Dumaine in the Quarter, put his .38 revolver and shoulder holster, his vodka and cigarettes in a paper bag and was walking back down the balcony when I saw the apartment manager sweeping dust out his doorway through the railing into the courtyard below. He was a dark-skinned, black-haired man with bad teeth and turquoise eyes. I opened my badge and asked him if he had seen the men who had beaten Clete.

"Yeah, sho' I seen them. I seen them run down the stairs," he said. He had a heavy Cajun accent.

I asked him what they looked like.

"One man, I didn't see him too good, no, he walked on down Dumaine. I didn't pay him no mind 'cause I didn't know nothing was wrong, me. But there was a little one, a blond-haired fella, he pushed by me on the stair and run out on the street and got on a motorcycle wit' another fella."

"What did this fellow on the motorcycle look like?"

"Big," he said. Then he tapped on his biceps with one finger. "He had a tattoo. A tiger. It was yellow and red. I seen it real good 'cause I didn't like that little fella pushing me on the stair."

"Who'd you tell this to?"

"I ain't said nothing to nobody."

"Why not?"

"Ain't nobody ax me."

After I dropped off the paper sack with Clete's gun, cigarettes, and vodka at the hospital, the sun was low in the sky, red through the oak trees on St. Charles Avenue, and swallows were circling in the dusk. I checked into an inexpensive guesthouse on Prytania, just two blocks off St. Charles, and called Bootsie and told her that I would have to stay over and that I would be home tomorrow afternoon.

"What is it?" she asked.

"I have to run down a couple of things. It's grunt work mostly. Will you be all right?"

"Yes. Of course."

"Are you all right, Boots?"

"Yes. Everything's fine this evening. It was hot today, but it's cooling off this evening. It might rain tonight. There's lightning out over the marsh."

I could feel the day's fatigue in my body. I closed and widened my eyes. The long-distance hum in the telephone receiver was like wet sand in my ear.

"Would you call the dispatcher for me?" I said.

"All right. Don't worry about anything, Dave. We're just fine."

After I hung up I said a prayer to my Higher Power to watch over my home in my absence, then I called Clarise, an elderly mulatto woman who had worked for my family since I was a child, and asked her to look in on Bootsie that evening and to return in the morning to do house chores.

I showered in a tin stall with water that was so cold it left me breathless, put back on the same clothes I had worn all day, ate a plate of rice, red beans, and sausage at Fat Albert's on St. Charles, then began a neon-lit odyssey through the biker bars of Jefferson and Orleans parishes.

It's a strange, atavistic, and tribal world to visit. Individually its members are usually hapless, bumbling creatures who were born out of luck and whose largest successes usually consist of staying out of jail, paying off their bondsmen, and keeping their appointments with their probation officers and welfare workers. It's probably not coincidence that most of them are ugly and stupid. But collectively they are both frightening and a source of fascination for those who wonder what it might be like if they traded off their routine and predictable lives for a real fling out on the ragged edge.

The first bar I hit was one out on Airline Highway. Think of a shale parking lot covered with chopped-down Harleys whose chrome and lacquered-black surfaces seem to glow with a nocturnal iridescence; a leather jackboot stomping down on a starter pedal, the ear-splitting roar of straight exhaust pipes, the tinkle of a beer bottle flung through the limbs of an oak tree, a man urinating loudly on the shale in front of a pickup truck's headlights, his muscular, blue-jean-clad legs spread with the visceral self-satisfaction of a gladiator; the inside of a clapboard building crowded with men in sleeveless Levi jackets, boots sheathed with metal plates, black leather cutouts that etch the genitals and flap on the legs like a gunfighter's chaps; bodies strung with chains and iron crosses, covered with hair and tattoos of swastikas and snakes with human skulls inserted between the fangs; an odor of chewing tobacco, snuff, cigarette smoke rubbed like wet nicotine into the clothes, grease and motor oil, reefer, and a faint hint of testosterone and dried semen.

I was sure that the man with the tiger tattoo who had ridden away from Clete's apartment was Eddy Raintree, but he was not the same biker who had put the bribe money in my mailbox. Which meant that in all probability there was a connection between bikers, the Aryan Brotherhood, ex-convicts, and Bobby Earl or Joey Gouza. It made sense. Most outlaw bikers I had known were sexual fascists, and they were always seeking new and defenseless targets for the anger and dark blood that were trapped in their loins like throbbing birds.

But I got virtually nowhere at the bar on Airline Highway or at any of the other bars I cruised until 3 A.M. No one knew Eddy Raintree, had ever heard of him, or even thought his photograph vaguely familiar. But at the last place I visited, a narrow brick poolroom that used to be run by blacks between two warehouses across the river in Algiers, a drunk woman at the bar let me buy her a bowl of chili, and in her sad way she tried to be helpful.

Her hair was platinum, dark at the scalp, and the number 69 was tattooed on her arm. She wore a sleeveless yellow T-shirt with no bra, and a pair of Clorox-faded Levi's that hung as low as a bikini on her hips. (I had never been able to understand the women who hung with outlaw bikers, because with some regularity they were gang-raped, chain-whipped, and had their hands nailed to trees, but they came back for more, obedient, anesthetized, and bored, like spectators at their own dismemberment.)

She kept lifting spoonfuls of chili to her mouth, then forgetting to eat them, her eyes trying to focus on my face and the photograph of Eddy Raintree I held in my palm.

"What do you want with that dumb shit?" she asked. Her words were phlegmatic, like dialogue in a slow-motion film.

"Could you tell me where he is?"

"In jail, probably. Or out fucking goats or something."

"When did you see him last?"

She drew in on her cigarette and held the smoke down like she was taking a hit off a reefer.

"You don't want to waste your time with a dumb shit like that," she said.

"I'd really like to talk with Eddy. I'd really appreciate it if you could help me."

"He's into astronomy or something. He's weird. I've got enough weirdness in my life without a dumb fuck like that."

Then her boyfriend came back from the men's room. He was huge, with a wild beard, and he wore striped overalls with no shirt. His massive shoulders were ridged with hair; his odor was incredible.

"What do you think you're doing, man?" he said.

"Just finishing my conversation with this lady."

"It's finished. Good-bye."

I left two dollars on the bar for the chili and walked back out into the night. The heat of the day had finally lifted from the streets and the cement buildings, the wind was cool blowing from across the river, and I could see the red and green running lights of the oil barges on the water, and the glow of New Orleans against the clouds.

▼

I slept until nine the next morning, had coffee and *beignets* at a cool table under the pavilion at the Café du Monde, and watched the water from the sprinklers click against the piked fence around the park in Jackson Square and drift in a rainbow haze through the myrtle and banana trees. Then I went over to First District head-quarters a few blocks away and read Joey Gouza's file. It was another study in institutional failure, the kind of document that makes you doubt your own convictions and conclude that perhaps the right-wing simpletons are correct when they advocate going at social complexities with a chainsaw.

Since age thirteen, he'd had forty-three arrests. He was in the Louisiana reformatory when he was seventeen, he went up the road twice to Angola, and he did a federal three-bit in Lewisburg. He had been arrested for breaking-and-entering, auto theft, assault and bat-tery, possession of burglar tools, armed robbery, strong-arm rob-bery, sale of stolen food stamps, possession of counterfeit money, procuring, tax fraud, and murder. He was one of those career criminals who early on had gone about investigating and participat-ing in every kind of illegal activity that a city offered. But, unlike most petty thieves, pimps, smalltime fences, and smash-and-grab artists, Joey had gravitated steadily upward in the New Orleans mob and had developed a skill that was at one time revered in the underworld, that of the safecracker. Evidently he had peeled and cut up safes with burnbars in four states, although he had fallen on only one job, a box in a Baton Rouge pawnshop that netted him eighty-six dollars and a two-year jolt in Angola.

He wasn't hard to find. He owned a small Italian café and delicatessen in an old brick, iron-scrolled building shaded by oak trees on Esplanade. The inside smelled of oregano and meat sauce, crab-boil, sautéed shrimp, cheese and salami, the fried oysters and sliced tomatoes and onions that went into the poor-boy sandwiches on the counter, the steamed coffee from the espresso machines. The café was empty except for a black cook, the counterman, and a couple having breakfast at one of the checkercloth tables.

I asked for Joey Gouza.

"He's back in the office. What's the name?" the counterman said.

"Dave Robicheaux."

"Just a minute." He walked to the end of the counter and spoke through a half-opened door.

"Who's the guy?" a peculiar thick voice inside said.

"I don't know. Just a guy." The counterman looked back at me.

"Then ask him who he is," the voice said.

The counterman looked back at me again. I opened up my badge.

"He's a cop, Joey," the counterman said.

"Then tell him to come in, for Christ's sake."

I walked around the counter and through the door. Joey Gouza looked up at me from behind his desk. He was deeply tanned, tall, his face elongated, almost jug-shaped, his salt-and-pepper hair cut military style and brushed up stiffly on his scalp, his eyes as black as wet paint. He wore pleated gray slacks, a lavender polo shirt, ox-blood loafers; a cream-colored panama hat sat crown down on the corner of his desk. His neck was unnaturally long, like a swan's, hung with gold chains and medallions, and his open shirt exposed the web of veins and tendons in his shoulders and chest, like those in a long-distance runner or javelin thrower.

But it was the eyes that got your attention; they were absolutely black and they never blinked. And the voice: the accent was Irish Channel, but with a knot tied in it, as though the vocal cords were coated with infected membrane.

His smile was easy, as relaxed as the matchstick he rolled on his tongue. A fat dark man in a green visor, who smoked a cigar, sat at a card table in the corner, adding up receipts on a calculator.

"I got some unpaid parking tickets again?" Gouza said.

I held my badge out for him to see. "No, I'm Dave Robicheaux with the Iberia Parish sheriff's office, Mr. Gouza. It's just an informal visit. Do you mind if I sit down?"

If he recognized my name, it didn't show in his eyes or his smile.

"Help yourself, if you don't mind me working. We got to get some stuff ready for the tax man."

"I'm looking for Jack Gates," I said.

"Who?"

"Or Eddy Raintree."

"Who?"

"How about Jewel Fluck?"

"*Fluck?* Is this some kind of put-on?"

"Let's start with Jack Gates again. You never heard of him?"

"Nope."

"That's funny. I heard he fed your brother-in-law into an airplane propeller."

He took the matchstick out of the corner of his mouth and laughed.

"It's a great story. I've heard it for years. But it's bullshit," he said. "My brother-in-law was killed in a plane accident on his way to Disneyland. A great family tragedy."

The man at the other table was grinning and nodding his head up and down without interrupting his count of receipts. Then Joey Gouza put the matchstick back in his mouth and leaned his chin on his knuckle. His eyes were filled with an amused light as they moved up and down my person.

"You say Iberia Parish?" he said.

"That's right."

"You guys gave up shaving or something?"

"We're casual out in the parishes. Let's cut to it, Joey. You're an old-time pete man. Why do you want to give Weldon Sonnier a lot of grief?"

"Weldon Sonnier?"

"You don't know him, either?"

"Everybody in New Orleans knows him. He's a bum and a welsher."

"Who told you that?"

"That's the word. He borrows big dough, but he doesn't come up with the vig. That'll get you into trouble in this town. You saying I'm connected with him or something?"

"You tell me."

"I know your name from a long time ago. You were at the First District, weren't you?"

"That's right."

"So I think maybe you heard stories about me. You probably read my rap sheet before you came here this morning, right? You know I've been up the road a couple of times, you know I burned a box or two. You heard that old bullshit story about how I got this voice, how a yard bitch put a capful of Sani-Flush in my coffee cup. How the yard bitch got his cherry split open in the shower two days later? You heard that one, didn't you?"

"Sure."

He smiled and said, "No, you didn't, but I'll give it to you free, anyway. The point is it's not true. I was never a big stripe, I did easy time, I made full trusty in every joint I was in. But the big word there is *did*. Past tense. I *did* my time. I've been straight seven years. Look—"

He bounced his palm on top of a paper spindle and gazed reflectively out the window at some black children skateboarding by under the oaks.

"I'm a businessman," he continued. "I own a bunch of restaurants, a linen service, a movie theater, a plumbing business, and half a vending-machine company. Are we on the same wavelength here?"

He flexed his nostrils as though there were an obstruction in them and rubbed the grained skin of his jaw with one finger.

"I'll try again," he said. "You said it a minute ago, I was a pete man. I punched, peeled, and burned 'em. I went down for it twice, too. But safecracking became a historical art a long time ago. Today it's all narcotics."

"Bad stuff?" I smiled back at him.

He shrugged his shoulders and turned his palms up.

"Who am I to judge?" he said. "But go out to the welfare projects and see who's running the action. They're all colored kids. They scrape out crack pipes, they call it bazooka or something, and sell it for a buck a hit. Nobody who could think his way out of a wet paper bag is gonna try to compete with that."

"Maybe my information isn't very good. Or maybe I'm a little bit out of touch. But it's my understanding that you've got connections with Bobby Earl, that Jack Gates is a button man for you."

He leaned back in his chair and looked out the window again. He took the matchstick out of his mouth and dropped it in the waste can.

"I've tried to be polite," he said. "You're from out of town, you had some questions, I tried to answer them. You think maybe you're abusing the situation here?"

"I came here to pass on a couple of observations, Joey. When you try to get a cop on a pad and you don't know anything about him, get somebody to lend him money, don't leave it in his mailbox."

"What are you talking about?"

"The two thousand is in the Iberia Parish sheriff's desk drawer. At the end of the year it'll probably be donated to the city park program."

He was grinning again.

"You're saying I tried to bribe you? You drove all the way over here to tell me somebody's two thou is wasted on you? That's the big message?"

"Read it like you want."

"It's been a lot of fun talking to you. Hey, I didn't tell you I own a couple of goony golf courses. You like goony golf? It's catching on here in New Orleans. Hey, Louis, give him a couple of tickets."

The man with the cigar and green visor was grinning broadly, nodding his head up and down. He took a thick pack of tickets from his shirt pocket, popped two out from under the rubber band, and placed them on the desk in front of me.

Joey Gouza made a pyramid out of his hands and tapped the ends of his fingers together.

"I heard you were an intelligent man, Joey. But it's my opinion you're a stupid shit," I said.

His eyes went flat, and his face glazed over.

"You fucked with Cletus Purcel. That's probably the worst mistake you ever made in your insignificant life," I said. "If you don't believe me, check out what happened to Julio Garcia and his bodyguard a few years back. I think they wished they had stayed in Managua and taken their chances with the Sandinistas."

"That's supposed to make me rattle? You come in here like you fell out of a dirty-clothes bag, making noise like you got gas or something, and I'm supposed to rattle?" He pointed into his breast-bone with four stiff fingers. "You think I give a fuck about what some pissant PI's gonna do? Tell me serious, I'm supposed to get on the rag because he whacked out a spick nobody in New Orleans would spit on?"

"Clete didn't kill Garcia. His partner did."

I saw the recognition grow in his eyes.

"Tell those three clowns they're going down for the murder of a sheriff's deputy," I said. "Stay out of Iberia Parish. Stay away from Purcel. If you fall again, Joey, I'm going to make sure you go down for the bitch. Four-time loser, mandatory life."

I flipped the goony golf passes on his shirt front. The man in the green visor sat absolutely still with his cigar dead in his mouth.

When I got back to New Iberia I showered, shaved, put on fresh clothes, and ate lunch with Bootsie in the backyard. I should have felt good about the day; it wasn't hot, like yesterday, the trees were loud with birds, the wind smelled of watermelons, the roses in my garden were as big as fists. But my eye registered all the wrong things: a fire burning in the middle of the marsh, where there should have been none; buzzards humped over a dead rabbit in the field, their beaks hooked and yellow and busy with their work; a little boy with an air rifle on the bank of the bayou, taking careful aim at a robin in an oak tree.

Why? Because we were on our way back to the specialist in Lafayette. The treatment of lupus, in our case, had not been a matter of finding the right medication but the right balance. Bootsie needed dosages of corticosteroid to control the disease that fed at her connective tissue, but the wrong dosage resulted in what is called steroid psychosis. For us her treatment had been like trying to spell a word correctly by repeatedly dipping a spoon into alphabet soup.

There were times I felt angry at her, too. She was supposed to avoid the sun, but I often came home from work and found her weeding the flower beds in shorts and a halter. When we went out on the salt to seine for shrimp, she would break her promise and not only leave the cabin but strip nude, dive off the gunnel, and swim toward a distant sandbar, until she was a small speck and I would have to go after her.

We got back from Lafayette at 4 P.M. with a half-dozen new prescriptions in her purse. I sat listlessly on the front porch and stared at the smoke still rising into the sky from the cypress trees burning in the marsh. Why had no one put it out, I thought.

"What's wrong, Dave?" Alafair said.

"Nothing, little guy. How you doing?" I put my arm around her small waist and pulled her against me. She had been riding her horse, and I could smell the sun in her hair and horse sweat in her clothes.

"Why's there a fire out there?"

"Dry lightning probably hit a tree during the night," I said. "It'll burn itself out."

"Can we go buy some strawberries for dessert?"

"I have to go by the office a few minutes. Maybe we'll go to town for some ice cream after supper. How's that?"

"Dave, did the doctor say something bad about Bootsie?"

"No, she's going to be fine. Why do you think that?"

"Why did she do that with those, what d'you call them, those things the doctor gives her?"

"Her prescriptions?"

"Yeah. I saw her dump her purse all over her bed. Then she wadded up all those 'scriptions. When she saw me she put them all back in her purse and went into the bathroom. She kept running the water a long time. I had to go to the bathroom and she wouldn't let me in."

"Bootsie's sick, little guy. But she'll get better. You just got to do it a day at a time. Hey, hop on my back and let's check up on Batist, then I have to go."

She walked up on the steps and then climbed like a frog onto my shoulders, and we galloped like horse and rider down to the dock. But it was hard to feign joy or confidence in the moment or the day.

The wind changed, and I could smell the scorched, hot reek of burnt cypress in the marsh.

▼

I drove to the office, talked briefly with the sheriff about my visit to New Orleans, my search through biker bars for Eddy Raintree, and my conversation with Joey Gouza.

"You think he's pulling the strings on this one?" the sheriff said.

"He's involved one way or another. I'm just not sure how. He controls all the action in that part of Orleans Parish. The guys who beat up Clete wouldn't have done it without Gouza's orders or permission."

"Dave, I don't want you putting a stick in Gouza's cage again. If we nail him, we'll do it with a warrant and we'll work through New Orleans P.D. He's a dangerous and unpredictable man."

"The New Orleans families don't go after cops, sheriff. It's an old tradition."

"Tell that to Garrett."

"Garrett stumbled into it. In 1890 the Black Hand murdered the New Orleans police chief. A mob broke eleven of them out of the parish prison, hanged two from street lamps, and clubbed and shot the other nine to death. So cops like me get bribe offers and guys like Clete get brass knuckles."

"Don't start a new precedent."

I went to check my mailbox next to the dispatcher's office. It was five-fifteen. All I had to do was glance at my mail and thumb through my telephone messages and make one phone call, and I was sure that when Drew picked up the phone she would be calm, perhaps even apologetic for her distraught behavior of yesterday, and I would be on my way home to dinner.

Wrong.

The dispatcher had written Drew's message in blue ink across the first pink slip on the stack: *Dave, don't you give a damn?*

Her house was only two blocks from the drawbridge that I would cross on my way home, I told myself. I would give myself fifteen minutes there. Friendship and the past required a certain degree of obligation, even if it was only a ritualistic act of assurance or kindness, and it had nothing to do with marital fidelity. Nothing, I told myself.

She was barbecuing in the backyard. She was barefoot, and she wore white tennis shorts and a striped blue cotton shirt. Her face looked hot in the smoke, and the back of her tan neck was beaded with perspiration. The picnic table was covered with a flowered tablecloth, and in the middle of it was a washtub filled with crushed ice and long-neck bottles of Jax. The oaks and myrtle trees in the yard were full of fireflies, and through the gray trunks of the cypresses along the bank I could see some kids waterskiing behind a motorboat on Bayou Teche.

"Maybe I dropped by at the wrong time," I said.

"No, no, it's fine. I'm glad you're here," she said, waving the smoke away from her face. "Weldon and Bama are coming over at eight. Stay for supper if you like."

"Thanks. I have to be getting on in a minute. I'm sorry I didn't get back to you, but I had to go to New Orleans. Did a uniformed deputy come out yesterday?"

"Yes, he read magazines in my living room for three hours."

She picked up an opened bottle of beer from the table and drank out of it. The bottle was beaded with moisture, and I watched the foam run down inside the neck into her mouth.

"There's some soda in the refrigerator," she said.

"That's all right."

She put the bottle in her mouth again and looked at me. I glanced away from her, then picked up a fork and flipped one of the chickens on the grill. The *sauce piquante* flared in the fire and steamed off in the breeze.

"Why didn't you report the break-in, Drew?"

"I don't know who it was. What good would it do?"

"Was it your father?"

"If he's alive, he'd have no interest in me."

"Do you think it was one of Joey Gouza's people?"

"That gangster in New Orleans?"

"That's right. I have a feeling he and Weldon are on a first-name basis."

"If I knew who it was, I'd tell you."

"Cut it out, Drew. You can't get strung out one day, then the next day go back to the deaf-and-dumb routine."

"I don't like you talking to me like that, Dave."

"You made a point of relaying your feelings through the dispatcher. It's a small department, Drew. It's a small town."

"I don't have those kinds of concerns, thank God. I'm sorry if you do."

She took a bandana from her pocket and wiped the perspiration off the back of her neck. Her face suddenly looked soft and cool in the mauve-colored light off the bayou.

"I wasn't doing very well yesterday," she said. "Maybe I shouldn't have called you. I shouldn't have made it so personal, either."

"Look, when somebody creeps your house, it's for one of two reasons: either to steal from you or do you bodily harm, or perhaps both. When it happens, it frightens you. You feel violated. You want to take everything out of your closets and dresser drawers and wash them."

She unsnapped the cap on another bottle of Jax and sat down on the picnic bench. But she didn't drink from the bottle. She just kept drawing a line down through the moisture with her finger.

"I was in northern Nicaragua," she said. "When the contras 'violated' someone, they cut the person up in pieces."

"I was just trying to say that your reaction was understandable, Drew."

"I bought a pistol this morning. The next time someone breaks into my house, I'm going to kill the sonofabitch."

"That's not going to make the bigger problem go away. You're protecting Weldon from something, and at the same time you know if he doesn't get help, he's going to take a fall. I think you've got another problem, too. Weldon's done something that goes against your conscience, and somehow he's pulled you into it."

"I wish I could be omniscient. It must be wonderful to have that gift."

"Has he been mixed up with the contras?"

"No."

I looked her steadily in the eyes.

"I said no," she repeated.

"I'm going to say something you probably won't like. Weldon worked for the CIA. Air America flew in and out of the Golden Triangle. Sometimes they ferried around warlords, who were in reality transporting narcotics. The station chiefs knew it, the pilots knew it. Weldon's been involved in some nasty stuff. Maybe it's time he took his own fall. I think he's a chickenshit for hiding behind his sister."

"Why'd you let everything go between us?"

"Excuse me?"

"You were talking about chickenshit. I thought you were the sun coming up in the morning. That's what I thought you were."

I felt the skin of my face tighten in the humid air.

"I went to Vietnam. Do you remember what you thought about people who went to Vietnam?" I said.

"That wasn't it at all, and you know it. You blew it with Bootsie, and I was 'just passing through.' That's what chickenshit means."

"You're wrong."

She took a drink from the bottle and looked away toward the bayou so I couldn't see her face.

"I always respected you," I said. "You got upset yesterday because under it all you have a tender heart, Drew. Nobody is expected to be a soldier every day of his life. I start every other day with a nervous breakdown."

Her face was still turned away from me, but I could see her back shaking under her shirt.

I put my hand lightly on her shoulder. Her fingers came up and covered mine, rested there a moment, then she lifted my hand up and released it.

"It's time for you to go, Dave," she said.

I didn't reply. I walked across the thick Saint Augustine grass, through the shadows and the tracings of fireflies in the trees. When I turned and looked back at her, I didn't see a barefoot woman pushing at her eyes in the smoke but a little Cajun girl of years ago whose bare legs danced in the air while a switch whipped across them.

▼

Early the next morning I sent two uniformed deputies to check the missions and the shelters in Iberia and Lafayette parishes for a man who had been disfigured in a fire. I also told them to check the old hobo jungles along the S.P. tracks.

"What do we do when we find him?" one deputy said.

"Ask him to ride down with you."

"What if he don't want to come?"

"Call me and I'll come out."

"Half the guys in that hobo camp look like their mothers beat on them with a baseball bat."

"This guy's face looks like red rubber."

"Can we take him out to lunch?" He was grinning.

"How about getting on it?"

"Yes, sir."

Then I called Clete's hospital room in New Orleans, but was told by a nurse that he was in X-ray. I asked her to have him call me collect when he got back to his room. Fifteen minutes later I was drinking coffee, eating a doughnut, and looking out the window at a black man who was selling rattlesnake watermelons and strawberries off the back of his pickup truck, when my phone extension rang. It was Weldon Sonnier.

"What's the idea of leaning on my sister?" he said.

"I think you've got it turned around."

"What did you say to her?"

I set my doughnut down on a napkin.

"I think that's none of your business," I said.

"You'd damn well better believe it is."

"Then why don't you stop dumping your garbage in her life?"

"Listen, Dave—"

"I got a bribe offer from an anonymous letter writer. This guy mentioned your name. He also said you're a prick and a welsher."

He was silent.

"Then I talked with Joey Gouza. He also called you a welsher."

"Consider the source."

"The interesting question is why I keep seeing or hearing the word 'welsher' when your name is mentioned."

"When did you see Gouza?"

"None of your business."

"He's a candidate for a lobotomy. I wouldn't mash on his oysters."

"Why are you mixed up with Gouza?"

"Who says I know him? The guy's notorious. Gouza is to New Orleans what monkey flop is to a zoo."

"Weldon, the real problem is you've tracked through your own shit and you're laying it off on other people. I think you've put your sister in jeopardy. In my opinion that's a lousy thing to do."

"Yeah? Is that right? Maybe if you ever get your nose out of the air long enough, I'll clue you in on the facts of life down in the tropics."

"I think you've sought out the trouble in your life. Nobody forced you to fly for Air America. You were dirty in Indo-China, I think you're dirty now."

"I wish I had the patent on righteousness. I guess you never called in any 105s on a ville. Stay the fuck away from my sister if you can't handle it any better than you did yesterday."

He hung up. This time I was the one whose words and anger were caught in my throat like a tangle of fish hooks. Unconsciously I wadded up a sheet of paper on top of my desk and threw it toward the wastebasket, then realized it was my time log for my paycheck.

▼

It was just after one o'clock and it had started to rain again when Clete returned my call. I had opened my windows, and the wind blew a fine spray through the screens.

"Can you come to New Orleans this evening?" he asked.

"I was coming tomorrow."

"How about today?"

"What's up?"

"I got some information on Bobby Earl that might lead us to those farts who worked me over."

"Wait a minute, where are you?"

"At home."

"The hospital cut you loose?"

"I cut myself loose. Somehow the smell of bedpans just doesn't go together with mashed potatoes and boiled carrots. Forget about the hospital. Look, you remember Willie Bimstine and Nig Rosewater?"

"The bondsmen?"

"That's right. I chase down jumpers for them sometimes. So I called them this morning to see if they might have some work for me, since I don't have any medical insurance and my hospital bill is a nightmare. But these guys are also a gold mine of information on the lowlifes of New Orleans. So when I had Nig on the phone I asked him what he knew about the buttwipes who put stitches all over my head. No help there, though. In fact, he said he thought Raintree and Fluck weren't around the city anymore, because when they're in town you hear about it. Fluck in particular. Evidently he likes beating the shit out of people.

"So I asked Nig what kind of action Bobby Earl might be involved in, and he told me this interesting story. Nig went a twenty-five-thousand-dollar bond for this broad over in Algiers. The broad got nailed with four kees of pure Colombian nose candy. But Nig's not worried about her. She's got a high-priced lawyer, it's her first bust, and she knows she can cut a deal and not do any time, so Nig's money is safe. It's her two brothers who are the problem. Nig put up big bucks to get them out on a robbery beef, and they both skipped on him.

"Smart businessman that he is, Nig tells the broad that she either delivers up her brothers or he yanks her bond and she waits for her trial in the parish jail. Which is not what she envisioned for herself, because this broad is one beautiful hot-assed piece of equipment who the bull dykes will cannibalize. So Nig thinks he's got her and she'll have both her brothers in his office in twenty-four hours. But the broad pulls one on Nig that he doesn't expect.

"She says if he messes with her bond, threatens her again, or gets in her face about anything, she'll have a bedtime chat with Bobby Earl, and Willie and Nig's state license is going to be hanging out in the breeze. Nig checked it out. She's Bobby Earl's regular punch across the river. Once a week he's at her pad like clockwork. She brags it around among the lowlifes that she fucks him cross-eyed on the ceiling."

"I'm not following you, Clete. Who cares? This doesn't get us any closer to Fluck, Gates, or Raintree. Tell Nig to give his story to the *Picayune* about election time."

"Here's the rest of it. Nig says the broad's brothers are bikers and they were both in the AB in Angola and Huntsville."

"I don't know if that's a big lead."

"You got anything else? It's Thursday. Nig says Thursday is poontang night for Bobby in Algiers. We tail him over there and see what happens. Come on, Bobby Earl's an amateur. We'll make drops of blood pop on his forehead."

I looked out at the rain denting the trees and thought for a moment. The rain was blowing across the truck awning of the black man selling strawberries and watermelons, and in the south, against a black sky, lightning was striking against the Gulf.

"All right," I said.

"Why all the thought?"

"No reason. I'll be at your apartment in about three hours."

Clete had enough problems of his own and didn't need to know everything about a police investigation, I told myself. I called Bootsie and told her that I had to go to New Orleans, but I promised to be back that night, no matter how late it was. I meant it, too.

▼

We used Clete's battered Plymouth for the tail. It was 7:30, and we were parked a block down the street from Bobby Earl's driveway; the sky was still black with clouds and rainwater ran high and dark in the gutters. Out on Lake Pontchartrain I could see the lighted cabins of a yacht rocking in the swell. Clete smoked a cigarette and blew the smoke out his window into the rain-flecked air. He wore his porkpie hat over the scalped divots and stitches in his head, and a purple-and-white-striped shirt and seersucker trousers that rode up high on his ankles. He kept rubbing the back of his thick neck and craning his head.

"Is something wrong?" I asked.

"Yeah, there is. I hurt from head to foot. Man, I must be getting old to let punks like that take me down."

"Sometimes you lose."

"You're always quoting Hemingway to me. Do you know what he told his kid when his kid asked something about the importance of being a good loser? He said, 'Son, being a good loser requires one thing—practice.'"

"Clete, we do it by the numbers tonight."

"Who said different? But you got to make 'em sweat, mon. When they see you coming, something inside them should try to crawl away and hide."

"There he goes. Try to stay a block behind him," I said.

Clete started up the Plymouth's engine. The rusted-out muffler, which was wired to the frame with coat hangers, sounded like a garbage truck's. The white Chrysler headed up the street with its lights on and turned at the corner toward Lakeshore Drive.

"Don't worry, he's not going to make us," Clete said. "Our man's got his mind on getting his Johnson serviced. I've got to scope out this broad. Nig says she looks like a movie star. When I was in Vice—"

"He's not going to Algiers. He's turning the wrong way."

"He's probably picking up some rubbers."

"Clete—"

"I didn't drag you down here just to fire in the well. Take it easy."

We watched the Chrysler speed down the wet boulevard along the lakefront, then slow and turn through the iron gates of the yacht club. The taillights disappeared down a palm-lined drive that led to an enormous white glass-domed building by a golf course. Clete pulled to the curb and stared glumly through the windshield. The waves out on the lake were dark green and blowing with strips of froth. He breathed loudly through his nose.

"It's all right," I said.

"The hell it is. I'm going to take that cocksucker down."

"We don't need him to talk to the girl."

"I don't know where she is. He meets her in different bars, then they go to a motel."

"We'll give it a little while. Maybe he'll head over to Algiers later."

"Yeah, maybe," he said. His eyes moved over the rolling fairways and oak trees, the parking lot in front of the main building, the sailboats rising and falling in their slips. "There're two or three exits to this place. We'd better park inside. I'm going to have a talk with Nig later about credibility. That's the problem with this PI stuff, you've got about the same clout as the lowlifes. I always feel like I'm picking up table scraps."

We drove through the gate and parked at the back of the lot, where we could see the Chrysler two rows away, under a sodium lamp. Clete reached into the back seat for his Styrofoam cooler, pulled out two fried-oyster poor-boy sandwiches, a can of Jax for himself, and a Dr. Pepper for me. He kept brushing crumbs off his shirtfront while he ate. When he finished a beer he crushed the can in his huge hand, threw it out onto the parking lot, and snapped open another one. He squinted one eye at me.

"Dave, have you got something else on the agenda?" he said.

"Not really."

"You're not going to see Joey Meatballs again and forget to invite your old partner to the party, are you?"

"Gouza doesn't rattle. We're going to have to take down somebody around him."

"It's been tried before. They're usually a lot more afraid of Joey than they are of us. I heard he busted out a snitch's teeth in Angola with a ballpeen hammer. Every punk and addict and pervert in New Orleans knows that story, too."

"How heavy do you figure he's into the crack trade?"

"He's not. It's pieced off too many times before it gets to the projects. Gouza's on the other end. Big shipments, pure stuff, out of Florida or South America. I hear his people distribute to maybe four or five guys in Orleans Parish, they make their profit on quantity, then they're out of the chain with minimum risk. Even the greaseballs won't go into the welfare projects. I had to go after a jumper for Nig at the St. Thomas. Two kids on the roof filled up a thirty-gallon garbage can with water and dropped it on me, bottom end down. It missed me by a foot and flattened a kid's tricycle like a half-dollar. . . . But you didn't really answer my question, noble mon. I think you've got something else on the dance card and you're not cutting ole Cletus in on it."

"This case has been all dead ends, Clete. When I learn something, I'll tell you. My big problem is the Sonniers. I feel like locking them all up as material witnesses."

"Maybe it's not a bad idea. Taking showers with child molesters and mainline bone smokers helps get your perspective clear sometimes.

"I couldn't make it stick. They weren't actually witness to anything."

"Then let them live with their own shit."

"I'm still left with a dead cop."

We sat for a long time in the rain. The band of cobalt light on the horizon gradually faded under the rim of storm clouds, and the lake grew dark and then glazed with the yellow reflection of ballroom lights in the club. I could taste salt in the wind. I pulled my rainhat down over my eyes and fell asleep.

I see Bootsie when she's nineteen, her hair as bright as copper on the pillow, her nude body as pink and soft as a newly opened rose. I put my head between her young breasts.

When I awoke the rain had stopped completely, the moon had broken through a rip in the clouds over the lake, and Clete was not in the car. I could hear orchestra music from the ballroom. Then I saw him, in silhouette, his wide back framed in the opened driver's door of Bobby Earl's Chrysler, his elbows cocked, both his arms pointed down toward his loins. He rotated his head on his neck as though he were standing indifferently at a public urinal. Even at that distance I could see the spray splashing on the dashboard, the steering wheel, the leather seats. Clete shook himself, flexed his knees, and zipped his fly. He cupped his Zippo in his hands, lit a cigarette, and puffed it in the corner of his mouth as he walked back toward the car and squinted up approvingly at the clearing sky overhead.

"I don't believe it."

"You got to let a guy like Bobby know you're around," he said, slamming the door behind him. "Ah, lookie there, our man scored after all. I think he's one of these guys who plans on marrying up and screwing down."

Bobby Earl walked across the parking lot in a white suit, charcoal shirt, and white-and-black striped tie. A red-headed woman in a sequined evening gown held on to his arm and tried to step across the puddles in her high heels. Both she and Bobby Earl balanced champagne glasses gingerly in their hands. The woman was laughing uncontrollably at something Bobby Earl was telling her.

Earl opened the passenger door for her, then got behind the wheel. The light from the sodium lamp shone through his front window, and I saw his silhouette freeze, then his shoulders stiffen, as though he had just become aware that a geological fissure had opened up below his automobile. Then he got out of the car, staring incredulously at his upturned palms, the wet streaks in his suit, the damp imprints of his shoes.

Clete started the engine, and the rusted-out muffler thundered off the asphalt and reverberated between the rows of cars. He turned out into the aisle and drove slowly past the Chrysler, the engine and frame clanking like broken glass.

"What's happenin', Bob?" he asked, then flipped his cigarette in a high, sparking arc, punched in a rock tape, and gave Bobby Earl the thumbs-up sign.

Bobby Earl's face slipped by the window like an outraged balloon. The woman in the sequined evening gown walked hurriedly back toward the clubhouse, her spiked heels clicking across the puddles.

▼

All men have a religion or totems of some kind. Even the atheist is committed to an enormous act of faith in his belief that the universe created itself and the subsequent creation of intelligent life was simply a biological accident. Eddy Raintree's votive attempt at metaphysics was just a little more eccentric than most. Both the gunbull in Angola and the biker girl in Algiers had said that Raintree was wired into astronomy and weirdness. In New Orleans, if your interest ran to UFOs (called "ufology" by enthusiasts), Island voodoo, witchcraft, teleportation through the third eye in your forehead, palm reading, the study of ectoplasm, the theory that Atlanteans are living among us in another dimension, and herbal cures for everything from brain cancer to impacted wisdom teeth, you eventually went to Tante Majorie's occult bookstore on Royal Street in the Quarter.

Tante Majorie was big all over and so black that her skin had a purple sheen to it. She streaked her high cheekbones with rouge and wore gold granny glasses, and her hair, which was pulled back tightly in a bun, had grayed so that it looked like dull gunmetal. She lived over her shop with another lesbian, an elderly white woman, and fifteen cats who sat on the furniture, the bookshelves, and the ancient radiator, and tracked soiled cat litter throughout the apartment.

She served tea on a silver service, then studied the photo of Eddy Raintree. Her French doors were open on the balcony, and I could hear the night noise from the street. I had known her almost twenty years and had never been able to teach her my correct name.

"You say he got a tiger on his arm?" she asked.

"Yes."

"I 'member him. He use to come in every three, four mont's. That's the one. I ain't forgot him. He's 'fraid of black people."

"Why do you think that?"

"He always want me to read his hand. But when I pick it up in my fingers, it twitch just like a frog. I'd tell him, It ain't shoe polish, darlin'. It ain't gonna rub off on you. Why you looking for him?"

"He helped murder a sheriff's deputy."

She looked out the French doors at the jungle of potted geraniums, philodendron, and banana trees on her balcony.

"You ain't got to look for him, Mr. Streak. That boy ain't got a long way to run," she said.

"What do you mean?"

"I told him it ain't no accident he got that tiger on his arm. I told him tiger burning bright in the forests of the night. Just like in the Bible, glowing out there in the trees. That tiger gonna eat him."

"I respect your wisdom and your experience, Tante Majorie, but I need to find this man."

She twisted a strand of hair between her fingers and gazed thoughtfully at a calico cat nursing a half-dozen kittens in a cardboard box.

"Every mont' I send out astrology readings for people on my list," she said. "He's one of them people. But Raintree ain't the name he give me. I don't 'member the name he give me. Maybe you ain't suppose to find him, Mr. Streak."

"My name's Dave, Tante Majorie. Could I see your list?"

"It ain't gonna he'p. His kind come with a face, what they get called don't matter. They come out of the womb without no name, without no place in the house where they're born, without no place down at a church, a school, a job down at a grocery sto', there ain't a place or a person they belong to in this whole round world. Not till that day they turn and look at somebody at the bus stop, or in the saloon, or sitting next to them in the hot-pillow house, and they see that animal that ain't been fed in that other person's eyes. That's when they know who they always been."

Then she went into the back of the apartment and returned with several sheets of typing paper in her hand.

"I got maybe two hundred people here," she said. "They're spread all over Lou'sana and Miss'sippi, too."

"Well, let's take a look," I said. "You see, Tante Majorie, the interesting thing about these guys is their ego. So when they use an alias they usually keep their initials. Or maybe their aliases have the same sound value as their real names."

Her list was in alphabetical order. I sorted the pages to the "R's."

"How about Elton Rubert?" I asked.

"I don't 'member it, Mr. Davis. My clerk must have put it down, and he don't work here anymore."

"My name is Dave, Tante Majorie. Dave Robicheaux. Where's your clerk now?"

"He moved up to Ohio, or one of them places up North."

I wrote down the mailing address of Elton Rubert, a tavern in a small settlement out in the Atchafalaya basin west of Baton Rouge.

"Here's my business card," I said. "If the man in the photo shows up here again, read his palm or whatever he wants, then call me later. But don't question him or try to find out anything about him for me, Tante Majorie. You've already been a great help."

"Give me your hand."

"I beg your pardon?"

She reached out and took my hand, stared into my palm and kneaded it with her fingers. Then she stroked it as though she were smoothing bread dough.

"There's something I ain't told you," she said. "The last time that man was in here, I read his hand, just like I'm reading yours. He axed me what his lifeline was like. What I didn't tell him, what he didn't know, was he didn't have no lifeline. It was gone."

I looked at her.

"You ain't understood me, darlin'," she said. "When your lifeline's gone, his kind get it back by stealing somebody else's." She folded my thumb and fingers into a fist, then pressed it into a ball with her palms. I could feel the heat and oil in her skin. "You hold on to it real hard, Mr. Streak. That tiger don't care who it eat."

▼

I had had trouble finding a parking place earlier and had left my pickup over by Rampart Street, not far from the Iberville welfare project. When I rounded the corner I saw the passenger door agape, the window smashed out on the pavement, the flannel-wrapped brick still in the gutter. The glove box had been rifled and the stereo ripped out of the panel, as well as most of the ignition wires, which hung below the dashboard like broken spaghetti ends.

Because First District headquarters was only two blocks away, it took only an hour to get a uniformed officer there to make out the theft report that my insurance company would require. Then I walked to a drugstore on Canal, called Triple A for a wrecker, and called Bootsie and told her that I wouldn't be home as I had promised, that with any luck I could have the truck repaired by late tomorrow.

"Where will you stay tonight?" she asked.

"At Clete's."

"Dave, if the truck isn't fixed tomorrow, take the bus back home and we'll go get the truck later. Tomorrow's Friday. Let's have a nice weekend."

"I may have to check out a lead on the way back. It might be a dud, but I can't let it hang."

"Does this have to do with Drew?"

"No, not at all."

"Because I wouldn't want to interfere."

"This may be the guy who tried to take my head off with a crowbar."

"Oh God, Dave, give it up, at least for a while."

"It doesn't work that way. The other side doesn't do pit stops."

"How clever," she said. "I'll leave the answering machine on in case we're in town."

"Come on, Boots, don't sign off like that."

"It's been a long day. I'm just tired. I don't mean what I say."

"Don't worry, everything's going to be fine. I'll call in the morning. Tell Alafair we'll go crabbing on the bay Saturday."

I was ready to say goodnight, then she said, as though she were speaking out of a mist, "Remember what they used to teach us in Catholic school about virginity? They said it was better to remain a virgin until you married so you wouldn't make comparisons. Do you ever make comparisons, Dave?"

I closed my eyes and swallowed as a man might if he looked up one sunny day and felt the cold outer envelope of a glacier sliding unalterably into his life.

When I was recuperating from the bouncing Betty that sent me home from Vietnam, and I began my long courtship with insomnia, I used to muse sometimes on what were the worst images or degrees of fear that my dreams could present me with. In my innocence, I thought that if I could face them in the light of day, imagine them perhaps as friendly gargoyles sitting at the foot of my bed, even hold a reasonable conversation with them, I wouldn't have to drink and drug myself nightly into another dimension where the monsters were transformed into pink zebras and prancing giraffes. But every third or fourth night I was back with my platoon, outside an empty ville that stunk of duck shit and unburied water buffalo; then as we lay pressed against a broken dike in the heated, breathless air, we suddenly realized that somebody back at the firebase had screwed up bad, and that the 105 rounds were coming in short.

The dream about an artillery barrage can be as real as the experience. You want to burrow into the ground like an insect; your knees are pulled up in a fetal position, your arms squeezed over your pot. Your fear is so great that you think the marrow in your skull will split, the arteries in your brain will rupture from their own dilation, blood will fountain from your nose. You will promise God anything in order to be spared. Right behind you, geysers of mud explode in the air and the bodies of North Vietnamese regulars are blown out of their graves, their bodies luminescent with green slime and dancing with maggots.

I had seen Vietnamese civilians who had survived B-52 raids. They were beyond speech; they trembled all over and made mewing and keening sounds that you did not want to take with you. When I would wake from my dream my hands would shake so badly that I could hardly unscrew the cap on the whiskey bottle that I kept hidden under my mattress.

As I slept on Clete's couch that night, I had to deal with another creation of my unconscious, one that was no less difficult than the old grainy filmstrips from Vietnam. In my dream I would feel

Bootsie next to me, her nude body warm and smooth under the sheet. I would put my face in her hair, kiss her nipples, stroke her stomach and thighs, and she would smile in her sleep, take me in her hand, and place me inside her. I would kiss the tops of her breasts and try to touch her all over while we made love, wishing in my lust that she were two instead of one. Then as it built inside of me like a tree cracking loose from a riverbank, rearing upward in the warm current, she would smile with drowsy expectation and close her eyes, and her face would grow small and soft and her mouth become as vulnerable as a flower.

But her eyes would open again and they would be as sightless as milk glass. A scaled deformity like the red wings of a butterfly would mask her face, her body would stiffen and ridge with bone, and her womb would be filled with death.

I sat up in the darkness of Clete's living room, the blood beating in my wrists, and opened and closed my mouth as though I had been pulled from beneath the ocean's surface. I stared through the window and across the courtyard at a lamp on a table behind a curtain that was lifting in the breeze from a fan. I could see someone's shadow moving behind the curtain. I wanted to believe that it was the shadow of a nice person, perhaps a man preparing to go to work or an elderly woman fixing breakfast before going to Mass at St. Louis Cathedral. But it was 4 A.M.; the sky overhead was black, with no hint of the false dawn; the night still belonged to the gargoyles, and the person across the courtyard was probably a hooker or somebody on the downside of an all-night drunk.

I put on my shirt and slacks and slipped on my loafers. I could see Clete's massive form in his bed, a pillow over his face, his porkpie hat on the bedpost. I closed the door softly behind me. The air in the courtyard was electric with the smell of magnolia.

The bar was over by Decatur, one of those places that never closes, where there is neither cheer nor anger nor expectation and no external measure of one's own failure and loss.

The bottles of bourbon, vodka, rum, gin, rye, and brandy rang with light along the mirror. The oak-handled beer spigots and frosted mugs in the coolers could have been a poem. The bartender propped his arms impatiently on the dish sink.

"I'll serve you, but you got to tell me what it is you want," he said. He looked at another customer, raised his eyebrows, then looked back at me. He was smiling now. "How about it, buddy?"

"I'd like a cup of coffee."

"You want a cup of coffee?"

"Yes."

"This looks like a place where you get a cup of coffee? Too much, too much," he said, then began wiping off the counter with a rag.

I heard somebody laugh as I walked back out onto the street. I sat on the railway tracks behind the French Market and watched the dawn touch the earth's rim and light the river and the docks and scows over in Algiers, turn the sky the color of bone, and finally fill the east with a hot red glow like the spokes in a wagon wheel. The river looked wide and yellow with silt, and I could see oil and occasionally dead fish floating belly up in the current.

My truck was not repaired until six o'clock Friday evening. By the time I hit South Baton Rouge the sun was a red molten ball in the western sky. I crossed the Mississippi and swung off the interstate at Port Allen and continued through the Atchafalaya basin on the old highway. The bar that Eddy Raintree may have been using as his mail drop was on a yellow dirt road that wound through thick stands of dead cypress and copper-colored pools of stagnant water.

It was hammered together from clapboard, plywood, and tarpaper, its screens rusted and gutted, the windows pocked from gravel flung against the building by spinning car tires; it sat up on cinder blocks like an elephant with a broken back. A half-dozen Harleys were parked on the side, and in the back a group of bikers were barbecuing in an oil drum under an oak tree. The yellow dust from the road drifted across their fire.

The Atchafalaya basin is the place you go if you don't fit anywhere else. It encompasses hundreds of square miles of bayous, canals, sandspits, willow islands, huge inland bays, and flooded woods where the mosquitoes will hover around your head like a helmet and you slap your arms until they're slick with a black-red paste. Twenty minutes from Baton Rouge or an hour and a half from New Orleans, you can punch a hole in the dimension and drop back down into the redneck, coonass, peckerwood South that you thought had been eaten up by the developers of Sunbelt suburbs. It's a shrinking place, but there's a group that holds on to it with a desperate and fearful tenacity.

I slipped my .45 in the back of my belt, along with my handcuffs, put on my seersucker coat, and went inside the bar. The jukebox played Waylon and Merle; the men at the pool table rifled balls into side pockets as though they wanted to drive pain into the wood and leather; and a huge Confederate flag billowed out from the tacks holding it to the ceiling.

A metal sign, the size of a bumper sticker, over the men's room door said WHITE POWER. I used the urinal. Above it, neatly written on a piece of cardboard, were the words THIS IS THE ONLY SHITHOUSE WE GOT, SO KEEP THE GODDAMN PLACE CLEAN.

The bartender was a small, prematurely balding, suntanned man with thin arms who wore a wash-frayed suit vest with no shirt. On his right forearm was a tattoo of the Marine Corps globe and anchor. He didn't ask me what I wanted; he simply pointed two fingers at me with his cigarette between them.

"I'm looking for Elton Rupert," I said.

"I don't know him," he said.

"That's strange. He gets his mail here."

"That might be. I don't know him. What do you want?"

"How about a 7 Up?"

He took a bottle out of the cooler, snapped off the cap, and set it before me with a glass.

"The ice machine's broken, so there's no ice," he said.

"That's all right."

"That's a dollar."

I put four quarters on the bar. He scraped them up and started to walk away.

"It looks like you have some letters in a box up there. Would you see if Elton's picked up his mail?" I said.

"Like I told you, I don't know the man."

"You're the regular bartender, you're here most of the time?"

He put out his cigarette in an ashtray, mashing it methodically, then his eyes went out the open front door and across the road as though I were not there. He picked a piece of tobacco off his tongue.

"I'd appreciate your answering my question," I said.

"Maybe you should ask those guys barbecuing out back. They might know him."

"You were in the corps?"

"Yeah."

"You're only in the crotch once."

"You were in the corps?"

"No, I was in the army. That's not my point. You're only in the AB once, too."

He lit another cigarette and bit a hangnail on his thumb.

"I don't know what you're saying, buddy, but this is the wrong fucking place to get in somebody's face," he said.

A barmaid came in the side door, put her handbag in a cabinet, and carried a sack of trash out the back.

"You're saying you don't understand me, my words confuse you?" I asked.

"What's with you, man? Somebody shoved a bumblebee up your ass?"

"What's your name, podna?"

"Harvey."

"You're treating me like I'm stupid, Harvey. You're starting to piss me off."

"I don't need this shit, man." He looked out the back door at the men in jeans, cutoff denim jackets, and motorcycle boots, who were drinking canned beer in the barbecue smoke under the tree.

"It's just you and me, Harvey. Those guys don't have anything to do with it," I said.

The barmaid came back inside. She looked like she had dressed for work in a dime store. Her blond hair was shaved on one side, punked orange on the tips; she wore black fingernail polish, a pink top, black vinyl shorts, owl glasses with red frames, earrings made from chromed .38 hulls.

"Give this guy a free 7 Up if he wants one. I'm going to the head," Harvey said to her.

I waited a moment, then followed him into the men's room and shot the bolt on the door. He was in the single stall, urinating loudly into the toilet bowl.

"Zipper it up and come out here, Harvey," I said.

He opened the stall door and stared at me, his mouth hanging open. I stuck my badge up close to his face.

"The man's real name is Eddy Raintree," I said. "Now don't you bullshit me. Where is he?"

"You can bust me, you can kick my ass, it don't matter, I don't know the sonofabitch," he said. "Guys get their mail here. They go behind the bar and pick it up. I don't know who they are, I don't ask. Check out those cats behind the building, man. There's one guy drove a pool cue through another guy's lung out there."

"Where's my man live, Harvey?"

He shook his head back and forth, his mouth a tight line. I rested one hand on his shoulder and looked steadily into his face.

"What are you going to do when you walk out of here?" I said.

"What do you mean going—"

"You think you're going to make some mileage with my butt?"

"Look, man—" He started to shake his head again.

"Maybe ease on over to the phone booth and make a call? Or take a round of beers to the outdoor geek show and mention that the heat is drinking 7 Up inside?"

"I'm neutral. I got no stake in this."

"That's right. So it's time for you to go. To tell the lady behind the bar you're taking off early tonight. We're understood on this, aren't we?"

"You're the man. I do what you say."

"But if I find out you talked to somebody you shouldn't, I'll be back. It's called aiding and abetting and obstruction of justice. What that means is I'll take you back with me to the Iberia Parish jail. The guy who runs it is a three-hundred-pound black homosexual with a sense of humor about which cells he puts you guys in."

He rubbed his mouth. His hand made a dry sound against his whiskers.

"Look, I didn't see you, I didn't talk to you," he said. "Okay? I'm going home sick. What you said about the AB, it's true, it's lifetime. If one guy doesn't take you out, another does. I'm a four-buck-an-hour beer bartender. I've got ulcers and a slipped disc. All I want is some peace."

"You've got it, partner. We'll see you around. Stay away from phones tonight, watch a lot of television, write some letters to the home folks."

"How about treating me with a little dignity, man? I'm doing what you want. I ain't a criminal, I ain't your problem. I'm just a little guy running around in a frying pan."

"You've probably got a point, Harvey."

I unbolted the door and watched him walk to the bar, say something to the barmaid, then leave by the side door and drive up the dirt road in a paintless pickup truck. The dust from the parking lot drifted back through the rusted screens in the late-afternoon sunlight. Once he was out of sight, it would not take Harvey long to decide that his loyalties to the bikers and Eddy Raintree were far more important to his welfare than his temporary fear of me and the Iberia Parish jail.

I returned to the bar and asked the barmaid for a pencil and a piece of paper. She tore a page from a notepad by the telephone and handed it to me. I scribbled two or three sentences on the back and folded it once, then twice.

"Would you give this to Elton for me?" I said.

"Elton Rupert?"

"Yeah."

"Sure." She took the note from my hand and dropped it in the letter box behind the bar. "You probably just missed him. He usually comes in about four o'clock."

"Yeah, that's what Harvey was saying. Too bad I missed him."

"Too bad?" She laughed. "You got stopped-up nostrils or something? Trying to open up your sinuses?"

"What?"

"The guy's got gapo that would make the dead get up and run down the road."

"He has what?"

"Gorilla armpit odor. You sure you know Elton? He stays in that shack by the levee and doesn't bathe unless he gets rained on. I don't know where he gets off knocking the niggers all the time."

"I like your earrings."

"I got them just the other day. You really like them?"

"Sure. I've never seen any made out of .38 shells."

"My boyfriend made them. He's a gun nut but he's real good at making jewelry and stuff. He's thinking of opening up a mail-order business."

"Elton doesn't have a phone, does he?"

"He doesn't have any plumbing. I don't know why he'd have a phone."

I looked at my watch.

"Maybe I have time to stop by his place just a minute. It's not far, is it?" I said.

"Straight down the road to the levee. You can't miss it. Just follow your nose. Hah!"

"By the way, how's Elton's eye?"

"It looks like worms ate it. Are you doing some kind of missionary work or something?"

The violet air was thick with insects as I drove down the yellow road toward the levee and the marsh. The road crossed the Southern Pacific tracks, then followed alongside a green levee that was covered with buttercups. On the other side of the levee were a canal, a chain of willow islands and sandbars, and a bay full of dead cypress. Three hundred yards from the track crossing was a fishing shack, a small box of a place with a collapsed gallery, an outhouse, an overflowing garbage barrel in back. Both a pirogue and a boat with an outboard engine were tied to wood stobs driven into the mudflat. A chopped-down Harley was parked on the far side of the gallery, its chrome glinting with the sun's last red light. The sky was black with birds.

I parked the truck down the levee, took my World War II Japanese field glasses from my locked toolbox, which the kids from the Iberville project hadn't gotten into, and waited. It was going to be a hot night. The air was perfectly still, heated from the long afternoon, stale with the smell of dead water beetles and alligator gars that fishermen had thrown up on the bank. I studied the shack through the field glasses. The garbage barrel boiled with flies, an orange cat was eating a fishhead in a bowl on the shack step, a man walked past a window.

Then he was gone before I could focus on his face.

Finally it was dark, and the man inside the shack lit an oil lamp, opened a tin can at a table, and ate from it with a fork, hunched over with his back toward me. Then he urinated off the back steps with a bottle of beer in one hand, and I saw his big granite head in the light from the door, and the muscles that swelled in his shoulders like lumps of garden hose.

When he was back inside I got out of the truck with my .45 in my hand, crossed the levee, and moved through the darkness toward the shack. The willows were motionless, etched against a yellow moon, and I saw a moccasin as thick as my wrist uncoil off a log, drop into the water, and swim in a silvery V toward a dead neutria who had been hit by a boat propeller. The man moved in silhouette across the window, and I slid back the receiver on the .45, eased a hollow-point into the chamber, and walked quickly up the mud-bank to the back steps. I heard train cars jolt together, then a locomotive backing along the tracks on the far side of the levee.

Now, I thought, and I cleared the three steps in one jump, burst into the shack, into a reek of stale sweat that was as close and gray as a damp cotton glove. His head looked up from the comic book that was spread on his knees. I aimed the .45 straight into the face of Eddy Raintree.

"Hands behind your neck, down on the floor! Do it, do it, do it!" I shouted.

The skin around his right eye was puckered with white sores. I shoved him off the chair amid a litter of newspapers, beer cans, and fast-food containers. His weight bowed the floor planks. I put the .45 behind his ear.

"All the way down on your face, Eddy," I said, and began to pull the handcuffs from the back of my belt.

That should have been the end of it. But I got careless. Maybe my alcoholic dreams and sleeplessness of the previous night were to blame, or the eye-watering body odor that filled the room, or the sudden slamming of freight cars out in the darkness. But in the time it took the handcuffs to drop from my fingers, my vision to slip off the back of his head, he spun around like an animal turning in a box, grabbed the .45 with both hands, and locked his teeth on the knuckle of my right thumb.

His eyes were close-set like a pig's in the lamplight, his jaws knotted with cartilage, trembling with exertion. Blood spurted across the back of my hand; I could feel his teeth biting into the bone. I clubbed desperately at the back of his thick neck. His coarse, oily skin felt like rubber under my knuckles.

I was almost ready to drop the gun when he rammed his shoulder into my chest and dove headlong through the front window curtain.

My right hand quivered uncontrollably. I picked up the .45 with my left and went out the front door after him. He was running along the levee next to a stopped freight that must have been a mile long. The locomotive was haloed with white light and wisps of vapor, and in front of it gandy walkers were repairing track in the red glare of burning flares.

Eddy Raintree must have received his dishonorable discharge from the Marine Corps before a DI could teach him to stay off the crests of hills and embankments and never run in a straight line when someone is making a study of you through iron sights.

It felt strange to fire the .45 with my left hand. It leaped upward in my grasp as though it had a life of its own. Both rounds whanged and sparked off the sides of a gondola, and Eddy Raintree kept running, his head hunched into his shoulders. I knelt in the weeds, sighted low to allow for the recoil, let out my breath slowly, and squeezed off another round. His right leg went out from under him as though it had been struck with a baseball bat, and he toppled down the far side of the levee to the railroad bed.

When I slid down the embankment and got to him he had his palm pressed tightly against his thigh and was trying to pull himself erect on a metal rung at the end of a boxcar. His hand was shining and wet, and his face had already gone white with shock. A sweet, fetid odor came from the car, and then I saw that it was actually built of slats and contained cages.

"Sit down, Eddy," I said.

He breathed hard through his mouth. His eyes were bright and mean, the whites flecked with blood.

"It's over, partner. Don't have any wrong thoughts about that. Now sit down and give me your wrist," I said.

He tried not to grimace as he eased himself down on the gravel. I cuffed one wrist, looped the chain through the iron rung on the car, and cuffed the other wrist. Then I patted him down.

"What the fuck's this train carrying?" he said.

I split open his pants leg with my Puma knife. The entry hole in the skin was black and no bigger than the ball of my index finger. But it took my wadded handkerchief to cover the exit wound. I slipped my belt around his thigh and tightened it with a stick.

"What the fuck is in that car?" he said. His long hair hung from his head like string on a pumpkin.

"I'm going to give you the lay of the land, Eddy. You're leaking pretty bad. I'm going to run up ahead and ask those train guys to radio for an ambulance. But if we can't get one out here right away, I think we should dump you into my truck and head into Baton Rouge."

The side of his face twitched.

"What's the game?" he said.

"No game. You've got a big hole in you. You're going to need some blood."

"That's it? I'm suppose to get scared now? I had a nigger gunbull sweat me with a cattle prod till he ran out of batteries. Go fuck yourself."

"Read it like you want. I'm going to the head of the train, then I'll be back and we'll load you in my truck."

He twisted his head around at a sound inside the railroad car.

"There's fucking lions or tigers in there, man," he said.

"It's part of a circus. They're in cages. They can't hurt you."

"What if they back up the fucking train while you're taking a walk?"

"You dealt the play, Eddy. Live with it. Keep that belt tight and don't move your leg around."

"Hey, man, come here. Cuff me to that light over there."

"It's too far to move you."

"What the fuck's with you? You enjoy people's pain or something?"

"I'll be back, Eddy."

"All right, man, I'll trade. Jewel smoked the cop in the basement. But I didn't have any part in it. We were just there to creep the joint. You saw me, I didn't have a piece."

"That's not much of a trade."

He waited a moment, then he said, "There's a whack out. On Sonnier and the broad, both."

"Which broad?"

"His sister." He wet his lips. "I can't swear it, but I think the whack's out on you, too. You're a hair in the wrong guy's nose."

"Which guy?"

"That's all you get, motherfucker. I cut a deal, it's in custody, with a lawyer and the prosecutor there."

"I think you're a gasbag, Eddy, but I don't want to see you die of fright." I uncuffed one wrist, then locked both of his arms behind him. "Lie quietly. I'm going to ask a couple of those gandy walkers to help me put you in the truck."

"Hey, man, those animals smell my blood. Hey, man, come back here!"

He lay on his side in the gravel and weeds, his face sallow and slick with sweat in the humid air. His manacled arms were ropy with muscle, as though he were being hung from a great height, as though his tattoos were about to pop from his skin. A breeze blew across the levee, and I could smell the moist odor of animal dung and almost taste Eddy Raintree's fear of his own kind.

I walked three hundred yards to the head of the train, showed my badge to the engineer, and told him to radio to Baton Rouge for an ambulance. Then I asked two black gandy walkers to help me with Eddy Raintree. They wore dirt-streaked undershirts, and their black skin was beaded with sweat in the red light of the track flares. They looked at their crew foreman, who was white.

"Go ahead, boys," he said.

They walked behind me, back toward where Eddy Raintree lay on his side in the weeds and gravel. I heard the deep-throated sound of a tiger or lion in the wind. I turned to say something light to the black men, when one of them pointed into the distance.

"You got somebody coming yonder on a motorcycle," he said.

I saw the headlight and the starlit silhouette of the bike and a small rider bounce down the side of the levee and come hard along the line of train cars. I could already see Eddy Raintree trying to rise to one knee, as he realized that he might still have another frolic in the funhouse.

It was very quick after that.

I pulled the .45 from my belt and broke into a run. The motorcycle passed Eddy Raintree, skidded in the gravel, and circled back in the direction it had come from, the headlight beam bouncing off the sides of the train. At first I thought the small rider was trying to swing Eddy up behind him, the way a rodeo pickup man scoops up a thrown cowboy. Then I saw a rigid object about two feet long in his hand, saw him extend it out beside him, and in my naïveté I thought it might be bolt cutters, that Raintree would lift up his manacled wrists, and the small rider would snap him free and I would be left breathless and exhausted while they disappeared over the levee into the darkness.

But I was close enough now to see that it was a shotgun, with the barrel sawed off right in front of the pump. Eddy Raintree had made it to one knee and was frozen in the headlight's radiance, like an armless man trying to genuflect in church, when the shotgun roared upward three inches from his chin.

Then the small rider opened up his bike, one boot skipping along the rocks for balance, and wove the bike up the levee in a shower of dirt and divots of grass and buttercups. My chest was heaving, my arm shaking, when I let off two rounds at his toylike silhouette just before he hit it full-bore, his head bent low, and disappeared in a long roll of diminishing thunder between the levee and the willow islands.

Eddy Raintree's buttocks were collapsed on his heels. His head was turned away from me, as though he were trying to hide his facial expression or a secret that he wished to take with him to another place. The animals in the circus car crashed wildly about in their wire cages. I touched Eddy Raintree lightly on the shoulder, and it rotated downward with gravity on the severed tendons in his neck.

One of the gandy walkers vomited.

"Oh Lord God, look what they done to that po' man," the other said. "His face hanging off the wrong side of his head."

9

It was after midnight before I finished with the paramedics, local sheriff's deputies, an angry detective who accused me of operating in his jurisdiction without first contacting his office, and the parish medical examiner, who, like many of his kind, had aspirations to be a comedian.

"You could can that guy's B.O. as a chemical weapon and bring the Iranians to their knees," he said. "I'd consider rabies shots."

When I got into my truck I knew I should drive straight back to New Iberia. That would have been the reasonable thing to do. But my late-night hours had never been characterized by reason, neither as a practicing or as a recovering drunk.

Less than an hour later I was on Highland Drive, west of the LSU campus in Baton Rouge, and I turned out of the long corridor of oaks into a brick-paved driveway lined with a rick fence and rosebushes. It led to an enormous white house with antebellum pretensions that might have been built five minutes ago on a Hollywood movie set. The trim on the front door was pink, the brasswork as bright and portentous as gold.

When he opened the front door in his pajamas, the breeze made the chandelier over his head ring with sound and light.

"Bootsie needs your help," I said. "No, that's not really true. I need it for her. I'm out there on the rim, Lyle."

10

The next morning was Saturday, and I should have been off for the day, but the dispatcher called at 9 A.M.

"What do you want to do with these four guys Levy and Guillory brought in?" he asked.

"What four guys?"

"The bums Levy and Guillory brought in from the shelters. Levy said you were looking for guys who'd been in an ugly-man contest. You've got some beauts here, Dave."

I had completely forgotten.

"Where are they now?" I said.

"In the drunk tank."

"How long have they been there?"

"Since yesterday."

"Get them out of there. I'll be right down."

Fifteen minutes later I was at the office. I walked down a corridor to a holding cell, where the four men patiently waited for me on a single wood bench. In the center of the cell floor was a

urine-streaked drain hole. The men all had the emaciated character-
istics of people whose lives existed on a straight line between the
blood bank and the wine store. Like most professional tramps, they
had a strange chemical odor about them, as though their glands had
long ago stopped functioning properly and now secreted only a
synthetic substitute for natural body fluids. I opened up the barred
door.

One man's head was misshapen, broken on one side like a
dented walnut; the second's face was eaten with a skin disease that
looked like skin cancer; the third had a bad harelip and virtually no
cartilage in his nose; but it was the face of the fourth man on the
bench that made me wince inside.

"Have you guys eaten?" I said.

They nodded that they had, except the man on the end. His eyes
never blinked and never left my face.

"I'm sorry about what happened," I said. "I didn't mean for you
to be locked up. I had just wanted to talk to you, but I went out of
town and my orders got a little confused."

They made no reply. They shuffled their shoes on the concrete
floor and looked at the backs of their hands. Then the man with the
skin disease said, "It ain't bad. They got TV."

"Anyway, I apologize to you guys," I said. "A deputy will drive
you back to wherever you want to go. He'll also give you a voucher
for a meal at a café in town. Here's my business card. If you ever
want to pick up a dollar or two sanding down some boats, call that
number."

They rose as one to go out the open cell door.

"Say, podna, would you stay a minute with me?" I said to the
last man on the bench.

He sat back down indifferently and began rolling a cigarette. I
took a chair from the corridor and sat opposite him. His whole head
looked like it had been put in a furnace. The ears were burnt into
stubs; the hairless red scar tissue looked like it had been applied in
layers to the bone with a putty knife; part of the lips had been
surgically removed so that the teeth and gums were exposed in a
permanent sneer.

He rolled the tobacco into a tight cylinder, wet down the glued seam, and crimped the edges. He lifted his eyes up to mine. They looked as lidless, as reptilian and liquid as a chameleon's. He popped a match aflame on his thumbnail. It was as thick and purple as tortoise shell.

"You like my face?" he asked.

"What's your name?"

"Vic."

"Vic what?"

"Vic Who-gives-a-shit? One name's good as another, I figure."

"How about giving me your last name?"

"Benson."

"How'd you get hurt, podna?"

He put his cigarette in the hole where his lips were pared away at the corner of his mouth. He blew smoke out toward the bars. "In a tank," he said.

"You were in the service?"

"That's right."

"Where'd you serve?"

"Korea."

"Your tank got nailed?"

"You got it."

"Where in Korea?"

"Second day, at Heartbreak Ridge. What's all this stuff about?"

"There're some people who say they've seen a man with your description looking through their windows."

"Yeah? Must be my twin brother." He laughed, and saliva welled up on his gum.

"There's a preacher in Baton Rouge who thinks a man who looks like you might be his father."

"I had a son once. But I didn't raise no preacher."

"You ever hear of a woman called Mattie?"

He took his cigarette carefully off his lip and tipped the ashes between his knees.

"Did you hear me, podna?" I said.

His eyes regarded me quietly.

"You guys got nothing else to do except this kind of stuff?" he asked.

"Did you know a woman named Mattie?"

"No, I didn't."

He picked at a scab inside his wasted forearm.

"How often do you go the blood bank?" I asked.

"Once or twice a week. Depends on how many is in town. They keep records."

"Where do you receive your VA checks?"

"What?"

"Your disability payments."

"I don't get them no more. I ain't gone in to certify in five or six years."

"Why not?"

" 'Cause I don't like them sonsabitches."

"I see," I said, then I spoke to him in French.

"I don't speak it," he said.

"I think you're not telling me the truth, Vic."

He dropped his cigarette to the cement and mashed it out with his foot.

"You interested in my life story, run my prints," he said, and turned up his palms. "We were buttoned down when they put one up our snout. I was the only guy got out. The hatch burned me all the way to the bone when I pushed it open. I don't know no preacher, except at the mission. You saying I look in people's windows, you're a goddamn liar."

His breath was stale, his eyes like heated marbles inside his red, manikinlike face.

"Where are you staying?" I said.

"At the Sally, in Lafayette."

"I don't have anything to hold you on, Vic. But I'm going to ask you to stay out of Iberia Parish. If these same people are bothered by a man who looks like you, I want to know that you were somewhere else. Do we have an agreement on that?"

"I go where I want."

I tapped my fountain pen on the back of my knuckles, then stood up and swung the door wide for him.

"All right, podna. The deputy at the end of the corridor will drive you back to Lafayette," I said. "But I'll leave you with a thought. If you're Verise Sonnier, don't blame your children for your unhappiness. They've had their share of it, too. You might even learn to be a bit proud of them."

"Get out of my way," he said, and walked past me, tucking in his shirt over his skinny hips.

▼

I went home, turned on the window fan in the bedroom, and slept for four hours. On the edge of my sleep I could hear Alafair and Bootsie weeding the flower beds under the windows, walking through the leaves, scraping ashes out of the barbecue pit. When I awoke, Bootsie was in the shower. Her figure was brown and softly muted through the frosted glass, and I could see her washing her arms and breasts with a rag and a bar of pink soap. I took off my underwear and stepped into the stall with her, rubbed the smooth muscles of her back and shoulders, worked my thumbs up and down her spine, kissed the dampness of her hair along her neck.

Then I dried her off like she was a little girl, although it was I who often had the heart of a child while making love. We lay on top of the sheets, and the fan billowed the curtain and drew its breeze across us. I kissed her thighs and her stomach and put her nipples in my mouth. When I entered her, her body was so hot she felt like she was burning with a high fever.

Later, I took Alafair to Saturday evening Mass at the cathedral, then attended an AA meeting. When it was my turn to talk, I did a partial fifth step before the group, which consists of admitting to ourselves, to another human being, and to God the exact nature of our wrongs.

Why?

Because I had gone to Lyle Sonnier's house in Baton Rouge and compromised my faith in my Higher Power. I had let Him down, and by doing so—seeking out the help of a man whom I had considered a charlatan—I had let Bootsie down, too. Even Lyle had said so.

When he had hit the light switch in his kitchen, the chrome, yellow plastic, white enamel, and flowered wallpaper leaped to life with the brilliance of a flashbulb. He took a bottle of milk and pecan pie from the icebox, set forks, plates, and crystal glasses on the table, then sat across from me, wan-faced, tired, obviously unsure of where he should begin.

"We can talk a long time, Dave, but I guess I ought to tell you straight out I can't give you what you want," he said.

"Then you *are* a fraud."

"That's a tough word."

"You said you can heal, Lyle. I'm calling you on it." I felt a bubble of saliva break in my throat.

"No, you don't understand. I *was* a fraud. I was strung out on rainbows and purple acid, black speed, you name it, street dealing, breaking into people's cars, hanging in some of those gay places on South Los Angeles Street in L.A., you get my drift, when I met this boozehead scam artist named the Reverend Jimmy Bob Clock.

"Jimmy Bob and me went on the tent circuit all over the South. He'd whip up a crowd till they were hysterical, then he'd walk down that sawdust aisle in a white suit with the spotlight dancing on it and grab some poor fellow's forehead in his hands and almost squeeze his brains out his ears. When he'd let go, the guy would be trembling all over and seeing visions through the top of the tent.

"Before the show he'd have me go to the rear of the line and ask some of the old folks if they wouldn't like a wheelchair to sit in, and wouldn't they like to be right down on the front row? I'd wheel them down there, and halfway into his sermon he'd jump off the stage, take them by the hands, and make them rise up and walk. Then he'd shout, 'What time you got?' And they'd shout back, 'It's time to run the devil around the block with the Reverend Jimmy Bob Clock.'

"Jimmy Bob was a pistol, son. On camera he'd grab a handful of somebody's loose flesh and shake it like Jell-O and say he'd just cured it of cancer. He'd lift up somebody's legs from a wheelchair and hold them at an angle so one looked shorter than the other, then he'd straighten them out, praying all the time with his eyes squeezed shut, and holler out that a man born lame could now walk without a limp.

"Except they got Jimmy Bob on a check-writing rap in Hattiesburg, and I had to do the next show in Tupelo by myself. The tent was busting with people, and I was going to try to get through the night with the wheelchair scam and maybe curing somebody of deafness or back pain or something else that nobody can see, because if that crowd doesn't get a miracle of some kind they're not shelling out the bucks when the baskets go around. But right in the middle of the sermon this old black woman comes up the aisle on two canes and I know I've got a problem.

"She started pulling on my pants leg and looking up at me with these blue cataracts, opening and closing her mouth like a baby bird in its nest. Then everybody in the tent was looking at her, and there wasn't any way out of it, I had to do something.

"I said, 'What's brought you here, auntie?' And I held the microphone down to her.

"She said, 'My spine's fused. They ain't nothing for the pain. 'Lectric blanket don't do it, chiropractor don't do it, mo'phine don't do it. I wants to die.'

"She had on these big thick glasses that were glowing from the spots, and tears were running down her face. I said, 'Don't be talking like that, auntie.'

"And she said, 'You can cure this old woman. God done anointed you. It ain't no different than touching the hem of His garment.' And she dropped her canes and set her hands on the tops of my shoes.

"I thought my conscience had been eaten up with dope a long time ago. But I wanted God to take me off the planet, right there. I wanted to tell everybody in that tent they were looking at a man who had gone as low as spit on the sidewalk. I didn't have any words, I didn't know what to do, I couldn't see anything but those spots burning in my eyes. So I got down on my knees and I put my hands on that old woman's head. Her hair was gray and wet with sweat and I could feel the blood beating in her temples. I prayed to God, right up through the top of the canvas, 'Punish me, Lord, but let this lady have her way.'

"That's when I felt it for the first time. It kicked through both my arms just like I grabbed hold of an electric fence. It made my teeth rattle. She straightened her back, and the pain and misery drained out of her face like somebody had poured cool water through her whole body. I'd never seen anything like it. I was trembling so bad I couldn't get off my knees. Something broke inside me and I started crying. The whole tent went crazy. But I *knew,* even at that moment, the power had come up through that old woman, through the faith in that old, sweaty, tormented black head. Sometimes in my sleep I can still feel her hair on my palms.

"It won't work for you, Dave. You came here for magic. You don't believe in the world I belong to. It's going to make you remorseful later, too."

I hadn't eaten any of the pie. I pushed it away from me with the back of my wrist and looked through the side window at the headlights of a car clicking whitely along the dark line of oak trees on Highland Drive.

"What I'm saying is, you gave up on your own belief," he said. "But don't beat up on yourself about it. You got desperate and you came here to get help for somebody else, not yourself. Just go back to doing what you were before. Sometimes you got to hump it a long way before you get out of Indian country, Loot."

I looked down between my knees at the linoleum. I didn't think I had ever been so tired.

"I appreciate your time, Lyle," I said.

He touched the teardrop scar tissue that ran from his right eye.

"Long as you're here, there's something I want to own up to," he said. "The last time I saw you, I tried to push buttons on you. I mean, when I mentioned that stuff about you poking my sister."

"I already forgot it."

"No, you don't know everything involved, Dave. Drew had the hots for you back in college, and maybe she's still got them. But maybe for a reason you don't understand. You're a lot like Weldon."

I raised my head and looked at him.

"You're both big, nice-looking guys," he said. "You were both officers in the war. Neither one of you likes rules or people telling you what to do. Both of you have electric sparks leaking off your terminals."

I stared into his eyes.

"Growing up, we didn't have anybody but ourselves," he said. "It screws you up. What's sick behavior to one person is love to another. We didn't care what other people said was right or wrong. They were the same people burning us with hot cigarettes or sticking us in foster homes. Weldon and Drew weren't just brother and sister for each other. And I'm not innocent in this, either. But it was always Weldon she loved."

I looked away from the fine bead of pain in his eyes.

"Why do you think I've had three wives?" he asked. "Or why's Weldon married to an addict who hangs on him like a child? Or why does Drew get it on with anybody who's got hair sticking out the top of his shirt? It's like your feelings and your head are never on the same wavelength. Every time you make love with somebody, you get mad at them and resent them. Figure that one out.

"Dave, you've got a lock on sanity. Don't come to the likes of us for insight."

He forked a piece of pie into the back of his mouth and chewed it silently, his eyes never leaving my embarrassed averted face.

▼

Sunday morning Bootsie, Alafair, and I went crabbing down by the coast. We tied chicken necks inside the weighted wire traps, whose sides would collapse on the bottom of the bay and then snap back into place with a jerk of the cord that was strung through a ring on the top. In three hours we filled a washtub with bluepoint crabs, washed them later with a garden hose in the backyard, and boiled them in a black iron pot on top of my brick barbecue pit. There was a breeze through the oaks, and the sky had a blue sheen to it, like stretched silk, and white clouds were piled high as a mountain on the western horizon.

It was a wonderful day. I had been to Mass and communion the previous evening, I had done a fifth step on my lapse of faith in my Higher Power, and I had determined once again to stop keeping score in my ongoing contention with the world, time, and mortality, and to simply thank providence for all the good things that had come to me through no plan of my own.

Eddy Raintree, with all the instincts of a mainline con and trapped animal, had tried to trade off information about a hit on Weldon, Drew, and perhaps even me. So far I hadn't talked with either of them about Raintree's possible knowledge of a contract on them, primarily because it was a waste of time; I had already warned them repeatedly about the possible consequence of not cooperating with the investigation, and I was tired of being dismissed as an adverb in their lives.

Also, I didn't take Raintree seriously. Every sociopath or recidivist about to go down for a serious jolt suddenly has access to information about armored-truck scores, judges on the pad for the syndicate, the assassination of John Kennedy, or dope sales to a U.S. vice president.

I would leave Sunday intact, keep it the fine day it was, and let tomorrow and its uncertainties take care of themselves. We drove into New Iberia in the purpling light and ate ice cream under a spreading oak by Bayou Teche and listened to a Cajun band play in the park. I hugged Bootsie and Alafair against me.

"What's that for?" Alafair said, her eyes squinting with her grin.

"I have to make sure you guys don't get away from me," I said.

At eleven o'clock that night, just as raindrops started to splash on the window fan in our bedroom, the sheriff called and said that Drew Sonnier had been found nailed to the gazebo in her backyard.

A neighbor had found her seated on the steps, half conscious, white with shock, her left hand impaled on the gazebo floor with a sixteen-penny nail, a pool of vomit in her lap.

"Hey, are you all right?" the sheriff said.

"Yes."

"She's at the hospital, she's doing okay. At least under the circumstances."

"Who did it?"

"I don't know if you're ready for this."

"The guys from the Garrett killing?"

"Joey Gouza himself. Or at least he gave the orders and watched while two of his goons held her down and drove it through her hand."

"What?" I said incredulously.

"She said it was Gouza. She can identify him, she'll testify against him. Maybe we just hit the big one. . . . What's the matter?"

"She can make Joey Gouza? How does she know him?"

"All I know is what the city cops told me, Dave."

"What's the motive?"

"Since it's your day off, I was going to send somebody else to take her statement. But I think maybe you'd better do it. Or had you rather somebody else do it?"

He was a good man, but he was basically an administrator and more conscious of the need for professional civility than dealing with realities.

"I'll go on over there in a few minutes," I said. "Besides the neighbor, who was the first person at the scene?"

"I think the paramedics got there first, then the city cops." He paused a moment. The rain was clattering on the tin roof of the gallery now. "They're cutting a warrant on Gouza now. I don't care if he's in the city jail or ours, but I want that sonofabitch in a cage. Nobody's going to do that to a woman in this parish while I'm sheriff."

I was surprised. He wasn't given to profanity or anger. I had an idea that Joey Meatballs was about to wish that he had not gotten involved with the Sonnier family and the rural unsophistication of Iberia Parish.

▼

I went to the hospital, but I didn't go up to Drew's room. Instead, I questioned one of the paramedics who had brought her in. I sat next to him on a wood bench by the emergency-room entrance while he drank coffee out of a Styrofoam cup. He told me he had been a navy corpsman before he had gone to work for the parish as a paramedic. His face was young and clean-shaved, and he reminded me of most medics, firemen, or U.S. Forest Service smoke jumpers whom I had known. They were enamored of the adrenalin rush, living on the edge, but they tended to be quiet and self-effacing men, and unlike many cops they didn't have self-destructive obsessions.

"What'd you see at the scene besides Ms. Sonnier?" I asked.

"I beg your pardon?"

"Did you see a hammer?"

He looked out the glass door at the rain falling on the bayou. "No," he answered. "I don't think so. But it was getting dark."

"What do you think they used to nail her hand down?"

"I don't know. But whoever did it drove it all the way down to the skin. It was a son of a gun to pull out of the boards. I had to press her hand down flat while my partner worked the nail out with a pair of vise grips. She passed out while we were doing it, poor lady."

"Did she look like she had fought with them? Was she bruised or scratched?"

"She could have been, I didn't notice. I was thinking about getting that nail out of her hand."

"Did she tell you anything?"

"She was in trauma. When something like that happens to them, it's like they've been drug behind a car. Maybe you ought to talk with the city cops. They were up there a little while ago."

"I will. Thanks for your time. Here's my telephone number in case you think of anything later that might be important."

"She's a nice lady. She jogs by my house sometimes. She must have got messed up with a bad guy. Maybe they were *both* drunk when he did it to her. I've seen some bad stuff since I came to work here, but not one like this."

"What do you mean *drunk?*"

"She must have puked up a fifth of gin and vermouth. There's no mistaking the smell."

I decided not to take a statement from Drew right then. Sometimes trial attorneys use the axiom "Never ask a question you don't know the answer to." The same is not absolutely true for a police officer, but you do have to know some of the answers in advance in order to gauge the accuracy or truthfulness of the others.

I drove to the city police station and read the report written up by the investigating officer. It was one paragraph long, ungrammatical, full of misspellings, and described almost nothing about the crime scene or the crime itself except the nature of the injury to the victim and the fact that in the hospital she had identified her assailants as two white males of medium height and build and a third white male by the name of Joey Gouza, who had watched the assault from the driver's window of his automobile.

The only evidence recovered or noted at the crime scene was the sixteen-penny nail.

Drew's house was dark and the rain was slanting through the trees as I walked through her sideyard with a six-battery flashlight. I squatted down on the floor of the gazebo and shined the beam on the planks by the top of the steps. They were smeared with miniature horsetails of dried blood, and one was centered with a blond nail hole. I walked back into the rain and searched in the myrtle bushes around the gazebo. The light flicked across a pop bottle impacted with dirt, two broken bricks, and what looked like a shattered slat from an apple crate that lay propped against some myrtle branches at the base of the gazebo.

But there was no hammer.

I stooped into the wet bushes and examined the bricks by turning them over with my pocket knife and shining the light on all their surfaces. But I saw no chip marks or scratches that would indicate that either had been used to drive a nail into a hardwood surface.

I searched among the oak trees, in the flower beds, and over the lawn, and found no hammer there, either, not that I should, I told myself. But it was something else that I didn't see that bothered me most. According to the report, she had told the city cops that Gouza had watched the assault from the window of his automobile. I returned to the gazebo's steps and shined the flashlight back toward the house. The long driveway and garage were obscured from view by a hedge and two huge clumps of banana trees. If Gouza had had a direct line of vision from his car to the gazebo, he would have had to pull it around the garage and park it on the grass behind the house.

And there were no tire tracks on the lawn. But it had rained, I thought, and maybe the depressed blades of grass had sprung back into place.

What I did find, in the weeded area around a lime tree, was a wet handkerchief spotted with blood. I put it in a Ziploc bag, and I had no idea what it meant, if anything.

The next morning I sat by Drew's hospital bed and put a half dozen mug shots face down on the sheets next to her good hand. Her other hand, her left, was wrapped thickly with bandages and rested on top of a pillow. She wore no makeup, and her hair was unbrushed and her face still puffy with sleep.

"I thought you might wait until after breakfast," she said. "Would you excuse me a minute?"

She went into the bath, then came back out a few minutes later, touching at her face with a towel and widening her eyes. She got back in the bed and pulled the sheet up to her stomach.

"Look at the pictures, Drew."

She turned them over mechanically, one by one. Then she picked up one and dropped it in front of me.

"You have no doubt that's the guy?" I asked.

"Why don't you tell me, Dave? Is that Joey Gouza or not?"

"It's Joey Gouza."

"So arrest him."

"Somebody else is taking care of that. Did the city cops show you mug shots last night?"

"No."

"Then how did you know it was Gouza?"

"He was at a party Weldon gave in New Orleans."

"When I mentioned his name once before, you seemed a little vague about it, Drew."

"That's the man who smoked a cigarette while his two pieces of shit tried to crucify me."

I picked up the photographs and put a rubber band around them. The grass outside the window was bright green, and the sunlight looked hot on the trees, which were still wet from last night's rain.

"Why do you think they did it?" I asked.

"Gouza said, 'Tell your brother to pay his debts.' "

"What's his voice sound like? Does he have an accent?"

"Why are you asking me things like this?"

"A prosecutor is going to ask you, his defense attorney is. Why do you object to me asking you?"

"He has an accent like any other New Orleans lowlife."

"I see. That'd make sense, wouldn't it?"

"No, what you're really asking is something else. There's something wrong with his voice. He sounds like he has a strep throat. No, it's worse than that. He sounds like his vocal cords were burnt with acid."

"Here are some other mug shots, Drew. See if any of these guys look like the two men who hurt you."

She went through them one at a time, looking carefully at each one. Among the six mug shots were the faces of Jewel Fluck, Eddy Raintree, and Jack Gates. She shook her head.

"I've never seen any of these men," she said. She touched the tops of my fingers as I gathered up the photographs from the sheet. "What happened to your thumb?"

"A man bit it the other night."

"Maybe it's catching."

"He used to be a bodyguard for Bobby Earl."

"What did you do with him, put him in the dog pound?"

"No, I didn't get the chance, Drew. I had him cuffed by a railroad track when a guy named Jewel Fluck blew most of his face off with a shotgun. His name was Eddy Raintree. He was one of the guys I just showed you. Would you describe the two men who hurt you?"

"Do you know what victim rape is?" she asked.

"Yes."

"I'm a little bit used up right now. You said something before about me being a soldier. I'm not. I'm still shaking inside. I don't know if I'll ever stop. If you want to take me over the hurdles, you can. But I think you're acting like a shit."

"The sheriff told me to come up here last night and take a statement. But I didn't. I figured the city cops had pretty well worn you out. Maybe you ought to consider who your real friends are, Drew."

She turned her head on the pillow and looked out the window. I could see a tear secrete brightly in the corner of her eye.

"I'll come back later," I said.

She nodded, her head still turned toward the window. Her skin looked dull in the sunlight.

I paused before I went out the door.

"You're willing to testify against Gouza at a trial, Drew?"

"Yes," she said quietly.

"You know they'll put Weldon on the stand, too, don't you?"

She twisted her head back toward me on the pillow. I saw that her projections about the future had not yet reached the last probability. She drank from a glass of water and pulled her knees up under the sheet. Her face had the divorced, empty look of a person who might have lived one way all her life only to awake one morning and discover that none of her experience counted, that she was cut loose and voiceless in a place where no other people lived.

On the way out of the hospital I stopped by the gift shop and sent a vase of flowers to her room. I signed the card "From your many friends in Amnesty International."

▼

They brought Joey Gouza from New Orleans in leg and waist chains, got him arraigned that afternoon, and amidst a crowd of photographers, news reporters, and onlookers, who behaved like spectators at a cockfight, virtually trundled him from the courtroom to a city jail cell. Bail was set by Judge James Lefleur, an ill-tempered right-wing coonass also known as Whiskey Jim.

When Gouza came out of the court, in pink shirt, cream slacks, and wide black tie with white polkadots, with cops holding him by both arms, he managed to get one hand loose, grab his phallus, and spit into the lens of a television camera.

I checked my .45 with a guard before he worked the levers that slid the barred door on a corridor that led past three holding cells and the drunk tank.

"I'd like to go inside with him," I said.

"Then you'd better take a stun gun with you," the guard said. "What's he done?"

"Look for yourself, look at the floor. The sonofabitch."

The corridor in front of one cell was splattered with spaghetti, coffee, and cobbler that had obviously been flung with the plastic tray and Styrofoam containers from the iron apron in the cell door.

I walked down the corridor and propped one arm against the bars of Joey Gouza's cell. Tieless and beltless now, he sat on a bunk that was suspended from wall chains; he smoked a cigarette methodically, his fingers pinched on the paper, his furious black eyes staring into the center of the gloom.

Then he saw me. "It's you."

"What's happenin', Joey?"

"I should have figured your nose was in this someplace."

"You're wrong. I'm not a player. It looks like it's between you and other people this time."

"What people? What the fuck is going on, man?"

"You should have stayed out of Iberia Parish."

"Are you out of your mind? You think I got an interest in some shithole that counts the mosquitoes in the population? You tell me what the fuck is going on." His voice rasped and broke wetly in his throat. He breathed deeply to regain his momentum. "Look, I don't sit still while people ream me. You got that, Jack? You tell me what the fucking game is."

"I don't think there is one, Joey. I just think you paddled too far up shit creek this time. That's the way it breaks sometime."

"The way it breaks? What do you got, yesterday's ice cream for brains? That judge, I've never seen him before and he's got a hard-on for me before they unlock me off the chain. He called me a wild animal, in front of all them people. Bail, one-point-seven-million dollars! That's a hundred and seventy thousand large for a bondsman. You telling me these people ain't trying to run a hook through my balls? Those two guys who busted me, they stuck guns in my face in my own restaurant. You've got a real problem here, some people that's totally out of control."

"You've got good lawyers. They'll get your bail reduced."

He flipped his cigarette in a shower of sparks off the wall and kneaded his hands together. His long neck and shoulders were webbed with veins.

"What are you down here for, to toss peanut shells at the

monkeys?" he said. "Go tell that screw there's no toilet paper in here."

"I thought you might want to talk to me."

He rose from the bunk, breathing hard through his nose, and came toward me.

"That broad's lying," he said.

"She's been pretty convincing."

His eyes looked hard into mine and narrowed.

"You know it's a ream. I see it in your face, man," he said. "You offering me something?"

"Somebody did it to her. I don't think it was anybody around here. Everybody I talk to thinks you're the number-one candidate, Joey. I think they've got the right person in the cell."

His hand shot out of the bars, knotting my shirt in his fist. His breath was rife with jailhouse funk. My collar button popped loose on the floor.

"I ain't going down on a phony beef. You tell that broad that," he said. "You tell her brother to get her off my back."

I tore his hand loose.

"You understand me, man?" he said. "I don't roll over. You push me, I'll leave your hair on the wallpaper."

"Tell that to everybody at your trial, Joey. It makes good court-room theater."

He hit the bars with the heel of his fist. His face was livid, popping with cartilage.

"You're twisting me, man. What's your stake? What's your fucking stake?" he said.

"Why did those guys creep Weldon Sonnier's house?"

He paced back and forth, his nostrils dilating.

"I'll print it out for you in big letters," he said. "I'm a business-man, I don't creep houses, I don't drive out to some hole in the road to stoke up a bunch of small-town jackoffs. They're the kind who send you to the electric chair and then go back to watering their plants. Look, you were a New Orleans cop. You know how it gets done. Somebody keeps getting in your face and don't listen to reason, you tell another guy about it, then you forget it. You don't even want to know who does it. If you're a sick guy, with a real bone on for somebody, you get Polaroids, then you burn them.

"That's how it works. You don't drive into some broad's back-yard and nail her to a gazebo. You don't end up in a hick court with Elmer Fudd dropping a one-point-seven-million-dollar bond on your head. The point is, when people got dog food between their ears they're dangerous, and I don't fuck with them. Is it starting to clear up for you now?"

He stuck a cigarette in his mouth and hunted in his shirt pockets for a match.

"Gimme a light," he said.

"How'd you get involved with Bobby Earl?" I said.

He pulled the cigarette out of his mouth and shook it at me.

"You quit trying to jerk my chain, man," he said. "You want to know how I got this voice? A swinging dick tried to make me his punk when I was a seventeen-year-old fish. I caught him in the shower with a string knife. Except he was a made guy, and I didn't know the rules about made guys back then, and his friends hung me up in my cell with a coat hanger. They crushed my voice box. But I didn't roll over then, man, and I don't roll over now.

"Explain to the broad I'm a three-time loser. If I go down on the bitch, I got nothing to lose. That means I can cop to anything they want and take Sonnier with me. I'll make sure he gets heavy time, and I'll be inside with him when he does it. Let her think about that."

"You're a hard man, Joey."

"Tell that screw down there to get me processed or send up some toilet paper."

He scratched at the inside of his nostril with his thumbnail and blew air through his nasal passages. He had already lost interest in my presence, but a dark light remained in his face, as though he were breathing bad air, and his heated eyes, the nests of veins in his neck, his unwashed smell, the soft scud of his loafers on the cement, his jug head in silhouette against the cell window, made me think of the circus creatures who pawed the dark while they watched the dé-nouement of Eddy Raintree from their cages.

Later, I called Weldon at his office and was told that he was with a drilling crew at the old Sonnier farm.

I drove down the dirt road past the rusted windmill and crumbled brick supports where the house had stood before Weldon had hired a gang of drunken blacks to tear it apart with crowbars and sledgehammers. I parked my truck by a sludge pond and an open-sided shed stacked with pipe and sacks of drilling mud, and walked up the iron steps of a rig that roared with the noise of the drilling engine.

The roughnecks on the floor were slimy with mud, bent into their work at the wellhead with the concentration of men who know the result of a moment's inattention on a rig, when the tongs or a whirling chain can pinch off your fingers or snap your bones like sticks.

A tool pusher put a hard hat on my head.

"Where's Weldon?" I shouted at him.

"What?"

"Where's Weldon Sonnier?" I shouted again over the engine's roar.

He pointed up into the rig.

High up on the tower I saw Weldon in coveralls and hardhat, working with the derrick man on the monkey board. The derrick man was clipped to the tower with a safety belt. I couldn't see one on Weldon. His face was small and round against his yellow hat as he looked down at me.

A moment later he put one foot out on the hoist, grabbed the cable with one hand, and rode it down to the rig floor. There was a single smear of bright grease, like war paint, on one of his cheekbones.

"Coffee time," he yelled at the floormen.

Somebody killed the drilling engine, and I opened and closed my mouth to clear my ears. Weldon pulled off his bradded gloves, unzipped his coveralls, and stepped out of them. He was wearing slacks and a polo shirt, and his armpits and the center of his chest were dark with sweat.

"Let's go over here in the shade," he said. "It must be ninety-five today."

We walked to the far end of the platform and leaned against the railing under a canvas awning. The air was sour with natural gas.

"I thought you'd pretty well punched out this field," I said.

"Anyplace there was an ocean, there's oil. You just got to go deep enough to find it."

I looked out at the wells pumping up and down in the distance and the long spans of silver pipe that sweated coldly from the natural gas running inside.

"With the low price of crude, a lot of outfits are shut down now," I said.

"That's them, not me. What are you out here for, Dave?"

"To deliver a message."

"Oh?"

"Actually I'm just passing on an observation. Have you been up to see Drew today?"

"Yeah, a little while ago."

"You know you're going to end up testifying at Gouza's trial, then?"

"So?"

"I get the feeling you think somebody's going to wave a wand over your situation and you won't ever have to explain your dealings with Gouza. He's not copping a plea. He's facing life in Angola. His defense attorneys are going to use a chain saw when they get you and Drew on the stand."

"What am I supposed to do about it?"

"Give some thought to what Drew's doing."

He wiped at the grease on his face with a clean mechanic's cloth.

"Tell Gouza he doesn't want to make bond," he said. "Believe me, he doesn't want to see me unless he's got some cops around him."

"Then you buy it?"

"You think she did it to herself? You've got the right guy in jail. Just make sure he stays there."

"Here's the problem I have, Weldon. Joey Gouza is what they call a made guy. That's unusual in his case. He wasn't born to it, he didn't have any patrons or political allies greasing the wheels for him. He worked his way up from a reformatory punk. That means that in his world he's a lot smarter than a lot of the people around him. Come on, you know him, Weldon, do you think he'd set himself up for a fall like this?"

He folded the pink mechanic's cloth in a neat square and balanced it on the rail. Then he moved it and balanced it again.

"Stonewall time is over," I said. "Your sister just put the tape on fast forward."

"So you've come out here to tell me she's a liar?"

"No, I've come out here to tell you she's a victim. I'm using the word in a broad sense, too. There's a certain kind of victimization that starts in childhood. Then the person grows older and never learns any other role. Except maybe one other. The word for that one is enabler."

"You better get to it, Dave." He turned toward me and rested his hand on the metal rail.

"Lyle understands it and he never finished high school."

"I'm going to ask you to choose each of your words carefully, Dave."

I took a deep breath. The air was pungent with gas, acrid with the smell of oil sludge and dead weeds in the sunlight.

"Look, Weldon, if I know about your family history, about some of the complexities in it, do you believe that Gouza's attorneys won't have access to the same information, that they won't use it to tear your sister apart?"

"Say it or shut the fuck up and get out of here."

"She's not just your sister. In her mind she's your wife, your lover, your mother. She'll do anything for you. It's a way of life for her. You know it, too, you rotten sonofabitch."

His feet were already set when he swung. He caught me on the chin, and my head snapped back and my hard hat rolled across the rig floor.

I straightened up, held the rail with one hand, and looked into his face. It was stretched tight on the bone, and the suntanned skin at the corners of his eyes was filled with white lines.

The roughnecks on the floor stared at us in disbelief.

I pushed at the side of my chin with my thumb.

"They'll melt you into lard in the courtroom, Weldon," I said. "Gouza won't even have to take the stand. Instead, you and Drew will be on trial, and those defense attorneys will make you sound like a pornographer's wet dream."

I saw his hand move, his eyes click again as though he'd been slapped.

"Don't even think about it," I said. "The first one was free. You come at me again, and I'll make sure you do time for assaulting a police officer." I picked up the hard hat from the rig floor and shoved it into his hands, jammed it into his chest. "Thanks for the tour of the rig. My recommendation is you hire a good lawyer and get some advice about the wisdom of suborning perjury. Or apply for a pilot's job in a country that doesn't have an extradition treaty with the United States. See you around, Weldon."

I walked down the iron steps to my truck. I could hear the canvas awning flapping in the hot wind, a chain clinking brightly against a piece of pipe, in the embarrassed silence of the roughnecks on the rig floor.

▼

The next morning I drove across the I-10 bridge over the Mississippi to Baton Rouge. The river was high and muddy, almost a mile across, and the oil barges far below looked as tiny as toys. Huge oil refineries and aluminum plants sprawled along the east bank of the river, but what always struck my eye first when I rolled over the apex of the bridge into Baton Rouge was the spire of the capitol building lifting itself out of the flat maze of trees and green parks in the old downtown area. All the state's political actors since Reconstruction had passed through there: populists in suspenders and clip-on bow ties, demagogues, alcoholic buffoons, virulent racists, a hillbilly singer who would be elected governor twice, another governor who broke out of a mental asylum in order to kill his wife, a recent governor who pardoned a convict in Angola, who repaid the favor by murdering the governor's brother, and the most famous and enigmatic player of them all, the Kingfish, who might have given FDR a run for his money had he not died, along with his supposed assassin, in a spray of eighty-one machine-gun bullets in a hallway of the old capitol building.

I parked my truck and sat in the gallery during the morning session of the legislature. I watched the regard with which Bobby Earl was treated by many of his peers, the warm handshakes, the pats on the arm and shoulder, the expression of gentlemanly goodwill by men who should have known better. It reminded me of the deference sometimes shown to a small-town poolroom bully or redneck police chief. The people around him well know his hatred of Jews, intellectuals, news people, Asians, blacks; no one doubts his potential with the leaded baton or the hobnailed boot across the neck. But they make friends with the ape in their midst, no matter how violently the tuning fork vibrates inside them; consequently they absorb his dark powers, and secretly gloat at the fear he inspires in others.

They recessed for lunch, and I followed Bobby Earl and a group of his friends one block to the entrance of an expensive restaurant with an awning that extended out over the sidewalk. The windows were filled with ferns and hanging copper pots. After Earl and his group had entered the restaurant, I put on my seersucker coat, tightened my necktie, and walked inside, too. Most of the tables were filled, the air loud with conversation and scented with the smell of gumbo from the kitchen, bourbon and tropical drinks from the bar.

"I don't think we have a seating for one, sir. Would you like to wait in the bar?" the maître d' said.

"I'm with Mr. Earl's party. Ah, there he is right over there," I said.

"Very well. Please follow me, sir," he said.

I walked with the maître d' to Bobby Earl's table. The maître d' set a menu down for me at an empty place setting and walked away. Earl turned away from his conversation with another man, then his mouth opened silently as he looked up and realized who was sitting down at his table.

"Hello, Mr. Earl. I apologize for bothering you again, but I'm just in town briefly and I didn't want to disturb you at the legislature," I said. "How are you gentlemen? I'm Detective Dave Robicheaux, with the Iberia Parish sheriff's office. I just need to ask Mr. Earl a question or two. Y'all go right ahead with your lunch."

They went on talking to each other, as though my presence was perfectly natural, but I could see their eyes, the positions of their bodies, already disassociating themselves from the situation.

Bobby Earl wore a brown pinstripe suit and a yellow silk tie, and his thick hair looked blow-dried and recently cut.

"What are you doing here?" he said.

"Do you know that Joey Gouza's in custody?"

"No."

I set my notebook on the tablecloth and peeled back several pages. It contained nothing but notes from old investigations and a grocery list I had made out at the office yesterday.

"I interviewed him in his cell yesterday and your name came up," I said.

"What?"

"Gouza is charged with ordering two men to nail Drew Sonnier's hand to a gazebo. When I questioned him your name came up in the conversation. That fact bothered me, Mr. Earl. Is it your statement that you don't know Joey Gouza?"

"I'm not making a statement. What are you trying to do here?"

A man at the end of the table coughed quietly into his fist and went to the restroom.

"You and Joey Gouza seem to have the same friends. Your lines keep crossing in this case, Mr. Earl. Originally I questioned you about Eddy Raintree. Now someone has blown Eddy's face off with a shotgun. You knew that, didn't you?"

"No, I don't know anything about this. You listen—"

His voice level rose, and the man next to him excused himself to talk with friends at the bar.

"You're harassing me," Earl began again. "I can't prove it, but I suspect you have a political motivation for what you've been doing. It won't work. It just makes my cause stronger. If you doubt me, call the *Morning Advocate* and check the polls."

"Let me tell you what Gouza said and you can come to your own conclusions. We were talking about *you,* then he begins to tell me that if he goes down for what is called the 'bitch,' which is a life sentence given to habitual criminals, he's going to take others down with him. What does that seem to suggest to you, Mr. Earl?"

"It suggests you're going to have a lawsuit against you for slander." His monocular right eye, with the enlarged pupil like a spot of India ink, was fixed on my face. The skin along the bottom rim was trembling with anger.

I folded my notebook and put it in my shirt pocket. I picked up a package of crackers from the breadbasket, then dropped it in the basket again.

"You're an intelligent man, and I'll tell you the truth, Mr. Earl," I said. "I think Joey might be in on a bum rap. But unfortunately for him, nobody cares if a guy like Joey is innocent or not. People just want him put away in a cage for a long time, and they don't care how it's done. The prosecutor will probably get a new political career out of it, his lawyers will get rich on his appeals while he's chopping sugarcane at Angola, his wife and mistresses will clean out his bank accounts and sell everything he owns, and his hired stooges will go to work for his competitors and forget they ever heard of him. In the meantime, there are probably some sadistic gunbulls who will ejaculate at the thought of busting Joey's hump on their work gangs.

"Now, if you were Joey Meatballs and facing a prospect like that, wouldn't you be willing to cut a deal, any deal, including maybe putting your mother in harness on a dogsled team?"

The other men at the table had gone quiet now and had given up the pretense of conviviality. They looked at their watches, touched nervously at their mouths with their napkins, stared at a remote part of the restaurant. The cost of their lunch with Bobby Earl was not one they had anticipated.

I rose from the table.

"You like primitive law and vigilante solutions to complex problems, Mr. Earl," I said. "Maybe you've stumbled into one of your own creations this time. But I wouldn't end up as Joey Gouza's fall partner. He doesn't care about political causes. He had his own brother-in-law fed into an airplane propeller. What do you think his lawyers might have planned for you?"

The tables around Bobby Earl's had now become quiet, too. He turned to speak to the men seated next to him, but their eyes were fixed on the flower arrangement in the center of the table. But I learned then that Bobby Earl was not easily undone in a public situation. He rose from the table, put his napkin neatly by his plate, and walked toward the men's room, pausing to let a black drink waiter pass. His gaze was level, his face handsome, almost pleasant-looking, his thick brown hair tousled by the cool currents from the air-conditioner.

I realized then that Bobby Earl might burn inside with banked fires, and that perhaps I had indeed inserted some broken glass in his head that would saw through brain tissue later; but in front of an audience he was a tragedian actor, a protean figure who could create an emanation of himself out of will power alone and become as benign, photogenic, and seemingly anointed by history as Jefferson Davis in defeat.

I had a feeling this one would go into extra innings.

12

That evening Bootsie, Alafair, and I went to a shrimp boil in the park on Bayou Teche. The air smelled of flowers and new-cut grass, the clouds were marbled with pink, the oak trees around the wood pavilion were dark green and thick with birds. School was out for the summer, and Alafair and some other kids played kickball on the baseball diamond with the sense of dusty, knee-grimed joy that's the special province of children during summer. In fact, Alafair's aggressiveness at play made me wonder if she didn't have a bent for adversarial roles. Her cheeks were dirt-streaked and flushed with excitement; she charged without blinking at the kicker and took the volleyball full in the face, and then ran after it again, sometimes knocking another child to the ground.

The last four days with Bootsie had been wonderful. The new balance of medicine seemed to be working. Her eyes smiled at me in the morning, her posture was erect and self-assured, and she helped me and Batist at the dock and in the bait shop with cheerful eagerness. Only an hour ago I had looked up from my work and caught her in a moment when she was unconscious of my glance, just as though I had clicked the camera lens and frozen her in the pose of the healthy and unworried woman that I prayed she would become again for both of us. She had just emptied the bait tanks, her denim shirt stuck wetly to her uplifted breasts, and she was staring abstractedly out the screen window at the bayou, eating a carrot stick, her hair touched by the breeze, one hand set jauntily on her hip, the muscles in her back and neck as strong and firm as a Cajun fishergirl's.

At that moment I realized the error of my thinking about Bootsie. The problem wasn't in her disease, it was in mine. I wanted a lock on the future; I wanted our marriage to be above the governance of mortality and chance; and, most important, in my nightly sleeplessness over her health, and the black fatigue that I would drag behind me into the day like a rattling junkyard, I hadn't bothered to be grateful for the things I had.

She peeled the shell off a shrimp, dipped the shrimp in a horseradish sauce and put it in her mouth. She reached out and touched my chin lightly with two fingers, as though she were examining for a skin blemish.

"Is that where Weldon hit you?" she asked.

"I beg your pardon?"

"Oh my, such innocence."

I cleared my throat.

"I was in the supermarket this morning," she said. "A woman whose husband is a floorman on Weldon's rig couldn't stop herself from asking about your welfare."

Her eyes crinkled at the corners.

"Weldon's not always a rational man," I said.

"Why didn't you arrest him?"

"He's a tormented man, Boots. He carries a burden nobody should have to carry."

She stopped chewing. Her eyes looked into mine.

"Lyle told me some things about their childhood, about Weldon's relationship with Drew," I said.

A crease went across her brow, and she set her half-eaten shrimp back on the paper plate. The children out on the baseball diamond were tumbling in the dust, their happy cries echoing off the back-stop.

"They're messed up in the head real bad," I said. "Weldon's a pain in the butt, all right, but I suspect he wakes up each morning with the Furies after him."

"He and Drew?" she said, the meaning clear and sad in her eyes now.

"Probably Lyle, too. I said something pretty rough to Weldon about it. So he had a free one coming."

"That's an awful story."

"They'll probably never tell all of it, either."

She was quiet for a few moments. Her eyes were flat and turned inward; her hair looked like it was touched with smoke in the broken light through the tree.

"When this is over, maybe we can invite them to dinner," she said.

"That'd be fine."

"You wouldn't mind?"

"No, of course not."

"Why didn't anyone—" she began. Then she stopped, coughed in the back of her throat, and said, "I never guessed. Poor Drew."

I squeezed her hand; but it felt dry and pliant inside mine. Her mouth had the down-turned expression of someone who might have opened a bedroom door at the wrong moment. Then she stood up and began clearing the table, her face concentrating on her work.

"I'm going to invite her to go shopping with me in Lafayette," she said. "You think she'd like that?"

"You bet," I said.

You'll always be a standup lady, Boots, I thought.

Out on the baseball diamond a shout went up from the children as someone fired the volley ball into the backstop.

▼

It was dusk when we returned home, and the air was heavy and cool, motionless, loud with the croaking of frogs out in the cypress.

I parked under the pecan trees in the front yard, and Bootsie and Alafair walked up to the house while I rolled up the truck's windows. The sky had turned blue-black, the color of scorched iron, and I could feel the barometer dropping again, and smell sulfur and distant rain. As I started up the incline toward the gallery, a beat-up flatbed truck bounced through the chuckholes in the dirt road and turned in to my drive. On the back was a huge chrome-plated cross, with the top end propped on the cab's roof and the shaft fastened to the bed with a boomer chain.

Lyle Sonnier cut the ignition and stepped down, grinning, from the running board. He wore a pair of striped overalls without a shirt, and his thin chest and shoulders were red with sunburn.

"I thought I'd take your time just for a minute," he said. "What do you think of it?"

"It looks like it's made of car bumpers."

"It is. Me and this ole boy in Lafayette welded a shell all around the wood beams. What do you think?"

Batist had left on the string of electric bulbs over the dock, and the cross rippled and glowed with a silver and blue light.

"It looks like an artwork. It's beautiful," I said.

"Thanks, Loot. It's the only thing the Reverend Jimmy Bob Clock left me before they sent him off to Parchman Farm. One time we were outside New Albany, Mississippi, where some Klan uglies had burned a cross in a field, and Jimmy Bob was eating a hamburger in the truck across the road, looking out at that black cross, when he says, 'No sense letting good building material go to waste.' Then he walks across the road and gives this colored farmer who was out there plowing a dollar for it.

" 'What in the world are we gonna do with that?' I say.

"He says, 'Son, the most exciting place in a shithole like this is the Dairy Queen on Saturday night. When you run a hallelujah tent show, you gotta give them lights in the sky.'

"He went into a supermarket, bought eight rolls of aluminum foil, and wrapped the cross in it, then we drove out to a junkyard and he got a guy to string it with electric bulbs. That night we put it up on a hill, way up the slope from the tent, and hooked it up to the generator, and you could see that cross glowing in the mist for five miles."

I nodded absently and looked up toward my lighted gallery.

"Well . . . I didn't mean to take up a lot of your evening," he said. "I just wanted to tell you I didn't feel good about the other night in Baton Rouge. You came to me for help and I couldn't offer you very much."

"Maybe you did, Lyle."

He looked at me curiously, then lifted one of his overall straps off his sunburn with his thumb.

"I'm going to put the cross up on my new bible college," he said. "I was going to call it the Lyle Sonnier Bible Institute. Now I'm just going to call it the South Louisiana Bible College. How's that sound?"

"It sounds pretty good."

"I told you I ain't as bad as you think."

"I think maybe you're not bad at all, Lyle."

His eyes looked into the corners of mine, then he brushed at the dirt and leaves in the drive with his shoe.

"I appreciate it, Loot," he said.

"You want to come in?" I asked.

"No, thanks anyway. I just came into town to see Drew at the hospital and pick up my cross in Lafayette. Weldon told me about him taking a swing on you. I'm sorry that happened. I know you've been as good and fair as you can to both him and Drew. But you really stuck a garden rake in his head."

"Weldon has to stop jerking everybody around. Maybe it's time he takes his own fall."

Lyle etched lines in the leaves and dust with the point of his shoe. He rested his mutilated hand, which in the deepening shadows looked almost like part of an amphibian, on the truck's door handle.

"Weldon told me last night what he's been involved in. It's a mess, it surely is," he said. "I think he wants to tell you about it. He's pretty well worn-out with it."

"Do you want to tell me what it is?"

"It's his grief. You'll have to get it from him. No offense meant." He got up in the cab of his truck and clicked the door shut

with his underarm. He smiled. "I better get out of here before I get
in some kind of legal trouble. You know why I keep that burnt
cross, why I'm gonna put it up on top of my Bible college? It don't
let me forget where I've been and what I'm fixing to be. It's like that
ole boy says in the song, 'I might be an old chunk of coal but I'm
gonna be a diamond someday.' Give Weldon a chance. Maybe
inside that cinder-block head of his he wants you to like him."

"What I think is unimportant, Lyle. Your brother's problem is
going to be with the court. Anyway, there's something I should tell
you before you go. We brought in an old-timer from the Sally in
Lafayette, a fellow who'd been in a fire. He might be the same man
you saw in your audience."

"He told you his name was Vic Benson?"

"You know him?"

"Sure. I drove to Lafayette and talked to him the other day. We
run a shelter in Baton Rouge and a couple of new guys told me
about him."

"He's not your father, then?"

He smiled again and started his truck.

"It's him, all right. He denied it, said he had only one son and
not some diddly-squat TV preacher he wouldn't waste his jizzum
on." He shook his head good-naturedly. "That old bas— . . . that
old son of a buck still knows how to rub a little pain into you. But
he's a wet-brain now, been in and out of jails and insane asylums all
over Texas, Louisiana, and Mississippi, at least that's what the other
wet-brains say. They say maybe he's got cancer in the lungs, too. So
what are you gonna do except feel sorry for a guy like that? I gotta
deedee, Loot. Hang loose."

He drove down the dirt road through the dark tunnel of oak
trees, the chrome-plated cross vibrating against his cab, just as the
first raindrops dimpled the bayou.

▼

I was tired, but I had to drive to Lafayette that night and pick up
a new aluminum shiner tank and water pump for the bait shop. On
my way back out of town I saw one of Weldon Sonnier's company

trucks pull out of the traffic and park under the trees in front of the Catholic home for handicapped children.

Weldon, in a pair of knife-creased brown slacks and a form-fitting T-shirt like a 1950s hood would wear, walked up the sidewalk to the front entrance with a stuffed shopping bag hanging from each hand.

I stopped at the traffic light, clicked my fingernails on the horn button, turned the radio on and off at least three times, resolved under my breath that I would continue on home and not intrude any more than necessary on Weldon's pride, hard-headedness, and carefully nursed store of private misery.

The light turned green, and I went around the block and parked across the street from Weldon's truck. The moon was up, and the sky in the north, where it hadn't yet started to rain, looked like a lighted ink wash. I headed up the walk toward the entrance.

Why?

Because he needs to know that you don't get the heat off your back by punching out a police officer on an oil rig floor, I told myself.

But that wasn't it. The truth was I wanted to believe in Weldon, in the same way that sometimes you encourage someone you care about to lie to you. Or perhaps I wanted somehow to dispel the fear that one day I would have to make him Joey Gouza's fall partner.

But what would I find in a Catholic children's home that would be of any value in eventually cutting Weldon loose from the investigation or prosecuting the executioners of a deputy sheriff or taking down a racist politician?

Answer: Nothing.

I walked through the front door into a softly lit and immaculately clean oak-floored hallway, with statues of St. Anthony, St. Theresa, and Jesus resting on pedestals against the walls, and looked through a set of open French doors into a large recreation room.

It was filled with the children whom nobody wanted. They were retarded, spastic, mongoloid, born with deformed limbs, locked in metal braces, wired to electronic devices on wheelchairs. Scattered about on the floor was a tangle of torn wrapping paper, colored ribbon and bows, and boxes that had contained all kinds of toys. He must have made several trips back and forth to the truck.

Neither the nuns nor the children looked in my direction. Weldon had taken off his shoes and was walking on his hands in the middle of the room. His face was almost purple with blood, his muscles quivering with tension, while coins and keys from his pockets bounced all over the rug and the children screamed in delight.

When he finally flipped himself over on his back, his mouth grinning crazily, his eyes bright with exertion, the children and nuns clapped as though they had just witnessed the world's greatest aerialist at work.

He sat up and rubbed his knees, still grinning. Then he saw me.

I waved at him with two fingers. His eyes lingered on mine a moment, bemused, faintly embarrassed perhaps, then he turned back to the children and said, "Hey, you guys, the ice cream man made a big delivery this evening. Sister Agnes says it's time to fang it down."

I turned and walked back outside into the night and a snap of lightning across the sky and the odor of rain striking warm concrete.

▼

It rained hard during the night, and in the morning the sun came up yellow and hot and wreathed with mist over the marsh. I got up early and went down to the dock to help Batist open up, then had breakfast with Bootsie and Alafair in the kitchen. The backyard was wet and still blue with shadow, and the bloom of the mimosa was as bright as blood where the sun struck the treetop.

"What are you going to do today, little guy?" I said to Alafair.

"Bootsie's taking me to buy a new swimsuit, then we're going have a picnic in the park."

"Maybe I can join you guys later," I said.

"Why don't you, Dave? We'll be under the trees by the pool."

"I'll head over about noon, or a little earlier if I can," I said. Then I winked at Alafair. "You keep Boots out of the sun, little guy. She's already got enough tan."

"It's bad for her?"

Bootsie looked at me and made an impatient face.

"Well, she doesn't listen to us sometimes and we have to take charge of her," I said.

Bootsie rapped me across the back of the hand with her spoon, and Alafair's eyes squinted with delight. I grinned back at her, then when Bootsie was putting dishes in the sink I came up behind her and hugged her hard around the middle and kissed her neck.

"Later, later," she whispered, and patted me quietly on the thigh.

It was going to be a fine day. I kissed Alafair good-bye, then flipped my seersucker coat over my shoulder and was almost out the door when the phone on the counter rang and Bootsie picked it up.

"It's the sheriff," she said, and handed it to me.

I put my hand over the receiver and touched her shoulder as she walked away. "The picnic is at noon. I'll be there, I promise, unless he sends me out of town. Okay?" I said.

She smiled without replying and began washing dishes in the sink.

"I just talked to the city chief," the sheriff said. "They had to take Joey Gouza to Iberia General at seven last night. He went apeshit in his cell, crashing against the bars, rolling around on the floor, and kicking his feet like he was having a seizure, slurping water out of the toilet."

"You mean he had a psychotic episode?"

"That's what they thought it was. They got him in a van to take him to the hospital and he puked all over it. The doc at emergency receiving said he acted like he'd been poisoned, so they pumped his stomach out. Except by the time they got the tube down his throat there was hardly anything left inside him except blood from his stomach lining. Evidently the guy's got ulcers on top of his other problems."

"What do you think happened?"

"A guard found an empty box of ant poison in the food area. Maybe somebody dumped it into his mashed potatoes. But to tell you the truth, Dave, I don't believe the city people are in a hurry to admit they can't provide security for a celebrity prisoner. They're having more fun with Joey Gouza than pigs rolling in slop."

"What do you want me to do?"

"If he's connected with Garrett's murder, let's nail his butt before they take him out in a body bag. Not that half of New Orleans wouldn't get drunk in the streets."

I drove over to Iberia General and walked down the hall to Joey Gouza's room. A uniformed cop was reading a magazine outside the door.

"How you doin', Dave?" he said.

"Pretty good. How's our man?"

"I have a fantasy. I see him running down the hall in his nightshirt. I see me parking a big one in his brisket. Does that answer your question?"

"Is he that bad?"

"It probably depends on whether or not you have to clean up his piss."

"What?"

"He took a piss off the side of the bed, right in the middle of the floor. He said he doesn't use bedpans."

I went inside the room and closed the door behind me. Gouza's right wrist was cuffed to the bed rail and one ankle was locked to a leg chain. His elongated face was white on the pillow, his lips caked at the corners with dried mucus. In the middle of the floor was a freshly mopped damp area. The room smelled bad, and I tried to open the window but it was sealed with locks that could only be turned with an Allen wrench.

He rubbed his nose with his finger. His eyes were black and cavernous in his drawn face.

"You don't like the smell?" he asked. His voice sounded like air wheezing out of sand.

"It's kind of close in here, partner."

"They told you I took a leak on the floor?"

"Somebody mentioned it."

"They told you they keep me chained to the bed, they don't even let me walk to the toilet?"

"I'll see what I can do about it."

"I can't raise my voice. Come closer."

I moved a chair to his bedside and sat down. His sour breath and the odor from under his sheet made me swallow.

"It's a whack," he said.

"On who?"

"Who the fuck you think?"

"Maybe it was an accident. It happens. The people who prepare jailhouse food haven't worked in a lot of five-star restaurants."

"I jailed too long, man. I know when the whack's out. You feel it. It's in people's eyes."

"You're a superstar, Joey. They're not going to lose you."

"You listen to me. Yesterday afternoon a trusty, this punk, a kid with mushmelons for buns, is sweeping out the corridor. Then he looks around real careful and walks over to my cell and says, 'Hey, Joey, I can get you something.'

"I go, '*You* can get me something? What, a case of AIDS?'

"He says, 'Stuff you might could use.'

"I go, 'The only *stuff* I see around here is you, sweetcakes.'

"He says, 'I can get you a shank.'

"I go, 'What I need a shank for from a punk like you?'

"He says, 'Sometimes there's some badasses in the shower, man.'

"I go, 'You clean the shit out of your mouth when you talk to me.'

"He says, 'It's just a city jail, but there's a couple of bad guys here. You don't want the shank, you don't want a friend, that's your business. I was only trying to help out.'

"I go, 'What guys?' But he's already walking off. I go, 'Come back, you little bitch,' but he clanks on the door for the screw to open up and shoots me the bone."

"Like you say, Joey, he's probably just a punk who wants a job when he gets out. What's the big deal?"

"You don't get it. A guy like that don't shoot the bone at a guy like me. Something's happening. There's been some kind of change. . . ." His hand motioned vaguely at the air, at the sunlight through the window. "Out there somewhere. It's a whack. Look, I want a hot plate and canned food brought in."

Then I saw something in his eye that I hadn't seen before, in the corner, a tremolo, a moist, threadlike yellow light, like a worm feeding.

He and his kind spent a lifetime trying to disguise their self-centered fear. It accounted for their grandiosity, their insatiable sexual appetites, their unpredictable violence and cruelty. But almost always, if you were around them long enough, you saw it leak out of them like a sticky substance from a dead tree.

"I owe you a confession, Joey," I said.

"You owe me a——" He turned his head on the pillow to look at me.

"Yeah, I haven't been honest with you."

His brow became netted with lines.

"I cooked the books on you a little bit," I said. "You wanted me to tell Weldon you weren't going down by yourself. I did as you asked, but I told the same thing to Bobby Earl."

His head lifted an inch off the pillow.

"You told Earl——" His breath was rasping. "You told Earl *what?*"

"That you're going to take other people down with you."

"Why you trying to tie me with Earl?"

"You seem to know a lot of the same people, Joey."

His face was gray and dry. His eyes searched in mine.

"I got you figured," he said. "You're trying to put out word to the AB I'm gonna roll over. That's it, ain't it? You're gonna keep squeezing me till I cop to some bullshit plea. Do you know what you're doing, man? The AB's not part of the organization. They think somebody's gonna rat-out a member, it's an open contract. They're in every joint in the country. You do time when there's an AB hit on you, you do it in lockup. I mean with a solid iron door, too, man, or they'll get you with a Molotov through the bars. That's what you're trying to bring down on me? That's why you're pulling on Bobby Earl's crank? That's a lousy fucking thing to do, man."

"Would Jewel Fluck try to whack you, Joey?"

His eyes narrowed and grew wary.

"I saw him take out Eddy Raintree. It was pretty ugly."

"I got no more to say to you."

"I can't blame you. I'd feel the same way if all the doors were slamming around me. But think about it this way, Joey. You're a made guy. There're cops who respect that. Are you going to do major time while a guy like Bobby Earl sips Cold Duck and gets his picture on the society page? He's a Nazi, Joey, the honest-to-God real article. Are you going to take a jolt for a guy like that?"

He leaned over the side of the bed and spit in the wastebasket. I looked the other way.

"Drop dead, man. I don't know anything about Bobby Earl."

I studied his face. His skin was grained, unshaved, filled with twitches.

"What are you staring at?" he said.

"Give him up."

"You must have some kind of brain tumor or something. Nothing I say seems to get in your head. You guys ain't gonna do this stuff to me. You tell these local bozos I'm walking out of this beef. I'm not doing time, I'm not getting whacked in custody, either. I ain't getting whacked. Can you handle that, Jack?"

"The local bozos aren't taking a lot of interest in your point of view, Joey. Every once in a while a token guy gets dropped in the skillet, and this time it looks like you're it. It might not be fair, but that's the way it works. You never saw a mob run across town to do a good deed, did you?"

He tried to turn away from me, but his wrist clanked the handcuff chain against the bed rail. He hit the mattress with his other fist, then clenched his arm over his eyes.

"I want you to leave me alone," he said.

I got up from the chair and walked to the door. His chained right foot stuck out from under the sheet. He tried to clear his throat and instead choked on his saliva.

"I'll see about the canned goods and the hot plate," I said.

He worked the sheet up to his chin, kept his arm pressed tightly across his eyes, and didn't reply.

▼

I arrived in the park before Bootsie and Alafair and walked idly along the bayou's edge under the trees. Desiccated gray leaves were scattered along the mudbank. I squatted down and flipped pebbles at several thin, needle-nosed garfish that were turning in the current.

I was troubled, uncomfortable, but I couldn't wrap my hand around the central concern in my mind.

Joey Gouza was in custody, where he belonged. Why did I worry?

Policemen often have many personal problems. TV films go to great lengths to depict cops' struggles with alcoholism, bad marriages, mistreatment at the hands of liberals, racial minorities, and bumbling administrators.

But my experience has been that the real enemy is the temptation to misuse power. The weaponry we possess is awesome—leaded batons, slapjacks, Mace, stun guns, M-16s, scoped sniper rifles, 12-gauge assault shotguns, high-powered pistols and steel-jacketed ammunition that can blow the cylinders out of an automobile's engine block.

But the real rush is in the discretionary power we sometimes exercise over individuals. I'm talking about the kind of people no one likes—the lowlifes, the aberrant, the obscene and ugly—about whom no one will complain if you leave them in lockdown the rest of their lives with a good-humored wink at the Constitution, or if you're really in earnest, you create a situation where you simply saw loose their fastenings and throw down a toy gun for someone to find when the smoke clears.

It happens, with some regularity.

I saw Bootsie and Alafair setting out picnic food on a table by the baseball diamond and I walked over to join them. Alafair streaked past me, her face already flushed with expectation.

"Hey, where you going, little guy?" I said.

"To play kickball."

"Don't blind anyone."

"What?"

"Never mind."

Then she turned and plunged into the midst of the game, knocking another child to the ground. I sat down in the shade with

Bootsie and ate a piece of fried chicken and two or three bites of dirty rice before my attention wandered.

"Did something happen this morning?" Bootsie asked.

"No, not really. Joey Gouza's probably having his day in the Garden of Gethsemane, but I guess that's the breaks."

"Do you feel bad about him for some reason?"

"I don't know what I feel. I suppose he deserves anything that happens to him."

"Then what is it?"

"I think he's in jail for the wrong reasons. I think Drew Sonnier is lying. I also think nobody cares whether Drew is lying or not."

"That doesn't make sense, Dave. If he didn't do it to her, who did?"

Out on the field the kids had torn loose a base pad from its fastening in the sand, where it served as the home base for one side. Alafair had the volleyball under one arm and was trying to replace the wooden peg in the sand without anyone else taking the ball from her.

"I don't know who did it," I said. "Maybe Gouza ordered it done as a warning to Weldon, then Drew lied to put him at the scene. But a guy like Gouza doesn't go out on a job himself."

"It's the city's case. It's not your responsibility."

"I twisted him. I made Bobby Earl think Gouza was going to drop the dime on him, then I told Gouza about it. The guy's experiencing some real psychological pain. He thinks a hit's out on him."

"Is there?"

"Maybe. And if there is, I might be responsible."

"Dave, a man like that is a human garbage truck. Whatever happens to him is the result of choices he made years ago. . . . Are you listening?"

"Sure," I said. But I was watching Alafair. She couldn't hold the wooden peg with one hand and tamp it down in the sand without releasing the volleyball with the other, so she balanced the peg against her folded knee, then knocked it down with the heel of her free hand.

"What is it?" Bootsie said.

"Nothing," I said. "You're right about Joey Gouza. It would be impossible to be more than a footnote in that guy's life."

"Do you want another piece of chicken?"

"No, I'd better get back to the office."

"Let the city people handle it, *cher.*"

"Yeah, why not?" I said. "That's the best idea."

She squinted one eye at me, and I averted my gaze.

▼

Ten minutes after I was back at the office, my phone rang.

"Dave?" His voice was cautious, almost deferential, as though he were afraid I'd hang up.

"Yeah, what is it, Weldon?"

He waited a moment to reply. In the background I could hear "La Jolie Blonde" on a jukebox and the rattle of pool balls.

"You want to have a bowl of gumbo down at Tee Neg's?" he asked.

"I've already eaten, thanks."

"You shoot pool?"

"Once in a while. What's up?"

"Come down and shoot some nine-ball with me."

"I'm a little busy right now."

"I'm sorry," he said.

"About what?"

"For taking a punch at you. I'm sorry I did it. I wanted to tell you that."

"Okay."

"That's all . . . 'okay'?"

"I pushed you into a hard corner, Weldon."

"You're not still heated up about it?"

"No, I don't think so."

"Because I wouldn't want you mad at me."

"I'm not mad at you."

"So come down and shoot some nine-ball."

"No more games, podna. What's on your mind?"

"I've got to get out of this situation. I need some help. I don't know anybody else to ask."

After I hung up I drove over to Tee Neg's pool hall on Main Street. The interior had changed little since the 1940s. A long mahogany bar with a brass rail and cuspidors ran the length of the room, and on it were gallon jars of cracklings (which are called *graton* in southern Louisiana), hard-boiled eggs, and pickled hogs' feet. Wood-bladed fans hung from the ceiling; green sawdust was scattered on the floor; and the pool tables were lighted by tin-shaded lamps. In the back, under the blackboards that gave ball scores from all around the country, old men played dominoes and *bourée* at the felt tables, and a black man in a porter's apron shined shoes on a scrolled-iron elevated stand. The air was thick and close with the smell of gumbo, boiled crawfish, draft beer, whiskey, dirty-rice dressing, chewing tobacco, cigarette smoke, and talcum from the pool tables. During football season illegal betting cards littered the mahogany bar and the floor, and on Saturday night, after all the scores were in, Tee Neg (which means "Little Negro" in Cajun French) put oilcloth over the pool tables and served free robin gumbo and dirty rice.

I saw Weldon shooting pool by himself at a table in back. He wore a pair of work boots, clean khakis, and a denim shirt with the sleeves folded in neat cuffs on his tan biceps. He rifled the nine ball into the side pocket.

"You shouldn't ever hit a side-pocket shot hard," I said.

"Scared money never wins," he said, sat at a table with his cue balanced against his thigh, knocked back a jigger of neat whiskey, and chased it with draft beer. He wiped at the corner of his mouth with his wrist. "You want a beer or a cold drink or something?"

"No thanks. What can I do to help you, Weldon?"

He scratched at his brow.

"I want to give it up, but I don't want to do any time," he said.

"Not many people do."

"What I mean is, I *can't* do time. I've got a problem with tight places. Like if I get in one, I hear popsickle sticks snapping inside my head."

He motioned his empty jigger at the bar.

"Maybe your fears are getting ahead of you," I said.

"You don't understand. I had some trouble over there."

"Where?"

"In Laos." He waited until the barman had brought him another shot and a fresh draft chaser. He tipped the whiskey into the beer and watched it balloon in a brown cloud off the bottom of the glass. "We operated a kind of flying taxi service for some of the local warlords. We were also transporting some of their home-grown organic. Eventually it got processed into heroin in Hong Kong. For all I know, GIs in Saigon ended up shooting it in their arms. Not too good, huh?"

"Go on."

"I got sick of it. On one trip I told this colonel, this half-Chinese character named Liu, that I wasn't going to load his dope. I pushed him off the plane and took off down the runway. Big mistake. They shot the shit out of us, killed my copilot and two of my kickers. I got out of the wreck with another guy, and we ran through jungle for two hours. Then the other guy, this Vietnamese kid, said he was going to head for a village on the border. I told him I thought NVA were there, but he took off anyway. I never found out what happened to him, but Liu's lice heads caught me an hour later. They marched me on a rope for three days to a camp in the mountains, and I spent the next eighty-three days in a bamboo cage just big enough to crawl around in.

"I lived in my own stink, I ate rice with worms in it, and I wedged my head through the bamboo to lick rainwater out of the mud. At night the lice heads would get drunk on hot beer and break the bottles against my cage. Then one morning I smelled this funny odor. It was blowing in the smoke from the campfire. It smelled like burned hair or cowhide, then, when the wind flattened out the smoke, I saw a half-dozen human heads on pikes around the fire. I don't want to tell you what their faces looked like.

"Liu's buttholes probably wanted to ransom me, but at the same time they were afraid of our guys because they'd shot up the plane and killed three of my crew. So I figured eventually they'd get tired of busting bottles on my cage and pissing on me through the bars, and my head was going to be curing in the smoke with those others.

"I used to wake with fear in the morning that was unbelievable. I'd pray at night that I would die in my sleep. Then one day some other guys came into the camp, guys who knew I was money on the hoof and who wanted to make some toady points with the CIA. They bought me for a case of Budweiser and six cartons of cigarettes."

He drank from his boilermaker, his eyes glazed faintly with shame.

"It's a funny experience to have," he said. "It makes you wonder about your worth."

"Cut it loose, Weldon."

"What?"

"We already paid our dues. Why run the same old tape over and over again?"

"I volunteered for Air America. I can't blame that on somebody else."

"You didn't volunteer to be a heroin mule."

He pulled the cellophane off a cigar and rubbed it between his fingers until it was a small ball.

"If you were going to cut a deal with the feds, who would you go to?"

"It depends on what you did."

"We're talking about guns and dope."

"You mean you got into it again?"

"Yes and no."

I looked at him quietly. He made a series of wet rings on the table with his jigger.

"The guns and the dope didn't get delivered, but I burned some guys for one hundred and eighty grand," he said.

His eyes flicked away from mine.

"This is straight? You actually ripped off some traffickers for that kind of money?" I said.

"Yeah, I guess it was sort of a first for them."

"One of the guys you burned is right there in the city jail, isn't he?"

"Maybe, maybe not."

"There's no maybe about it. My advice is you should talk to the DEA or to Alcohol, Tobacco and Firearms. I know a pretty good agent in Lafayette."

"That's about all you can suggest, huh? No magic answers."

"You won't confide in me. I'm at a loss to help you."

"If I did confide in you, I'd probably be under arrest."

He smiled wanly and started to drink from his glass, then set it back down.

"I'll give what you said some thought, Dave."

"No, I doubt that, Weldon. You'll go your own way until you beat your head into jelly."

"I wish I always knew what was going on inside other people. It'd be a great asset in the oil business."

▼

Before I drove back to the office I walked across the drawbridge over the Teche and watched the current running through the pilings and the backs of the garfish breaking the water in the sunlight. The air was hot, the sky bright with haze, the humidity so intense that my eyes burned with salt and my skin felt like insects were crawling on it. Even under the trees by the old brick firehouse in the park, the air felt close and moist, like steam rising off a stove.

Weldon had his problems, but I had mine, too. This case went far beyond Iberia Parish, and it appeared to involve people and power and politics of a kind that our small law-enforcement agencies were hardly adequate to deal with. Once again, I felt like the outside world was having its way with us, that it had found something vulnerable or weak or perhaps even desirous in us that allowed the venal and the meretricious to leave us with less of ourselves, less of a way of life that had been as sweet in the mouth as peeled sugarcane, as poignant and heartbreaking in its passing as the words to "La Jolie Blonde" on Tee Neg's jukebox:

> Jolie blonde, gardez donc c'est t'as fait.
> Ta m'as quit-té pour t'en aller,
> Pour t'en aller avec un autre que moi.

Jolie blonde, pretty girl,
Flower of my heart
I'll love you forever,
My jolie blonde.

Still, Joey Gouza was in the city of New Iberia's custody, and if the prosecutor's office had its way he would be hoeing sweet potatoes on Angola Farm the rest of his life.

But something that had bothered me at noon while I had watched Alafair playing in the park was troubling me again, this time because of an idle glance across the bayou at a young man fishing under a cypress tree. I was watching him because he reminded me of so many working-class Cajun boys I had grown up with. He stood while he fished, bare-chested, lean, olive-skinned, his body knotted with muscle, his Marine Corps utilities low on his stomach, smoking a cigarette in the center of his mouth without taking it out. His bobber went under, and he jerked his pole up and pulled a catfish through the lily pads. Then I noticed that his left hand was gone at the wrist and he had to unhook the catfish and string it with one hand. But he was quite good at it. He laid the fish across a rock, pressed the sole of his boot down on its stomach, slipped the hook loose from the corner of its mouth, and worked a shaved willow fork through the gills until the hard white point emerged bloody and coated with membrane from the mouth. Then with his good hand he flopped the fish into the shallows and sank the willow fork deep into the mud.

▼

The sheriff was sitting sideways in his swivel chair, reading a diet book, punching at his stomach with three fingers, when I walked into his office. He looked up at me, then put the book in his drawer and began fiddling with some papers on his blotter. Like many Cajun men, his chin was round and dimpled and his cheeks ruddy and flecked with small veins.

"I was thinking about going on a diet myself," I said.

"Somebody left that in here. I don't know who it belongs to."

"Oh."

"What's up?"

I told him I was going out to Drew Sonnier's again and my suspicions about what had happened at the gazebo.

"All right, Dave, but make sure you get her permission to look around on the property. If she won't give it to you, let's get a warrant. We don't want any tainted evidence."

He saw me raise my eyebrows.

"What?" he said.

"You're talking about evidence we might use against her?"

"It's not up to us. If she's filed false charges against Joey Gouza, the prosecutor might want to stick it to her. You still want to go out there?"

"Yes."

"Then do it. By the way, she was discharged from the hospital this morning, so she's back home now."

"Okeydoke."

"Dave, a little advice. Try to put the lid on your personal feelings about the Sonniers. They're grown-up people now."

"All right, sheriff."

"There're a couple of other things I need to tell you. While you were out the jailer called. It seems one trusty decided to snitch on another one. The night Joey Gouza went apeshit and vomited all over his cell, the trusty preparing the food got swacked on paregoric and accidentally knocked a box of ant poison off the shelf onto a table. It probably got in Gouza's food. Except the trusty didn't tell anybody about it. Instead he wiped off the table and served the trays like nothing had happened."

"Gouza's convinced there's a hit on him."

"That might be, but this time it looks like it was an accident."

"Where's the trusty now?"

"They're moving him over to the parish jail. I'd hate to be that guy when Gouza finds out who fired up his ulcers."

"There's no chance an AB guy was involved?"

"The guy who spilled the ant poison is a migrant farm worker in for DWI. . . . You almost look disappointed."

"No, I just thought maybe the guys in the black hats were

starting to cannibalize each other. Anyway, was there something else?"

"Yeah, I'm afraid there is." He kept putting one hand on top of the other, which was always his habit when he didn't want to say something offensive to someone. Then he pressed his glasses more tightly against his eyes. "I got three phone calls, two from state legislators and one from Bobby Earl's attorney. They say you're harassing Earl."

"I don't read it that way."

"They say you gave him a pretty bad time in a Baton Rouge restaurant."

"I had five minutes' conversation with him. I didn't see anything that unusual in it, considering the fact that I think he's involved with a murder."

"This is another thing that bothers me, Dave. We don't have any evidence that Earl is connected with Garrett's death. But you seem determined to tie Earl to it."

"Should I leave him alone?" I looked him straight in the face.

"I didn't say that. I'm just asking you to look at your motivations."

"I want—"

He saw the heat in my face. "What?" he asked.

"I want to turn the key on the people who killed Garrett. It's that simple, sheriff."

"Sometimes we have an agenda we don't tell ourselves about. It's just human."

"Maybe it's time somebody 'fronts a guy like Earl. Maybe he's gotten a free pass too long."

"You're going to have to ease up, Dave, or it'll be out of my hands."

"He's got that kind of juice?"

"No, he doesn't. But if you try to shave the dice, you'll give it to him. You got into it at his house, then you created a situation with him in a public place. I don't want a suit filed against this department, I don't want a couple of peckerwood politicians telling me I've got a rogue cop on my hands. It's time to take your foot off the accelerator, Dave."

My palms were ringing with anger.

"You think I'm being too hard on you?" he asked.

"You have to do what you think is right."

"You're probably the best cop we ever had in this department. Don't walk out of here thinking my opinion is otherwise, Dave. But you've got a way of kicking it up into overdrive."

"Then the bottom line is we're cutting Bobby Earl some slack."

"You once told me the best pitch in baseball is a change of pace. Why not ease up on the batter and see what happens?"

"Ease up on the wrong guy and he'll drill a hole in your sternum with it."

He turned his hands up on the blotter.

"I tried," he said, and smiled.

When I left the room, the back of my neck felt as though someone had held a lighted match to it.

▼

Drew answered her door in a print sundress covered with yellow flowers. Her tan shoulders were spotted with freckles the size of pennies. Even though her left hand was swathed in bandages as thick as a boxing glove, she had put on eye shadow, lipstick, and dangling earrings set with scarlet stones, and she looked absolutely stunning as she stood with one plump hip pressed against the doorjamb.

I had called fifteen minutes earlier.

"I don't want to keep you if you're on your way out, Drew," I said.

"No, it's fine. Let's sit on the porch. I fixed some tea with mint leaves in it."

"I just need to look around back."

"What for?"

"I might have missed something when I was out before."

"I thought you might like some tea."

"Thanks just the same."

"I appreciated the flowers."

"What flowers?"

"The ones you sent up to my hospital room with the Amnesty

International card. One of the pink ladies saw you buy them."

"She must have been mistaken."

"I wanted to act nice toward you."

"I need to look around back. If you don't want to give me your permission, I have to get a warrant."

"Who lit your fuse today?"

"The law's impersonal sometimes."

"You think I'm trying to get you in the sack?"

"Give it a break, Drew."

"No, give me an honest answer. You think I'm all heated up for you, that I'm going to walk you into my bedroom and ruin your marriage? Do you think your old girlfriends are lining up to ruin your marriage?"

"Can I go in back?"

She put her good hand on her hip. Her chest swelled with her breathing.

"What do you think you'll find that no one else did?" she asked.

"I'm not sure."

"Whose side are you on, Dave? Why do you have to spend so much time and effort on me and Weldon? Do you have any doubt at all that an animal like Joey Gouza belongs in jail? Of all the people in the parish, why are you the only one who keeps turning the screws on us? Have you asked yourself that?"

"Should I go after the warrant?"

"No," she said quietly. "Look anywhere you want to. . . . You're a strange man. You understand principle, but I wonder how well you understand pain in other people."

"That's a rotten thing to say."

"Too bad."

"No, you're not going to get away with that, Drew. If you and Weldon weren't my friends, both of you would have been in jail a long time ago for obstruction of justice."

"I guess we're very fortunate to have a friend such as you. I'm going to shut the door now. I really wish you had had some tea. I was looking forward to it."

"Listen, Drew—"

She closed the door softly in my face, then I heard her turn the bolt in the lock.

I went back to my truck, took a screwdriver and three big Ziploc bags off the seat, and walked through the side yard to the gazebo. The latticework was thick with bugle and grapevine, and the myrtle bushes planted around the base were in full purple flower. I knelt down in the moist dirt and probed through the bushes until I found the two pieces of brick I had seen previously. I dropped them both in a plastic bag, then found the broken slat from an apple crate and picked it up carefully by the edges. There was a split from the top down to a nail hole in the center of the slat. I turned it over between my fingers. Even in the deep shade I could see a dark smear around the hole on the opposite side. I slipped the slat into another bag and worked my way back out of the myrtle bushes onto the grass.

I glanced behind me and saw her face at a window. Then it disappeared behind a curtain.

Each of the steps on the gazebo had been carpentered with a two-inch gap between the horizontal and perpendicular boards. I tried looking through the openings into the darkness below the gazebo but could see nothing. I used the screwdriver to unfasten a section of latticework at the bottom of the gazebo and lifted it out with my fingers. It was moist and cool inside and smelled of standing water and pack-rat nests. I reached underneath the steps and touched the cold metal head of a ball-peen hammer.

I wondered if she had tried to remove it before I had arrived. I worked it out from under the steps with the screwdriver and carefully fitted it into the third plastic bag, then walked up to the screened-in porch on the side of the house.

When she didn't answer, I banged louder with the side of my fist against the wall.

"What is it?" she said, jerking open the door, her face pinched with both anger and defeat.

I let her take a hard look at the two broken bricks, the split apple-box slat, and the ball-peen hammer.

"I'm going to tell you a speculation or two, Drew, but I don't want you to say anything unless you're willing to have it used against you later. Do you understand that?"

Her mouth was a tight line, and I could see her pulse beating in her neck.

"Do you understand me, Drew? I don't want you to say anything to me unless you're completely aware of the jeopardy it might put you in. Are we perfectly understood on that?"

"Yes," she said, and her voice almost broke in her throat.

"You punched the nail through the slat, and you laid the slat across the two bricks. Then you put your hand under the nail and drove it all the way through into the step. The pain must have been terrible, but before you passed out, you splintered the slat away from the nail and shoved it and the bricks into the myrtle bushes. Then you pushed the hammer through the gap in the step."

Her eyes were filming.

"Your prints are probably all over the bricks and the slat, but that won't mean anything in itself," I said. "But I have a feeling there won't be any prints on the hammer except yours. That one might be hard to explain, particularly if there are blood traces on the hammer and we know for sure it's the one that was used to drive the nail into the gazebo floor."

She was breathing hard now, her throat was aflame with color, and her eye shadow had started to run. She licked her lips and started to speak.

"This time listen to me for a minute," I said. "I'm going to take this stuff down to the prosecutor's office and they can make of it what they want. In the meantime I recommend you drop the charges against Joey Gouza. Do it without comment or explanation."

She nodded her head. Her eyes were glistening, and she kept shutting them to clear the tears out of the lashes.

"It happens all the time," I said. "People change their minds. If anyone tries to build a case against you, you keep an attorney at your side and you turn to stone. You think you can do that?"

"Yes."

I wanted to put my arms around her shoulders. I wanted to press her against me and touch her hair.

"Will you be okay?" I asked.

"Yes, I believe I'll be fine."

"Call Weldon."

"I will."

"Drew?"

"Yes."

"Don't mess with Gouza anymore. You're too good a person to get involved with lowlife people."

She kept closing and unclosing her good hand. Her knuckles were white and as tight against her skin as a row of nickels.

"You liked me, didn't you?" she said.

"What?"

"Before you went away to Vietnam. You liked me, didn't you?"

"A woman like you makes me wish I could be more than one person and have more than one life, Drew."

I saw the sunlight bead in her eyes.

A few minutes earlier she had asked me whose side I was on. I felt I knew the answer now. The truth was that I served a vast, insensate legal authority that seemed determined to further impair the lives of the feckless and vulnerable while the long-ball hitters toasted each other safely at home plate.

▼

That night the sheriff called me at home and told me that Joey Gouza was being moved from the hospital back to a jail cell. He also said that in light of the evidence I had found at Drew Sonnier's, the prosecutor's office would probably drop charges against Gouza in the morning.

When I got to the jail on East Main early the next morning, the sun was yellow and hazy through the moss-hung canopy of oak trees over the street, and the sidewalks were streaked with dew. I left my seersucker coat on when I went inside and stopped in the men's room. I took my .45 out of the holster, pulled the clip out of the magazine, ejected the round in the chamber, and slipped the pistol and the clip in the back of my belt under my coat. Then I unclipped the holster from my belt and dropped it in my coat pocket.

I waited for the guard to open the barred door that gave onto the row of cells where Joey Gouza was housed.

"You want to check your weapon, Dave?" he asked.

"They've got it up front."

"Somebody said he might walk. Is that true?"

"Yep."

"How the hell'd that happen?"

"Long story."

"The sonofabitch is eating his soft-boiled eggs now. Can you beat that? Fucking soft-boiled eggs for a piece of shit like that."

He opened the door, then walked with me down the corridor to Gouza's cell and turned the key in the lock.

"You sure you want inside with this guy?" he asked. "He won't shower. He thinks somebody's gonna shank him if he leaves his cell."

"It's all right. I'll yell when I'm ready," I said.

The guard closed the door behind me and went away. Gouza lay on his bunk in his jockey underwear. A band of dark hair grew in a line from his navel to his sternum. An empty bowl streaked with egg yolk and a wastebasket filled with torn and stained newspaper sat on the floor by his bunk. His face looked as pale as it had been in the hospital. His seemingly lidless black eyes studied me as I pulled up the single chair in the cell and sat on it.

"They're going to kick you loose," I said.

"Yeah, I owe you one."

"You really believe that somebody is going to do you in the shower?"

"Put it this way. One guy in this place got poisoned. Me. Your people say it was an accident. Maybe so. But I don't want any more accidents. Does that seem reasonable?"

I leaned forward with my forearms on my thighs. "I've got a problem," I said.

"You've got a problem?"

"Yeah, a serious one, Joey."

"What are you talking—"

"You're a made guy. A made guy worries about respect, about what people think of him."

"So?"

"When you get out of here, you'll probably have a nice dinner somewhere, maybe drink a glass of wine, maybe do a few lines with one of your whores. Then after a while all kinds of thoughts will start to turn over in your head. Are you with me?"

"No."

"You'll think about how you were humiliated, how a woman set you up for a fall, how Elmer Fudd and company turned you into a sideshow. Then you'll remember how you got scared and asked for your own hot plate and canned food and told the screw you wanted to stay in lockup. You'll wake up thinking about it in the middle of the night, then you'll wonder if the people around you are figuring you for a guy who's about to lose it, maybe a guy who's ripe for replacement. That's when you'll decide it's time for an object lesson. So that's what's been on my mind, partner. Sooner or later we'll have a visit from one of your people, a button man from Miami or maybe some AB sex deviate you turn loose on women."

He leaned over the bunk and spat into the wastebasket, then took a sip from a brown bottle of chalky medicine and screwed the cap back on.

"Think anything you want," he said. "I got nothing on my mind except getting treatment for my ulcers before they have to cut out half my stomach. Any beef I got against this shithole I let my lawyers handle with a civil suit. You can thank Fudd and the broad if y'all have to pass a sales tax to pay off the damages."

"What I'm really trying to do is apologize to you, Joey."

He raised his elongated head up on his elbow. The skin at the corner of his mouth wrinkled with a smile.

"You're gonna apologize? You're good, man. You ought to get yourself some kind of nightclub act. I can probably book you into a couple of places."

"Because I was going to pull a cheap ruse on you. I was going to treat you like a punk instead of a made guy. So I'm apologizing."

"You talk like you got clap in your brain or something. What's with you? You never make sense. Can't you talk to people like you got sense?"

I reached behind me and pulled the .45 from under my coat. I rested it on my thigh.

"You ain't supposed to have that in here, man," he said.

"You're right. That's what I've been trying to tell you. I want to apologize for what I had in mind."

He was rigid in the bunk. I stared intently at the floor, then cocked the hammer with my thumb and raised the barrel and fitted it into the hollow of his cheek. His eyes closed, then opened again, and his Adam's apple worked up and down with a dry click in his throat.

I squeezed the trigger, and the hammer snapped on the empty chamber. He gasped, and his face jerked like he'd been slapped.

"I was going to pull a cheap trick like that to scare you," I said. "But you're a made guy, Joey, and you deserve more respect than I've shown you. And even if I rattled you a little bit, you'd be back, wouldn't you?" I winked at him. "You'd really rip some ass, right or wrong?"

A sweat had broken on his ashen face.

"You're a head case, man," he said. "You stop this shit. You get the fuck out of my life."

I pulled the clip from my belt and let it rest against my thigh. The hollow-points were loaded tightly against the spring. I rubbed my thumb casually over the top round in the clip. The fingers of both my hands made tiny, delicate prints in the thin sheen of oil on the steel surfaces of the pistol and the clip. I could hear him breathing loudly through his nose and smell the odor of fear that rose from his armpits.

"You weren't in the service, were you?" I said.

"Who gives a shit?"

"Did you ever kill anybody close up?"

He didn't answer. His eyes went from my hands to my face and back to my hands again. I inserted the clip in the magazine, pulled back the receiver, and slid a hollow-point round into the chamber.

"I'm going to give you your chance," I said.

"What?"

"To do me. Right in this cell. I lied to the guard and told him I'd already checked my weapon. So everybody will believe you when you tell them I tried to kill you, that you got the weapon away from me and did me instead."

"I ain't playing this game."

"Yes, you are."

"I want the screw."

"It's just you and me, Joey. Here," I said, and I laid the .45 on the striped mattress next to his arm.

His hands were shaking. A drop of sweat fell from the point of his chin.

"I ain't touching it," he said.

"It's the only chance you'll get at me. If you send anybody back to Iberia Parish to square a beef, I'll be coming through your door two hours after it happens. It'll be under a black flag, too, Joey. No warrant, no rules, just you and me and maybe Clete Purcel as a Lucky Strike extra. Are you going to pick it up?"

He pressed one hand against his naked stomach and grimaced with a spasm that made his eyes close.

"You quit doing this to me. You fucking lay off," he said hoarsely.

I reached out and took the .45 back and eased the hammer back down. I tried to hide the deep breath that I drew into my lungs.

He leaned his head over the bunk and vomited into the wastebasket. The hair on his bare shoulders was damp with sweat. I wet some paper towels in the washbasin and handed them to him.

"Any vendetta you have against the Sonniers ends here, Joey," I said. "Are we understood on this?"

He sat up on the bunk and took the crumpled towels away from his mouth.

"I'll give you what you want," he said.

"I'm not quite following you."

"I'll give you the guy you want. You get the guy."

"Which guy?"

"I'll deliver him up. Packaged. You get the guy."

" 'Packaged'? What do you mean 'packaged'?"

"Don't act like a stupid fuck. You know what I mean."

"You're coming to some wrong conclusions. You don't make terms, you don't do our job."

"You got a dead cop. You want it squared. So the beef gets squared. Now, you stop pulling my insides out."

He hung his head over the wastebasket, one hand trembling on his temple. His long neck looked like a bent swan's.

"You can't walk out of here with that kind of misunderstanding, Joey. Do you hear me? This isn't a barter situation. Are you listening to me? Look at me."

But he continued to stare between his legs, his eyes glazed and dull, focused inward on his own pain.

▼

That evening, eleven hours after Joey Gouza was kicked loose from custody, someone tried to garrote Weldon Sonnier in his boathouse with a strand of piano wire.

13

The AA meeting room upstairs in the Episcopalian church is foul with cigarette smoke. On the walls are framed photographs of our founders, whom we still affectionately call Dr. Bob and Bill W., as though their anonymity need be protected even in death. Also on the wall are the twelve steps of AA recovery and the simple two axioms that we attempt to live by: ONE DAY AT A TIME and EASY DOES IT. The meeting is over now, and volunteers are washing coffee cups, emptying ashtrays, and wiping down the tables. I sit by a big floor fan that is blowing the smoke out the windows into the early-morning air. My AA sponsor, Tee Neg, who looks like a mulatto, sits across from me. Before he bought the bar and poolroom that he now owns on East Main, he was a pipeliner and oil-field roughneck, and three fingers on his right hand were snipped off by a drilling chain. He's uneducated, can barely read and write, but he's tough-minded and intelligent and unfailing in his loyalty to me.

"You mad at somet'ing again, Dave. That ain't good," he says.

"I'm not mad."

"We get drunk *at* somebody. Or maybe *at* somet'ing. That's the way it works. It's them resentments mess us up. Don't be telling me different, no."

"I know that, Tee Neg."

"It ain't worrying about Bootsie this time. It's somet'ing else, ain't it?"

"Maybe."

"You want to know what I t'ink's on your mind, podna?"

"I have a feeling you're going to tell me, anyway."

"You're studying on this case all the time. You t'ink that's it, but it ain't. You bothered by the way t'ings are, the way we got trouble with the colored people all the time, you bothered 'cause it ain't like it used to be. You want sout' Lou'sana to be like it was when you and me and yo' daddy went all day and went everywhere and never spoke one word of English. You walk away when you hear white people talking bad about them Negro, like that bad feeling ain't in their hearts. But you keep pretend it's like it used to be, Dave, that these bad t'ings ain't in white people's hearts, then you gonna be walking away the rest of yo' life."

"That doesn't mean I'm going to get drunk over it."

"I had seven years sobriety, me. Then I started studying on them fingers I left on that drill pipe. I'd get up with it in the morning, just like you wake up with an ugly, mean woman. I'd drag it around with me all day. I'd look at them pink stumps till they'd start throbbing. Then I went fishing one afternoon, went into a colored man's bait store to buy some shiners, told that man I was gonna catch me a hunnerd *sac-a-lait* befo' the sun get behind them willow tree. Then I told him I changed my mind, just give me a quart of whiskey and don't bother about no shiners. I got drunk five years. Then I spent one in the penitentiary. Get mad about what you can't change and maybe you'll get to do just what Tee Neg done."

He looks at me reflectively and rubs his palms in a circular motion on his thighs. I twirl my coffee cup on my finger, then one of the cleanup volunteers reaches down and takes it from me.

"That doesn't mean you always have to like what you see around you," I say.

"It don't mean you got to be miserable about it, neither."

"I'm not miserable, Tee Neg. Give it a break, will you?"

"It ain't never gonna be the same, Dave. That world we grown up in, it's gone. *Pa'ti avec le vent,* podna."

I look down from the window at the brick-paved street in the morning's blue light, the colonnades over the sidewalks, a black man pushing a wooden cart laden with strawberries from under the overhang of a dark green oak tree. The scene looks like a postcard mailed from the nineteenth century.

▼

I went out to Weldon's home on Bayou Teche at 9 A.M. the morning after he was attacked in his boathouse. When he opened the door he was dressed in Levi's, a pair of old tennis shoes, and a T-shirt. A folded baseball glove protruded from his back pocket.

"You're headed for a game or something?" I asked.

A red welt ran around his throat, like half of a necklace.

"I've got an apple basket nailed up on the barn wall," he said. "I like to see if my fork ball's still got a hop on it."

"You've been throwing a few?"

"About two hours' worth. It beats smoking cigarettes or fooling around with early-morning booze."

"How close was it?" I said.

"He came across my throat and I remember I couldn't breathe, that I was trying to get my fingernails under the wire. Then the blood shut off to my brain, and I went down on the deck like I was poleaxed. It all happened real quick. It makes you think about how quick it can happen."

"Walk me down to your boathouse."

"I don't know who it was, Dave. I didn't see him, he didn't say anything, I just remember that wire popping tight across my wind-pipe." He blew out his breath. "Man, that's a hard feeling to shake. When I was overseas and I thought about buying it, I always figured I'd see it coming somehow, that I'd control it or negotiate with it some way, maybe convince it it that I had another season to run. That's a crazy way to think, isn't it?"

"Let's see if we find anything down at your boathouse."

We strolled across the lawn toward the bayou. When we were abreast of the old barn on the back of his property, he stooped down and picked up a scuffed baseball with split seams.

"Watch this, buddy," he said.

He wet two of his fingers, took a windup, and whipped the ball like a BB into the apple basket.

"Not bad," I said.

"I should probably get out of the oil business and start my own baseball franchise. You remember the old New Iberia Pelicans? Boy, I miss minor-league ball." He picked up another baseball from the ground.

"The report says some kids scared the assailant off."

He threw the ball underhanded against the barn door, stuck his hands in his back pockets, and continued walking with me toward the boathouse.

"Yeah, some USL kids ran out of gas on the bayou and paddled in to my dock. Otherwise I would have caught the bus. But they couldn't describe the guy. They said they just saw some fellow take off through the bushes."

We walked out onto his dock and into the boathouse. Oars and life preservers were hung from hooks on the rafters, and the whole interior rippled with the sunlight that reflected off the water at the bottom of the walls.

"Are you sure he didn't say anything?" I said.

"Nothing."

"Did you see a ring or a watch?"

"I just saw that wire loop flick down past my nose. But I know it was one of Joey Gouza's people."

"Why?"

"Because I've got some stuff Joey wants. Joey's been behind all this from the beginning. The guy with the wire was probably Jewel Fluck or Jack Gates. Or any number of mechanics Joey can hire out of Miami or Houston."

"So you are hooked up with them?"

"Sure, I am. But I've had it. I don't care if I take a fall or not. I can't keep endangering or fucking up other people anymore. Give me a minute and we'll go to the movies."

"What?"

"You'll see," he said, moving a pirogue that was upended on sawhorses. Then he knelt on one knee and lifted up a plank in the floor of the boathouse. A videocassette tightly wrapped in a clear plastic bag was stapled to the bottom of the plank. He sliced the cassette out of the bag with his pocketknife. "Come on up to the house and I'll give you a private screening from Greaseball Productions."

"What's this about, Weldon?"

"Everything you want is on this tape. I'm going to give it to you."

"Maybe you should think about calling your lawyer."

"There's time for that later. Come on."

I followed him up to his house and into his living room. He turned on his television set and VCR; he plugged in the cassette and paused with the remote control in his palm.

"This is what it amounts to, Dave," he said. "I hit two dusters in a row, I was broke, and I was about to lose my business. I borrowed everything I could at the bank, but it wasn't enough to stay afloat. So I started talking with a couple of shylocks in New Orleans. Before I knew it I was dealing with Jack Gates and he made me an offer to do a big arms drop in Colombia."

"Colombia?"

"That's where it's happening. Bush is sending a lot of arms down there to fight the druglords, but the Colombian government has a way of whacking out some of the peasants with it at the same time. So there are antigovernment people down there who pay big money for weapons, and I figured I could make a couple of runs, twenty thou a drop, and not worry about the political complexities involved. Why not? I dropped everything in Laos from pigs to napalm homemade from gasoline and soap detergent.

"Then Jack Gates offered me the big score, eighty thou for one run. The plan was for me to fly an old C-47 into Honduras, pick up a load of arms, land at this jungle strip in Colombia, where these guys process large amounts of coke, load about eight million dollars worth of flake on board, then do the arms drop up in the mountains and head for the sea.

"But I told Gates I wanted the payoff when I loaded the coke. He said I'd get paid on this end, and I told him it was no deal, then, because I didn't exactly trust the kind of people he represented. So he made a couple of phone calls and finally said all right, since eighty thou is used Kleenex to these guys. Also, Gates and Joey Gouza thought we'd be in business together for a long time. Except I took them over the hurdles. Sit down. You'll enjoy this."

He pressed the remote button, and for fifteen minutes the screen showed a series of scenes and images that could have been snipped from color footage filmed in Southeast Asia two decades earlier: wind whipping the canvas cargo straps and webbing in the empty bay of a plane; the shadow of the C-47 racing across yellow pasture-land, hummocks, earthen dikes, and brown reservoirs, the dark green of coffee plantations, a village of shacks built from discarded lumber and sheets of tin that looked as bright and hot as shards of broken mirror in the sun; then the approach over the crest of a purple mountain and the descent into a long valley that contained a landing strip bulldozed out of the jungle so recently that the broken roots in the soil were still white and pink with life.

The next images looked like they had been taken at an oblique angle from the pilot's compartment: sweat-streaked Indians in cutoff GI fatigues dragging crates of grenades, ammunition, and Belgian automatic rifles into the bay, a man who looked like an American watching in the background, a straw hat shadowing his face; then suddenly an abrupt shift in the location and cast of characters. The second cargo was loaded at twilight, and the bags were pillow-size, wrapped in black vinyl, the ends tucked, folded, and taped, carried on board as lovingly as Christmas packages.

"The next thing you should see is a lot of parachutes popping open in the dark and those crates floating down toward a circle of burning truck flares in the middle of some mountains," Weldon said. "That's where I made a change in the script. Watch this."

The screen showed a moonlit seacoast, the waves sliding up on the beach in a long line of foam, humps of coral reef protruding from the surf like the rose-colored backs of whales. Then the kickers began shoving the cargo out of the C-47.

"I call this part 'Weldon pickles the load and says get fucked to the greaseballs,' " Weldon said.

The wind ripped apart the bags of cocaine and covered the black surface of the water with a floating white paste. The crates of arms tumbled out into the darkness like a flying junkyard. Some of the crates sent geysers of foam out of the groundswell; others burst apart on the exposed reef, bejeweling the coral with belts of .50 caliber shells.

The screen went white.

"That's it?" I said.

"Yeah. What do you think of it?"

"This is what Gouza's been after?"

"Yeah, I told both of them I had their whole operation on tape. I told them to get out of my life. I figured they owed me the eighty thou for the earlier runs, anyway. I took thirty-seven holes in the fuselage on one of them. What do you think of it?"

"Not much."

"What?"

"What else have you got besides this tape?" I asked.

"This is the whole show."

"Have you got something connecting Gouza to arms and dope trafficking?"

"I've just got this tape."

"Will you make a sworn statement that you were flying for Joey Gouza?"

"I can't."

"Why not?"

"I made all the arrangements with Jack Gates. Gouza stayed out of it."

I looked out the ceiling-high window at the live oaks in Weldon's sideyard.

"What's Bobby Earl's part in this?" I said.

"He's got no part."

"Don't tell me that, Weldon."

"Bobby doesn't have anything to do with it."

"Now's not the time to cover for this guy, podna."

"Bobby's mind is on the U.S. Senate and his putz. Use your head, Dave. Why would he want to get mixed up with dope and guns?"

"Money."

"He gets all he wants from right-wing simpletons and north Louisiana rednecks. Besides, that's not what he's after. You liberals have never figured him out. Bobby doesn't care about black people one way or another. He's never known any. How could he be upset by them? It's educated and intelligent white people he doesn't like. In his mind you're all just like his parents. I don't think a day went by in his life that they didn't let him know he was a piece of shit. He's got two loves in this world, porking the ladies and provoking the press and people like yourself."

"That might all be true, but he's hooked up with Joey Gouza and that means he's in this bullshit right up to his kneecaps."

"You're wrong."

"I'm weary of you holding out on me, Weldon."

"I'm not. I've told you everything. What else do you want out of me? A guy tried to take my head off with a piano wire. I can't think about it without shuddering all over. It really got to me, man. I can even smell the guy."

"What do you mean?"

He stopped, and his eyes looked into space.

"I didn't think about it before," he said. "The guy had a smell. It was like embalming fluid or something."

"Say it again."

"Embalming fluid. Or chemicals. Hell, I don't know. It was there just a second, then my light switch clicked off."

"It wasn't one of Gouza's people, Weldon."

His brow furrowed, and he fingered the red line around his neck.

"I think your brother, Lyle, was right all along," I said. "I think your father has made a spectacular reappearance in your life. Take this tape to the DEA or the U.S. Customs office, if you want. It doesn't fall under my jurisdiction."

"You're not interested in it?"

"We already have a murder warrant out on Jack Gates. You

haven't shown or told me anything that will help put any of the other players in jail."

"You mean I've been holding this evidence and taking all this heat for nothing? And all you can tell me is that my poor demented brother has been right all along, that my own father wants to put my head on a pike?"

"I'm afraid that's about it."

"No, that's not it, Dave," he said. "I think this time I finally read you. You're not interested in Joey Gouza or Jack Gates or any of these Aryan Brotherhood clowns. You want to staple my brother-in-law's butt to the furniture. In fact, if you had your way, you'd blow up his shit big time, wouldn't you? Just like a Gatling gun locking down on Charlie in the middle of a rice field."

We stared at each other in the silence like a pair of bookends.

▼

I drove to the Salvation Army transient shelter in Lafayette to try and find Vic Benson. A portly, red-cheeked, kindly man with big sideburns who ran the shelter said that Benson had had a fistfight with another man two days ago and had been asked to leave. He had responded by packing his duffel bag quietly and walking out the door without a word; then he had stopped, snapped his fingers as though he had forgotten something, and returned to the dormitory long enough to stuff his bed sheets in the toilet bowl.

"Where do you think he went?" I asked.

"Anywhere there's Southern Pacific tracks," the Salvation Army officer said.

"Can I talk to the other men?"

"I doubt if they know anything. You can try, though. They were a little afraid of Vic. He wasn't like the rest. Most of our men are harmless. Vic always made you feel he was working on a dark thought, like he was grinding sand between his back teeth. One time he was watching television . . ." He stopped, smiled, and shook the memory out of his face.

"Go on," I said.

"He and some of the other men were watching this minister,

then Vic said, 'I'd pour lye down that one's throat if his brother didn't deserve it worse.' "

"Which minister?"

"That fellow in Baton Rouge, what's-his-name."

"Lyle Sonnier?"

"Yeah, that's the one. I tried to make a joke out of it, and I said, 'Vic, what could you possibly have against that man up there?' He said, 'The same thing the rooster's got against the baby chick that thinks the brooder house is his.' Talking with Vic could be a little bit like walking through cobwebs. Or accidentally raking your hand across a yellow-jacket nest."

We talked to a half-dozen men in the dormitory, and they all had the same vacant response and benign, vacuous expressions that they wore and used as habitually as the identities and personal histories that they had created for themselves in hundreds of drunk tanks and trackside jungle camps. They reminded me of figures in a van Gogh or Munch painting. Palm fronds and the sunlit leaves of banana trees rustled against the screen windows, but in contrast the men inside looked wind-dried, the color of cardboard, weightless in their emaciation, their hollow chests devoid of heartbeat, the skin of their arms wrapped as tight as fish scales around their bones. Their squared-away bunks, which cast no shadows because of the sun's position, looked in their exactitude like a line of coffins.

Why the morbidness over a bunch of drunks? Because they brought back the ever-present knowledge in my life that I was one drink away from their fate—despair, murder of the soul, insanity, or death—and that realization was like someone working my heart muscle with an angry thumb.

The Salvation Army officer and I walked out of the dormitory into the sunlight, into the clean sweep of wind through oak and myrtle trees and a twirling water sprinkler on the grass.

"How would you describe that odor they have?" I asked.

"I beg your pardon?"

"That smell. They all have it. How would you describe it?"

"Oh. It's those short-dogs they drink. It's one step above paint-thinner."

"It's like they have liquefied mothballs in their blood, isn't it?" I said.

"Yeah, yeah, something like that."

"Would you say it smelled like embalming fluid?"

He scratched one sideburn with a fingernail.

"I was never a mortician," he said, "but, yeah, that seems to come pretty close. Yeah, some of those ole boys are mite near dead and don't know it yet. Poor fellows."

He didn't understand the direction of my questions, and I didn't explain it to him. I simply gave him my business card and said, "If Vic comes back here, call me. Don't mess with him. I think your intuitions about him are correct. He's probably a deranged and dangerous man."

"What's he done?"

"I think only Vic Benson and God could tell you that. I don't think the rest of us would even want to know. He's one of those who make you want to believe that all of us didn't fall out of the same tree."

"It's got something to do with children, doesn't it?"

"How did you know?"

"One of the old-timers told me Vic flipped a hot cigarette in the face of a little colored boy who was pestering him. I kind of put it out of my mind because I didn't want to believe it."

His face looked momentarily sad, then he shook hands with me and walked back across the wet, shining lawn into the gloom of the dormitory.

▼

I went back to the office, planning to call Lyle Sonnier in Baton Rouge to ask if he had any idea where his father might have gone. Just as I picked up the phone, I looked through the window and saw Clete Purcell park his automobile in a yellow zone, step out on the street, and stretch his arms like a bear coming out of hibernation. Two fishing rods were sticking out of a back window. I didn't wait for him to come into the office. At best, my colleagues thought of

Clete as a happy zoo animal; others had a way of disappearing from a room as soon as he entered it.

I met him outside on the walk.

"What's happening, Dave?" he said. "Did you eat lunch yet?"

"Nope."

"Let's eat some red beans and rice, then drown some worms after you get off work."

He wore a sleeveless tropical shirt, Budweiser shorts that hung off his navel, and his powder-blue porkpie hat slanted over one eye. His huge biceps were glowing with sunburn.

"We're going down to Cypremort Point for crabs tonight. You're welcome to go with us," I said.

He looked disappointed.

"That's all right," he said. "I thought I'd fish a little bit more today, that's all. Anyway, let's get something to eat and I'll fill you in on some stuff I found out about Joey Gouza and the white man's hope."

We drove down the street to a small café run by a black man. Crushed beer cans littered the floor of Clete's car, and I could smell beer on his breath.

"Are things slow at your office?" I asked.

"I just felt like taking off, that's all. Hey, let's eat."

We took paper plates loaded with red beans, rice, and links of sausage to a plank table under a live-oak tree. The café owner didn't have a beer license, and Clete went to the trunk of his car and came back with a sweating six-pack of Jax. It was warm in the shade of the trees, and smoke from a barbecue fire floated in a blue haze through the overhead limbs.

"I did some checking on Joey's business connections around town," Clete said. "I'm talking about his legitimate businesses—a linen service, a movie house up on Prytania, a bunch of dago restaurants, places where he launders his drug money for the IRS. Anyway, the word is Joey and his people are putting up big gelt for Bobby Earl's U.S. Senate campaign. In other words, the greaseballs are into PACs now."

I nodded. "Yeah?"

"That's it."

"So what's new in that? It's what we thought all along."

"You're reading it wrong, noble mon."

"How's that?"

"If Joey Meatballs was piecing off his drug action to Bobby Earl, he wouldn't have to give him money through a bunch of PACs. He'd already own the guy."

"Maybe that's the way he launders Earl's cut."

"They don't do it that way, Streak. They give the guy something he can't resist, they bring him in on one of their deals, their shylocks lend him money, they set him up with some hot-ass broad on video tape. But they don't go into the drug business with the guy, then create a lot of public records to show everybody they got the guy's tallywacker tied around their neighborhood fireplug."

"You drove all the way to New Iberia to tell me Bobby Earl is clean?"

"Oh, they know all the same people, and Joey would like to put a U.S. senator in his pocket, but there's no law against that, mon."

"Bobby Earl's dirty."

"Maybe so. I'm just telling you what I found out and what I think. The guy's a sonofabitch but so are half the politicians in Louisiana."

"I get the feeling something else is bothering you, Clete."

He ripped open another beer and lit a cigarette, his food unfinished.

"It comes with the territory. It's nothing new," he said.

"What is it?"

"I might get my PI ticket pulled."

"What for?"

He bit one of his fingernails and shrugged.

"I've had two or three beefs since I opened my office. It's my own fault," he said.

"You're always in a beef, Clete. Why is somebody giving you trouble about your ticket now?"

"That's what I asked this bozo who called me up from Baton Rouge."

"Which bozo?"

"With the state regulatory agency." His eyes moved around on my face.

"It's Bobby Earl, isn't it?" I said.

"Maybe."

"There's no 'maybe' about it."

"Anyway, they got these complaints and they're talking about a hearing before their board."

"What complaints?"

"Well, there was this button man, a real bag of shit out of Miami, a guy who whacked out two Cuban girls who were going to send this greaseball dealer up to Raiford. He jumped a two-hundred-thou bond, and word had it he was hiding out in Ascension or St. James Parish. So the bondsman in Miami calls me and tells me he'll pay me a five-grand finder's fee if I can bring in this guy before the bondsman has to come up with the two hundred thou. But the only lead he can give me on the shit bag is that he's somewhere between New Orleans and Baton Rouge, he loves pink Cadillacs, smoking dope, and being a big man around lowlife broads.

"So I spend two weeks cruising these dumps along Airline Highway. Just when I'm about to give up, I see this beautiful, flamingo-pink Cadillac convertible, with Georgia plates, parked in front of this club that's got both white and mulatto broads on stage. I go inside, and the place is filled with smoke and about two hundred geeks that look like somebody beat up on them with an ugly stick. But I don't see my man. So I go back out to the parking lot and pop the door lock on the Caddy with a slim jim. The inside smells like somebody rubbed hash oil into the upholstery. In the glove compartment I find a box of rubbers, a match cover from a Fort Lauderdale bar, an ice pick, and a dozen loose .38 shells. What does that tell me? This has got to be the shit bag's car.

"Except I look all over the bar and I can't find the guy, which means he's probably wearing a disguise. Then it's three in the morning, still no shit bag, and I'm bone-tired. So I kind of hurried things along by setting fire to the pink Caddy."

"You did what?"

"What was I supposed to do, spend the rest of the week there? I was working on spec. Anyway, the Caddy was burning beautifully in the parking lot, and the geeks came pouring out of the building to watch it, happy as pigs rolling in slop, except of course for the guy who owned the Caddy. Guess what?"

"He wasn't your guy."

"Right. He was a traveling sporting-goods salesman from Waycross. But guess what again? There, standing in the crowd, is my shit bag. In two minutes I had him in cuffs and locked to a D-ring in the back of my car. So it all worked out all right, except somebody saw me messing around the Caddy and told the cops and the firemen, and I had to come back the next day and answer some questions that made me a little bit uncomfortable. Then Nig got me into a scrape—"

"Nig?" I had finished eating and was glancing at my watch.

"Yeah, Nig Rosewater, the bondsman. I'm sorry to bore you with this stuff, Dave, but I don't get a regular paycheck. I depend upon guys like Nig to keep me afloat."

I took a breath and let him continue.

"Nig decides to go into the saloon business," Clete said. "So he opens a bar on Magazine right next to a black neighborhood. What kind of sign does he put in his window? 'HAPPY HOUR 5 TO 7—HAVE A SWIG WITH NIG.' So the first night somebody flings a burning trash can through the plate glass. Then they did it two more nights, even after Nig got rid of the sign. Who did it, you ask. The fucking Crips, not because they're big on civil rights but because it impresses the other punks in the neighborhood. Have you dealt with any of these guys? They knocked off a kid on Calliope, then, to make sure everybody got the message, they walked into the mortuary, in front of his family, and blew his coffin full of holes. They're a real special bunch.

"So I found out the kid who had been remodeling Nig's bar was named Ice Box. They call him that because he pushed a refrigerator on top of his grandmother. I'm not making this up. This kid could blow out your light like he was turning a page in a comic book. Anyway, I had a talk with Ice Box while I held him by his ankles off a fire escape, five stories up from the pavement. I think he's back in California these days. But his grandmother, can you dig it, with dents still in her head, filed charges against me.

"Anyway, somebody in Baton Rouge wants to cut a piece out of my butt. Like I say, I brought it on myself. I learned in the corps you don't mess with the pencil pushers. You stay invisible. You piss off some corporal in personnel and two weeks later you're humping it with an ambush patrol outside Chu Lai."

"Give me the name of the guy in Baton Rouge who's after you."

"Leave it alone. It'll probably go away."

"Bobby Earl won't."

"That's the point, mon. Earl's got no handles on him. We sent the shit bags up the road because they were born to take a fall. Earl's part of the system. There're people who love him. You think I'm giving you a shuck? Did you see him on *The Geraldo Rivera Show*? Some of those broads were ready to throw their panties at him. It's me and you who've got the problem. We're the geeks, Dave, not this guy. He's a fucking hero."

His breath was heavy with the smell of beer and cigarettes.

He crushed a beer can in his palm and dropped it on the table, then studied the tops of his big, coarse, red hands. He had tried to comb his sandy hair back over the divots where his stitches had been, but I could still see crusted lesions like thin black worms on his scalp.

"Oh, hell, what do I know?" he said, and looked down the street at the traffic in the hot sunlight, as though it somehow held the answer to his question.

▼

Back in my office, I got hold of Lyle Sonnier at his church.

"Hey, Loot, I'm glad you called," he said. "I've been thinking about throwing a big dinner here at the church, actually more like a family reunion, and I wanted to ask you and Bootsie."

"Thanks, Lyle, but right now I'm looking for Vic Benson, the fellow you think might be your father."

"What do you want him for?"

"He's part of an investigation."

"You don't have to look far, then. He's right here."

"What?"

"We had lunch together just a little while ago. He's out back painting some furniture for our secondhand store right now."

"How long has he been there?"

"He came in this morning."

"I think he tried to take your brother's head off last night with a piece of piano wire."

"Get real, Dave. He's a wino, a bundle of sticks. He has to wear lead shoes on a windy day."

"Tell that to Weldon."

"I already talked to Weldon. He says it was a Joey Gouza hit."

"Believe me, Lyle, Joey has no desire for more trouble in Iberia Parish."

"So if it wasn't Gouza, it was probably one of the walking brain-dead who follow Bobby Earl around. But no matter how you cut it, it wasn't the old man. Good God, Dave, what's the matter with you? Weldon could beat that poor old drunk to death with his shoe."

"Why do you think Bobby Earl might be involved in it?"

"He's bad news, that's why. He stirs up grief and hatred among the very people that's sitting out there in my flock—poor white and black folk. I'm tired of that character. Somebody should have stuffed his butt in a garbage can a long time ago."

"That may be true, Lyle, but that doesn't mean he's trying to whack out your brother."

I waited for him to say something, to offer me the linkage to Bobby Earl.

"Lyle?"

"Well, anyway, in my opinion the old man's harmless. You gonna arrest him?"

"No, I don't have enough for a warrant."

"Then what's the big deal?"

"I'll be over there later today or at least by Monday to talk to

him. Tell him that for me, too. In the meantime you might ask
yourself why he's shown up after all these years? Does he seem like
a man of goodwill to you?"

"Maybe he wants to atone but he hasn't learned the words yet.
It takes a while sometimes."

"Like we used to say out in Indian country, don't let them get
behind you."

"That's what somebody said at My Lai, too. Give all that Vietnam stuff to the American Legion, Dave. It's a drag."

"Whatever you say, Lyle. Hang loose."

"Hey, I'll get back to you with a date for that dinner. I want
your butt there, with no excuses. I'm proud to be your friend, Dave.
I look up to you, I always did."

What do you say to someone who talks to you like that? In order
to get a jump-start on the day I used to go on dry drunks that were
the equivalent of inserting my head in a microwave for ten minutes.
I had come to learn that a conversation with any one of the Sonniers
worked just as well.

▼

It was Friday afternoon, and it was too late and I was too tired for
a round-trip to Baton Rouge to interview Vic Benson, who was
probably Verise Sonnier, particularly in view of the fact that I had
no tangible evidence against him and talking to him was like con-
versing with a vacant lot, anyway.

The heat broke temporarily with a thirty-minute rain shower
that evening, then the wind came up cool out of the south, scatter-
ing dead pecan leaves up on my gallery, and the late sun broke
through the layered clouds as red and molten as if it had been poured
flaming from a foundry cup. We had a short-lived crisis at the bait
shop. I was filling up the bowls in the rabbit hutches by the side of
the house when I heard a loud yell in the shop, then saw Tripod
racing out the door, his loose chain slithering across the planks, with
Alafair right behind him. Then Batist came through the door with
a broom raised over his head.

Alafair caught Tripod up in her arms at the end of the dock, then turned to face down Batist, whose black, thick neck was pulsing with nests of veins.

"I gonna flatten that coon like a bicycle patch, me," he said. "I gonna wipe up that bait shop wit' him."

"You leave him alone!" Alafair shouted back.

"I cain't be running' a sto', no, with that nasty coon wreckin' my shelves. You set him down on that dock and I gonna golf him right over them trees."

"He ain't did anything! Clean up your own mess! Clean up your own nasty cigars!"

In the meantime, Tripod was trying to climb over her shoulder and down her back to get as much geography between him and Batist as possible.

Oh Lord, I thought, and walked down to the dock.

"It's too late, Dave," Batist said. "That coon headed for coon heaven."

"Let's calm down a minute," I said. "How'd Tripod get into the bait shop again, Alf?"

"Batist left the screen open," she said.

"I left the screen open?" he said incredulously.

"You were fishing out back, too, or he wouldn't have gotten up on the shelf," she said. Her face was flushed and heated, her eyes as bright as brown glass.

"Look his face, look his mouth," Batist said. "He eat all the sugar in the can and two boxes them Milky Ways."

Tripod, whose fur was almost black except for his silver-ringed tail and silver mask, didn't make a good witness for the defense. His muzzle and whiskers were slick with chocolate and coated with grains of sugar. I picked up the end of his chain. The clip that we used to fasten him to the clothesline was broken.

"I'm afraid we've got Tripod on a breaking-and-entering rap, Alf," I said.

"What?" she said.

"It looks like he's going to have to go into lockdown," I said.

"What?"

"That means let's put him in the rabbit hutch until tomorrow when I can fix his chain. In the meantime, Batist, let's close down the shop and think about going to the drive-in movie."

"It ain't my sto', it ain't my Milky Way. I just work here all day so I can clean up after some fat no-good coon, me."

Alafair was about to fire off another shot when I turned her gently by the shoulder and walked her back through the pecan trees in front of the house.

"He was mean, Dave," she said. "He was gonna hurt Tripod."

"No, he's not mean, little guy," I said. "To Batist, running the bait shop is an important job. He just doesn't want anything to go wrong while he's in charge."

"You didn't see what he looked like." Her eyes were moist in the deep shade of the trees.

"Alafair, Batist grew up poor and uneducated and never learned to read and write. But today he runs a business for a white man. He wants to do everything right, but he has to make an 'X' when he signs for a delivery and he can't count the receipts at the end of the day. So he concentrates on things that he can do well, like barbecuing the chickens, repairing the boat engines, and keeping all the inventory squared away. Then Tripod gets loose and makes a big mess of the shelves. So in Batist's mind he's let us down."

I saw her eyes blinking with thought.

"It's kind of like the teachers at school giving you a job to do, then someone else comes along and messes it up and makes you look bad. Does that make sense?"

She shifted Tripod in her arms, so that he lay on his back with his three paws in the air, his stomach swollen with food.

"I guess so. We going to the show?"

"You bet."

"Batist is going, too?"

"I don't know, you think he should go?"

She thought about it.

"Yeah, he should go with us," she said, as though she had just reached a profound metaphysical conclusion.

"You're the best, little guy."

"You are, too, big guy."

We popped Tripod into the hutch, then I swung Alafair up on my back and we walked beneath the sparking of fireflies onto the gallery and into the lighted house, where Bootsie was deep-frying *sac-a-lait* and listening to a Cajun song that was playing on the radio propped in the kitchen window. The western sky looked like a blood-streaked ink wash, and I could hear the cicadas in a distant woods, all the way across the waving field of green sugarcane at the back of my property.

▼

The next morning Alafair helped Batist and me open the bait shop. She earned her weekly allowance of five dollars by seining the dead shiners out of the bait tanks, seasoning the chickens that we barbecued on a split oil drum for our midday customers, draining the coolers, and pouring fresh ice over the beer and soda pop. But her favorite Saturday-morning job was sitting on a tall stool behind the cash register, her Astros baseball cap low on her head, ringing up worm and shiner sales with a loud bang on the keys.

It was a wonderful morning to fish. The air was still cool and windless, the early pink light muted in the cypress trees, the moon still visible in one soft blue corner of the sky. After we had rented most of our boats, I started the barbecue fire in the oil drum, then fixed coffee and hot milk and bowls of Grape-Nuts for the three of us, and we ate breakfast on one of the telephone-spool tables under an umbrella out on the dock. I had managed to push the Sonnier case completely out of my mind when the phone rang inside the shop and Alafair got up and answered it.

I could see only the side of her face through the screen window as she held the receiver to her ear, but I had no doubt that she was listening to something that she had never expected to come through our telephone. Her eyes were blinking rapidly and her tan cheeks were filled with white discolorations, and I saw her look at me with her mouth parted as though a childish bad dream had become real in the middle of her day.

I went quickly inside the shop and behind the counter and took the receiver from her hand.

"Dave, he called you real bad names," Alafair said. She was breathing hard through her mouth.

"Who is this?" I said into the receiver.

"You know who it is. Don't act stupid," a high, metallic voice, like that of a midget, said. "You cut a deal with Joey Meatballs, didn't you?"

"You're not shy about frightening a little girl. How about giving me your name?"

"You don't know my name?"

I picked up a pencil and scribbled across the top of a lined notepad: "Boots, call office, tell them to trace call in shop." Then I put the pad in Alafair's hands and pushed her toward the door.

"What's the matter, you got nothing wise to say?" the voice asked.

"What do you want, Fluck?"

"I want to know what you're giving Joey Gee so that he puts a whack out on me."

"There's no deal with Joey."

"You lying sonofabitch. He's out of the bag one day and every-body in New Orleans hears there's a five-grand open contract on me. You telling me you don't have anything to do with it?"

"That's right."

"What is it, you guys want to wipe your books clean with my ass? Or is it a personal beef because I almost cooled you out in Sonnier's house?"

"You're going down because you killed a police officer and Eddy Raintree."

"I'm shaking."

"To tell you the truth, Fluck, I'm busy right now and you're a boring man to talk to."

"The only reason somebody from the AB didn't take you out is you're not worth the trouble. But I'm going to give you a deal, one that'll make you big shit in your little town. I get immunity on that dead cop in the Sonnier house, I don't know anything about Eddy Raintree's problems next to a train track, and I give you everything you want on Joey Meatballs. I'm talking about guys he's whacked, the marshmallow Jack Gates shoved into the plane pro-peller, the crack they're selling to the niggers in the projects, gun deals with spics, you name it, I'll give it to you. . . . Are you listening to me, man?"

"I hear you just fine."

"Then you set it up. I want protective custody, too. Maybe in another state."

"I think you're overestimating your importance, Fluck. You're not the kind of witness that prosecutors get excited about."

"Look, I can take you to two graves down by Terrebonne Bay. Two guys that Joey made kneel down on the edge of a trench and suck on a barrel of a .22 mag before he dumped a big one down their throats."

"It's not a sellers' market these days."

"What's with you, man? You want to see Joey Gee go down or not?"

"Where are you?"

"Are you kidding?"

"What I mean is, you're probably not too far from a police station of some kind. Turn yourself in. It's the only deal you're going to get from me or probably anybody else. You executed a police officer. You get caught by the wrong guys and you'll never make the jail, Fluck."

"You're getting off on this, aren't you?"

Through the screen window I saw Bootsie wave at me from the gallery of the house.

"Nope. I'm tired of talking to you," I said.

"I'm messing up your morning, huh?"

"No, you just made a big mistake today."

"What mistake, what are you talking—"

"You phoned me at my home. You frightened my little girl. You did it because inside you're a small, scared man, Fluck. That's why you wanted Garrett to see it coming. For just a second you felt you were as big a man as he was."

"You're talking yourself into something real bad."

"Call the DEA. They cut deals with snitches all the time."

I could hear him breathing into the receiver.

"Where you from, outer space? You're fucking with the AB.

We're everywhere, man. There ain't anybody we can't clip. Even if I go down, even if I'm in a max unit somewhere, I can have your whole family taken out."

"For five grand your AB buddies will have you in a soap dish."

I could almost hear a wet, gastric click in his throat. Then he hesitated a moment, as though he were squeezing his anger back into a small box down in his chest.

"I want you to remember everything you said to me," he said. "Keep running the words over and over in your head. I'm gonna think up something for you, something special, something that you didn't think could ever happen in your life. I was in Parchman, man. You don't know how much pain a wise-ass fuck like you can go through before he dies."

Then the line went dead. I looked at my watch. I didn't know if there had been enough time for the dispatcher at the office to get a successful trace on the call or not. I dipped a wad of paper towels into the floating ice in the beer cooler and rubbed my face with it, then wiped my skin dry and flung the towels into the trash basket, as though I could somehow rinse and clean the voice of Jewel Fluck out of my day.

I waited ten more minutes, then called the dispatcher.

"They traced it to a pay phone on Decatur in New Orleans," he said. "We called First District headquarters, but the guy was gone when they got there. Sorry, Dave. Who was it?"

"The guy who killed Garrett."

"Fluck? Oh man, if we'd just been a little bit faster—"

"Don't worry about it."

I walked up through the shade of the pecan trees to the gallery. Bootsie was sitting in the swing with Alafair beside her. Alafair looked up at me from under the brim of her ball cap, her face filled with a pinched light.

"It was just a drunk man, little guy," I said. "He thought I was somebody else."

"His voice, it was—" she began. "It made me feel bad inside." She swallowed and looked out into the deep shadows of the trees.

"That's the way drunk people sound sometimes. We just don't pay any attention to them," I said. "Anyway, Bootsie had the call traced to New Orleans, and the cops went to pick this guy up. Hey, let's don't waste any more time worrying about this character. I need you to help me get ready for our lunch customers."

I felt Bootsie's eyes searching my face.

I went inside the house, took my .45 out of the dresser, slipped it down into my khakis, and pulled my shirt over it. At the dock I put Alafair in charge of turning the sausage links and split chickens on the barbecue grill. Her shoulders barely came above the top of the pit, and when the grease and *sauce piquant* dripped onto the coals her head and cap were haloed in smoke.

I put the .45 on a top shelf behind a stand-up display of Mepps spinners. I wouldn't need it, I told myself, not here, anyway. Fluck had too many problems of his own to worry about me. His kind took revenge only when they had nothing at risk, when it came to them as a luxury they could savor. I was sure of that, I told myself.

14

The sheriff learned of Fluck's phone call early Monday from the dispatcher. As soon as I walked into my office, he tapped on the doorjamb and followed me in.

"Jewel Fluck called you at your house?" he said.

"That's right." I opened the blinds and sat down behind my desk.

"Why do I have to hear that from the dispatcher?"

"I didn't see any point in disturbing you on the weekend."

"What'd he say?"

"Most of it was douche water. His clock's running out."

"Come on, Dave, why'd he call you?"

"He wanted to give up Joey Gouza for immunity on Garrett and Eddy Raintree. I told him the store's closed."

"You did what?"

"I indicated that cop killers don't get any slack, sheriff."

He sat down in the chair across from me and brushed one hand across the top of the other. He puffed out his cheeks.

"Maybe that's not yours to decide, Dave. There're a half-dozen agencies that want Joey Gouza salted away. The DEA, U.S. Customs, the FBI, Alcohol, Tobacco, and Firearms—"

"Cut a deal with the lowlifes and in the long run you always lose."

"In law enforcement every man's vote doesn't count the same. Wyatt Earp belongs in the movies, Dave."

"I tried to keep him on the phone so we could trace the call. You lose the edge on these guys as soon as you let them think they have something you want. That's the way it works, sheriff."

"What else did he say?"

"He believes Gouza's got a five-grand open contract on him. If you want, you can tell NOPD about it, but I don't think they'll wring their hands over the news."

"It's still Bobby Earl, isn't it?" he said.

"What?"

He scratched his clean-shaven soft cheek with a fingernail.

"Fluck, Gouza, this button man Jack Gates, I think they're all secondary players for you, Dave. It's Bobby Earl who's always on your front burner, isn't it?"

"Fluck frightened my little girl, sheriff. He also threatened me. You figure who's on my mind."

"You sound a little sharp, podna."

"This is the second time you've told me maybe it's me who's got a problem."

"It wasn't my intention to do so."

"Look, sheriff, we haven't turned the key on one guy in this case, except Gouza, and that was on a bum charge. When something like that happens, everybody gets impatient. Then a guy like Bobby Earl marshals a little pressure and convinces a few political oil cans that he's a victim, a federal agency decides that it's more interesting to throw a net over a mainline wiseguy like Gouza than a termite like Jewel Fluck, we local guys go along with it, and before you know it, half the cast is on the beach in the Virgin Islands and we're trying to figure out why people think we're schmoes."

"Maybe after this one's over, you should take a little vacation time."

"It won't change who's out there."

He did a *rat-a-tat-tat* on his thighs with his palms, then stood up, smiled, and walked out of my office without saying anything else.

▼

I drove to Baton Rouge that afternoon to question the burned man who called himself Vic Benson. It wasn't to be the kind of interview that I had planned. I parked my truck at the end of Lyle's brick driveway on Highland and walked up onto the columned porch to lift the brass door knocker that rang a set of musical chimes deep in the interior of the house, when Lyle walked out of the sideyard with a garden rake in his hand, wearing a T-shirt and jeans that hung off his hips. There were flecks of dirt and leaves in his mussed hair.

"Hey, Dave, what's happening?" he said. "You're just in time to fang down some barbecued pork chops. Come on around back."

"Thanks anyway, Lyle. I just need to ask Vic Benson a few questions. Is he staying over at your mission?"

"No."

"He took off?"

"No." He was smiling now.

"He's here?"

"In the backyard. We just put in some pepper plants. It's a little late but I think they'll take."

"He's living with you?"

"Out in the garage apartment."

"I think what you're doing isn't smart."

"I've never done anything smart in my life, Dave. Like Waylon says, 'I might be crazy but it's kept me from going insane.' "

"I'm not sure you want to hear everything I have to say to this man."

"The words ain't been made that's gonna upset me, son . . . I mean Loot. Come on around back."

The sweeping expanse of backyard was dotted with live oaks, lime trees, myrtle bushes, and circular weedless beds of roses and purple hydrangeas. Meat smoke from a stone fire pit drifted across the lawn and hung in the trees, and the Saint Augustine grass was so thick, so deeply blue and green in the evening shadows, that you felt you could dive into it as you would a deep pool of water.

Vic Benson was cutting back a clump of banana trees with a pair of garden shears. The blades of the shears were white and gummy with pulp. Each time he snapped the blades on a dead frond, the muscles in his face and neck flexed like snakes under his red scar tissue.

A thick-bodied black woman in a maid's uniform began setting a table on the flagstone patio.

"Let's sit down to eat, then you can ask the old man whatever you want," Lyle said.

"This isn't what I had in mind, Lyle."

"Quit trying to plan everything. What the Man on High plans for you is better than anything you could plan for yourself. Isn't that what y'all learn in AA? Look out yonder." He pointed across the brick wall and bamboo that bordered his property. "See it, just above the trees out on Highland, my cross, right up there on top of my Bible college. Look, it's silver and pink in the sunlight. Inside all that chrome is a charred wooden cross that was burned by Klansmen to terrorize black folk. Then the Reverend Jimmy Bob Clock made it his so me and him could run scams on a bunch of north Miss'sippi country people who didn't have two quarters to rub together in their overalls. Now it's on top of a Bible college where kids go to school free and study for the ministry. You think that's all accident? I read a poem once that had a line in it about a white radiance that stains eternity. That's the way I like to think about that cross up there."

"I don't like to cut into your sense of religiosity, Lyle, but how in the name of God do you justify all this?" I gestured at his house, his manicured lawns.

"I don't own it. I'm mortgaged up to my eyeballs. It all went into the college. That ain't a shuck, either, Loot."

"What do you pay that black woman with?"

He laughed.

"I don't pay her anything. She works three hours a day for room and board. She just got out of St. Gabriel. She did five years for murdering her pimp."

"What you do is your business, Lyle, but I think you have a

dangerous and psychotic man staying at your home."

"That black gal, Clemmie, might cut my throat, but a good fart would blow ole Vic off the planet like a dandelion. Come on, let's eat. You're too serious about everything, Dave. That's always been your problem. Treat the world seriously and in turn it'll treat you like a clown. You ought to learn that, Loot."

"How about saving it for a wider audience, Lyle?"

"It's just one guy's opinion," he said, and shrugged his shoulders. Then he waved at the man who called himself Vic Benson and who was now flinging a pile of dried banana fronds into a trash fire by a brick wall at the back of the property. His body was silhouetted like a figure cut from tin against the puffs of sparks and plumes of black smoke. He walked toward us, out of the shade, his eyes red-rimmed, unblinking, welded on mine, his puckered face as unreal as rubber twisted around a fist.

I didn't look directly at him while the black woman served us plates of black-eyed peas, dirty rice, and barbecued pork chops. But I could smell him, an odor like turpentine, tobacco smoke, wind-dried sweat.

Because part of his lips had been pared away, you could see everything in his mouth when he chewed his food. He reached across the table for a second pork chop, and a patch of black hair on his arm brushed the rim of my iced-tea glass.

"The way I eat, it bothers you?" he asked.

"No, not at all," I said.

"I seen them a lot worse than me. In an armed service hospital," he said. "They had to eat their food out of toothpaste tubes."

He drank from his glass. The iced tea gurgled across his teeth. His splayed fingers looked like gnarled and baked tubers.

"Someone used a piano wire on Weldon Sonnier and tried to remodel him into a stump," I said. "Do you know anything about that, Vic?"

"About what?"

"You heard me."

"Piano wire? That's a good one. The last time I seen you, you ax me if I was looking in somebody's windows. Maybe you got a bump on the brain or something."

The black maid had put on a Walkman headset and was dusting the patio furniture by slapping it with a dish towel, one hand propped on her hip, while she jiggled to music that no one else could hear. Vic pushed a piece of meat back into his mouth with his thumb and studied her undulating curves.

"I talked with the gentleman who runs the Sally in Lafayette," I said. "He said you were watching Lyle on TV one time and you mentioned how you'd like to pour lye down his throat."

Lyle's fork paused over his food a moment, then he continued eating with his eyes askance.

"What a drunk man says don't have no more meaning than horse piss on a rock," Vic said.

"He says you flipped a hot cigarette into a child's face."

"Then I say I don't have no recollection of him being there to say what I done and what I ain't done in my life."

"People sure seem to know when you've been around, though, Vic," I said.

"How about we ease it down a notch, Dave?" Lyle said.

"It don't bother me none," Vic said. "One guy like me gives a job to a hunnerd like him. He knows it, too."

"You're wrong about that, partner," I said. "You become a job for me when I have to cut a warrant on you. But right now I can't prove that you tried to take your son's head off with a piece of piano wire. That means you have another season to run. If I were you, I'd take advantage of my good fortune and change my ways. *Change ta vie, t'connais que je veux dire?*"

"I'm tired of this. Where'd you put that tobacco at?" he said, and pushed his plate away with the heel of his hand.

"I think I set it up on the brick wall. Stay where you're at. I'll get it," Lyle said, rose from his chair, and walked across the lawn.

Vic Benson stared straight into my face. His thin nose was hooked, like a hawk's beak.

"It looks like you drove up here for nothing, don't it?" he said.

I looked back into his face. His puttylike skin was incapable of wearing an expression, and his surgically devastated mouth was cut back into a keyhole over his teeth; but his eyes, which seemed to water as though they were smarting from smoke, contained a malevolent, jittering light that made me want to look away.

"I've got a feeling about you, partner," I said. "I think you not only want revenge against your children. I think you want to do something spectacular. A real light show."

"Go shit in your plate."

"You might even be thinking about torching Lyle's house, particularly if you could get Weldon and Drew inside with Lyle at the same time. I suspect fire stays on your mind quite a bit."

His red eyes shifted to the maid, her large breasts, her dress that tightened across her rump as she reached upwards to dust cobwebs off a bug lamp. He took a lucifer match out of his shirt pocket and rolled it across his teeth with his tongue.

"Fire don't know no one place. Fire don't know no one man," he said.

"Are you threatening me, Vic?"

"I don't waste my time on twerps," he said.

▼

The moon was down that night, but the pecan trees in the yard seemed to shake with a sudden white-green light when the wind blew out of the south and dry lightning trembled in the marsh. I couldn't sleep. I thought of fire, the vortex of flame that had swirled about Vic Benson (or Verise Sonnier) in a Port Arthur chemical plant, the sheets of hot metal that had buried him alive and branded his soul, the hateful energies that he must have carried with him like a burning chain draped around his neck. He was one of those for whom society had no solution. His life was ashes; he was morally insane and knew it; and his thoughts alone could make a normal person weep. The sight of pity in our eyes made him grind his back teeth. Years ago his kind were lobotomized.

He had nothing to lose. He was a living nightmare to hospital employees; prisons didn't want him; psychiatrists considered him pathological and hence untreatable; and even if he was convicted of a capital crime, judges knew that he could turn his own execution into an electronic carnival of world-class proportions.

Would he take an interest in my home and family? I had no

answer. But I was convinced that, like Joey Gouza or Bobby Earl, he was one of those who had gone across a line at some point in his life and had declared war on the rest of us. Whether we elected to recognize that fact or not, Vic would be at work with a penny book of matches or a strand of wire that he would pop musically between his fists. The time of his appearance in our lives would be of his choosing.

I fixed a cup of coffee and walked down the slope of my yard to the dock. The stars looked white and hot in the sky; on the wind I could smell the sour reek of mud and rotted humus in the marsh, and the wet, gray odor of something dead. A white tree of lightning splintered across the southern sky. Sweat ran down my sides. It was going to be a scorching day.

I unlocked the door of the bait shop and went inside and pulled the chain on the electric bulb that hung over the counter. Then I saw the diagonal slash across the back screen window that gave onto the bayou.

But it was too late. He rose up from behind the bait tanks and gently pressed the barrel of a pistol behind my ear.

"No, no, don't turn around, my friend. That'd get both of us in trouble," he said.

The light threw both of our shadows on the floor. I could see his extended arm, the pistol rounded by his fist, and an object, a sack perhaps, that seemed to dangle from his other hand.

"The till's empty. I've got maybe ten dollars in my wallet," I said.

"Come on, Mr. Robicheaux. Give me a little credit." The accent was New Orleans, the voice one I had heard before.

"What do you want, partner?"

"To give you something. You just shouldn't have come to work so early. . . . No, no, don't turn around—"

He shifted his position so that his face was well behind my range of vision. But when he did I saw his distorted silvery reflection on the aluminum side of a horizontal lunch-meat and cold-drink cooler. Or rather I saw the reflected metal caps and fillings in his mouth.

Then he stooped, set something on the floor, and nudged me toward the counter.

"Lean on it, Mr. Robicheaux. You probably don't pack when you come down to your bait shop, but a guy can't take things for granted," he said, and moved his free hand down my hips and pockets and over my ankles.

"Look, a black man who works for me is going to be here soon. I don't want him to walk in on this. How about telling me what's on your mind and getting out of here?"

"Your ovaries don't get heated up too easy, do they?" He clicked off the light. "What time's the colored man get here?"

"Anytime now."

"That sure would change your luck in a bad way, believe me." Then he said, "Listen, the man I work for has fixations. Right now you're one of them. Why? Because you keep bugging the shit out of him. It's time you lay off, man. This is an important guy. There's people up in Chicago don't want him puking blood all over New Orleans because of nervous anxiety. . . . No, no, eyes forward—"

He rubbed the pistol barrel along my jawbone.

"Is that it?" I said.

"No, that's not it, man. Look, nobody's got a beef with you, Mr. Robicheaux. Nobody had a beef with that cop who walked into Sonnier's house, either. That dumb fuck Fluck went out of control. We don't whack cops, you know that, man. So we're making it right.

"But it doesn't have to end here. You're a bright guy and you can have a lot of good things. Nothing illegal, no strings, just good business. Like maybe a nightclub down in Grand Isle. It's yours for the asking. All you got to do is call the right Italian restaurant on Esplanade. You know the place I'm talking about."

Through the slashed screen I could see the false dawn lighting the gray tops of the cypress trees in the marsh. I heard a fish flop loudly in the lily pads.

"I'll think about it," I said.

"Good . . . good. Now—"

I felt him shift his weight, felt the dangling object in his hand brush against my pants leg.

"What?" I said.

"I got to figure what to do with you. You keep walking in on me at the wrong time. Nothing personal but you've really fucked up my plans twice now."

"Like you say, so far it's not personal. . . . Don't do the wrong thing, partner."

I could hear him breathing in the dark. The back of my neck and head felt naked, as though the skin had been peeled away from all the nerve endings.

"What's inside that door, the one with the lock on it?" he said.

"It's just a storage room."

"Well, that's where you're going."

From behind, he put his left hand on my shoulder and guided me toward the door. I felt the sacked object bump back and forth below my shoulder blade.

"Unlock it," he said.

I found the key on my ring and snapped open the long U-shaped shaft on the lock. I wiped the sweat out of my eyes with the back of my wrist.

"Come on, get inside, man," he said.

"I want to give you something to think about when you leave me."

"You're gonna give me something to think about? I think you've got it turned around." He started to push me inside.

"No, I don't. I didn't see your face, so I can't identify you. That means you're home free on this one. But I know who you are, Jack. Don't go near my house. God help you if you get anywhere near my house."

"You don't know who your friends are. Hey, the man in New Orleans sent you a present. You'll like it. He's not a bad guy. He's got his own problems. How'd you like to have boils all over the lining of your stomach? Why don't you have a little compassion?"

With his knuckles he shoved me into the storage room, then snapped the lock shut. I heard him go out the front door, then moments later a car engine start out on the road.

I braced my back against a stack of beer cases and kicked as hard as I could against the door; but it was sheathed in tin, and the lock and hasp were solid. Then in the dark I tripped over an old twenty-five-horsepower Evinrude engine. I balanced it over my head by the shaft and the housing and hurled it against the slat wall next to the door. Two slats burst from the studs, and I splintered the others loose until I could squeeze through a hole back into the shop. I could hear the diminishing sound of Gates's car on the dirt road that led to the drawbridge over the bayou. I pulled the chain on the light bulb over the counter and started punching the office number on the phone. Both my hands were shaking.

"Sheriff's Department—"

"This is Dave. . . . Jack Gates just tore out of my bait shop. . . . He's armed and dangerous. . . . Call the bridge tender and tell him to lift the bridge. . . . I'll meet you guys at the—"

Then I stopped.

"What is it, Dave?"

I looked at the weighted clear plastic bag hanging from a nail on a post in the center of my shop.

"I'll meet you guys at the bayou," I said.

"What's wrong, Dave? Are you hurt?"

"No, I'm all right. Get hold of the bridge tender and seal the whole area off. Don't let this guy get out of town."

I put the receiver back in the cradle and stared numbly at the severed head inside the plastic bag. The eyes were rolled, the tongue lolled out of the mouth, the nose was mashed against the folds of plastic, and the blond hair was matted with congealed blood; but even in death the face looked like it belonged on a toy man. And to preclude the possibility that I could ever mistake Jewel Fluck for someone else, one of his fingers had been inserted in the thick, purple residue at the bottom of the bag.

I ran to the house, through the front door and into the bedroom, and grabbed the .45 out of the dresser drawer. Bootsie sat up in bed and clicked on the table lamp.

"What is it?" she said.

"Jack Gates was in the shop. I'm going after him. Don't go in the shop, Boots. Call Batist and tell him not to come to work right now."

"What is it? What did he—"

"We might have to dust for prints. Let's just keep people out of there for a while."

I saw her eyes trying to read my expression.

"Everything's all right," I said. "Just don't go out of the house, Boots, till we get this guy in custody."

Then I was out the front door and in the truck, banging over the chuckholes in the dirt road that led to the drawbridge over the bayou, the .45 bouncing on the seat beside me, the early red sun edging the marsh with fire.

I could hear sirens in the distance now. I rounded a corner in second, where the bayou made a wide bend, and through the oak trees which lined the road I could see the drawbridge extended high in the air, a quarter of a mile away.

Jack, I think you're about to be hung out to dry, I thought, and this time Joey the Neck is going down with you. Welcome to Iberia Parish, podjo.

Vanity, vanity, vanity. Jack Gates was an old-time Mafia soldier and thriving button man in a state whose system of capital punishment involved as much charity as you would expect in the deep-frying of pork rinds. Jack was not one you would simply drive into a bottleneck and cork inside the glass and put on display like a light bug.

I heard his car before I saw it the transmission wound up full-bore, the engine roaring through a defective muffler like a garbage truck, gravel exploding like grapeshot under the fenders. Then the TransAm skidded around the corner in a cloud of yellow dust, low on the springs, streaked and ugly with dried mud, ripping a green gash out of a canebrake.

I looked full into his face through his windshield—into his regret that he didn't take me out when he had the chance, his rage at the cosmic conspiracy that had made him the long-suffering soldier of an ulcer-ridden paranoid like Joey Gee.

I pulled the truck diagonally across the road, leaped from the seat, and aimed the .45 across the hood, straight at Jack Gates's face. He stomped on the brakes, and the TransAm bucked sideways in a chuckhole and fishtailed against the trunk of an oak tree, pinwheeling a hubcap down the center of the road. He stared at me momentarily through the open passenger's window, a blue revolver balanced in one hand on top of the steering wheel, his metal-capped teeth glinting in the sun's hot early light, the engine throttling open and subsiding and then throttling open again under the hood.

"Give it up, Jack," I said. "Gouza's a psychotic sack of shit. Let him take his own fall for a change."

The rooster tail of dust from behind the car drifted across his window, and in the second it took for me to lose eye contact with him, he aimed the revolver quickly out the window and popped off two rounds. The first one was low and kicked up dirt three feet in front of the truck, but the second one whanged off the hood and showered leaves out of the tree behind me.

Then he dropped the transmission into reverse and floored the TransAm back down the road, the tires burning into the dirt, spinning with circles of black smoke. He veered from side to side, clipping bark out of the tree trunks, bursting a tail light, ripping loose his bumper. But evidently he had an eye for detail and had remembered passing a collapsed wire gate and a faint trace of a side road that led through a sugarcane field, because he slammed on his brakes, slid in a half circle, then roared over the downed gate—cedar posts, barbed wire, and all.

I ran up the incline by the far side of the road, through a stand of pine trees, splashed across a coulee, and came out on the edge of the field just as the TransAm spun around the corner, rippled back a fender on a parked tractor, and mowed through the short cane toward a flat-topped levee that led back to the main parish road.

He hadn't expected to see me on foot in the field. He started to cut the steering wheel toward me, to drive me back into the trees or the coulee, then he changed his mind, spinning the wheel in the opposite direction with one hand and firing blindly out the window with the other. In the instant that the TransAm flashed by me, his face looked white and round and small through the window, like a spectator's in a theater, as though he had suddenly become aware that he was witnessing his own dénouement.

I went to one knee in the wet grass and began firing. I tried to keep the sights below the level of his window jamb to allow for the elevation caused by the recoil, but in reality it was unnecessary. The eight hollow-point rounds, which flattened to the size of quarters with impact, destroyed his automobile. They pocked silvery holes in the doors, spiderwebbed the windows, blew divots of upholstery into the air, exploded a tire off the rim, gashed a geyser of steam out of the radiator, and whipped a single streak of blood across the front windshield.

His foot must have locked down on the accelerator, because the TransAm was almost airborne when it roared along the lip of an irrigation ditch and sliced through the fence surrounding a Gulf States Power Company substation. The front end crashed right into the transformers, and the tiers of transmission wires and ceramic insulators crumpled in a crackling net on the car's roof.

But he was still alive. He let the revolver drop outside the window, then started to push open the door with the palms of his hands like a man trying to extricate himself from the rubble of a collapsed building.

"Don't get out, Jack! Don't touch the ground!"

He sat back down on the seat, his face bloodless and exhausted, then the sole of one shoe came to rest on the damp earth.

The voltage contorted his face as if he were having an epileptic seizure. His body stiffened, shook, and jerked; spittle flew from his mouth; electricity seemed to leap and dance off his capped teeth. Then his car horn and radio began blaring simultaneously, and a scorched odor, like hair and feces burning in an incinerator, rose from his clothes and head in dirty strings of smoke.

I turned and walked back to the road. The grass was wet against my trouser legs and swarming with insects, the sun hot and yellow above the treeline in the marsh. The drawbridge was down now, and ambulances, firetrucks, and sheriff's cars were careening toward me, emergency lights blazing, under the long canopy of oaks. My saliva tasted like copper pennies; my right ear was a block of wood. The .45, the receiver locked open on the empty clip, felt like a silly appendage hanging from my hand.

Paramedics, cops, and firemen were rushing past me now. I kept walking down the road, by the bayou's edge, toward my house. Bream were feeding close into the lily pads, denting the water in circles like raindrops. The cypress roots along the far bank were gnarled and wet among the shadows and ferns, and I could see the delicate prints of egrets in the damp sand. I pulled the clip from the automatic, stuck it in my back pocket, and let the receiver slam back on the empty chamber. I opened and closed my mouth to clear my right ear, but it felt like it was full of warm water that would not drain.

The sheriff came up behind me and gently put his hand inside my arm.

"When they deal the hand, we shut down their game," he said. "If it comes out any different, we did something wrong. You know where I learned that?"

"It sounds familiar."

"It should."

"We could have used Gates to get Joey Gee."

"Yeah, so we'll catch up with Fluck and use *him*. Six of one, half dozen of the other."

I nodded silently.

"Right?" he said.

"Sure."

"It's just a matter of time."

"Yeah, that's all it is," I agreed, and looked away into the distance, where I could almost feel the sun's heat cooking the tin roof on the bait shop.

15

I locked up the bait shop and let no one in it for the rest of the day. I thought about the events of that morning for a long time. Things had worked out for Joey Gouza in better ways than he could have ever planned. I had been responsible for springing him on the phony assault-and-battery charges filed by Drew Sonnier; Weldon's long-sought-after film evidence had turned out to be worthless; Eddy Raintree, a superstitious dimwit as well as pervert, who would have probably ratted out Joey Gee for an extra roll of toilet paper in his cell, had had his face blown into a bloody mist by Jewel Fluck while he was locked in my handcuffs; then Gates had gotten to Fluck, and I in turn had killed Gates, the only surviving person who could implicate Joey in the Garrett murder.

I wondered if Joey Gee got up in the morning and said a prayer of thanks that I had wandered into his life.

In the meantime one of his hired sociopaths had terrified my daughter, then he had ordered his chief button man to deliver a human head and severed finger to our family business.

I suspected that today had proved special for Joey, a day in which he took an extra pleasure in chopping up lines with his whores, sipping iced rum drinks with them by the pool, or maybe inviting them out to the clubhouse at the track for lobster-steak dinners and rolls of six-dollar parimutuel tickets. I suspected at this moment that Joey Gee did not have a care in the world.

After I wrote up my report at the office, I went back home and sat in the shade on the dock by myself, staring at the sun's hot yellow reflection on the bayou, the dragonflies that seemed to hang motionless over the cattails and lily pads. Even in the shade I was sweating heavily inside my clothes. Then I unlocked the bait shop and used the phone inside to call Clete Purcel. The heat was stifling, and the plastic bag that hung from the post in the center of the room had clouded with moisture.

When I had finished talking with Clete, the damp outline of my hand looked like it had been painted on the phone receiver.

I worked in the yard the rest of the afternoon, and when it rained at four o'clock, I sat on the gallery by myself and watched the water drip out of the pecan trees and *tick* in the dead leaves and *ping* on top of Tripod's cage. Then at sunset I went back into the bait shop with a hat box, and five minutes later I was on my way to New Orleans.

▼

"**Y**ou look tired," Bootsie said at the breakfast table the next morning.

"Oh, I'm just a little slow this morning," I said.

"What time did you come in last night?"

"I really didn't notice."

"How's Clete?"

"About the same."

"Dave, what are you two doing?"

I kept my eyes on Alafair, who was packing her lunch kit for a church group picnic.

"Be sure to put a piece of cake in there, Alf," I said.

She turned around and grinned.

"I already did," she said.

"Do you want to talk about it later?" Bootsie said.

"Yeah, that's a good idea."

Ten minutes later Alafair raced out the screen door to catch the church bus. Bootsie watched her leave, then came back into the kitchen.

"I just saw Batist carrying some lumber into the shop. What's he doing?" she asked.

"A few repairs."

"Did that man Gates do something in our shop? Is that why you wouldn't let anybody in it yesterday?"

"It just wasn't a day for business-as-usual."

"What's Clete's involvement with this?"

"It was Gouza's goons who put him in the hospital. That makes him involved, Boots."

She took the dishes off the table and put them in the sink. She gazed out the window into the backyard.

"When you go to see Clete, it always means a shortcut," she said.

"You don't know everything that's happened."

"I'm not the problem, Dave. What bothers me is I think you're hiding something from the people you work with."

"Joey Gouza ordered this man Gates to throw Gouza's brother-in-law into an airplane propeller. Then he sent this same man to our house with a—"

"What?"

I caught my breath and pinched my temples with my fingers.

"Gouza has a furnace instead of a brain," I said. "He's left his mark on our home, and I can't touch him. Do you think I'm going to abide that?"

She rinsed the plates in the sink and continued to look out the window.

"Two of the men who murdered the deputy are dead," she said. "One day it'll be Joey Gouza's turn. Can't you just let events take their course? Or let other people handle things for a while?"

"There's another factor, Boots. Gouza's a paranoid. Maybe today he feels wonderful, he's hit the daily double, the dragons are dead. But next week, or maybe next month, he'll start thinking again about the individuals who've hurt or humiliated him most, and he'll be back in our lives. I'm not going to let that happen."

She dried her hands on a dish towel, then used it to mop off the counter. She brushed back her hair with her fingers, straightened the periwinkles in a vase. Her eyes never looked at mine. She turned on the radio on the windowsill, then turned it off and took a pair of scissors out of a drawer.

"I'm going to cut some fresh flowers. Are you going to the office now?" she said.

"Yes, I guess so."

"I'll put your lunch in the icebox. I have to run some errands in town today."

"Boots, listen a minute—"

She popped open a paper bag to place the cut flowers in and went out the back door.

▼

That afternoon the sheriff came into my office with my report on Gates's shooting in his hands. He sat down in the chair across from me and put on his rimless glasses.

"I'm still trying to puzzle a couple of things out here, Dave. It's like there's a blank space or two in your report," he said.

"How's that?"

"I'm not criticizing it. You were pretty used up when you wrote this stuff down. But let me see if I understand everything here. You went down a little early to open up your bait shop?"

"That's right."

"That's when you saw Gates?"

"That's correct."

"You called the dispatcher, then you went after him in your truck?"

"Yeah, that's about it."

"So it was already first light when you saw him?"

"It was getting there."

"It had to be, because the sun was up when you nailed him."

"I'm not following you, sheriff."

"Maybe it's just me. But why would a pro like Gates come around your house at sunrise when he could have laid for you at night?"

"Who knows?"

"Unless he didn't mean to hurt you, unless he was there for some other reason—"

"Like Clete once told me, trying to figure out the greaseballs is like putting your hand in an unflushed toilet."

He looked down at the report again, then folded his glasses and put them in his shirt pocket.

"There's something that really disturbs me about this, Dave. I know there's an answer, but I can't seem to put my hand on it."

"Sometimes it's better not to think about things too much. Just let events unfold." I placed my hands behind my neck, yawned, and tried to look casually out the window.

"No, what I mean is, Gouza just got off the hook in Iberia Parish. Is this guy crazy enough to send a hit man after another one of our people, right to his house, right at the break of day? It doesn't fit, does it?"

"I wish Gates were here to tell us. I don't know what else to say, sheriff."

"Well, I'm just glad you didn't get hurt out there. I'll see you later. Maybe you ought to go home and get some sleep. You look like you haven't slept since World War II."

He went out the door. I tried to complete the paperwork that was on my desk, but my eyes burned and I couldn't concentrate or keep my thoughts straight in my head. Finally I shoved it all into a bottom drawer and fiddled absently with a chain of paper clips on top of my desk blotter.

Had I lied to the sheriff, I asked myself? Not exactly. But then I hadn't quite told the truth, either.

Was my report dishonest? No, it was worse. It concealed the commission of a homicide.

But some situations involve a trade-off. In this case the fulfillment of a professional obligation would require that my home and family become the center of a morbid story that would live in the community for decades, and Joey Gouza would succeed in inflicting a level of psychological damage on my daughter, in particular, that might never be undone. Saint Augustine once admonished that we should never use the truth to injure. I believe there are dark and uncertain moments in our lives when it's not wrong for each of us to feel that he wrote those words especially for us.

▼

I left the office and drove home on the oak-lined dirt road that followed the bayou past my dock. The first raindrops were starting to fall out of a sunny sky, as they did almost every summer afternoon at three o'clock, and I could feel the air becoming close, suddenly cooler, as the barometric pressure dropped, and the bream and goggle-eye perch started feeding on the bayou's surface by the edge of the lily pads. I passed the collapsed wire gate that Jack Gates had shredded when he had pointed the TransAm into the sugarcane field, and I avoided looking at the trashed substation and the bullet-pocked car that a wrecker had winched loose from the transformers and left upside down amid a litter of broken cane stalks. But I wasn't going to brood upon the death of Jack Gates; I had already turned over yesterday to my Higher Power, and I was determined not to relive it. My problems with Bootsie as well as the sheriff were sufficient to keep my mind occupied today. And if that was not enough, a man ahead of me in a pickup truck was stapling Bobby Earl posters on the tree trunks along the road.

By the time I turned in to my drive, he had just smoothed one to the contours of a two-hundred-year-old live oak at the edge of my yard and hammered staples into each of the corners. I closed the truck door and walked over to him, my hands in my back pockets. I even tried to smile. He looked like an innocuous individual hired out of a labor office.

"Say, podna, that tree's on my property and I don't want any nail holes in it."

A foot above my head was Bobby Earl's chiseled face, with stage lights shining up into it so that his features had the messianic cast of a Billy Graham. Below was his most oft-quoted statement, LET ME

BE YOUR VOICE, LET ME SPEAK YOUR THOUGHTS. Then farther down was some information about a rally and barbecue with Dixieland bands on Friday night in Baton Rouge.

"Sorry," the man with the hammer and staples said. "The guy just said to stick 'em up on all the trees."

"Which guy?"

"The guy who give me the signs."

"Well, just don't nail any more up till you get around that next corner, okay?"

"Sure."

I tried to free the staples from the bark, then I simply tore the poster down the middle, handed it to him, and walked up to the house.

Bootsie was in town and Alafair had not gotten home from her picnic yet. I undressed in the bedroom, turned on the window fan, lay down on top of the sheets with the pillow over my head, and tried to sleep. I could hear the rain hitting the trees in large, flat drops now and *tink*ing on the blades of the fan.

But I couldn't sleep, and I kept trying to sort through my thoughts in the same way that you pick at a scab you know you should leave alone.

No matter how educated a southerner is, or how liberal or intellectual he might consider himself to be, I don't believe you will meet many of my generation who do not still revere, although perhaps in a secret way, all the old southern myths that we've supposedly put aside as members of the New South. You cannot grow up in a place where the tractor's plow can crack minié balls and grapeshot loose from the soil, even rake across a cannon wheel, and remain impervious to the past.

As a child I had access to few books, but I knew all the stories about General Banks's invasion of southwestern Louisiana, the burning of the parish courthouse, the stabling of horses in the Episcopalian church on Main Street, the union gunboats that came up the Teche and shelled the plantation on Nelson's Canal west of town, and Louisiana's boys in butternut brown who lived on dried peas and gave up ground a bloody foot at a time.

Who cared if their cause was just or not? The stories made your blood sing; the grooved minié ball that you picked out of the freshly plowed row and rolled in your palm made you part of a moment that happened over a century ago. You looked away at the stand of trees by the bayou, and rather than the tractor engine idling beside you, you heard the ragged popping of small-arms fire and saw black plumes of smoke exploding out of the brush into the sunlight. And you realized that they died right here in this field, that they bled into this same dirt where the cane would grow eight feet tall by autumn and turn as scarlet as dried blood.

But why did large numbers of people buy into a man like Bobby Earl? Were they that easily deceived? Would any group of reasonable people entrust the conduct of their government to an ex-American Nazi or Ku Klux Klansman? I had no answer.

I wondered if any of them ever asked themselves what Robert Lee or Thomas Jackson might have to say about a man like this.

I finally fell asleep. Then I heard the brakes on the church bus and a moment later the screen door slam. Other sounds followed: a lunch kit clattering on the drainboard, the icebox door opening, the back screen slamming, Tripod racing up and down on the chain that was attached to the clothesline, the screen slamming again, tennis shoes in the hallway outside the bedroom door, then a pause full of portent.

Alafair hit the bed running and bounced up and down on her knees, lost her balance, and fell across my back. I raised my head up from under the pillow.

"Hi, big guy. What you doing home early?" she said.

"Taking a nap."

"Oh." She started bouncing again, then looked at my face. "Maybe you should go back to sleep?"

"Why would I want to do that, Alf?"

"Are you mad about something?"

I put on my trousers, then sat back down on the side of the bed and tried to rub the sleep out of my face.

"Hop up on my back," I said. "Let's check out what Batist is doing. It's not a day for lying around in bed."

She put her arms around my neck and clamped her legs around my ribcage, and we walked down through the wet leaves to the dock. It was raining lightly out of a gray sky now, the lily pads were bright green and beaded with water, and the bayou was covered with rain rings.

Batist had slid the canvas awning out on wires over the dock, and several fishermen sat under it, drinking beer and eating *boudin* out of wax paper. He had also allowed someone to put Bobby Earl posters in the bait-shop windows and on the service counter.

I let Alafair climb down off my back. Batist was taking some *boudin* out of the microwave. He wore canvas boat shoes without socks, a pair of ragged, white cutoffs whose top button had popped off, and a wash-faded denim shirt tied under his chest, which reminded me of black boilerplate. His shirt pocket was bursting with cigars.

"Batist, who put these posters here?"

"Some white man who come ax if he could leave them."

"Next time send the man up to the house."

"You was sleepin', you." He put a dry cigar in his mouth and began slicing the *boudin* on a paper plate and inserting matchsticks into each slice. "Why you worried about them signs, Dave? People leave them here all the time."

"Because they're for Bobby Earl, and Bobby Earl's a shit!" Alafair said.

I looked down at her, stunned.

"Put the cork in that language, Alf," I said.

"I heard Bootsie say it," she answered. "He's a shit. He hates black people."

Two men at the beer cooler were grinning at me.

"Dave, that's right. Them is for that fella Earl?" Batist said.

"Yeah, but you didn't know, Batist," I said. "Here, I'll throw them in the trash."

"I ain't never seen him on TV, me, so I didn't pay his picture no mind."

"It's all right, podna."

The men at the cooler were still grinning in our direction.

"Do you gentlemen need something?" I said.

"Not a thing," one of them said.

"Good," I said.

I took Alafair by the hand, and we walked back up the slope to the gallery. The wind was cool blowing out of the marsh and smelled of wet leaves and moldy pecan husks and the purple four-o'clocks that were just opening in the shadows. Alafair's hand felt hot and small in mine.

"You mad, Dave?" she said.

"No, I'm real proud of you, little guy. You're what real soldiers are made of."

Her eyes squinted almost completely shut with her smile.

▼

That evening Alafair went to a baseball game with the neighbors' children, and Bootsie and I were left alone with each other. It had stopped raining, and the windows were open and you could hear the crickets and the cicadas from horizon to horizon. Our conversation, when it occurred, was spiritless and morose. At nine o'clock the phone rang in the kitchen.

"Hello," I said.

"Hey, Streak, I thought I'd pass on some information in case you're wondering about life down here in the Big Sleazy."

"Just a minute, Clete," I said.

I took the telephone on its extension wire out on the back steps and sat down.

"Go ahead," I said.

"I found the perfect moment to drop the dime on our man. His dork just went into the electric socket big time."

In the background I could hear people talking loudly and dishes clattering.

"Where are you?"

"I'm scarfing down a few on the half shell and chugging down a few brews at the Acme, noble mon. There's also a French lady at my table who's fascinated with my accent. I told her it's Irish-coonass. She also says I'm a sensitive and entertaining conversationalist. She's talking about painting me in the nude. . . . Hey, trust me, Dave, everything's copacetic. It'll never go down in a manual on police procedure, but when it's time to mash on their scrots, you do it with hobnailed boots. Hang loose, partner, and come on down this weekend and let's catch some green trout."

I replaced the receiver in the phone cradle and went back inside the house. Bootsie had just put away some dishes in the cabinet and was watching me.

"That was Clete, wasn't it?" she said. She wore a sundress printed with purple and green flowers. She had just brushed her hair, and it was full of small lights.

"Yep."

"What have you two done, Dave?"

I sat down at the breakfast table and looked at the tops of my hands. I thought about telling her all of it.

"Back at the First District, we used to call it 'salting the mine shaft.' "

"What?"

"The wiseguys have expensive lawyers. Sometimes cops fix it so two and two add up to five."

"What did you do?"

I cleared my throat and thought about continuing, then I made my mind go empty.

"Let's talk about something else, Boots."

I gazed out the back screen at the fireflies lighting in the trees. I could feel her eyes looking at me. Then she walked out of the kitchen and began sorting canned goods in the hallway pantry. I thought about driving into town and reading the newspaper at the bar in Tee Neg's poolroom. In my mind I already saw myself under the wood-bladed fan and smelled the talcum, the green sawdust on the floor, the flat beer, and the residue of ice and whiskey poured into the tin sinks.

But Tee Neg's was not a good place for me to be when I was tired and the bottles behind the bar became as seductive and inviting as a woman's smile.

I heard Bootsie stop stacking the canned goods and shut the pantry door. She walked up behind my chair and paused for a moment, then rested her hand lightly on the back of the chair.

"It was for me and Alafair, wasn't it?" she said.

"What?"

"Whatever you did last night in New Orleans, it wasn't for yourself. It was for me and Alafair, wasn't it?"

I put my arm behind her thigh and drew her hand down on my chest. She pressed her cheek against my hair and hugged me against her breasts.

"Dave, we have such a wonderful family," she said. "Let's try to trust each other a little more."

I started to say something, but whatever it was, it was better forgotten. I could hear her heart beating against my ear. The sun-freckled tops of her breasts were hot, and her skin smelled like milk and flowers.

▼

By nine o'clock the next morning I had heard nothing of particular interest out of New Orleans. But then again the local news often featured stories of such national importance as the following: the drawbridge over the Teche had opened with three cars on it; the school-board meeting had come to an end last night with a fistfight between two high school principals; several professional wrestlers had to be escorted by city police from the National Guard armory after they were spat upon and showered with garbage by the fans; the drawbridge tender had thrown a press photographer's camera into the Teche because he didn't believe anyone had the right to photograph his bridge.

So I kept diddling with my paperwork, looking at my watch, and wondering if perhaps Clete hadn't simply spent too much time at the draft beer spout in the Acme before he had decided to telephone me.

Then, just as I was about to drive home for lunch, I got a call from Lyle Sonnier.

"Sorry to be so late getting back to you, Loot, but it was hard getting everybody together. Anyway, it's on for tomorrow night," he said.

"What's on?"

"Dinner. Actually, a crab boil. We're gonna cook up a mess of 'em in the backyard."

"Lyle, that's nice of you but—"

"Look, Dave, Drew and Weldon feel the same way I do. You treated our family decent while we sort of stuck thumbtacks in your head."

"No, you didn't."

"I know better, Loot. Anyway, can y'all make it or not?"

"Friday night we always take Batist and Alafair to the drive-in movie in Lafayette."

"Bring them along."

"I don't know if your father is anxious to see me again."

"Come on, Dave, he operates on about three brain cells, poor old guy. Have a little compassion."

"That's the second time this week somebody has said that to me about the wrong person."

"What?"

"Never mind. I'll ask Boots and Batist and get back to you. Thanks for the invitation, Lyle."

I drove home, and Bootsie and I fixed a pitcher of iced tea and poor-boy sandwiches of shrimp and fried oysters and took them out on the redwood picnic table under the mimosa tree.

"You sure you don't mind going?" I said.

"No. Why should I mind?"

"Their father may be there. He's terribly disfigured, Boots."

She smiled. The wind in the mimosa tree made drifting, lacy patterns of shadow on her skin.

"What you mean is, Drew will be there," she said.

"Well, she will be."

"I think I can survive the knowledge of your college romances, Dave." Her brown eyes crinkled at the corners.

I was late getting back to the department. When I walked through my office door the sheriff was sitting in my chair, one of his half-topped boots propped on the corner of my desk. A videotape cassette rested on his belt buckle. He looked at his watch, then his eyes glanced at my damp hair and shirt.

"You look like you just got out of the shower," he said.

"I did."

"You go home to take a shower in the middle of the day?"

"I had to change a tire."

"I'll be," he said, clicking his nails on the plastic cassette case. "What's up, sheriff?"

"An FBI agent dropped this tape by about an hour ago. It was shot last night in front of a home that's under surveillance out by Lake Pontchartrain. The home is owned by one of the Giacanos, the head greaseballs in New Orleans."

"Yeah?"

"They had a big party there last night. The Vitalis crowd from three states was milling around on the lawn, including Joey the Neck and a couple of his whores. Did you know that he makes his whores carry validated health certificates because he's terrified of catching AIDS from them? That's what this FBI agent said."

"I didn't know that."

"Anyway, this FBI agent knew we had a vested interest in Joey's career, and that's why he dropped off this tape." The sheriff removed his foot from my desk and swiveled the chair around to face me. "So I watched the tape. It's quite a show. You don't want to get up and go for popcorn on this one. And while I was watching it, I kept remembering something you said to me the other day."

He sucked on his bottom lip and stared into my face, his rimless glasses low on his nose.

"Okay, I'll bite, sheriff. What did I say to you?"

"You mentioned something about letting events unfold. So when I finished watching the tape, I got to thinking. Is Dave omniscient? Does he have insight into the future that none of the rest of us have? Or does he know about things that I don't?"

"I'm not good at being a straight man, sheriff. You want to cut to it?"

"Let's take a walk down to my office and stick this in the VCR. These guys do quite a job. It's even got sound. I sure wish we had their equipment."

As we went down the hallway I kept looking into the faces of other people. But there was nothing unusual in their expressions that I could see.

"I think there should be some screen credits on this," he said, clicking on his television set and fitting the cassette into the VCR.

"Maybe something like 'Directed by Cletus Purcel and Unnamed Friend.' "

"What about Purcel?"

He sucked in his cheeks, and his eyes looked into the corners of mine.

"You don't know?"

"I'm truly lost."

"Gouza pulled up to the house and parked. A couple of minutes later Purcel cruised by. It looked like he'd been following Gouza."

"How do they know it was Purcel?"

"A fed made him. Also they ran his tag. Then about twenty minutes later NOPD gets this anonymous phone call that Joey Gouza has got a body in the trunk of his car and his car can be found at this address out on the lake. That's where our film starts, Dave. Sit down and watch, then tell me what you think."

The sheriff closed the blinds, sat on the corner of his desk, and activated the VCR with a remote control in his palm. In the first black-and-white frames the screen showed an enormous Tudor house with lines of Cadillacs, Lincolns, Mercedes, and Porsches parked in the circular driveway and at the curbs. The oak trees in the sideyard were strung with Japanese lanterns, and through the piked fence and myrtle bushes you could see perhaps a hundred people milling around the food and drink tables.

Then a solitary city patrol car cruised down the street, its emergency lights off, slowed, and stopped. The driver got out with a clipboard and flashlight and walked up and down the line of cars at the curb, shining his light on the tags. He paused by a white Cadillac limo with black-tinted windows just as a dog unit pulled into the camera lens from the opposite end of the block.

The action was very quick after that. A uniformed cop, with a German shepherd straining at its leash, approached the back of the limo. Then the dog took one sniff and went crazy, leaping against its leash, clacking its nails on the bumper and trunk.

One of the cops used his radio, and moments later city police cars, with emergency lights flashing, poured into the block. They parked sideways in the street and blocked both driveway entrances; then uniformed cops swarmed across lawns and through hedges, shined their flashlights into cars, wrote down the numbers on every license tag in the neighborhood, arrived with more leashed dogs, and turned a quiet residential lakefront street into a carnival.

Two plainclothes detectives walked up to the rear of the limo and inserted a crowbar in the jamb of the trunk. By now the guests at the lawn party had started drifting out toward the curb, led by Joey Gouza and, behind him, a bald-headed barrel of a man in a white sports coat with a carnation, dark trousers, and white shoes.

"How you enjoying it so far?" the sheriff said.

"It's great stuff."

He paused the VCR.

"You recognize the guy in the sports coat?" he said.

"No."

"That's Dominic the Pipe Gabelli. He got his name from bashing a fellow inmate in Lewisburg. He's also a member of the Chicago commission. What do you think those cops are going to find in the trunk?"

I didn't answer.

"It's not a body," he said.

"You asked me down here to watch this, sheriff. If you want to make an implication about my involvement in the events in a surveillance film, then you should go ahead and do that. But you're going to have to get somebody else to listen to it."

"That's a little strong, don't you think?"

"No, I don't."

"Well, let's see what happens."

He started the tape again and increased the volume. The two plainclothes cops leaned their weight down on the crowbar, and you could hear the tip biting into metal, peeling back the lip of the trunk from the latch, snapping bolts loose from a welded surface. Gouza tried to grab one of the plainclothes cops and was shoved backward by a patrolman.

The audio wasn't the best; the voices of the crowd, the cops, the squawk of radios, the beating of helicopter blades overhead, a peal of thunder out on the lake, sounded like apples rolling around in a deep barrel. But Joey Gouza's furious, arm-waving outrage came through the television set with the painful clarity of a rupturing ulcer. "What the fuck you guys think you're doing?" he said. "You got to have a warrant to do that. You got to have probable cause. You get that fucking dog away from me. Hey, I said get him away!"

The trunk sprang open, and the faces of the two plainclothes cops blanched and snapped back as though they had been slapped. A woman in an evening dress vomited on the grass.

"Jesus Christ, I don't believe it," somebody said.

"Get a shovel or a broom or something. I ain't picking that up with my hands."

"What the fuck you guys talking about?" the man in the white sports coat said, pushing his way, along with Gouza, to get a better view of the trunk. Then he pressed his hand over his mouth and nose.

"Put in a call for the ME," one of the plainclothes cops said.

A uniformed sergeant, his hands inside a vinyl evidence bag, reached into the trunk of the car, took out Jewel Fluck's head, and laid it on the grass. Joey Gouza's face was stunned; his mouth dropped open; he stared speechless at the man in the white sports coat. He gestured emptily with both hands at the air.

"I don't know what it's doing there, Dom," he said. "It's a setup. These fuckheads are working with some pisspot cops over in Iberia Parish. I swear it, Dom. They been trying to put an iron hook through my stomach and tear my insides out."

"Shut up, Joey. You're under arrest," one of the plainclothes cops said. "Put your hands on the car and spread your legs. You know the drill. The rest of you people go back to your lasagne."

The uniformed sergeant shoved Joey face-forward against the side of the Cadillac and hit him under both arms. Joey's face went livid with rage, and he whirled and drove his elbow into the sergeant's nose.

Then NOPD went to work with the subtlety of method for which they're famous. While the sergeant tried to cup his hands over the blood that fountained from his nose, two other uniformed cops rained their batons down on Joey's back.

"We got a perp on dust," somebody yelled.

Then as though that one declaration justified any means of restraint, another cop ran from the far side of the street with a Taser gun. The cops flailing with their batons jumped back just as he fired.

But Joey had seen what was coming, too, and he drove sideways and the dart embedded in the thick, fat neck of the man in the white sports coat. He went down as though he had been bludgeoned with an ax, his body convulsing, his arms writhing in the damp grass with the electric shock.

Then a cop garroted Joey across the throat with his baton and lifted him, strangling, to his feet while two other cops cuffed his wrists behind him. The last frames in the film showed Joey being stuffed behind the wire screen of a patrol car, one foot kicking wildly at the window glass.

The sheriff put the VCR on rewind.

"The anonymous call was traced to the Acme Oyster Bar on Iberville," he said. "When the arresting plainclothes got there, they ran into none other than Cletus Purcel, bombed on boilermakers with seven dozen empty oyster shells piled on his table. The plainclothes don't think it's coincidence that Purcel was sitting in the Acme."

"But they didn't take him in, did they?"

"No."

"They won't, either."

"Why not?"

"Because they don't care, sheriff. Gouza won't go down on a murder beef, but they'll put him away for resisting arrest and assault and battery on a police officer. The court considers him a habitual. That means this time he goes into lockdown with the big stripes at Angola and they weld the door shut on him. Why should they worry about Clete?"

"You misunderstand me, Dave. I don't care about Purcel. I'm bothered by the possibility that one of my men shaved the dice. You know that was Jewel Fluck's head, don't you?"

"Maybe."

"You want to tell me what really happened with you and Jack Gates?"

I rubbed my palms together between my legs. The sunlight outside was white and hot through the cracks in the blinds.

"The evidence was found on the right person, sheriff. There's no way around that conclusion. You have my word on it."

He picked at his thumbnail, then raised his eyes to mine.

"That's about all I'm going to get from you, huh?" he said.

"Yeah, I guess that's about it."

"Well, maybe it's time I talk to Garrett's family again over in Houston."

I studied his face and waited.

"I think you wrote your signature on this case with a baseball bat, Dave. But anyway we're closing the file on it. The three men who killed Garrett are dead. The man they worked for is in the New Orleans city prison under a two-million-dollar bond. I think the slate's wiped clean." He gave me a measured look. "For everybody, you got my drift?"

"That's for other people to decide."

"I figured you might say that. Pride can be a sonofabitch sometimes, can't it?"

He pulled up the blinds. The hot, white radiance off the cement outside and the violent green of the trees and shrubs and grass made my eyes water. As I walked out of the office, I heard him pull the cassette from the VCR and drop it carelessly into a metal file drawer, then slam the drawer shut.

16

I took a vacation day from work the next day. Alafair and I packed a lunch, iced down some soft drinks, paddled a pirogue deep into the green light of the marsh, and fished with red worms and spinners for bluegill and goggle-eye. The morning air was moist and cool among the flooded trees, and in the shadows and mist rising off the water you could hear big-mouth bass flopping on the edge of the lily pads, hear a heron lift and flap his wings as he flew down a canal through a long corridor of trees and disappeared like a black cipher in a cone of sunlight at the end.

But as I pulled the paddle through dark water, heard it knock against a wet cypress knee, watched the earnestness in Alafair's face as she cast her baited spinner next to the water lilies and slowly retrieved it through a nest of bream, I knew that something else was taking hold of me, too. Age had finally taught me that there was a time to go with the season, to let go of the world's seriousness, to leave the terrible obligation of defining both yourself and the world to others.

Yesterday at the dock I had told Batist that Lyle Sonnier had invited him to the crab boil in Baton Rouge.

"What for he ax a black man?" he said.

"Because he likes you, because he'd like us *all* to come over."

He cocked one eye at me.

"You sure he want me there, Dave?"

"Yeah, or I wouldn't ask you, Batist."

He looked at me and reflected a moment.

"All right, that sounds nice. I'd like to go wit' y'all," he said.

Then, when I turned to go back up to the house, he added, "Dave, why *you* want to go? I had the feeling for a while you might want to put all them Sonniers in a tote sack with some bricks and t'row it in the bayou."

I smiled at his joke and didn't reply.

Did I indeed still feel guilt for letting Lyle go down a VC tunnel when we could have blown it and passed it by? Or did I feel obligated to Drew because of our young impetuosity in the back seat of my convertible on a summer night years ago? Was I so self-destructively flawed that I had taken on Weldon's problems only because I saw myself mirrored in him?

No, that wasn't it.

A therapist once told me that we're born alone and we die alone. It's not true.

We all have an extended family, people whom we recognize as our own as soon as we see them. The people closest to me have always been marked by a peculiar difference in their makeup. They're the walking wounded, the ones to whom a psychological injury was done that they will never be able to define, the ones with the messianic glaze in their eyes, or the oblique glance, as though an M-1 tank is about to burst through their mental fortifications. They drive their convertibles into automatic carwashes with the tops down, cause psychiatrists and priests to sigh helplessly, leave IRS auditors speechless, turn town meetings into free-fire zones, and even frighten themselves when they wake up in the middle of the night and think they've left the light on, and then realize that perhaps their heads simply glow in the dark.

But they save us from ourselves. Whenever I hear and see a politician or a military leader, a bank of American flags at his back, trying to convince us of the rightness of a policy or a deed that will cause harm to others; when I am almost convinced myself that setting humanitarian concern in abeyance can be justified in the interest of a greater good, I pause and ask myself what my brain-smoked friends would have to say. Then I realize that the rhetoric would have no effect on them, because for those who were most deeply injured as children, words of moral purpose too often masked acts of cruelty.

So that's when you let go of reason and slip deep into the wobbling, refracted green light of a marsh, with a child as your guide, and let the season have its way with your heart.

▼

Alafair decided to go to a movie with the neighbor's children that evening and spend the night at their house. So Bootsie fixed her an early supper, and just as the heat began to go out of the day, Bootsie, Batist, and I got in her car and, in the lengthening shadows, took the back road along the Teche, through St. Martinville, to the interstate and Baton Rouge.

We went over the wide sweep of the Mississippi at Port Allen, looked out over the crimson-yellow wash of sunlight on the capitol building and the parks and green trees in the center of Baton Rouge, and passed the old brick warehouses on the river that had been refurbished into restaurants and shops and named Catfish Town by the Chamber of Commerce (one block away from a black neighborhood of paintless cypress shacks, with sagging galleries and dirt yards, where emancipated slaves had lived during Reconstruction). Then we turned out onto Highland, toward the LSU campus, and began to see more and more posters advertising Bobby Earl's barbecue and political rally.

I slowed the car at a congested intersection where directional signs had been nailed to telephone posts pointing to the site of the rally at a public park two blocks away. Many of the cars around us had yellow ribbons tied on their radio aerials and Bobby Earl stickers plastered on their bumpers.

I felt Bootsie's eyes on my face.

"What?" I said.

"Don't be bothered by them," she said. "It's just Louisiana. Think about the Longs."

"It's not the same thing, Boots. The Longs weren't racists. They didn't sponsor legislation that would make it a twenty-five-dollar fine to beat up flag burners."

"Well, I'm just not going to let a person like that affect me."

"Yeah, I guess that's why you told Alafair that Bobby Earl was a shit."

My window was down. So was the window of the pickup truck next to me. The man in the passenger seat, whose chewing tobacco in his jaw looked as stiff as a biscuit, glanced directly into my face.

"You got a problem, partner?" I asked.

He rolled up his window and looked directly ahead.

"Dave . . ." Bootsie said.

"All right, I'm sorry. Sometimes I'm just not sure that democracy is the right idea."

"Talk about narrow attitudes," she said.

"Hey, Dave, that man Bobby Earl ain't been all bad," Batist said from the back seat.

"What?" I said.

"*Mais* black folk wasn't votin' for a long time. Now they is. I bet you ain't t'ought about that, no."

Bootsie smiled and punched me in one of my love handles, then reached across the seat and brushed a strand of hair out of my eyes. How do you argue with that kind of company?

▼

Lyle had tried to do it right. He had strung bunting in the trees, laid out a wonderful hors d'oeuvre and salad table, hired a professional bartender, piped music out onto the patio, and hung baskets of petunias from the ironwork on the upstairs veranda. The lawn had just been mowed, and the air was heavy with the smell of freshly cut grass and the wood smoke curling around the iron caldron on the brick barbecue pit.

He wore a pair of cream-colored pleated slacks, shined brown loafers, and a Hawaiian shirt outside his belt; his hair was wet and combed back on his collar, his cheeks still glowing from a fresh shave. His smile was electric when he greeted us in the sideyard and shook hands and walked us to the patio, where Weldon, his wife Bama, Drew, and several people whom I didn't know stood around the drink table. The deference, the unrelenting smile, the nervous light in Lyle's eyes made me feel almost as though he were trying to rearrange all the elements in his life in front of a camera so he could freeze-frame the moment and correct the inadequacies of a past, a childhood, that would never be acceptable to him or finally to anyone who had had a similar one imposed upon him.

But I didn't see Vic Benson, and while we fixed paper plates of chilled shrimp and popcorn crawfish and tried to be convivial, as though we had not all been brought together by a violent event, my eyes kept wandering to the garage apartment where he lived. Clemmie, the black maid who had done time in St. Gabriel, picked up a washtub filled with live bluepoint crabs and poured them skittering into the caldron on the fire pit.

"My, that surely smells good," Bama said. Her ash-blond hair was brushed out thick on her shoulders, and she wore a yellow sundress, gold earrings, and a tiny gold cross and chain around her neck. I never saw anyone with skin so white. You could see her blue veins as though they had been painted on her with the fine point of a watercolor brush.

"I'm real glad y'all could make it," Weldon said. He had already put out a cigarette in his plate and was drinking a beer out of the bottle, his eyes, like mine, glancing sideways unconsciously at the garage apartment. "I'm glad you brought Batist, too. It looks like he's making friends with Clemmie. I hope she doesn't pull a razor on him."

"Lyle is very good to people of color," Bama said.

"Lyle's known Batist since he was knee-high to a tree frog," Weldon said.

"I was speaking of Lyle's kindness to the woman, Weldon."

"Oh."

She turned toward me. Her face was as small as a child's. Her mouth made a red button before she spoke. There was a steady, serene blue light in her eyes, and I wondered how many downers she had dropped before her first highball.

"Weldon is overly conscious about who my brother is," she said.

"Dave gets a little upset on the subject of Bobby's politics," Weldon said.

"I don't subscribe to everything my brother stands for, but I don't deny that he's my brother, either," she said.

"I see," I said.

"He has many fine qualities of which the press is not aware or which they seem to have no interest in writing about."

Weldon idly twirled a shrimp on a toothpick between his fingers.

"Actually, today is Bobby's birthday," she continued. "We have to leave a bit early and drop off his present at the rally."

"Bama—" Weldon began.

"It'll take a few minutes. You can stay in the car," she said to him.

He made a face and looked away into the shadows. A moment later Clemmie passed our table.

"Go up and ask Vic to join us, would you, Clemmie?" Lyle said.

She began clearing paper plates off the glass-topped table as though she hadn't heard him. Her breasts looked like watermelons inside her gray-and-white uniform.

"Clemmie, would you please tell Vic all our guests are here?" Lyle said.

"I got to live on the other side of the wall from that nasty old man. That don't mean I got to talk to him," she said.

Lyle's face reddened with embarrassment.

"Maybe he doesn't want to come down. Leave him alone," Weldon said.

"No, he's going to come down here and eat with us," Lyle said. "He's paid for whatever he did to us, Weldon."

"You don't even know that it's him," Weldon said.

"Do you want me to go up there?" Drew said.

Good ole Drew, I thought. Always letter-high and right down the middle. She stood by the bar, her weight resting on one foot, her thick, round arms covered with tan and freckles.

"No, I'll do it," Lyle said.

"Why do you keep stirring up the past all the time?" Weldon said. "If it's not moving, don't poke it. Why don't you learn that?"

"Have another beer, Weldon," Lyle said.

"Lyle, this is your craziness. Don't act like somebody else is responsible," Weldon said.

Lyle got up from his chair and walked across the lawn toward the garage apartment.

"Lord h'ep me Jesus," he said to no one in particular.

Later, he came back down the stairs. Then, a few minutes later, the man who called himself Vic Benson stepped out the door and walked slowly down the stairs, a shaft of late sunlight breaking across his destroyed face.

He wore a frayed white shirt that was gray with washing and creaseless shiny black trousers that were hitched tightly around his bony hips. People glanced once at his face, then focused intensely on their conversations with the people next to them. He was smoking a hand-rolled cigarette without removing it from the corner of his mouth, and the paper was wet with saliva all the way down to the glowing ash. His eyes made you think he was being entertained by a private joke. He stopped by the edge of the patio, threw his cigarette into a flower bed, and picked up an empty glass off the bar. Then he knotted up a handful of mint from a silver bowl and bruised it around the inside of the glass.

"What you having, suh?" the black bartender asked.

Vic Benson didn't reply. He simply reached over the bar, picked up a bottle of Jack Daniel's and poured four fingers straight up.

Lyle rose from his chair and stood beside him awkwardly.

"This is Vic," he said to Bama and his brother and sister.

"Glad to meet you," Vic said.

Drew's and Weldon's eyes narrowed, and I saw Drew wet her lips. Weldon stuck an unlit cigarette in his mouth, then took it out.

"I'm Weldon Sonnier. Do you know me?" he said.

"I don't know you. But I heard about you," Vic said.

"What'd you hear?" Weldon asked.

"You're a big oil man here'bouts."

"I've got a record for dusters," Weldon said.

"You only got to hit a pay sand one in eight. Ain't that right?"

"You sound like you've been around the oil business, Vic," Weldon said.

"I roughnecked some. But I ain't ever run acrost you, if that's what you're asking. I seen *her* though." He lifted a shriveled forefinger at Drew.

I saw the side of her face twitch. Then she recovered herself.

"I'm afraid I don't recall meeting you," she said.

"I didn't say you'd met me. I seen you jogging on the street. In New Iberia. You was with some other people. But a man don't forget a handsome woman."

Her eyes looked away. Bama stared down at her hands.

"Lyle says you're our old man, Vic," Weldon said.

"I ain't. But I don't argue with it. People abide the likes of me for different reasons. Mostly because they feel guilty about something. It don't matter to me. What time we eat? There's a TV show I want to watch."

"Yeah, those crabs ought to be good and red now," Lyle said.

"You cook them in slow water, they taste better," Vic said. "There's people don't like to do it 'cause of the sound they make in the pot."

He took a long drink from his whiskey, his eyes roving over us as though he had just made a profound observation.

Batist and Lyle began dipping the crabs out of the boiling water with tongs and dropping them in the empty washtub to cool. Vic filled half of a paper plate with dirty rice, walked to the fire pit ahead of everyone else, picked up two hot crabs from the tub with his bare hand, and began eating by himself on a folding chair under an oak tree.

"Is that the man you saw at your window?" Drew said to Bama.

Bama's pulse was quivering like a severed muscle in her throat.

"I'm not sure what I saw," she said. "It was quite dark. Perhaps it was a man in a mask. To be frank, I've tried to put it out of my mind. I prefer not to talk about it, Drew. I don't know why we should be talking about these things at a dinner party."

Weldon smoked a cigarette and watched Vic Benson with a whimsical look on his face.

"Weldon?" Drew said.

"What?"

"Say something."

"What do you want me to say?"

"Is it him?"

"Of course it's him. I'd recognize that old sonofabitch if you melted him into glue."

▼

Bootsie and I got in the serving line, then tried to isolate ourselves from the Sonniers' conversation. But Bama was having her troubles with it, too. She made a mess of shelling the crab on her plate, spraying her dress and face with juice when she squeezed a claw between the nutcrackers, then rushing from the table as though the deck of the *Titanic* had just tilted under her.

When she returned from the bathroom, her face was fresh and composed and her eyes were rekindled with an ethereal blue light.

"My, I didn't realize it had gotten so late," she said. "We must be running, Weldon."

"Give it a minute. Bobby's not going anywhere," he said. But he wasn't looking at her. His eyes were still on Vic Benson, who was hunkered forward on the folding chair under the oak tree, drinking another glass of whiskey as though it were Kool-Aid.

"I don't want him to think we've forgotten his birthday," she said.

"Maybe he'd like for you to forget it, Bama. Maybe that's why he has the wrinkles chemically rinsed out of his face," Weldon said.

"I think that's an unkind remark to make, Weldon," she said. But he wasn't listening to her.

"You know, the old fart did a lot of bad things to us," he said. "But there's one that always stuck in my mind." He shook his head back and forth. "He caught me whanging it when I was about thirteen, and he clipped a clothespin on my penis and made me stand out in the backyard like that for a half hour."

"Hey, ease up, Weldon," Lyle said.

"I insist that we not continue this," Bama said.

Bootsie was already excusing herself from the table, and I was looking at my watch.

"You're right, damn it," Weldon said. "Let's drive the nail in this bullshit, give Bobby his present, then come back for some serious drinking."

Weldon got up from his chair and walked toward the tree under which Vic Benson sat.

"What are you going to do?" Lyle said. Then, "Weldon?"

But he paid no attention. He was talking to Vic Benson now, his back to us, his big hands gesturing, while Benson looked up at him silently. Then Benson set his glass down and rose to his feet. Clemmie poured the water from the caldron into the fire pit, and steam billowed out of the bricks and drifted across Benson and Weldon's bodies.

We couldn't hear what Weldon said, but the puckered skin of Benson's face was pulled back from his mouth in a leer of teeth and blackened gums, and his thin shoulders were as rectangular and stiff as if they were made of wire. Then Weldon walked back to the bar, pulled a sweating bottle of Jax out of the ice bin, and cracked off the cap.

"Quit staring at me like that, Lyle," he said.

"I ain't here to judge you," Lyle said.

"What'd you *think* I was going to tell him?" Weldon said.

"You got a lot of anger. Nobody can blame you for it."

"I offered him a job," Weldon said.

"Doing what?"

"Roustabout, driving a truck, whatever he wants to do. I also told him no matter what he decides the past between him and us is quits."

"What'd he say?" Lyle asked.

Weldon blew little puffs of air out his lips.

"I already forgot it," he said. "I tell you what, though. If I were you, I'd either buy that man an airplane ticket to Iraq or put bars over his doors and windows."

After Bama and Weldon were gone, Vic Benson stared at us for a long time from under the tree, then he turned and mounted the stairs to the garage apartment. The trees were deep in shadow, and down the street, against the lavender sky and amid the flights of swallows, you could see the sun's last red light reflecting on the chrome-plated cross atop Lyle's Bible college.

We were leaving also when we heard someone start a car engine immediately below the garage apartment.

"What's he doing with Clemmie's car?" Lyle said.

We turned and saw Vic Benson backing an ancient, dented gas guzzler, with red cellophane taped over the broken taillights, out the driveway. Smoke poured from under the frame.

"Oh, boy, I got a bad feeling," Lyle said.

He headed for the garage apartment, and I followed him.

We found Clemmie in her small living room, sitting very still in a lopsided stuffed chair, her right hand balanced carefully in the palm of the other, as though any movement would put her in peril. Her rouge was streaked with tears, and her nostrils and mouth were smeared with blood and mucus. Two fingers of her right hand were as bulbous as balloons at the joints.

"What happened?" Lyle said.

"He say, 'Gimme your car keys, you nigger bitch.' I say, 'You ain't getting them. I work hard for my car. I ain't giving it to no nasty white trash to drive round in.' He hit me in the face with his belt, hard as he could. I tried to run and throw my keys out the do', but he twisted them outta my hand, broke my fingers, Rev'end Lyle, just like twigs snapping. Then he spit in my hair."

Her shoulders were shaking. You could smell smoke, perfume, and dried sweat in her clothes. Lyle wet a towel and blotted her face with it. I lifted her hand and set it gingerly on the arm of the chair. A silver ring with a yellow stone was almost buried in the flesh below one knuckle.

"We'll take you to the hospital, Clemmie, then we'll get your car back," I said. "Don't worry about Vic Benson, either. He's going to be in the Baton Rouge city jail tonight. Do you know where he was going with your car?"

"He axed where that park at," she said.

"Which park?" I said.

"The place where Mr. Weldon gonna go see Bobby Earl. He got a pistol, Rev'end Lyle. He gone back in his room and come out with it, a little shiny pistol ain't no bigger than yo' hand. He say, 'You go down there and tell them people 'bout this I'll be back and cut off yo' nose.' That's what he say to me."

Lyle stroked her hair and patted her shoulders. I told Lyle to take her to the hospital, and I used the phone to call the Baton Rouge police department.

Outside, I asked Bootsie to wait for me, then I headed for the car. I didn't expect Batist to follow me.

But he did. And in so doing turned the two of us into a historical footnote.

I tried to dissuade him, too, as he stood with his huge hand on the door handle, about to get in the passenger's seat.

"It's just not a good idea," I said.

"You t'ink I scared, Dave? That's what you t'ink after all these years?"

His flower-print tie was knotted wrong; the top button of his white short-sleeved shirt had popped off; his seersucker slacks were stretched as tight as cheesecloth on his muscular thighs and buttocks. I don't think I ever loved a man more.

"Batist, there's some low-rent white people there," I said.

"There's places I still cain't go, huh? That's what you tellin' me, Dave, and I don't like to hear that, me."

"I'm asking you to stay with Bootsie, Batist."

"I ain't stayin' here no mo'. You don't want me wit' you, I'll walk back down to Catfish Town. Y'all can pick me up on your way back home."

I looked at the injury in his face, and I remembered my father admonishing me never to treat a brave man as anything other than a fire walker, and I wondered if I was guilty of that old southern white conceit that we must protect people of color from themselves.

"Well, I think the city cops will probably grab the old man before he does any more harm. But let's check it out, partner," I said. "It's really just the roller-derby crowd with a political agenda."

"What?"

"Never mind."

We drove back down Highland, through the LSU campus, to the park where Bobby Earl's constituency had come out in force. Amid the pin oaks, the pine and chinaberry trees, against the backdrop of tennis courts and a dusty softball diamond and picnic tables, it looked like a festive and innocent celebration of the coming of summer. A Dixieland band thundered under a pavilion; black cooks in white uniforms turned flank steaks on a huge portable barbecue pit that had been towed in on a truck; the back of the speaker's platform was lined with a thick row of American flags, and under trees that were strung with red, white, and blue bunting children raced breathlessly across the pine needles and queued up for free lemonade and ice cream.

Who were the parents? I asked myself. Their cars came from Bogalusa, Denham Springs, Plaquemine, Bunkie, Port Allen, Vidalia, and mosquito-infested dirt-road communities out in the Atchafalaya basin. But these were not ordinary small-town blue-collar people. This was the permanent underclass, the ones who tried to hold on daily to their shrinking bit of redneck geography with a pickup truck and gun rack and Jones on the jukebox and a cold Coors in the hand.

They were never sure of who they were unless someone was afraid of them. They jealously guarded their jobs from blacks and Vietnamese refugees, whom they saw as a vast and hungry army about to descend upon their women, their neighborhoods, their schools, even their clapboard church houses, where they were assured every Sunday and Wednesday night that the bitterness and fear that characterized their lives had nothing to do with what they had been born to, or what they had chosen for themselves.

But when you looked at them at play in a public park, in almost

a tattered facsimile of a Norman Rockwell painting, it was as hard
to be angry at them for their ignorance as it would be to condemn
someone for the fact that he was born disfigured.

Then on a side street we saw Clemmie's junker car parked in a
yellow zone. I found a parking place farther down the street, and
Batist walked back to Clemmie's car, raised the hood, disconnected
a fistful of sparkplug wires, and locked them in our trunk. I took my
holstered .45 out of the glovebox, clipped it onto my belt, and put
on my sports coat.

"You're sure you want to go?" I said.

"What else I'm gonna do, me? Stand here and wait for a man
that's got a pistol?"

"Well, I don't think anybody is going to give us any trouble,"
I said. "They feel secure when they're in numbers. But if anybody
gets in our face, we walk on through it. All right, Batist?"

"Dave, ain't nobody know these people better than a black man.
They ain't worried by the likes of me, no. They scared of the young
ones. They ain't gonna admit that, but that's what's on they mind.
They scared to death of some noisy kids whose mamas should have
whupped them upside the head a long time ago."

"They're scared of anybody who looks them in the eye, partner."

"We gonna set around here and wait for that man to shoot Mr.
Sonnier?"

"No, you're right. Let's go see what they're doing at the bottom
of the food chain these days."

Batist peeled the cellophane off a cigar, put it deep into his jaw,
and we walked back down the block and into the park, where
someone had just turned on the field lights over the softball diamond.

"Hey, Dave, wasn't there s'posed to be a lot of policemens
here?" Batist said.

"Yep."

"Where they at?"

I saw one uniformed cop directing traffic, another one eating a
barbecue sandwich under a chinaberry tree. I saw no one in the
crowd who looked like plainclothes. I walked up to the cop under

the chinaberry tree and unfolded my badge in my palm.

"I'm Detective Dave Robicheaux, Iberia Parish Sheriff's Department," I said. "Did you guys get a report about a man with a pistol?"

His face was round, and his mouth was full of bread and meat. He wiped his lips with the back of his wrist and shook his head.

"*I* didn't," he said. "There's a guy around here with a gun?"

"Maybe. Have you seen a man with a burned face? You can't miss him. His skin looks like red putty."

"No."

"Where's your supervisor?"

"He was over at the pavilion a while ago. This is no shit, some guy's after Bobby Earl?"

"No, not Earl. His brother-in-law, a man named Weldon Sonnier. Do you know him?"

"I never heard of him. Look, you want me to, we can get on the mike and find this guy."

"You can do what?"

"We can page him. We can get him out of the crowd."

I tried to hide the expression that must have been on my face.

"How about finding your supervisor for me, then calling for some more help?" I said.

"Sure." Then he looked over my shoulder. "Who's *he?*"

"Find your supervisor, podna. Okay?" I said.

Batist and I walked through the crowd toward the concrete band shell. The western sky was piled with purple clouds that were scorched black and crimson on the edges in the sun's fiery afterglow. In the distance an emergency siren was pealing through the streets. The band in the pavilion stopped playing a moment, then suddenly it struck up "Dixie," and a second band, inside the concrete shell, in candy-striped vests and straw boaters, joined in as though on cue, and in the deafening exchange of trombones, clarinets, trumpets, and martial drum rolls, the crowd went insane.

Then somebody released the restraining ropes on a huge net filled with red, white, and blue balloons, which rose by the hundreds into the windstream, and I realized what was going on. It was Bobby Earl's moment. Amid a throng of applauding people he was walking from the pavilion, dressed in a double-breasted tropical suit, his dry, wavy hair tousled by the breeze, toward the speaker's stand that had been constructed in front of the concrete shell, where the microphones, American flags, television cameras, and banks of loud-speakers waited for him. His smile had all the ease and confidence of a man who knew that he was loved, that he had truly found his place in this world.

We worked our way through the crowd. The bands were still blaring out "Dixie," and a drunk fat man in a sweat-stained pink shirt had climbed up on a picnic table and was screaming rebel yells at the speaker's platform. The smell of flat beer, deodorant, chewing tobacco, and talcum powder seemed to rise in a collective sticky layer from the people around us. I tried to push our way through the edge of the crowd into the picnic area behind the band shell. A uniformed police sergeant shouldered his way through a bunch of college kids and stood in front of me. He was a large man, with a ridged brow, sunken green eyes, a fresh sunburn on his face, and sweat rings under his arms. His love handles hung over his gunbelt, and he rested one palm on the butt of his .357 magnum.

"You the sheriff's detective from New Iberia?" he asked.

"That's right. I'm Dave Robicheaux."

His eyes shifted to Batist, then back to me.

"I just heard about this burned man with a gun," he said. "What's going on?"

"His name is Vic Benson. He's deranged, and I think he plans to harm Bobby Earl's brother-in-law."

"He's got a gun?"

"A chrome-plated revolver, caliber unknown."

"Hell of a fucking place to have a crazy man running loose with a gun. Every time I have to work one of these things, I have dreams the night before about earthquakes and tornados. My wife says I eat too much before I go to bed. Who's *this* man?"

"He's a friend."

"All right, I'm going to get some more uniforms into the crowd. In the meantime, you find Earl's brother-in-law, you get him out of here. A bunch like this can take to religion or flattening your town, either one, in about five minutes."

"Thanks for your help, sergeant."

"Don't thank me, podna. I worked a riot once at the stadium. The next time I get caught in one, I'm going home, open a beer, and sit in the backyard. Maybe listen to it on the radio." He smiled.

The crowd began to thin at the edges, and finally Batist and I stepped out into an area of pine trees, barbecue pits, overflowing trash barrels, and a small sandy stretch of playground with seesaws and swing sets.

There, sitting in a child's swing, sipping beer out of a deep paper cup, was Weldon Sonnier.

"I think you aged me about ten years tonight," I said.

He looked up at me.

"Hey, Dave. Hey, Batist. What's up?"

"Your father is around here somewhere with a pistol. Guess who he's looking for?"

"What?"

"After you left, he beat up the black maid and stole her car. It's parked about a block from here. He's got a revolver."

He made a clucking sound. "The old man's always up to new tricks, huh?" he said.

"The Baton Rouge cops want you out of the area. I do, too."

He sipped his beer and gazed lackadisically at some kids shagging flies on the softball diamond.

"Where's Bama?" I asked.

"She went to give Bobby his present. You got to get a number and wait. You'd think he was the pope."

"It's time for you to go back to Lyle's. I'll find Bama and bring her along."

"What the hell are you talking about, Dave?"

"You're leaving."

"Are you serious?"

"You're leaving on your own or you're leaving in custody. It's up to you, Weldon."

"I don't know about legal jurisdiction and that sort of thing, but I doubt you have much authority here, Dave. And I don't see any Baton Rouge cops, and I don't see any old man with a pistol. Take a break and get a soft drink over at the pop stand."

"You're starting to piss me off again, Weldon."

"That's your problem."

"No, it's yours. I think you were born with a two-by-four up your butt."

"I never said I was perfect."

"Do you have to prove that you're not afraid of your father? You flew hundreds of combat missions. Didn't you ever learn who you are?"

He raised his face and looked at me in an odd way. For just a moment in the fading light, his big ears, his square face, his close-cropped head made me remember the young boy of years ago, his bare feet gray with dust, his overalls grimed at the knees, swamping out the poolroom for two bits an hour.

Then the light in his eyes changed, and he took a drink of beer and looked down between his knees.

"You've done your job, Dave. Now let it go," he said.

I felt Batist pull my sleeve, felt the urgency in his hand even before I heard it in his voice.

"Dave, look yonder," he said.

Bobby Earl and his entourage of bodyguards and political aides had gone into the grassy area between the speaker's platform and the concrete shell. Bama had worked her way through the throng and was giving him an oblong box wrapped with satin-finish white paper and a pink ribbon. But that was not what Batist had seen.

On the other side of the concrete shell, Vic Benson had just exited one of the portable bathrooms that stood in a long row under the trees, a baseball cap on his head, dark glasses on his nose. And as quickly as I saw him, he disappeared behind the far wall of the shell.

Then it hit me.

He knows Bama went to the park with Weldon. Through the crowd he got a glimpse of Bama talking with Bobby Earl. At a distance he's mistaken Bobby Earl for Weldon.

"Good God, he's going to shoot Bobby Earl," I said.

"What?" Weldon said.

I took my badge from my coat pocket, held it open in front of me, and ran toward the grassy area behind the speaker's platform, the weight of the .45 knocking against my hip. I heard Batist hard on my heels. People paused in midsentence and stared at us, their expressions caught between laughter and alarm. Then Earl's bodyguards were moving toward us, spreading out, their faces heating with expectation and challenge.

Through their bodies I saw Earl's peculiar monocular vision focus on my face.

"Get that man out of here!" he said.

Two men in suits stepped in front of me, and one of them stiff-armed me in the shoulder with the heel of his hand. His coat hung at an odd angle because of a weight in the right-hand pocket.

"Where you think you're going, buddy?" he said. His breath was rife with the smell of cigars.

"Iberia Parish sheriff's office. There's a man in the crowd with—" I began.

"Yeah? Who's that with you? The African paratroopers?" he said.

"He's FBI, you peckerwood shithead," I said. "Now, you get the fuck out of my way."

Mistake, mistake, I thought, even as the words came out of my mouth. Don't humiliate north Louisiana stump-jumpers in front of either their women or the boss man.

"Iberia Parish don't mean horse piss on a rock here," the second man said. "You better haul your ass 'fore you get it hauled for you."

Then more of Earl's bodyguards and aides pressed toward me, as though I were the source of all their problems, the spoiler of a grand moment in which they had been allowed to participate.

I stepped back from them and held my palms outward. Then I pointed one finger at them.

"I'll make it brief," I said. "Get your man out of sight before he gets dusted. Second, I'm going to be back later and bust every one of you for interfering with an officer in the performance of his duty."

I moved out of the crowd and behind the concrete shell to the far side. Lines had formed in front of the portable bathrooms, and large numbers of people were now drifting out of the picnic areas and the pavilion toward the speaker's platform. The wind had suddenly died, and the air had grown close and hot, with a dusty, metallic smell to it, and the field lights were white and haloed with humidity against the darkening sky. I kicked over a trash barrel, rolled it snug against the concrete shell, stood on it, and tried to see Vic Benson's baseball cap among the hundreds of heads in the crowd.

It seemed impossible.

Then I heard a woman scream and I saw people separating themselves from some terrible or frightening presence in their midst, tripping on each others' ankles, falling backward to the ground. Not twenty feet from me, Vic Benson was racing through the crowd, the way a barracuda would slice through a school of bluefish, a small silver pistol in his upraised hand.

Bama saw him before Bobby Earl, whose back was turned as he signed autographs for children. Her face went white, and her mouth opened in a round red O.

I knocked a woman down, felt somebody bounce hard off my shoulder, crashed across a folding wheelchair, and dove headlong into the small of Vic Benson's back.

He hit the ground under me, and I heard the breath go out of his lungs in a gasp, and once again I smelled that odor that was like turpentine or embalming fluid, wind-dried sweat, nicotine, smoke rubbed into the skin and clothes. His baseball cap toppled off his head, his dark glasses were askew on his face, and his eyes stared into mine the way a lizard's might if it were trapped on top of a hot rock in the middle of a burning field.

His lips moved, and I knew he wanted to curse or wound me in some fresh way, but his breath rasped in his throat like a man whose lungs were perforated with holes. I slipped my hand along his arm and removed the unfired pistol from his fingers.

I thought it was over. It should have been.

But Batist, when he had seen what was about to happen, had plunged through the crowd from the other side, his arms outspread, and had flung both Bama and Bobby Earl to the ground and had landed with his huge weight on top of both of them. People were screaming and shoving one another; photographers and TV cameramen were trying to get Bobby Earl's prone body, with Baptist's on top of it, into their cameras' lenses; and three uniformed cops were fighting desperately to get through the rim of the crowd and into the center before a riot spread throughout the park.

Then I realized that most of the people pressed into the center of the grassy area had not seen Vic Benson or understood what he had tried to do. Instead, some of them obviously believed that Batist had attacked Bobby Earl.

As Batist tried to raise himself on his arms, a man on the edge of the crowd swung a doubled-over dog chain at his head, then two of Earl's bodyguards grabbed him by the belt and began tugging him backward.

"Put that fucking nigger in a cage," someone yelled.

Then the crowd surged forward, toppling over one another, trampling others who had already fallen to the ground. Between their legs I saw the desperation in Batist's face as he tried to shield his eyes from a solitary fist that was flailing at his head. A string of saliva and blood drooled from his lower lip.

I tore into their midst. I drove my fist as hard as I could into the back of a man's thick neck; I ripped my elbow into someone's rib cage and felt it go like a nest of popsicle sticks; I lifted an uppercut into another man's stomach and saw him cave to his knees in front of me, his face gray and his mouth hanging open as if he had been eviscerated.

Then they rolled over both Batist and me.

There are moments in your life when you think the last frames in your film strip have just snapped loose from the reel. When one of those moments occurs, you hear your own blood thundering in your ears, or a sound like waves bursting over a coral reef, or hundreds of feet pounding dully on the earth.

Or perhaps the last frame in the strip simply freezes and you hear nothing at all.

Then as though sound and sight, trees and sky and air had all been given back to me, I saw the sunburned police sergeant with the hard, green eyes, knocking people backward with his baton, gripping it horizontally with both hands, swinging it violently from side to side, pushing the crowd back into a wider and wider circle.

Then other cops were in the circle, and you could feel the

energies go out of the crowd the way air leaves a punctured balloon. When I got to my feet, I pulled my shirt out of my trousers and wiped my face on it. It was smeared with spittle and blood.

"I'm taking your piece and cuffing you and your friend together till I can get y'all out of here. Don't argue about it," the sergeant said.

"No argument, podna," I said.

He snapped one cuff of a set on my wrist and the other on Batist's. Batist's white shirt hung in strips off his massive shoulders.

Bobby Earl was standing among his bodyguards, his double-breasted tropical suit smudged with grass stains. He held a folded handkerchief to the corner of his mouth and combed back his wavy hair with his fingers. I felt the sergeant's hand tighten under my arm.

"Just a minute," I said to him. "Hey, Bobby, a black man just saved your worthless pink ass. You and your constituency might think that over. There's another thought I want to leave you with, too, and I don't want you to take it the wrong way. But if you ever try to hurt my friend Cletus Purcel again, they'll have to scrub you out of your garbage grinder with a toothbrush."

Batist and I walked to a squad car, surrounded by cops, our wrists chained together, our clothes in rags, just as lightning flickered across the sky and raindrops as heavy as marbles began to strike the leaves of the pin oaks above our heads.

Through the back window of another squad car, his arms manacled behind him, Vic Benson's destroyed face stared out at the cops, the milling crowd, the trees, the park, the slanting rain, the blackened sky, perhaps the earth itself, as though the invisible forces that had driven him all his life had gathered at this place, in this moment, to finally and irrevocably have their way with him.

EPILOGUE

We took our vacation in Key West in late summer, when the weather is hot and bright, prices are cheap, the streets are empty of tourists, and the Gulf is lime green and streaked with whitecaps as far as the eye can see, and dark patches of water, like clouds of India ink, drift across the coral reefs.

But it was more than simply a respite from police work. I had taken indefinite leave from the sheriff's department. I let other people's problems, the seriousness, all the fury and mire and complexity, pull out of my grasp, in the same way that you finally tire of grief or guilt or a bonegrinding ongoing contention with the world. One morning, perhaps just before sunrise, you turn your eyes in a different direction and notice a blue heron rising from the reeds along the bayou's edge, a gator's walnut-ridged eyes moving silently through a milky skim of algae and floating twigs, a glowing radiance on the earth's rim that suddenly breaks through the black trunks of the cypress trees with such a white brilliance that you want to shield your eyes.

Joey Gouza is back with the big stripes in Angola pen, but not for the murder of Garrett or Jewel Fluck, or even the assault-and-battery beef. Joey's final legal chapter was written in the New Orleans city prison. He set fire to his mattress, plugged up the commode with his clothes, flooded the whole cell block, and urinated through the bars on a gunbull. He tried to tell anyone who would listen that both the Aryan Brotherhood and the Mexican Mafia had put a hit on him. No one was interested, or perhaps, more accurately, no one cared.

Finally he was moved into an isolation cell with a solid iron door, because he was convinced that an AB member, with the consent of the Mafioso who had taken a Taser dart in the neck that had been intended for Joey, was going to turn him into a flaming object lesson by hurling a Molotov cocktail through his bars.

Two days later a new guard walked him down to the shower stalls and the small concrete room that contained barbells and a broken universal gym, where Joey was supposed to shower and exercise by himself. Then the guard let eight other men out of their cells. Joey Gouza broke off a five-inch shank, made from a jagged sliver of window glass, in another inmate's shoulder.

The investigator's report stated that the other inmate had celled with Jewel Fluck in Parchman, that his upper torso was tattooed with swastikas and iron crosses, and that at the time of the attack he had been carrying a razor blade mounted on a toothbrush handle.

But who cared?

Joey Gouza went down for attempted murder.

I'd like to be able to tell you that Bobby Earl's political career ended, that somehow the events in the park revealed him publicly as a fraud or a physical coward, or that his followers turned against him. But it didn't happen. It couldn't.

I had been determined to prove that Bobby Earl was fronting points for Joey Gouza, or that he was connected with arms and dope trafficking in the tropics. I was guilty of that age-old presumption that the origins of social evil can be traced to villainous individuals, that we just need to identify them, lock them in cages, or even march them to the executioner's wall, and this time, yes, this time, we'll catch a fresh breeze in our sails and set ourselves on a true course.

But Bobby Earl is out there by consent. He has his thumb on a dark pulse, and like all confidence men, he knows that his audience wishes to be conned. He learned long ago to listen, and he knows that if he listens carefully they'll tell him what they need to hear. It's a contract of mutual deceit by which they open up their flak vests and take it right through the breastbone.

If it were not he, it would be someone like him—misanthropic, beguiling, educated, someone who, as an ex-president's wife once said, allows the rest of us to feel comfortable with our prejudices.

I think the end for Bobby Earl will come in the same fashion as it does for all his kind. Unlike the members of The Pool and that great army of villainous buffoons trying to sneak through life on side streets, Bobby Earl's ilk want power so badly that at some point in their lives they make a conscious choice to embrace evil. It's not a gradual seduction. They do it without reservation, and that's when they leave the rest of us. You know it when it happens, too. No amount of cosmetic surgery can mask the psychological deformity in their eyes.

Then unbeknown to themselves they set about erecting their own scaffolds; their most loyal adherents become their executioners, just as Mussolini's people hanged him upside down in a filling station and Robespierre's followers trundled him over their heads to the guillotine.

Then the audience moves on and seeks a new magician.

But people like Bobby Earl don't read history books.

▼

As I watched Alafair dive off our rented boat, just the other side of Seven-Mile Reef, her tan body glazed with sunlight and saltwater, I thought of children everywhere, and I thought of the pain that can be inflicted on them like a stone bruise in the soul, like a convoluted, blood-red rose pushed deep into the tissue by a brutal thumb.

She floated above the reef, watching the schools of clown fish and mackerel, blowing saltwater out her snorkel, the small waves lapping across her back and thighs. Thirty feet below, the sand was like ground diamonds; you could see each black spike in the nests of sea urchins, and the fire coral was so bright it looked as if it would scorch your hand with the intensity of a hot stove.

Then I saw a long, tubular shadow ripple across the crown of the reef and flatten out on the ocean floor. It must have been eight feet long. A floating island of kelp obscured my angle of vision, then the shadow changed directions and I saw the glistening brown back of a hammerhead shark. When he turned and flipped his tail fin I could see one round, flat, glassy eye, his gash of a mouth, the jagged row of razor teeth, the obscene pale whiteness of his stomach.

I yelled at Alafair, but her ears were half underwater and she didn't hear me. I kicked off my canvas shoes, stepped up on the gunwale, hit the water in a long, flat dive, and reached her in three strokes. By now she had seen the shark, and her face was terrified when I grabbed her around the waist and began swimming back to the boat. Then a peculiar thing happened. She knew that we were fighting against each other, that our legs were thrashing impotently in a shimmering cone of wet light above the shark's murderous gaze, and I saw a quiet, almost naïve expression of resolution replace the fear in her face. She worked the mask and snorkel off her head, hooked them on her arm, and began to swim with me toward the boat ladder, her body horizontal, her head twisting from side to side so she could breathe above the chop.

I pushed her rump over the gunwale, then toppled over it myself onto the deck. I hugged her against me on the hot boards, and pressed her head tightly under my chin.

She looked up at me, and I saw concern coming back into her face.

"Wow!" I said, and tried to grin.

"What kind of shark was that, Dave?"

"It was a nurse shark. They're big wimps. But who wants to take any chances?"

"His head . . . it was ugly. It looked like he'd eaten a big brick." Then she smiled at her own joke.

"Those nurse sharks are not only wimps, they're dumb wimps. They're always swimming into the sides of boats and reefs and things," I said.

Her brown eyes were happy and full of light again.

"Hey, Dave, we gonna put out the lines and troll for mackerel?"

"Sure, little guy," I said, and squeezed her against my chest again, my eyes tightly shut, hoping that she would not feel the fearful beating of my heart.